THE
MAGIC
BULLET

By the same author:

ETHICS (AND OTHER LIABILITIES)

HOOPLA

ONE OF THE GUYS

THE MAGIC BULLET

HARRY STEIN

 Delacorte Press

Published by
Delacorte Press
Bantam Doubleday Dell Publishing Group, Inc.
1540 Broadway
New York, New York 10036

Library of Congress Cataloging in Publication Data
Stein, Harry.
The magic bullet / by Harry Stein.
p.   cm.
ISBN 0-385-31286-5
1. Cancer—Research—United States—Fiction.   2. Conspiracies—United States—Fiction.   3. Physicians—United States—Fiction.
I. Title.
PS3569.T366M3   1995
813'.54—dc20   94-34168
                                                            CIP

Designed by Rhea Braunstein

Manufactured in the United States of America
Published simultaneously in Canada

February 1995

10   9   8   7   6   5   4   3   2   1

BVG

For Charles and Abe,
who were also
pioneers

It's hard to imagine any author having a better experience writing a book than I had with this one. Leslie Schnur is a wondrous editor: smart, generous, and resourceful. Her colleagues at Delacorte—far too numerous to name—are likewise as good as they come. Joy Harris, my agent, was there throughout, ever wise and caring.

Particular thanks is owed to the respected oncologist who gave so unsparingly of both time and experience, thereby providing vast insight into the labyrinthian universe of high-stakes cancer research. Without this person, who chooses to remain anonymous, this book would not be remotely what it is.

THE
MAGIC
BULLET

The first change was infinitesimal—a mutation in a single nucleotide of a single cell, deep within her right breast. It is impossible to say what caused it, or even if it was necessarily destined to have any impact. Still, from that moment on, that cell was unique among the several trillion in her body.

She was seventeen years old.

Over the next decade, the cell mutated several times. It began to behave autonomously, independent of the controls governing its neighbors. Its shape became slightly irregular. The structure of its nucleus changed. Its metabolism increased.

Her career was going exceedingly well.

Eight years later, the cell undergoes a sudden, dramatic change. The DNA within its unstable nucleus begins mutating hourly. All the cell's energy is channeled into growth and reproduction. Normal signals directing it to stop are ignored. Immunological surveillance breaks down. Within a month, it has spawned close to a hundred daughter cells.

Sometimes she thinks she is living a fantasy. Between her two young children, her work, and her husband, she jokes that she doesn't have time for problems.

It takes four years for the next great mutation. The malignant cells now number in the hundreds of thousands; but even if taken all together, are no larger than the head of a pin. Some, however, have already learned how to live outside the breast.

One afternoon, doing laps in the White House pool, she feels a dull pain in her lower back. She ignores it; seemingly just a minor muscle spasm. The backache lasts twenty-four hours and disappears as suddenly as it arrived.

D aniel Logan lay, motionless, on a gurney in a dim cubicle off the emergency room in New York's Claremont Hospital. He'd been this way for an hour—alone in the dark, seemingly forgotten by the nurses moving in the corridor just a few feet away. Occasionally, in his semiconsciousness, he could hear a faint rumble of thunder; evidence that the storm battering the city this Sunday evening had not abated. As far as the emergency room personnel were concerned, he might as well not even exist.

Dr. Logan smiled. *Good,* this is just what he'd hoped for when he heard the forecast en route to the hospital, that business would be slow. God knows he needed the rest! He hadn't made it home from that damn party the night before until nearly dawn, and he'd had to report to the ER at noon; the senior resident in charge of a skeleton crew of one intern, a handful of nurses, and a half dozen support staff. More than ever, he appreciated the sweet truth behind that most cynical of medical maxims: Sickness takes a vacation during lousy weather.

But abruptly Logan sat up, roused by a commotion in the hallway. Swinging off the gurney to his feet, he poked his head into the corridor.

A pair of security men were restraining a large, unwieldy drunk.

"Hey, Doc," called one of the security men, "want some action on this guy?"

"Gimme a sec."

The Claremont emergency room was like many others in large city hospitals. Waiting patients could peer through a glass partition into the doctors' station where, in turn, the doctors and nurses could survey newcomers and assess which cases required immediate attention; meanwhile charting the heartbeats of those already under their care on a large EKG monitor suspended from the ceiling. Strolling over to the ER reception desk, Logan instinctively glanced up at the monitor. Nothing going on. Only one customer waited on the other side of the glass, a young Hispanic man staring blankly into the middle distance.

"What's his problem?" Logan asked Nurse Clancy—known as Nurse Amazon, even to her face.

"The drip. Dr. Richman's already taken a culture."

"Good."

She smirked. "Must be pretty bad to bring him out on a night like this."

Trust me, thought Logan, heading back down the corridor, *if you had green stuff coming out of your dick, you'd be in here too.*

The drunk was now sprawled out on the bed in a cubicle, held in check by four point restraints, one on each limb. Since the cubicle was designed to accommodate two people, one horizontal, the other vertical, Logan joined the group in the corridor peering within as a nurse drew a blood sample.

"You in, Doc?" asked an attendant named Ruben Perez.

"Wouldn't miss it." Looking the patient over, Logan tossed a quarter into the emesis basin that was serving as the bank; there were already half a dozen others inside.

Logan prided himself on his skill at "Guess the Alcohol Level." One early morning just the week before, a young Chinese man had been brought in appearing more inebriated than anyone they'd seen in months. The bids ranged from 400 milligrams per deciliter to 800; certain people would be *dead* at 700. Logan's colleagues laughed when he came in at 275—until the fellow registered 295 on the computer. Logan alone had taken note of the key fact: Orientals invariably have a very low tolerance for alcohol.

Now Logan turned to Janice Richman, the young intern on duty. Shy and unassuming though she was, Richman had crackerjack diagnostic skills; tonight he was liable to have some real competition. "Okay, Richman, you're up."

"Five twenty."

Logan nodded. "Put me down for four thirty."

Five minutes later, assorted medical personnel, more than half the staff on duty, crowded around the terminal as a nurse retrieved the winning number from the computer.

"Four thirty-five."

"Dammit!" snapped Richman, to Logan's amused surprise. She'd never before shown her competitive side.

"Logan," exclaimed Ruben Perez, "you're a medical animal!"

Logan laughed, pocketing the change. "Hey, everyone's gotta have a specialty. I happen to be a drunkologist."

He smiled at Richman. "Janice, will you keep an eye on things? I'm gonna grab a bite to eat."

"Yeah, yeah," she said, "go blow your winnings."

"I'll join you," said Perez. "I had a break due two hours ago."

"I'm starved," noted Logan as they headed downward in the elevator. "I open the refrigerator this morning and all I find is some moldy cheese and a bottle of beer. I'm telling you, if my patients saw how I live, they wouldn't let me near them."

"I thought all you Yuppie doctors know how to cook."

"Nah, that's the *new* cliché—I'm the old one. But I'm not complaining. I get to live on Chinese takeout and Hydrox cookies."

Only a corner of the cafeteria remained open, and the only food available at this hour was from vending machines. As Perez wolfed down a cup of something passing as chicken soup, Logan poked at a container of Jell-O cubes.

"What are you doing, man?" smiled Perez. "The idea is to eat it."

"Look, I'm trying to resuscitate some very sick Jell-O here."

"By the way," said the orderly, "I meant to ask—how's that old guy Friedman doing?"

"Which one is he?"

"Christ, you doctors. . . ." He shook his head. "Fever? Abdominal pain? Low hematocrit? I brought him in around three o'clock. He looked septic."

It was not unusual for orderlies to take an interest in their charges, but the depth of Ruben's concern was exceptional; as was his understanding of medicine. When things were hopping in the ER, Logan could always count on him to direct him to the patients most in need of care. Born in the Dominican Republic and raised in the South Bronx,

Perez was only a few years older than Logan; and the young doctor knew —and knew that Perez did too—that if he'd had more than a high school education, he'd have made a hell of a doctor himself. Though they rarely saw one another outside the hospital, over the course of dozens of conversations like this one, their mutual regard had slowly blossomed into firm friendship. Around Perez, Logan could readily drop the casual world-weariness that, on hospital grounds, so many wore as protective coloring.

"I stabilized him in the ER," Logan replied, "and sent him up to intensive care."

"He's a nice guy. Think he'll make it?"

Logan hesitated, then shook his head. "No." He paused. "You're right, after a while you almost do stop thinking of them as people. He's a nice guy, huh?"

Perez nodded. "He was in the first wave that landed on Normandy, can you believe that? Great stories to tell. You know what he tells me when I'm wheeling him in? 'This is what I get for eighty-seven years of bad living.' "

Logan smiled. "I'll look in on him before I go. Promise."

Perez stirred his soup. "So . . . tell me about the party."

"Not much to tell . . ."

" 'Not much to tell,' " echoed Perez sarcastically. "The man attends one of the social events of the season and makes me read about it in the *Daily News*."

"Hey, for me it was work." Logan smiled. "I just went as a courtesy."

In fact, the event in question, celebrating the thirty-five years in practice of Dr. Sidney Karpe, one of medicine's most celebrated names, had gone exceptionally well for Logan. Karpe was a one-man industry: he wrote books, provided medical commentary for network news shows, featured a roster of celebrity clients as long as that of William Morris. If, as it happened (and as Karpe's colleagues knew from firsthand experience), he was a mediocre doctor, that hardly seemed to matter. For his greatest skill lay in choosing associates—"accessory brains," his envious rivals called them—to handle the nuts and bolts.

Which is where Dan Logan came in. The most gifted young doctor emerging that year from the city's top medical facility, ideally suited for

Karpe's operation by training, temperament, and range of experience, he'd been wooed by the great man for months now; offered, in addition to a starting salary of $170,000, the kind of perks designed to dazzle a middle-class kid from the Midwest, from weekend yacht parties to regular trips to London, Paris, and the Middle East. And last night had been the clincher. At Karpe's elbow, he'd met movie stars, politicians, and financiers; he'd been introduced as a soon-to-be partner in the practice.

But there was no way Logan was about to report any of that—not to Perez, stuck here at Claremont with little hope of escape. The money was *too* good, the perks almost embarrassingly grand.

"Fine," said Perez, "did you enjoy the *work?*"

Logan smiled. "Some of the women," he conceded, "were quite attractive."

"Now we're getting somewhere."

"But you know how shy I am."

"Yeah, right."

"Really. A place like this, the women are way out of my league. Unless one of them has a medical complaint, I don't even know how to get started."

"Logan, you're the kind of guy the women's magazines are always talking about."

" 'How to Meet Terrific Eligible Bachelors'?"

Perez grinned, surprised his friend had strolled into so obvious a setup. "Guys Who'll *Never* Commit."

"Anyway," said Logan, brushing this off, "I felt incredibly awkward in that tuxedo. That's not me."

"You go to that place I told you? Did it fit right?"

"*Yeah,* it fit right. I wasn't about to look like a *total* jerk."

Indeed, Logan knew he'd seldom looked better. Still boyish at twenty-nine, he was aware that his loping gait, longish hair, and quick smile could lend him the air of a spirited undergraduate; charming, but as unserious professionally as he remained about his personal life. This was an impression he'd gone to great lengths to avoid. Last night, he knew, he'd looked like a comer.

"So did you commit to Karpe?"

"Not yet."

"Why not?"

Why not? The truth was, Logan fervently wanted it several irreconcilable ways at once. Ambitious for conventional success and status, he also clung to a brand of idealism that, had he advertised it, most of his colleagues would surely take as naive. Delighted as he'd be to find himself an object of envy, he also ached for plausible reasons to respect himself.

Too—and this was probably as vital as the rest—there was the matter of . . . *sport*. For Logan medicine at its best involved the skill and gamesmanship of basketball or high-stakes poker. It was *fun* to correctly diagnose an unusual condition or devise a creative treatment for an intractable malady; it could be nothing short of thrilling when a mix of intuition and hard work cracked a case that baffled other doctors. During the grind of internship and residency at one of the nation's most competitive and unforgiving hospitals, it was those occasions that had given him moments of professional satisfaction that approached pure joy.

Logan knew full well that within Karpe's practice the cynicism would be even more acute—and the opportunities for creativity even rarer.

"I guess," he began haltingly, answering his friend's question, "that clinical work, at this point . . ." He shook his head. "I mean, we both know how it can beat you up emotionally. That old guy—what's his name again?"

"Friedman?"

"You won't believe this, but there was a time when I'd have gotten incredibly involved with a guy like that." He smiled. "Back in college I used to cry all the time at movies."

"Hey, no one blames you. Big criers don't inspire a helluva lot of confidence in patients."

"I mean, even the way we talk about death around here. Notice how no one ever dies in a hospital?"

Perez smiled. "Right. They 'box' or 'crump.'"

"Or 'tube,'" added Logan. "Or 'have their subscription canceled.'" He paused meaningfully. "I've just been thinking about how nice it'd be to do something else."

"For instance?"

"Pure research."

Perez looked at him in surprise. "Like hell. You're going to Karpe's money factory."

Logan picked at his Jell-O a long moment, then looked up. "I want to show you something." He reached into the pocket of his white jacket and pulled out a crumpled envelope. "This was in my box this morning." He handed it across the table.

Perez withdrew the single page and put on his glasses to read. It turned out to be little more than a form letter, coolly impersonal, Logan's name slotted into the right place by a computer that, an instant later, had churned out the same letter to someone else.

> Dear Dr. Logan:
> Thank you for your application to the American Cancer Foundation. As you know, we are currently in the process of developing the roster of incoming fellows.
> I am pleased to inform you that you are among those selected for final consideration. As such, you are invited to visit the ACF to be interviewed by members of our staff. Please contact Dr. Shein, the supervisor of the Fellowship Program, at the number listed below to arrange for a mutually convenient date.
> We look forward to seeing you shortly.

The signature at the bottom belonged to Dr. Kenneth Markell, the director of the ACF, one of the world's greatest names in cancer research.

Perez let out a low whistle. "I'm impressed. Save that for your grandchildren." He folded the letter and replaced it in the envelope.

"That isn't why I showed it to you."

"What, you want my advice? How the hell should I know what to tell you? Just that you should be flattered."

"Hey, it's a form letter. They probably send out a couple of hundred of these."

Perez grinned. "You want sympathy? You're right, they probably do."

Logan rose to his feet. "Aren't we supposed to have some work to do around here?"

*   *   *

Back in the ER things had started to pick up. Four patients waited to be seen, among them a chest pain and a chronic asthmatic.

"Where's Richman?" demanded Logan of Nurse Clancy behind the desk.

She nodded toward the line of examining rooms. "With a dirtball" —hospitalese for malingerer.

Logan peered beyond the cubicle curtain. Richman was examining a woman of perhaps thirty, blond and very attractive. "Excuse me, Dr. Richman . . . ?"

Richman excused herself and joined him in the hallway.

"What's the story?"

"Why, you interested?" She smirked. "Divorcée, two kids, Park Avenue address. Probably has a *lot* of money."

Logan rolled his eyes. "I mean, what's her *problem?*"

"I don't know. Cough and fever. But the vital signs are okay."

"Well, don't take too long. They're starting to stack up out there."

Logan had the chest pain and the asthmatic placed in examining rooms and instructed a nurse to run the standard tests. He turned his attention to Mrs. Zaretsky and her three days of non-stop diarrhea. But abruptly there came a sharp knock on the examining room door: it was Clancy from reception reporting a crisis.

The patient had been brought in by ambulance. Forty-one years old and in apparent remission from Hodgkin's disease, she'd awakened with sharp abdominal pains. Logan glanced at her chart, then bent over the stretcher. He noted she was yellow-gray and her breathing was shallow. In the previous hour and a quarter she'd grown progressively shorter of breath.

Logan knew he had a very sick woman on his hands. Instinctively, he felt her condition had nothing to do with the cancer; it was atypical for the disease to present itself so acutely. All things considered—abdominal pains, circulatory collapse, the fact that she was on steroids—sepsis seemed the likeliest possibility.

Her husband hovered nearby. "What's wrong with her, Doctor?"

Logan led him to a corner. "I'm not sure. I'm going to put her on antibiotics. All indications are that she's septic."

"What does that mean?"

"There's an infection in the bloodstream. What we've got to do now is find its source. Until then, the drugs should hold the infection down."

The man went ashen. "Oh, God, I should have brought her in three days ago."

He was right—but the rule was to keep them, at the very least, from feeling guilty. "It probably wouldn't have made any difference. This seems to have happened quite suddenly."

The patient herself was fully conscious and scared to death. Logan placed his hand in her palm. "Listen, Helen, you're going to be okay. We're going to help you."

"But I'm having such trouble breathing."

"I know that. We're getting you some oxygen so you'll feel better soon."

Patting the patient gently on the arm, Logan headed for the nurses' station. He needed to know how much oxygen she had in her blood.

The station was vacant. "Nurse Clancy!" he called in frustration. He waited a long moment. "Goddammit, Clancy!"

"What is it, Dan?" said Ruben Perez. "I'll handle it."

He nodded. "Get me a blood-gas kit, and let's set up a hundred-percent oxygen mask."

Abruptly the night nurse appeared. "What is it?"

Though he was steaming, this clearly wasn't the time for a petty doctor-nurse squabble. "Just wheel the patient from the ER into a room, please."

She caught his tone anyway. "I was in the john, for Chrissakes."

"Ruben," he said, turning away, "I'm gonna need a set of X rays. And keep an eye on her blood pressure."

Logan rushed from the room and collared St. Pierre, the second night nurse. "Call up to the second floor—this lady needs a surgeon in a hurry. Pour in the normal saline, cover her with triple antibiotics, and give her a gram of steroid."

Ten minutes later she was wheeled off into surgery. Logan had been on the nose: a perforated duodenal ulcer, leading to septicemia and shock. No sweat—but another hour without proper treatment and she wouldn't have made it.

There was no time to savor it. As he headed back to the ER to check up on his chest pain, he was met by Janice Richman.

"Here you are. Could you have a look at this?" She couldn't quite hide the panic.

"What?"

Richman was already hustling back down the hall, leading the way. "That woman. I left her alone for a few minutes and . . ." Reaching the door, she opened it. The woman he'd seen earlier was totally transformed. Wild eyed, her blond hair damp with sweat, she was trying to climb over the raised railings of the bed. In her struggle, the blue hospital gown had come undone and was hitched up to her waist.

"What's her name?"

"Betsy Morse."

Logan rushed over to the bed. "C'mon, Betsy, take it easy! Tell me what the problem is."

She looked at him with wild, unfocused eyes; then flung an arm toward his face.

"Betsy, calm down. Stay in bed. We're here to help you."

He grabbed her by the shoulders and tried to ease her down; her skin was burning.

"Betsy, relax. Relax!"

Richman stood in the doorway, watching, shaken.

"Richman, I need your help, for Chrissakes!"

But the harder they tried to hold her down, the harder she fought. She was thrashing now, wholly out of control. People in delirium, stripped of the rational, are often astonishingly strong. It was all they could do to keep her in bed.

Now she began making noises, grunts, and unintelligible nonsense syllables. Her face contorted, she was kicking violently.

"Clancy," yelled Logan, "get in here!" This time the nurse appeared almost instantly. "Tie her down. Four-point restraints. Get security to sit on her. Get a rectal temperature, she's hot as a pistol. One milligram of Haldol IM stat!"

The doctors extricated themselves as security took over. "Let's get her someplace we can hook her up to the EKG."

It was what any good doctor most dreads: the utterly inexplicable. Benumbed, Logan retreated to the doctors' station.

The young woman's EKG tracing had already appeared on the overhead monitor: sinus tachycardia at 150 beats per minute. An instant later, Clancy's head appeared around the corner. "Forty-two degrees."

"Cool her down, use lukewarm water, not ice!" commanded Logan. "Six hundred fifty milligrams of acetamenophen per rectum!"

Above him, the monitor showed ventricular tachycardia—the chaotic fluttering of a severely injured heart.

He ran to her bed, joining Richman and two nurses. She was out cold. Logan punched at her chest. No blood pressure. No carotid pulse.

"Get a blood pressure cuff on her! Put a board under her back!" Furiously, Logan began cardiopulmonary resuscitation.

"Get everybody up here. Call a cardiac arrest and set up for a respirator!"

Seconds later the message thundered over the loudspeakers: *"Cardiac team, emergency room, Cardiac team, emergency room."*

At this hour, Logan knew, it would be ten minutes before anyone arrived. He ordered saline pads applied to her chest. "Run up the paddles to three hundred watt-seconds!"

The energy of the shock literally raised her from the bed. There was a sudden odor of seared flesh.

Logan looked at the monitor. Flat line.

"Keep pumping!" he screamed. "Where the hell's the goddamn respirator?"

One by one, bleary eyed, the cardiac team rushed in.

Logan and Richman stepped aside. While continuing to work at the young woman's chest, the cardiac team began administering drugs pall mall, desperately trying to flog the last living heart cells into action. One by one they failed.

"Well," spoke up Logan, with pretend calm, "anyone have any other ideas?"

Silence.

Logan snapped off the EKG. "Thank you, everybody."

"Another one in a box," said one of the cardiac guys softly, trying to maintain his sanity.

Glancing across the room, Logan caught Ruben Perez's eye. He reached into his pocket and felt the envelope.

The moment he entered the grounds of the American Cancer Foundation, crossing a narrow bridge over a meandering brook and steering the rented Taurus onto a long sloping drive lined with spruce and maple, Dan Logan understood why this place was always referred to as a campus. *The ACF campus.* With its vast manicured lawns and elegant Federal-style buildings, it instantly conveyed as strong a sense of dignity and purpose as any ivy-covered institution of higher learning.

Like everything else here, that was by design. The Federal style is *meant* to awe—and its power had long worked on visitors far more important than Dr. Daniel Logan. To the powerful politicians responsible for much of its funding, as well as to researchers the ACF hoped to lure away from other institutions, these *looked* like buildings where serious work was done, serious science.

Quite simply, there was no research institute, not in the United States or anywhere else in the world, remotely like the American Cancer Foundation. Founded in 1946, born of the boundless can-doism of the immediate post-war, the ACF now comprised some fifteen individual buildings. Here a small army of Ph.D.s and M.D.s worked toward the single goal of curing cancer. The ACF also contained its own hospital, the Eisenhower Medical Center, staffed by some of the finest oncologists in the world.

Driving past a series of smaller buildings that he supposed to be labs, making note of a pristine wood in the middle distance, Logan couldn't help but begin to muse: If he became a part of this place, he could *accomplish* something.

Not that he had any illusions. This was just a lark, a day trip to satisfy his own curiosity. If he made the two o'clock shuttle out of National, he'd be home before five; there'd still be time to take care of a few things at the hospital before dinner.

Still . . . behind the windows, moving about inside the labs, he could see people little older than he was. What important, even critical, questions were they working on this very moment? How many times, growing up, had he heard a TV reporter soberly intone "Researchers at the American Cancer Foundation today announced . . ."?

Now, as he drew closer to the imposing administration building where he was to be interviewed, the sense of déjà vu from his college days was even stronger. Dozens of people, a handful of the more than ten thousand technicians and secretaries, scientists and administrators, employed by the ACF, moved along the sidewalks and across the lawns this early March morning; some leisurely, others hurrying as if they were late for an important exam. Many carried leather satchels or notebooks; the vast majority were in their twenties or thirties.

Parking the car in the lot outside the administration building, he made his first appointment with five minutes to spare. It was with Raymond Larsen, the chief of the Department of Medicine.

He knew the name, of course. Dan had seen it often in the prestigious *Annals of Internal Medicine*. The journal came every month, its name embossed in authoritative black capital letters on a light green cover, its pages thick and glossy. At Claremont everyone with even a pretense to a serious career devoured every issue, not only for its instructive value but as a defensive weapon. When you quoted the *Annals,* you quoted Scripture.

And Larsen was one of the writers of Scripture.

In the outer office, Larsen's secretary, a charmless older woman, took his name and told him to take a seat. Before he'd even done so, Larsen himself hurried into the room. Tall and ramrod straight, he bore a distinct resemblance to Lee Marvin. He stopped and cast the secretary a look.

"He here to see me?"

"Dr. Logan," she replied evenly. "A candidate for the fellowship program."

Larsen gave him a quick once-over. There was no evidence he liked what he saw. Wordlessly, he reached toward the secretary for Dan's file. "Follow me."

For all his awe, Logan didn't much like what he saw either. Larsen looked and carried himself like nothing so much as a marine drill sergeant, all brusque impatience and snarly command. He even wore a brush crew cut straight out of a fifties movie. *How*, he wondered fleetingly, *does this guy manage to deal with patients?*

In his office, Larsen seated himself behind his desk and motioned for the younger man to take the seat opposite. As he leafed through the file, Logan studied the room. The walls were bare except for diplomas from Princeton and Harvard. The broad mahogany desk bore only a telephone and a neat stack of papers. No knickknacks. No photos of loved ones—if there were loved ones.

But there were books, shelf after shelf of books, on all aspects of cancer medicine. Logan recognized some of the titles; he had consulted more than a few. ACF Director Markell's tome—all four editions—were there. Sauerhaft's *Gynecological Malignancies*. Then there was a volume by Larsen himself, *Gastrointestinal Malignancies*, wedged between two others whose bindings, once clean and crisp, were fading and cracked. Museum pieces—Logan wondered why he'd even keep them around.

"I see you have a recommendation from L. D. Greiner," spoke up Larsen suddenly.

"Yessir." Logan had studied with the Nobel prize–winning chemist as a postdoc in molecular biology at Stanford, before he'd changed course and opted for medicine. The esteemed scientist had been exceptionally warm to him, almost paternal. Logan knew that Greiner's glowing report was one of the things that made his resume leap out from the pack.

And yet, he abruptly realized, Larsen was taking it as a liability. "May I ask why you opted out of molecular biology just six months after you got your doctorate? It doesn't say much for your stick-to-itiveness."

It took Logan just a moment to recover his wits. "I loved the work," he said. "Being in the lab with Dr. Greiner was terrifically exciting intellectually. It's just that there was a . . . coldness to it. A lack of connection between what I was doing and any practical application. Whereas with medical research—"

"You get to *help people*," Larsen finished the thought—and, with horror, Logan realized that he was mocking him.

"Something like that," he agreed.

"You realize, of course, that we have many promising applicants. And only a few slots to fill."

"Yes, I do."

"Good. I don't like people to have any illusions." He slammed the file shut. "Anything I can tell you?"

Actually, he'd had many questions. Beginning with precisely the sorts of research opportunities he might have as an incoming associate. But Larsen's invitation had been merely pro forma: it seemed that actual questions would only annoy him further.

"No, sir. I've already done a great deal of reading about the ACF."

"Tell me, Dr. Logan, are you married?"

The question caught Logan totally by surprise. What possible bearing could *that* have on anything? "No, sir, I'm not."

"I see." Larsen rose to his feet and extended his hand. "Well, thank you for coming by. You'll be hearing from us."

The interview, scheduled for half an hour, had taken less than ten minutes. It was forty minutes until the start of the next one. Shell-shocked, Logan was not even sure he wanted to bother going through with it. Over the course of his young career, he had been exposed to his share of unpleasantness: envy, duplicity, mean-spiritedness. He had come to understand that, by its very nature, big-time medicine tends to attract difficult personalities. But never before had he been the object of what he took to be outright contempt.

How could a man with Larsen's reputation as a physician and educator behave in such a way?

Taking a seat on a bench outside the administration building, he withdrew from his coat pocket the folded copy of *The Washington Post* he'd bought at the airport. But, though he stared at the page, his mind wouldn't fix on the words. He felt a dull pain behind the eyes, the beginning of a headache. Fleetingly—without even noting the irony— he wondered where he could get an aspirin in this place.

"Hi."

Logan looked up, startled. Before him stood a short, balding man in his early forties, his bright eyes and droopy little mustache lending him an almost comic appearance—if Dan Logan had been in a comic mood.

"Hello," he returned laconically.

"I work here," offered the other. He indicated his white lab coat, in case there was any doubt. "I saw you just came outta Larsen's office. What an asshole, right? Mind if I sit down?"

He immediately did so. Dan hesitated, searching for the appropriate answer. "I wouldn't say that," he replied finally.

"Oh, no? What, that bug that lives up his ass escaped this morning?" He snorted at his own joke. "You're at Claremont? Lotta rich SOBs for patients, I bet."

Logan's face reflected his surprise.

His companion pointed to the Claremont Hospital security pass dangling from the lapel of his coat. "I got a lotta talents. Mind reading ain't one of 'em."

For the first time, Logan allowed himself a smile. "I'd say that's a bit of an exaggeration." He paused. "But, yeah, we've got our share."

"You like New York? You're not from there originally."

"No. But I like it." He could hardly even figure out how to talk to this guy. "Actually, I'm from Decatur, Illinois."

"I am. From New York." He snorted again. "You wouldn't've guessed, right? You ever have a corned beef at the Carnegie Deli?"

"I'm afraid not."

"No? Why the hell else'd anyone live in that town? Tell me how you ended up at Claremont Hospital."

So—why not?—Dan found himself running through the story of his life in medicine. The excruciating first couple of years of medical school, where basically all he learned, aside from a little something about organ pathology, a ton of jargon, and the rudiments of cell biology, was to do exactly as he was told. The joy of liberation that came in the third year with the start of hospital rounds. Internship and residency and the sense, in the midst of exhausting eighteen-hour days, of actually beginning to emerge as a physician. His steadily growing interest in oncology.

"Why oncology?" asked the other. "What's the big deal about curing cancer? Lose a mother or something?"

Logan knew there was no cruelty intended in this. In fact, its very directness made him laugh. "No."

"Good. For a minute there, I thought you were a cliché."

Logan glanced at his watch. "My God!" He leapt to his feet. "Look, I've got to go. I'm ten minutes late for my interview." He started moving away. "Nice meeting you. Really."

"Just hold on a sec, Logan."

He turned. They'd never exchanged names. "You ain't late for your interview. You're in the middle of it."

For a long moment Logan was speechless. "Dr. Shein?" he said at last.

The other nodded. "Call me Seth. Beautiful day, time on my hands, figured I'd come to you."

Despite himself, Dan smiled. The day was overcast and unpleasantly cool. As the head of the ACF's clinical oncology program, Shein probably had less free time than the guy across the river in the Oval Office. "So what now?" asked Logan.

Shein rose to his feet and nodded toward the administration building. "There."

His office turned out to be immense—as large as the lab space in the basement of Claremont Hospital that Logan shared with twenty others. But Shein's personality seemed to instantly fill it.

"So . . ." he said, taking a seat in his antique wooden swivel chair and throwing his feet up on his desk, "tell me about this work you did with Greiner."

Left standing, Logan decided he should sit in the dilapidated upholstered chair at the foot of the desk. Immediately, he sank a foot into it. In fact, he was so low, and the clutter of reports and journals on the desk before Shein so high, that he could see only the top half of his face.

"Well," he began, repositioning himself for a better view, "we were trying to see if there were unique genes that expressed themselves in glioblastoma—"

"Stop moving, for Chrissakes. Goddamn chair's like a Venus-fly-trap."

"It's not very comfortable."

"Get out of it. Sit *there*." He indicated a plain wooden chair nearby. "So . . . ?"

"So," continued Logan, moving to the new chair, "the point was to take the DNA, slice it up with a restriction enzyme, and package it with a virus. Then you let—"

"Right," cut in Shein, "you let the goddamn virus infect the bacteria and so on and so forth." He paused, nodding toward the clutter on the desk. "Read about it years ago in *Proceedings of the National Academy of Sciences*. Just wanted to hear it in your own words. Good."

Logan looked at him curiously.

"You'd be surprised how many people try to bullshit me." He snorted. "Can you believe it—*me*?"

It didn't surprise Logan that Shein should flash a huge ego. A certain arrogance was in the makeup of every successful scientist he'd ever known. But he also knew that in this case, it was probably entirely justified; by reputation, Shein was among the most gifted researchers in the field.

"So," he added, "you were telling me outside how well you learned to follow orders in med school . . ."

Dan nodded. "I'm afraid so."

"*Afraid* so. What, you got something against following orders? What the hell you think makes an organization function?"

Logan hesitated. Where was Shein going now? Impulsively—at this point he seemed to have little to lose—he blurted out what he really felt. "Sure. But medicine's not the military. As a researcher, should you really always defer to a superior? Even if he's . . . you know, full of . . ."

"*Crap* is the word you're after, Logan. Or is it *shit*?"

"I really don't mean to—"

"Yes you do. I prefer *shit* myself. Why pussyfoot around?" He paused. "You must have some pretty good offers, no?"

Again, he'd play it straight. "A few."

Shein nodded. "Right, Karpe's got a great practice, all right. You'll be in the society columns in no time."

The younger man just stared at him. Was there anything this guy didn't know?

"But you know what?"

It wasn't so much a question as a challenge. "What?"

"You're not going there, you're coming here. You're gonna help us cure cancer."

"*What?!*" Logan wasn't even sure he could get the words out. "I'm . . . accepted?"

"I don't *want* butt kissers, Logan. What the hell kind of creativity am I gonna get with that?"

"But Dr. Shein—"

"Seth."

"Are you authorized to . . ." He hesitated. "I should tell you that Dr. Larsen—"

"Larsen's a schmuck, all right? He ask you if you were married?"

Logan nodded blankly. "He did."

Shein snorted. "You're not black, Jewish, or a woman. Gays are harder to tell. His private campaign"—he put on a German accent—"*to preserve the* Reich!"

"I'm not gay."

"Look, Larsen knows you're my kinda boy and he's out to protect his turf. You'll find that's the way it works around here."

Logan was nearly speechless. "It doesn't sound like a great work atmosphere."

"No?" This actually seemed to give Shein pause. "It depends how you look at it. The way I see it, you can tell even more about a guy by his enemies than his friends."

Logan nodded. Now that the shock had passed, he was aware of the excitement building. He tried hard to suppress it. This thing had to be discussed, negotiated. "Look," he began evenly, "I can't tell you how flattering this is—"

"Don't get so easily flattered either," cut in Shein, who evidently felt entitled to finish every one of the younger man's sentences. "You like baseball?"

"Yes." Logan tried not to look baffled.

"You're in luck, the ACF's got a box for the Orioles." He paused. "This is a draft, get it? And you're just a prospect. A good one, but still only a prospect. I can't promise you'll even make it to the pros."

"Look," Logan tried again, "I've already made something of a commitment to Karpe. There's a lot of solid hands-on medical work there."

"Right, rich people's diseases. Bet you get lots of chronic fatigue syndrome. And hemorrhoids. Nice work—look up someone's ass and pull out two hundred bucks."

"Actually, a lot of his patients have cancer."

Shein snorted. "You know why you're not gonna do that? 'Cause you're smart enough to know the two biggest secrets about cancer. One, that when it comes to treatment, we're still in the Dark Ages. So, two, even the best clinical oncologists are just glorified grease monkeys. They can only wait for us creative guys to give them some tools."

He was right and Logan knew it. He made no response.

"You'll start at fifty-one thousand."

Logan swallowed hard. "My offer from Karpe is more than three times that. I have a couple of others almost as high."

"No negotiation. This is a non-profit foundation, remember?"

Crestfallen, Logan remained silent.

"What," picked up the other, "you think this is a *bad* career move? This is the big time, Logan. Me, I got security clearance and everything. You know what even a couple of years at the ACF does for your resume? You wanna talk money, the big drug companies start top researchers from this place at three hundred grand, plus a piece of whatever patents they develop!"

Logan weighed this a long moment. "Why would you need security clearance?"

Shein waved the question away. "Are you kidding, where do you think the big shots"—he nodded vaguely in the direction of Washington—"come for treatment? Especially if they want to keep it under wraps? Who the hell do you think treats them?" He smiled at his own indiscretion. "You can get a nice autograph collection going. Think of it as one of the perks of the place."

Abruptly, Shein was on his feet, heading out of the room. "C'mon, I want to show you the main lab complex."

Mutely, Logan followed, his head spinning.

"Then I want you to see the satellite labs—you passed 'em on the way in. And let's not forget the Eisenhower Medical Center." He smiled.

"I mean, that's where you're gonna be spending most of your time, right?"

Late that night in his modest apartment, unable to sleep, Logan got out of bed and flicked on the living-room light. He found what he was looking for on the top row of the bookshelf: *Microbe Hunters,* about the pioneers of microbiology—the very copy that had so moved him as a child. It was a vintage edition, published in 1938, twelve years after the book's original appearance, and there was some damage to the binding. Gently, he opened it to the glossy section in the middle: old-fashioned engravings and ancient photographs of the geniuses honored on its pages. Stiff, serious men, wearing black suits and grim expressions.

All, that is, except the final one, Paul Ehrlich, the conqueror of syphilis. Slim, bearded, and bespectacled, appearing to be in his mid-sixties, he stared out from the page with a quizzical, almost childlike expression. On the desk before him sat the manuscript upon which he had apparently just been working. In one hand he held a cigar.

Studying the photograph, Logan smiled. As a kid, he'd lionized Ehrlich the way other kids did John F. Kennedy or Reggie Jackson. Even now, he found the story profoundly moving: this impish little man, for more than a decade working against incredible odds to find "the magic bullet" that would cure the ancient scourge.

Now Logan flipped backward to the title page. Yes, there they were, the twin inscriptions. The first was from his grandfather to his father on his ninth birthday; a curt admonition to read this book over the summer vacation. The second was from his father to himself on his eleventh: *Read this book for love, Dan, and learn more from it than I did.*

The buffet luncheon at Seth Shein's Arlington home had been billed as a social occasion—casual dress, spouses and significant others invited—but Dan Logan knew that career would be at the top of the agenda. In just two days the incoming fellows would begin working at the American Cancer Foundation, and this hazy June afternoon was the first time they would be meeting some key members of the hierarchy; their first shot, in brief, at making an impression—and of sizing up others as they tried to do the same.

"Dammit," muttered Logan as he stood in front of the open clothes closet of his new apartment. In general indifferent to how he dressed—clean was usually good enough—he realized that today this was not a matter to be taken lightly. Every detail of personal presentation might prove a potential edge—or liability.

He rejected shorts: too casual. Next he tried on the baggy, double-pleated Italian pants his last girlfriend had talked him into buying after dragging him into a chic men's shop in Manhattan. Staring at his reflection in the mirror, he tried hard to give the pants a fair shot, but wondered how any normal person could feel anything but silly wearing them.

This is ridiculous, he thought, not for the first time, *I'm a doctor, not a model*—and then began considering the merits of plaid.

After nearly an hour, he decided the wisest move was the safe one: he dimly recalled having once read in a men's magazine that khaki pants and a blue blazer were right for just about any occasion.

Seth Shein greeted him at the front door of his impressive Tudor home, a plastic cup of Scotch in his hand, wearing shorts and an extravagant Hawaiian shirt. "Kinda overdressed, wouldn't you say, Logan? It's a goddamn pool party."

Logan looked stricken. "I guess I am."

"Good thinking. You fit right in."

In fact, though the temperature hovered in the mid-eighties—and the party was indeed held around Shein's pool—all but two of the seven male junior fellows were also wearing jackets and most also had ties; while every one of the five women had shown up in a dress-for-success suit.

This made the distinction between the newcomers and the senior fellows—those who'd now been at ACF for a year—immediately apparent. All but a couple of *them* wore shorts.

Shein led Dan onto the patio, making introductions. Never good at names himself—a problem he knew he had to work on—Logan marveled that Shein not only knew who everyone was but the specifics of their backgrounds, their specialties, even their hobbies. "Allen Atlas," he said, moving him in the direction of a tall, hollow-cheeked young man in a tailored blue suit, "Dan Logan."

Dan and Atlas shook hands crisply, eyeing one another with interest.

"Allen went to school at Vanderbilt," noted Shein evenly—then suddenly assumed an exagerrated Southern accent. "In *Tennesseeeeee*. But we won't hold that against him, will we?"

The tall young man looked stricken—trying to figure out what the eminent Shein might possibly have against his alma mater.

"Now, Dan here," added Shein, in apparent comparison, "went to Princeton as an undergraduate and Stanford for his Ph.D. Number two in your class at Princeton, wasn't it?"

Logan nodded.

Shein shrugged. "We'd have gotten number one, but I'm told he went into law."

"Actually," Dan corrected, "*she* went into law."

"Ahhh," laughed Shein, slapping him on the back, "a person of precision *and* sensitivity. Good going—the girls must love that."

"Nice to meet you," mumbled Allen Atlas, eyeing him coolly.

"Same here," replied Dan. "Looking forward to working together."

"Oh, Seth . . ."

They wheeled to face a middle-aged woman bearing a pitcher of iced tea. Anxious looking and dowdily dressed, she was incongruously pretty.

"I'm sorry to interrupt you, dear," she said, "but you've got a telephone call."

He laughed. "Why sorry? What the hell you supposed to do, tell the guy to go screw himself?" He gave her a quick peck on the cheek—"Dan Logan, Allen Atlas, my wife, the endlessly patient and still beauteous Alice Shein"—and headed into the house.

There was an awkward pause. "Well," she said, "I do hope you young men will be happy here at the ACF."

They offered their thanks. It was only as she walked away that Logan became aware of her pronounced limp. He looked at his companion in surprise.

"She was one of the last kids to get polio," said Atlas blandly. And, without a further word of explanation, he wandered away.

Moving to the refreshment table, Logan poured himself a white wine and looked around. The newcomers seemed to be keeping almost entirely to themselves, clustered in groups. After a long moment, he headed toward one of these—three women and two men—at the far end of the pool.

He already knew one of them. John Reston was the other junior associate who had been recruited from Claremont. Though they'd never spent much time together, Logan had always liked him.

"Well," exclaimed Reston, brightening, "look who's here! Ladies and gentleman, Daniel Logan—a fellow escapee from Claremont Hospital hell."

As Reston made the introductions, Dan made a conscious effort to link the names to the faces. *Amy*—no last name necessary, she wasn't with the program, just Reston's girlfriend. *Barbara Lukas*—the tiny one, little more than five feet, with the staccato delivery and the degree from Duke. *Paul Bernstein*—quick with a smile, by the look of it a little too smooth. In fact, he seemed to be already putting the moves on *Sabrina Como*—the striking young Italian with the mane of black hair, large green eyes, and incredible accent upon whom Logan himself was suddenly interested in making an impression.

Abruptly, from out of nowhere, Seth Shein joined them. "You all making friends?"

They agreed they were.

"Good, you're gonna be working closely together." He smiled. "We like to leave the back-stabbing to the *senior* staff."

This brought an uncomfortable laugh. Dan began to suspect that perhaps the Scotch was getting to Shein.

A moment later, the thought was confirmed. Smiling at Sabrina Como, Shein announced, "Appearances to the contrary, we recruit our foreign associates only for their *scientific* potential."

Sabrina looked at him evenly, showing nothing, but Dan noticed Barbara shoot Shein a vicious look. Still, she was wise enough to remain silent—as they all were. He, Reston, and Bernstein, supposedly sensitive, postfeminist types all, simply stood there, grinning awkwardly.

It was Reston's petite blond friend Amy who broke the silence. "And I'm sure women are treated very well at the ACF," she offered breezily. "Appearances to the contrary."

Logan and the other associates turned to her, horrified. But they were stopped short by Shein's hearty laugh. "That's *great!*" He laughed some more. "I really mean it, I wish you were in the program."

This was so unexpected that Amy didn't know quite how to respond. "You know," she said after a long pause, "I'm not really sure I have much to contribute here. Why don't I leave you people alone to get acquainted?"

As she moved off in the direction of the buffet table, Reston offered a helpless shrug. "Sorry."

"Don't *apologize*, Reston," interjected Shein, "she's a riot. Believe me, hang around here long enough, you forget what someone with guts *sounds* like." And, chuckling to himself, he left them.

Among the four associates, there was a long silence. "You should know," offered Sabrina, "I really am not bothered by such things."

"Well, you should be," snapped Barbara Lukas. "A superior makes a lascivious remark like that in this country, it's called sexual harassment."

"Ah." She nodded, with a barely perceptible smile. "Well, then, perhaps it is because I am not from this country."

"You were *meant* to be insulted. As a woman. We all were."

"Because he says I am a good scientist and also pretty?"

"Exactly. Because he has no damn business commenting on your looks one way or the other."

"Ah," she said again, and paused thoughtfully. "I must study to learn to recognize such insults."

Logan, suppressing a smile, looked at her with even greater interest; but Lukas, unsure whether she was being heeded or gently mocked, quickly turned to Reston. "She your wife?" she said, nodding after Amy.

"My girlfriend," replied Reston. "She's a lawyer, she got a job with the FCC."

"He's right—she's got guts. I should've said something myself."

"I strongly suspect you'll get other chances," he said dryly.

"Well," noted Bernstein, "I hate to be a realist, but saying what you think isn't exactly the best policy around here. Not everyone's as tolerant as Shein. I had a long talk last night with one of the senior associates. There are a few people we're really going to have to watch out for."

Barbara Lukas focused on him intently. "Name names."

With a tilt of the head, Bernstein indicated a balding young man in horn-rimmed glasses standing near the buffet table. "See him?"

The others turned to look.

"Peter Kratsas. He's Larsen's number two."

"Larsen interviewed me," spoke up Logan. "If that's what you can call it. I was in and out of there in ten minutes."

"I also." They all turned to Sabrina. "I came all the way here for this interview, and he was just cold like anything."

"Tell me about it," agreed Bernstein. "But I hear Kratsas is even worse. For starters, he doesn't have Larsen's talent. But what you've really gotta watch out for is that he's *nice*. Always ready to chat about sports or old movies like he's your best pal."

Barbara Lukas rolled her eyes. "So you think he's on your side—and he's a pipeline right back to Larsen?"

"You got it," nodded Bernstein.

"Who else should we know about?" asked Dan.

"Who *shouldn't* we know about?"

Seeing how much Bernstein was enjoying this performance, Logan had a strong feeling he was purposely being overdramatic.

"Who else?" pressed Barbara Lukas.

"Greg Stillman."

There was a surprised silence. The name needed no explanation. Dr. Gregory Stillman, world-renowned specialist in breast cancer, was one of those chiefly responsible for the ACF's reputation.

"C'mon," said Logan finally, "someone's doing a lot of exaggerating here."

Bernstein snorted. "I'm talking personality, not medical acumen. Talk to the senior associates—this is a guy who describes *himself* as 'a vicious SOB.' He thinks other people respect him for it." He paused for effect. "And they do."

A few minutes later, Logan moved alongside Reston at the buffet table. "You buy any of that?"

Reston shrugged. "Hard to tell. Maybe we were just watching a guy working real hard to impress a good-looking woman." He smiled. "Who can blame him?"

"Well," said Logan, "we survived Claremont. . . ."

The remark called for no elaboration. The institution they'd just left was a political minefield, famous even in the cutthroat world of high-powered medicine for the willingness of young doctors to curry favor with their superiors and, when it came to that, to cut one another up; and, maybe even more so, for the readiness of senior personnel to shaft their subordinates in self-protection.

"Damn right," agreed Reston, "no way this could be as bad as that. At Claremont, you had the greed factor, everyone after the same big pot of gold at the end of the rainbow. Here—"

"It's for science," Logan finished the thought.

Reston laughed. "I was gonna say the only pot's the one we piss in."

"So what brought you into research? You don't really seem like the type."

"Me? I hate the sight of blood."

Logan smiled.

"You think I'm kidding? The first time I saw an autopsy—the way they folded that poor guy's scalp and used an electric saw to pop his top —I *knew* there had to be a better angle."

"Really? I always found autopsies pretty interesting."

"Another thing," said Reston, ignoring this, "—I think over the long run clinical work can have a disastrous effect on your libido. I mean, I love women. But you can take the most beautiful one in the world—someone you'd normally *fantasize* about—and stick her in one of those damn hospital gowns, with that harsh light showing every zit and blemish, and, sorry, the romance is gone. Especially if you catch her later in the autopsy room. You're not gonna *think* about sex for a week."

"Well . . ." If Logan didn't know quite how to respond, he at least had to admire the guy's candor, a trait he'd encountered all too rarely at their prior place of employment. "I'm pretty sure you won't have to suffer through too many autopsies here. That doesn't seem to be part of the drill."

"I hope not. Let's face it, the only reason they did so many at Claremont was so those weenies in the administration could keep their asses covered."

"Wasn't that everyone's main job at Claremont, keeping his ass covered? All you wanted to do was get out of that place unscathed."

Reston nodded. "So? How'd you manage it?"

"I don't know." He thought about it a moment. "Look, you have to be good. They don't screw people with real promise. That'd be screwing themselves, the whole basis of their reputation—"

"I get it, no one gave you a hard time cause you were so *talented*."

Logan smiled; no offense was meant, none taken. "I mean, sure, you don't go looking for trouble. You find out early who the key players are and make a point of staying on their good side. You make yourself helpful to attending physicians. You don't go around telling dirty jokes to senior administrators."

"Not unless you've seen someone else get ahead doing it first. See, now we're getting into my territory. It's called being obsequious."

"Being *careful*. There's a difference."

"Don't forget the patients. You *never*—even momentarily—leave John Eldridge Grump III in a room with a comatose ex–Pullman porter." He paused. "Actually, one of the nicest things about Claremont Hospital is that it's the socially acceptable place to check out—I could keep track of my patients through the *Times* obituaries. God forbid any of those people should be caught dead at Brooklyn Jewish!"

"Fine," acknowledged Logan, "*very* careful. I don't pretend to be selfless—in this business that's self-destructive. But," he added, meaning it, "I also don't think I ever violated my sense of integrity."

"All right, *strategically* obsequious. *Honorably* obsequious." He nodded, grinning. "Neither did I."

Logan laughed; this guy seemed to be a soulmate. "Well, then, who's to say that training won't be as valuable at this place as anything else?"

But abruptly they were cut off by the roar of a motorcycle zooming up the adjacent driveway. Skidding to a stop, the driver—in black leather, his face obscured by the black-tinted Plexiglas of his helmet—dismounted and strode into the midst of the gathering.

"Who the hell is *that?*" whispered Reston. "Talk about making an impression!"

"Stillman!" called out Seth Shein from across the patio, as if in response. "Get that goddamn thing off my lawn!"

Stillman removed the helmet, revealing a beet-red face, topped by thick black hair matted with perspiration. He looked to be in his late thirties. His surprisingly unimpressive features—a doughy face and droopy eyelids—lent him a sense of sleepy disengagement.

Almost instantly, a half dozen senior associates surrounded the eminent oncologist. "You guys I already know," he announced, loud enough for everyone to hear. "Let's see if we've got any scientists in this new bunch."

From then on, it was Stillman's show. Purposefully, he began making the rounds of the newcomers, introducing himself and exchanging a few words. Given Bernstein's earlier warning, Logan found himself surprised that the man seemed quite the opposite of an ogre.

"I read your recommendations," he told the young doctor. "We're looking for good things from you."

"Thank you, sir," said Logan, immensely pleased. "I'll try not to disappoint."

"Good. Don't." Unexpectedly, he flashed a smile. "Anything you need, I'm the guy—"

"Chicken, Greg?" offered Seth Shein, suddenly at their side, thrusting a plate of barbecued chicken Stillman's way. He smiled, but there was utterly no warmth in it.

Stillman speared a leg—"Why not?"—and started munching it. Suddenly he was a different man, his eyes alive, looking distinctly younger, *energized*.

"Why not a breast, Greg? Isn't that your specialty?"

"Not after you've been handling it, Seth. At that point the patient is usually beyond hope."

The other glared at him. "At least I don't run experiments that risk lives!"

"That's true," said Stillman. "Your experiments don't do anything at all."

Looking on, Logan was aghast. It wasn't merely that Shein had had far too much to drink, or even that these two so clearly loathed each other. What was remarkable, what even the wars at Claremont had not prepared him for, was how little effort either made to hide the fact.

Abruptly, Stillman turned back his way with an ingratiating smile. "Aren't you hot in those clothes, Doctor?"

"Leave him alone," snapped Shein.

"Well?" said Stillman, ignoring this.

Not knowing what to do, Logan nodded tentatively.

"I know I am," said Stillman, suddenly unzipping his leather jacket and tossing it at Shein's feet; quickly followed by his boots and leather pants. Underneath, he wore a pair of trunks.

"First rule of medical research," he announced, with a raised eyebrow, "—one a lot of people around here have yet to learn: Never shy away from the unorthodox because you're worried what people will say." He shot Shein a look. "You'll find that most people—including your colleagues—are idiots." He dived into the pool and with strong, even strokes began making his way to the other end.

"You," hissed Shein, in Logan's direction, "are going to have to choose sides." And, though still dressed, dived into the pool after the other man, racing frantically to overtake him.

Two days later, his first day of work, Logan reached the ACF grounds before seven. Though the initiation session for incoming associates was not scheduled to begin till eight-thirty, he didn't want to take the slightest chance of arriving late; or, for that matter, of drawing *any* undue attention to himself.

The encounter between the two senior scientists had thrown him badly. Sure, it was easy to rationalize, and he did, that the occasion had provided an unusually combustible set of circumstances: brutal heat, lots of alcohol, an audience of novice junior associates calling forth the basest competitive instincts of each. Logan had often seen gifted men under stress act like spoiled five-year-olds, and knew he would many times again; ego and insecurity almost always come as a matched set. Still, as he replayed the scene over and over in his mind, the question grew ever more insistent: *What the hell had he gotten himself into?*

Besides, heavy rain was predicted; and, though he'd studied a map of the campus, Logan's sense of direction was notoriously unreliable. He would surely need time to get his bearings.

It proved a wise precaution. The employee pass he'd received in the mail got him through the main gate, but he found himself turned away from the underground garage of the administration building by a uniformed guard. In the interest of sabotage prevention, it seemed one needed a special parking credential available only through ACF security. Then, just as he drew his newly purchased used Ford into the visitors' lot several hundred yards beyond, the heavens opened.

Cursing himself for forgetting his umbrella, he made a dash for the building, *The Washington Post* his only shield. By the time he got there, he was soaked.

"Christ," he muttered, staring at his matted hair in the men's room mirror. To his further annoyance, the paper-towel dispensers were empty —in fact, the bathroom seemed surprisingly poorly serviced in general, more like the one in his old high school than what he'd expected to find in the nation's top medical research facility. Doing the best he could with wadded toilet paper, he headed for the nearby cafeteria, got a cup of tea, and took a spot at a corner table to dry out.

He had just unfolded his soggy paper when he saw John Reston, moving his way with a full tray.

"Look at you," noted Reston, grinning. "No security pass, right?"

Logan shook his head. "Do you have one?"

He set down the tray and withdrew an official-looking laminated card from his jacket pocket. "Just have to know the right people. Talk to Shein's assistant, she'll take care of it." He smiled. "Or talk to Shein—if you dare."

"How'd you find out?"

"Hey, some of us got here a few days early and asked around." Sitting down, he indicated his plate, piled high with scrambled eggs and overdone bacon. "Hope you don't mind me making a pig of myself."

"Go ahead, it's your body."

"And I *looove* abusing it." Reston crammed a forkful of eggs into his mouth. "You feeling all right? You seem down."

"Aren't you? After the other day?"

"Naaah. Look, guys like this, we're hardly even in their field of vision. Anyway, they've already wrecked our personal and financial lives, what more can they do?"

Despite himself, Logan smiled. "So who's running this orientation meeting?"

"Larsen."

"Really?" Logan shuddered. "The guy hates me."

"Welcome to the club." He ran a napkin across his mouth. "But listen, I'm telling you, you can't take these things personally. Junior associates aren't important enough for a guy like Larsen to hate."

"You're probably right."

"Aren't you going to eat anything? That tea'll go right through you on an empty stomach."

"So?"

He shrugged. "Just a suggestion. My guess is Larsen won't much like it if you keep jumping up from the meeting."

Larsen was precisely as Logan remembered him. Sitting at the head of a large conference table, flanked on one side by his lieutenant Kratsas and on the other by his grim-faced secretary, the chief of the Department of Medicine ran the meeting with dry, humorless efficiency.

He opened by indicating the two thick spiral-bound notebooks that had been set down before each of the new associates. "For your first assignment, you will be expected to master the material in these books. All of it. No excuses or exceptions."

That was it. No word of welcome. No banter. Not even the pretense of collegiality.

"Now," continued Larsen, "you all know who I am and why we're here. You have been accepted into this program because somebody thinks you've got what it takes to eventually make a contribution toward curing cancer. But it is my job to inform you that, at least for the first year, your role is to provide support for senior physicians. You are to do what you're told, period. We are not looking to you for creativity."

This did not come as anything like news to Logan or the others, of course. They'd always known that the ACF was a rigid hierarchy; and that as first-year fellows their chief concern would be not research but basic patient care.

Still, Logan wondered if any of the others were as put off by Larsen's condescending manner as he was. He quickly glanced up from the legal pad where he was scribbling notes. All of the others, writing dutifully, kept their heads down.

"Each of you will be responsible for charting the progress of between one hundred twenty-five and one hundred and fifty patients," Larsen continued, "of whom about twenty will be on site at any given moment. As you know, our job here is to develop and test new cancer therapies. Every patient at the ACF has agreed to take part in a carefully controlled course of treatment. A large part of your job is to see to it your patients in no way deviate from the instructions they have been issued. That they understand that if they fail to follow through in any way, they will be dropped from the program." He paused. "Some lay people might see this as callous. As scientists, we know better. We understand that in a program of rigorous scientific inquiry, rules can never be bent."

He paused, nodding in the direction of Kratsas. "Some of you are familiar with Dr. Kratsas. He will give you a brief overview of the trials currently in progress. Everything you will hear is privileged information. Divulging any of it without authorization shall be regarded as grounds for immediate dismissal."

The threat was of course unnecessary, a pointless insult to the professionalism of the highly skilled young doctors present; yet Logan felt certain the man's loutishness was not even intentional. His style reflected his essence.

"Dr. Kratsas," he said, surrendering the floor.

Kratsas's sudden smile was ingratiating, a conscious effort to dispel the chill that had settled over the room.

"First," he began, "I want to extend a personal welcome. I'm sure I speak for the entire senior staff in saying that we are always available as colleagues and friends."

Logan glanced at Larsen, who stared straight ahead, showing nothing. *Sure,* he thought, *that guy'll be my friend, all right—the day jelly beans cure cancer.*

"Now, then," continued Kratsas, "some of you may know I'm an avid fan of the film director Alfred Hitchcock. I bring this up for a reason—because I believe Hitchcock would have made a magnificent cancer researcher. Why? He was canny, he was precise, he was resourceful and—a quality we must all nurture—he understood desperation and fear. Not only understood them, but knew how to *work* with them." As he scanned the table meaningfully, there was not a doubt in Logan's mind that he'd delivered these lines a dozen times before.

Kratsas smiled again and patted a notebook on the table before him. "Now, then, as I'm sure you know, our courses of experimental treatment fall into three categories. A Phase One trial is by definition a new and highly innovative form of treatment. Subjects' malignancies are highly advanced and we obviously recognize going in that the chances of meaningful success are remote." He paused and took a sip from the glass of water before him. "Indeed, in such trials our very definition of success changes. Usually, what most interests us is measuring toxicity—gauging the maximum dose of this new drug the human body will tolerate. Its impact on the malignancy is often of only secondary concern."

He held up a notebook. "As you read through your material, you will note that we are currently conducting only two Phase One protocols here at the ACF. Which is to say, no one will be dealing with more than two or three patients who are participating in such research. Still, given such patients' highly advanced levels of disease, they are likely to require a considerable amount of attention." He paused, glancing at Larsen. "Obviously, we do not lie to patients. Ethics is a serious concern here at the ACF. But neither, when a patient's situation is desperate, is it necessarily always the best policy to volunteer every scintilla of truth. Think of Hitchcock: patients who are led to feel there is no hope have precious little incentive to remain with the program."

He cleared his throat and took another sip of water. "Now, then, only a small number of the drugs that go through a Phase One test, perhaps ten percent, move on to a Phase Two trial—a more comprehensive test aimed at determining a compound's effectiveness against malignancy in a specific organ. In turn, no more than about ten percent of those drugs—*one* percent of the total—are sufficiently promising to warrant Phase Three trials, which test the new treatment against the best existing therapy. When a patient signs on, he does not know whether he will receive an established or an experimental treatment. I can tell you, however, that it is our policy to never give any cancer patient a placebo. That would constitute deception of the cruelest kind."

He paused. "We all know that lay people—and that includes our patients and their families—tend to have a wildly optimistic view of what can be achieved. They don't come here merely because everything's free; they're hoping to be cured. We, however, are scientists. Our hopes may be great, but our expectations are realistic: a successful Phase Three trial is defined as one that produces a response rate only slightly better than the standard treatment, or one that meaningfully improves quality of life.

"Now, then, that doesn't mean breakthroughs don't occur. I presume you are all familiar with the drug cisplatin . . .?" He paused, surveying the serious faces around the table, seeming to wait for a response.

"Active against testicular cancer," spoke up Reston.

"Yes, but that's hardly the full story. I suppose you're all too young to remember a movie called *Brian's Song*, but it was a great success when I was your age. It was based on the story of a football player who died of testicular cancer as a very young man."

"Brian Piccolo," said Logan softly, from his seat beside Larsen's secretary.

Larsen looked at him sharply. "This is not a free-for-all, Doctor. Or a television quiz program."

"Now, then," continued Kratsas, "in those years, the early seventies, the cure rate for metastatic testicular cancer was on the order of thirty percent. Today it is what?"

Silence.

It was Sabrina Como, the Italian, who finally spoke up. "I believe it is seventy-five percent," she said.

Kratsas nodded. "Actually, with cisplatin, it's closer to eighty."

He picked up one of the spiral notebooks and let it fall to the table with a bang. Several of the young associates started. "Heavy, huh? It contains, among other things, a rundown of all current protocols—thirty-six in all. You shall be expected to have familiarized yourself with them all by Wednesday. Because that is the day you assume charge of your full complement of patients."

Even during their long years as interns and residents, none of the younger doctors had ever heard anyone suggest such a workload: in two days each would be handed over one hundred patients desperately ill with cancer—patients whose course of treatment, whose very medicines, at this moment they knew *nothing* about.

"For your benefit," picked up Kratsas, "the senior associates have dictated a full history of each case. Later this afternoon, you will learn from the communications people how to do proper ACF evaluation dictation. Such an evaluation will be expected whenever a patient is discharged, or otherwise passes from the program." Logan could scarcely suppress a smile; *passes from the program*—the euphemism was a new one to him, even after Claremont. "These evaluations must be letter perfect," Kratsas droned on. "Master the form! By Wednesday, you will also be expected to have full command of the computer system."

Logan paused in his note taking to chance a quick smile in Reston's direction: this was so overwhelming, there seemed no other possible response.

"As for hospital duty, at least one of you must be on the patient floor at all times, day and night. It is expected that you will divide up the night coverage equitably among yourselves. If you want some sleep, I suggest you find an empty patient room."

He turned back to Larsen. "Now, then, I think that about covers it."

Larsen nodded crisply. "One thing I wish to emphasize. Every doctor here of course has a responsibility to his patients. But his primary responsibility—his overriding priority—must always be this institution. Is that understood?"

Larsen's fearsome gaze swept the table. Then, tentatively, a hand rose into the air. Barbara Lukas.

"What is it?" snapped Larsen.

Clearly, this was not easy, and her voice quavered slightly. "It's just a small thing. In referring to a doctor, you keep saying *his* responsibility and *his* priority. I was just wondering, since there are also quite a few of us women here, if you might be a bit more inclusive."

There was total, stupefied silence. Larsen's face visibly reddened, and Logan thought he could see a vein in his temple start to twitch. In an effort to distance themselves from this kamikaze mission, most of the other women present stared down at the table.

But, incredibly, Larsen seemed to keep his cool. "What," he said, tight lipped, "would you suggest?"

Lukas seemed to gain in confidence. "Perhaps *he or she*, something like that. Just a little more sensitivity."

He drummed his fingers on the table, appearing to consider this. "No, Dr. Lukas, NO!" With a sudden crack, his hand came crashing down on the polished wood. "Maybe young people get away with bullying their elders at Duke these days, but it will not happen here!"

He paused, then resumed his former tone. "After your patient-care year, you will in turn pass on your patient roster to next year's incoming fellows. And, assuming we are pleased with you"—here, stopping for a millisecond, he shot Lukas daggers—"you will then be attached to a laboratory in which to pursue your specific area of interest."

Abruptly, a bell sounded in the corridor outside the conference room, followed immediately by a commanding female voice on the loud-speaker. "Code blue. Twelfth floor. Room thirty-eight."

"Never mind that," snapped Larsen. "Let's continue."

"Dr. Larsen . . ." The words, the first his secretary had spoken, were barely above a whisper, but Logan picked them up.

Larsen leaned toward her.

"That's Mrs. Conrad."

He hesitated an instant, frowned, then rose to his feet. "Dr. Kratsas," he said, moving briskly toward the door, "take over, will you?"

"Who's Mrs. Conrad?" ventured Logan, several hours later.

Rich Levitt, the senior associate whose patient roster Dan was about to inherit, stared at him across his tidy desk. "She's an ovarian patient."

"That's it?"

"The wife of *Senator* Conrad . . . ?" He raised an eyebrow, waiting for it to sink in. ". . . North Carolina? The Senate Appropriations Committee?"

"Ahhhh."

"Why?"

Logan recounted the episode from the meeting.

"Don't tell me that's your first visit to the real world. How do you think this place gets most of its funding?"

Dan nodded. Of course, it made perfect sense. Every medical facility he knew of, no matter how supposedly democratic, provided treatment a bit *more* equal for the select few. What took him aback was the other's straightforwardness. Entry into an ACF program was widely believed to be solely on the basis of suitability for a treatment protocol.

"I guess I kind of thought the ACF was above that kind of politics," Dan admitted.

"Look, it's not like she wasn't a legitimate candidate. Let's say she just got more consideration than *other* legitimate candidates. The important thing for you to know is that it's not your problem: Mrs. Conrad's not on our patient roster." He smiled and shook his head. "Above politics? Some of these guys spend half their lives up on the Hill trying to shake money loose for their pet projects."

"Any big shots on our patient roster?"

Levitt held out a hand and ticked them off. "Two congressmen. The administrative aide for the number-two man on the Senate Armed Services Committee. One Labor Department spouse, one Defense Department staff spouse." He tapped his head and smiled. "It's all right here in case of emergency. But none of them are as important as Mrs. Conrad. You saw it, she makes even Larsen jump."

Logan didn't know quite what to make of Levitt. Rarely had he encountered so improbable a mix of selflessness and utter cynicism; then again, increasingly that seemed simply a reflection of the ACF itself.

"So Mrs. Conrad's the top VIP here now?"

"Absolutely." He paused. "As far as I know."

"What does that mean?"

Levitt exhaled deeply. Though he had no objection to answering the newcomer's wide-eyed questions, his real concern was handing over his patients so he could move on to better things.

"Sometimes—rarely, but sometimes—there are people who get seen only by the top guys. They might even check in under phony names."

"You're kidding me."

"Not that the rest of us don't usually know there's something going on."

He glanced at his watch and sighed. "Look," he said, rising to his feet, "I think it's about time you met some of my—soon to be your—patients."

"Well," said Logan, following suit, "at least this part will be familiar."

"Maybe. Although the patients you'll be dealing with here may not be what you're used to."

Logan was baffled. "Actually, I had a lot of experience at Claremont dealing with terminal cancer pat—"

"No," interrupted Levitt. "There are big differences. First, you were treating those patients individually, improvising as circumstances changed, right?"

"Of course."

"Well—I can't emphasize this strongly enough, Logan—here you have zero treatment options. None. Your job is to enforce the protocol. Period. Which means that sometimes you'll actually have to go *against* your better judgment."

Logan was silent as this hit home.

"It can be a huge psychological adjustment."

"What happens if a patient starts questioning the terms of the protocol?"

"Happens all the time. Your problem is just making sure the patient doesn't *leave* the protocol. Because then you're messing with the entire study: there'll be no way to know if that patient's responding to therapy or for how long. When patients start dropping out, people start saying the work was sloppy or the treatment was too toxic." He paused. "Trust me, if a protocol patient drops out on your watch, the senior guy running that study will have your ass. Some of those guys are killers."

"I get that impression."

Levitt nodded. "Yeah, I heard about that thing at Shein's the other day. Welcome to the ACF."

In fact, Logan had been thinking of Lukas's gruesome face-off with Larsen, but no matter. "Some of these guys . . ." he ventured, ". . . you get the impression they're liable to blow any minute."

"You learn to take it in stride."

"I mean, getting on the junior people is one thing. But they hate *each other*."

"Absolutely." He smiled. "When I first got here, another guy showed me a chart he'd done of the relationships between the big hitters. Each senior staffer was represented by a circle with lines representing normal interactions in black ink and lines representing *hate* interactions in red." He paused for effect. "I'm telling you, the thing looked like a wiring diagram for the phone company."

"But it doesn't make sense. Even at Claremont, there were—"

"You have any idea how fierce the competition is for funding? It's a zero-sum game: every time someone wins, someone else loses."

Levitt explained that in the case of Shein and Stillman, for instance, the animosity dated to Shein's long-ago support of a young ACF researcher who had come up with a novel approach to breast cancer: using a syringe to shoot monoclonal antibodies directly into the bloodstream in a kind of biochemical search-and-destroy mission. Stillman vigorously resisted (and won) on the ground that the data on which the conclusions were based were incomplete—though soon afterward he wrote a protocol himself based on the same idea. Quite simply, Stillman regarded breast cancer as his turf; in mucking around with *his* cancer Shein had earned an enemy for life. More than one enemy, in fact—for Stillman numbered among his allies a half dozen key figures at the ACF.

"That's par for the course. None of these guys can stand each other. Larsen—*he* probably hates Shein even more."

"What's the story there?"

He shrugged. "Nothing in particular. Just oil and water. To Larsen, Shein represents everything most loathsome not only about science but life. And vice versa."

Logan had already sensed as much. "Do Larsen and Stillman get along?"

"Get *along?*" he asked, surprised. "You mean, like *friends?*" He stopped, began again. "Look, I'll try and simplify things. The way it works is all the top guys have their own little fiefdoms and their own loyalists. The ultimate aim of each is to defeat all the others. But sometimes, for strategic reasons, they'll forge alliances against a common enemy. Get it?"

"You make it sound medieval."

He smiled. "Well, I've never actually heard of anyone using maces and boiling oil."

Logan nodded soberly. "So what you're saying is I'd better stay on *everyone's* good side. Consider me warned."

"And you'd better also be ready for some of what you're going to be running into from patients—"

"That I'm familiar with. I've dealt with some pretty bad attitudes."

"You think so? Because the ones at the ACF are a whole different breed. A lot of them have moved heaven and earth to get here; they've told their local doctors, 'I no longer want this shit you're giving me,' and traveled thousands of miles to undergo a course of treatment that might end up doing nothing. The ACF is a roll of the dice and not many shrinking violets take it."

"They're fighters. Nothing wrong with that."

Levitt nodded. "The truth is, if you've got cancer, there's no better place to be treated. It's just that full cooperation is *their* part of the bargain—and sometimes they make you pay for it." He started from the room, Logan trailing after. "What I'm trying to tell you is that conflicts are inevitable because we and the patients basically have different agendas. We're interested in finding ways to cure cancer. They want *their* cancer cured. No one ever uses the term *guinea pig,* but some patients eventually get the idea that's what they've signed up for."

"I see," said Logan soberly.

"No, but you're about to." Rounding a corner, they came to a bank of gleaming elevators. "Let's go see Rochelle Boudin."

"Which one's she?" Logan had already gone over several dozen of the patient files Levitt had prepared.

"Massive mediastinal Hodgkin's disease? She's one of Larsen's."

"Oh, right,"—as always, Logan had a better head for disease than for names—"she's in the control group for the test of the new drug combination they're trying against Hodgkin's—they have her on ACE chemo."

The protocol in question was a Phase Three. ACE chemotherapy, an acronym for the three compounds involved in the treatment, had been pioneered almost twenty-five years before by Dr. Kenneth Markell, current head of the ACF. If it was less than completely effective, it significantly reduced tumor mass eighty percent of the time.

"What's the problem? Didn't the report say she's doing well?"

"What does that have to do with it—this woman is the *mother* of all pains." He paused. "And there's also a *father.*"

The reference, as Logan soon learned, was to the patient's husband, Roger, who seemed to spend almost as much time at the hospital as his wife, hovering over her, seeing it as his role to challenge the doctors' every move.

After a couple of minutes in their presence, Logan had a hard time deciding which of them he liked less: the endlessly self-pitying Rochelle, who seemed to see her illness as some vast plot to undermine her happiness; or the arrogant Roger, a take-charge guy without a clue. For the moment, he was content to stand back and watch Levitt handle these two.

The problem today was that Rochelle was due to start a new round of chemotherapy in two days. For most every patient, of course, chemo is an ordeal approached with dread; but they swallow hard and take their medicine.

Not Rochelle.

"It will have to be postponed," her husband put it to Levitt. "She's not ready."

"I'm really sorry," she said mournfully.

"I'm afraid that's not possible, Mrs. Boudin. We've been through this."

"You docs can do whatever you damn well please," snapped Roger.

"Actually," came the measured reply, "you know very well we can't. According to the terms of the protocol—"

"Damn the protocol! Look at her—she's looking great, she's feeling fine! Why put her through this now?"

"I feel like I'm losing control," said Rochelle, her bottom lip trembling. "It's not fair that you make me feel that way. Just thinking about it makes me nauseous."

"They just take advantage of your good nature. They make allowances for other patients on this protocol."

"That's completely untrue."

"Easy to say—since you haven't let us meet any!"

"We're bound to protect their anonymity just as we do yours." Levitt exhaled deeply, trying to maintain his composure. "I understand, the treatment is extremely unpleasant. And, yes, thank God, the tumor does seem to be in remission. But we do this for a reason. We've been charting the lab values very closely and—"

"So have we," cut in Roger, "and *we* think it's unnecessary. At the least, we insist on a reduction of the dosage."

"I'm sorry, we can't do that."

Roger Boudin shook his head, as if scarcely able to believe the doctor's unreasonableness. "I didn't want to have to say this, but we've taken the numbers elsewhere for independent evaluation."

"You've *what?*" If he'd hoped to get Levitt's attention, he'd succeeded beyond all expectations; for a moment Logan thought his colleague might lose it. But almost instantly he recovered his professionalism. "Mrs. Boudin," he said blandly, turning toward the patient, "obviously it is your right to take that information to anyone you see fit. It is also your right to remove yourself from the protocol at any time." He stared at the floor a moment, then cleared his throat. "If you choose to do so, kindly inform me as soon as possible so I can prepare the appropriate paperwork."

Levitt was playing with fire, and Dan Logan knew it. Would he really let her go—or was he simply convinced they were bluffing?

Bingo! Almost instantly, Roger began backpedaling. "I don't mean . . . no, it's nothing like that. He's a cousin of mine. We just got to talking about it."

Levitt stared at him coldly. "As I say, it is your choice. You have been informed of the rules." He glanced at his watch. "I've got other patients to see."

He turned and began walking from the room. Logan followed.

"Doctor?"

They turned. It was Rochelle, her eyes moist. "Could you come back later?" she asked, a lost little girl. "Maybe tomorrow? Just to answer a few questions?"

He nodded crisply. "Certainly."

As soon as they reached the hall, Levitt clapped his hands together. "Meaning," he added, grinning broadly, "that *you'll* be back later."

The malignant cells now number in the tens of millions. Having successfully migrated from the breast, they prosper in new environments; even when completely autonomous, free of all contact with their fellows. They have proven particularly adept at infiltrating bone.

She tries hard to ignore the nagging pain. It is one more demand on her patience in a life full of such demands. For years she's been saying she doesn't believe in illness. Anyway, the Tylenol in her desk drawer still provides the temporary relief she needs.

The progression is relentless. A malignant cell observes none of the constraints that inhibit normal ones. Each is now the equivalent of a professional killer, plundering nutrients that normal cells need to survive, showing contempt for physiological equilibrium and tissue architecture. The tumor replicates itself every three weeks. Each new generation of malignant cells is even more aggressive.

Her husband knows her better than anyone. Before bed one evening he notices—not for the first time—that she is vigorously massaging the small of her back. Shrugging off her assurance, he insists she have it looked at.

Logan got very little sleep that night—but he didn't care. Propped up in bed, surrounded by piles of spiral-bound notebooks, sipping from a coffee cup—a gift from an old girlfriend, bearing a picture of Drs. Frankenstein, Kildare, and Mengele over the words Medicine, a straaaange businesss—he was so immersed in the notebooks, it was nearly dawn before he was even aware of the time.

This was no mere assignment to be grudgingly endured. The descriptions of the trials being performed at the ACF were more than just fascinating; after his introduction to the place, they were invigorating. This was what mattered, not all the personality conflicts and petty bureaucratic maneuverings. Those came with every job everywhere. But only at the ACF was it possible to do this kind of remarkable work.

The protocols were the heart and soul of the ACF, the very reason for its existence and wondrous reputation. For a young doctor, studying them was a chance to explore the thinking of the greatest minds in the field, to have the very future of cancer medicine laid out before him.

Each of the thirty-six protocol proposals ran at least twenty-five pages and was loaded with the kind of obscure language and arcane detail that would quickly put off anyone outside the field. But to Dan, every one was like a chapter of an epic detective story. For it suggested a new approach to the age-old mystery of cancer; a plausible theory about why and how malignant cells grow and change as they do; a daring hypothesis about how this or that drug might have an impact where nothing had ever worked before.

Logan was not surprised by the number of compounds that had

demonstrated activity against malignancy—at least in a test tube or a rat. Too, he was prepared for the staggering variety of problems that remained in almost every instance, most involving the complex issue of toxicity: fully a third of the trials focused on mechanisms for targeting tumor cells while leaving surrounding healthy cells intact. But what did take him aback, what he had never before fully grasped, was how many of the most promising drugs had in some form been known to scientists for decades. It was just that, among the hundreds of thousands of compounds available, with more being developed every day, their potential uses had never before been fathomed, let alone tested; no one, until now, having made the essential leaps of logic and imagination.

Logan found himself absorbed even by the specifics of patient eligibility, daily treatment plans, and statistical analyses of data. Able to see the desperate human beings beyond the cold numbers, he understood that a change of just a few percentage points in the survival rates represented the lives of thousands of individuals and the well-being of countless families.

The next morning, Reston caught the bounce in Logan's step as soon as he saw him approaching the administration building lobby.

"Who'd *you* sleep with?"

Logan laughed. "I have the feeling I'm not going to be sleeping with anyone for a long time—unless I find someone who gets turned on by randomized trials in Hodgkin's disease."

"Ah, you've been going through the protocols. . . ."

Logan nodded. "God, some of the stuff that's being done around here!"

"I know," smiled Reston. "Amazing, isn't it?"

"I mean, I'm reading this stuff and thinking, *What the hell do these people need* me *for?*"

"We went through that yesterday with Larsen—to do the scut work." He snickered. "But don't give me any of that false-modesty crap. You're thinking the same thing I am: *How soon before I get to run a protocol of my own?*"

Logan smiled. "Me? I'm a humble junior associate, I accept my station in life."

"Like hell."

"At least for public consumption." He glanced around the busy lobby. "Look, seriously, that kind of talk's not going to do either of us any good."

"Logan, they know we're ambitious. Ambition is part of what they were after when they brought us here."

"*Controlled* ambition. Ambition in the service of the greater good."

Reston nodded. "You're right. The first order of business"—his voice dropped slightly—"is figuring out which of the senior guys to try and get as a godfather."

"Reston, you're really out of your mind, you know that?"

"What are you, blind, deaf, and dumb or just pretending to be? You think you'll get anywhere around here without one?"

Logan shook his head. "Not me. I'm steering clear of that stuff. I want to stay on good terms with all of them."

"Not possible. Trust me, they're sizing us up, same as we are them. Every one of them's looking to put together the best team."

"Fine," said Logan, exasperated. "Who do you want?"

His friend grinned. "Me? Markell—why not shoot for the top?"

They both laughed; they hadn't so much as laid eyes on the august director of the ACF.

"Good morning, gentlemen."

They wheeled. There, to their intense discomfort, his motorcycle helmet under his arm, stood Gregory Stillman. How much had he heard? His small, hard smile gave away nothing.

"Hello, Dr. Stillman."

"Nice to see you again, sir."

"Logan and Reston, isn't it—the Claremont twins?"

"Actually, sir," said Dan, "we hardly knew each other there."

"Don't mind me, I play little tricks to remember names—something I picked up from a book on memory retention." His eyes narrowed slightly. "I try to make an effort to know each of the junior associates personally. Tell me, do you have some time right now?"

The two young doctors exchanged a quick glance. Logan knew full well that Shein would take it as a betrayal; he also suspected that this might be precisely what Stillman had in mind.

Reston quickly made the decision for him. "Sure, we were just going to grab a bite in the cafeteria."

Ten minutes later they were in Stillman's office, listening to the story of his own rapid rise within the ACF hierarchy. A mere fifteen years before, he blithely noted, he had been just a first-year fellow himself; today, "I've got eighteen people working for me." He smiled. "Going on thirty. We've been fortunate lately in attracting quite a bit of funding to our work on breast cancer."

Stillman's brilliant career, as the younger men well knew, was built on his pioneering work in the molecular origins of the horrific disease. While most earlier researchers had focused on surgical attacks on breast malignancy, or new versions of chemotherapy, Stillman aimed to attack it at its root. In his studies, he investigated possible derangement in DNA molecules; which proteins seemed to be overproduced in breast tumors and which were absent; the chemical agents within cancer cells that enabled them to replicate themselves with such deadly efficiency.

"Would you like to hear what I'll be working on next?" he asked. "This is going to be the next great breakthrough."

His visitors' faces lit up: this was like being invited to the unveiling of a Da Vinci masterpiece.

Stillman slowly rose to his feet. "Do you like opera?"

"I do," said Logan, confused.

"Any particular favorite?"

"Mozart. Especially *The Marriage of Figaro*."

Stillman chuckled with what seemed to be condescension. "Dr. Reston?"

He hesitated, then smiled. "Especially *Tommy*. By the Who."

Stillman turned to Logan, unsmiling. "Evidently, Dr. Reston does not share our reverence for the past. Too bad. That's where we're going to find many of the answers to today's problems."

Stillman had taken a CD from the corner of the bookshelf and placed it in a nearby machine. "This is *Nerone*, by Boito. It's probably more . . . *sophisticated* than what you're used to, but I hope you'll enjoy it."

As the opening chords of the piece filled the room, he returned to his seat behind the desk. Opening a drawer, he withdrew a manila folder.

"This began over a year ago," he said. "A patient came in and asked me to examine her tits."

The word had been intended to shock, and he was pleased to note a reaction from Logan.

"That's my job," he explained evenly. "I'm one of the top tit men around this place." Catching Reston's grin, he grinned back. "By the way, I'm no prude, like Larsen. I like 'em when they're healthy too."

Caught off guard by Stillman's aggressive tastelessness, Logan said nothing. What was going on here? If—as he'd allowed himself to believe —the point was to secure their allegiance, Stillman was going about it in a curious way.

But suddenly the senior man was all business again. "She had an inflammatory carcinoma, a particularly bad disease—the tumor was diffuse, it didn't form a lump. But the point is, there was something extremely unusual about this patient. I had given up hope on her, and then, to my surprise, some of her tumors—not all, but some—spontaneously disappeared." He paused meaningfully. "A lesson for you here, gentlemen: Be alert for crazy exceptions to the rule, they're the ones bearing secrets. It turned out this woman was taking a course of drugs and enhanced vitamins for a completely unrelated condition."

"May I ask what condition?" interjected Reston.

Stillman shot him an annoyed glance. "Sure. After I've had our work patented." He resumed his professorial tone—and changed the subject. "There are a number of interesting things we've been working on in this lab."

From the folder, he withdrew two eight-by-ten black-and-white photographs. "You'll note this is a photomicrograph of malignant breast cells growing in a culture dish."

Sure enough, the cells were arrayed in the familiar chaotic pattern characteristic of breast malignancies. Many were joined together in irregular swirls, like stars in a Van Gogh night sky. Others were of grotesque size and shape. In some places they were heaped together in piles.

"And this," he said, displaying the second photograph, "is the same cell growth after a six-week exposure to one of the new chemotherapeutic agents we've been developing." He paused. "I can tell you that it involves a new mycotoxin—one of the ones a field researcher brought back last year from the Amazon."

The change was uncanny! More than half the cells were clearly dead or dying, their nuclei shriveled. In whole sections of the photograph, there remained no living cells at all.

"That's unbelievable!" exclaimed Reston.

Stillman nodded crisply. "Yes. It is." He stood up, signaling the session was over. "I'm glad you enjoyed it."

He ushered Reston into the hall first, then turned back to face Dan. "Of course, we know it can be a long way from a culture dish to successful clinical trials."

"Yessir."

"You can probably see I'm a difficult personality, Dr. Logan. I don't give a good goddamn who I offend."

Logan, awkward, a silly grin plastered on his face, made no response. None was expected.

"Just bear this in mind. I've got more protocols going at the ACF than anyone. Almost twice as many as Shein."

Logan hardly had time to be anxious. He was obliged to spend the rest of this second day at the ACF in the computer room, trying to learn a system that beat anything he'd ever imagined for complexity, yet one that he couldn't leave the room without having mastered: every procedure at the ACF—from ordering antibiotics to tracking patients' progress—went through this machine.

When he was finally done, it was after 8:00 P.M. Yet he dragged himself back up to the twelfth floor and made his way to Rochelle Boudin's room.

"Sorry I took so long," he said apologetically. "I'm still pretty new here."

"Where's Dr. Levitt?" replied Roger, clearly not a man big on pleasantries.

"He's off service." Logan paused. "I'm sure you'll see him from time to time, but you'll be dealing primarily with me from now on."

The Boudins exchanged a glance. "What do you know about my wife's case?" demanded Roger.

"I'll be working under the senior physicians, of course. But, please, I want you to feel comfortable discussing anything at all with me."

Rochelle looked him over for the first time. "I'm not sure any doctor can ever understand how we feel."

"Try me."

And so, with his gentle prodding, she told the story of her illness, from the diagnosis eight months before, to the frustrations with local doctors in their hometown of Cincinnati, to their stormy relationship with the staff at the ACF. All the while, Roger mainly listened, cutting in only to make an acid remark about someone they'd had a particular problem with.

When she'd finished, Logan started asking questions: What was it about the ACF that gave them the most trouble? Were they unhappy with the course of treatment or was it mainly a communications problem?

"Both," said Roger. "This is Rochelle's life we're talking about, almost no one in this whole damn place seems to get that."

Logan nodded. "I heard what you said before about your sense of having no control. I understand that. And I think we on this side have to make a real effort to be more sensitive to it. I promise you I will."

But, he explained, he expected that they would make an equal effort to recognize the constraints under which he and every ACF employee were operating; that, in short, they not give him grief about observing the protocols.

"We've already agreed about the chemo," Roger shot back. "Isn't that enough for you people?"

Logan tried hard not to betray his irritation; *this* was what he got for his trouble? "Absolutely," he replied evenly. "Thank you."

It was, in any case, enough for the moment.

"Look," he said, "I've got to be running along. I'll come by and see you tomorrow."

Rochelle looked at him gratefully. "Thank you, Dr. Logan," she said softly.

So, he thought, allowing himself a smile as he moved from the room, maybe *that's* how to handle these two: divide and conquer.

He was still smiling when he spotted Shein, emerging from the room across the hall.

"You look pretty pleased for a guy we're working to death."

With relief, Logan saw that Shein was unaware of his visit with Stillman. "Actually, sir—"

"Seth . . . I'm the good guy around here, remember?"

"Actually, Seth, I'm enjoying it."

"This from a guy who just walked out of a chamber of horrors!" He nodded toward the Boudin room. "That's Larsen's protocol she's on. Ever hear the saying 'Like doctor, like patient'?"

"I'm trying to make the best of it. I work on the theory that there's some good in everyone."

Shein clapped a hand on his shoulder. "Ah, an optimist. We don't get very many of those around here." He paused. "So you're really doin' all right? I didn't sell you a bill of goods?"

"Not at all."

Shein positively beamed. "Keep up with this crazy attitude, I'm gonna have to adopt you!"

It always surprised Logan to hear himself described as a workaholic. Though in the hypercompetitive circles in which he operated the characterization could be useful—and he certainly never corrected such a misimpression—the truth was he was as good at chilling out as anyone. Karpe, at least, had been canny enough to see that; the element of his pitch the young doctor had found most seductive by far was the photo album of yachts, each owned by a patient, that the great doctor pulled from his desk toward the end of the interview. Logan had no trouble at all seeing himself lolling away weeks at a time on someone's deck in the Mediterranean.

It was not until the third Sunday after his arrival that Logan finally had more than a couple of hours for himself. He had planned to go furniture shopping—save for his bed, an overstuffed chair that dated back to his college years, and a pair of bookshelves, his small apartment was almost bare—but instead got distracted by a string of M*A*S*H reruns on the tube. Then, for more than an hour, he soaked in the tub, reading an odd little paperback on World War I flying aces he'd found when he unpacked his books. Then—*what the hell*, he decided, *furniture can wait*—he grabbed the Sunday *Washington Post* and headed for the small park he'd passed every morning en route to work.

It was, he discovered, known formally as M. Allen Smith Park, and it was exactly what he needed on this lazy summer afternoon: high grass, lots of shade trees, CLEAN UP AFTER DOGS signs that seemed to be respected.

He walked to a quiet area, kicked off his loafers, and lay down in the grass; then, through squinted eyes, gazed upward at the sun shafting through the trees. From a ballfield a hundred yards away came the sounds of a pickup softball game: dim exhortations aimed at the pitcher or batter, the crack of ball against aluminum, an occasional cheer. Closer by, in an enclosed playground area to his left, very young children on swings and slides made noises of abandon and joy so pure as to be almost beyond his understanding.

Logan propped himself up on an elbow to study the scene. He noted how many of the parents were fathers; and calculated—a safe bet —that most were divorced. The kids were incredibly appealing but, God, they were demanding! *Is this something he would ever do?* He'd always taken it as a given that he would. Someday. Long, long after he'd gotten past the demands of the ACF.

Now he opened the paper and began flipping through the news section. About midway through, a headline caught his eye: DOCTORS CLAIM BREAKTHROUGH ON PROSTATE CANCER.

"Researchers at New York's Memorial Sloan-Kettering Cancer Center report that a combination of radiation plus 'souped-up' chemotherapy has achieved dramatic results in patients with advanced prostate cancer," it began. "The trial, headed by Drs. Lawrence Boyles and Kenneth Rotner, involved thirty-eight patients deemed incurable by existing methods. 'Obviously, we are quite excited by these results,' said Dr. Rotner, who explained that the team is planning a series of more comprehensive trials."

It went on this way for another six or seven paragraphs, but Logan had seen enough. He didn't know the doctors involved personally, but he didn't have to: their game was clear enough. Prostate research is an extremely tough one to get funding for—no organized lobby, zero glamour—and if they didn't set off a few bells and whistles, who would?

The real problem was the press itself. Easily cultivated, readily flattered by the attention of prominent doctors, reporters injected themselves into medical politics without even being aware of the fact. Wouldn't these guys ever learn? How many years of reports of "breakthroughs" and "impending victories" would there have to be before they got it through their heads that medical miracles—Fleming's penicillin or Salk's vaccine—are, at best, once-in-a-generation events?

Yet the media keep the engine churning endlessly. Who could ever forget the hoopla over interferon? It wasn't the first time the medical press had found a cure for cancer, even that year, but rarely had it been quite so aggressive in its claims. When the drug proved a bust, they moved on; but countless doctors had to deal with the fallout, a level of despair that in many cases matched that brought on by the onset of the disease itself.

The problem, of course, is that the truth—that progress is incremental and painfully slow—won't get reporters their airtime or column inches. So the press reports medicine the same way it reports everything else, as high drama, a pitched battle between contending forces. "The War on Cancer," it's always called, "The Battle Against Crippling Childhood Illnesses," "The Continuing Fight Against Heart Disease." Never mind that there's no intent there, that those malignant cells don't *know* they're hurting anyone.

Logan lay back in the grass, closed his eyes, and smiled. It was a funny thought: the press almost made him ready to feel sorry for cancer. In its perpetual search for good guys and villains, it just *badgered* this poor disease unmercifully.

"Hey? Excuse me?"

Dan opened one eye and squinted at the silhouette looming over him. A guy with a baseball glove. "Yes?"

"You want to play some ball?" He nodded vaguely in the direction of the field. "A couple of our guys've left."

The offer was tempting; Logan was a softball player from way back. "I don't know." He raised one of his bare feet in the air. "I'm not really dressed for it."

"Don't worry about it, we're not exactly pros."

"You got a mitt I can borrow?"

"You can use mine."

Logan turned out to be one of the better players on the field. Intense as they were, these guys were basically weekend hackers; and it was amusing to note how ready they were to jump down one another's throats at every misplay in the field or missed opportunity at the bat.

For two innings they pretty much ignored Logan, exiled to the fourth outfielder spot. But when he finally came to bat, and lined a triple over third to drive in two runs, he was instantly transformed into a hero. As soon as he'd come around to score, Kevin—the catcher, the man in charge—sat down beside him on the rickety bench. "Nice shot. You field as good as you hit?"

"Depends on how hard the ball's coming at me."

"I'm thinking of moving you to first base."

"Sure, sounds good."

"So, you from around here? We play every Sunday, you know."

"I just moved here."

"Oh, yeah? You with the government?"

"I'm a doctor with the ACF."

The other, impressed, gave a low whistle. "Not bad."

"How about you?"

"Me? I'm with the IRS, an attorney. We got four or five other lawyers here. Also a couple of congressional aides, a few accountants. We all live in town." He paused, seemingly struck by a momentous thought. "Hey, Bruce Ryan's a doctor." He pointed at a rail-thin fellow in glasses coaching third base. "I'll introduce you guys."

The next inning, Kevin was as good as his word. "So," said Bruce Ryan, "you're at the ACF." Logan could not help but note this seemed less in the spirit of fellowship than sullen challenge.

"Right. How about you?"

"Just a radiologist. I'm with Prince William County Hospital, down in Manassas."

"Ah. That's supposed to be a good facility."

"Don't worry, I make good money."

What kind of answer did *that* call for? "Good. Glad to hear it."

"I knew another guy at the ACF."

"Oh, yeah, who's that?"

"I met him at a party a few years ago. A first-year fellow. I can't exactly remember the name—Cooper-something."

"It doesn't ring a bell. He must be gone by now."

"Coopersmith, I think. Real sharp guy. He was working on a protocol he'd set up."

Logan smiled indulgently. "No, that's not possible. First-year fellows don't run protocols. We get the scut work."

The other shook his head. "No, I'm sure of it. That's why it made such a big impression on me, 'cause he was so young."

"Well . . ." Logan shrugged. "I'm not going to argue with you."

"Anyway, that's some hot-shit place. That's the trade-off, isn't it: guys like you get the glory, guys like me get the dough."

Logan had run into this kind of nastiness more than once since making the decision to come to the ACF—mainly from doctors at Claremont headed to big-money practices. He knew it represented the most pathetic kind of insecurity; self-justification and envy masquerading as cockiness. But he hated it, and wished he were better at answering in kind.

"I don't see it that way" was all he could come up with now. "It's not like they make you take a vow of poverty."

The other smiled. "Don't take it wrong, someone over there must think you're pretty good."

What he was starting to feel toward this guy went beyond simple dislike; it approached stupefaction. "Actually," he said coolly, "a lot of people do. And they're right."

Just then the batter lined to center for the third out of the inning.

"What's your name again?" asked Bruce Ryan. "Dan Logan?"

"With a *D* and an *L*. Want me to write it down for you?"

"Don't worry," he said, turning to head back out to the field. "Just curious, in case I ever hear it again."

Logan walked up to Kevin behind home plate. "Look, I've really got to get going. I've got a couch to buy."

"Oh, really?" The guy looked genuinely disappointed. "Well, look, we're out here every Sunday, you know where to find us."

"Thanks."

As he walked from the field, Logan decided he'd stop by Baskin-Robbins for a coffee shake. He also made a mental note to check out a recent junior associate named Coopersmith.

Before the end of the summer Daniel Logan was entirely at home at the ACF. He found what was asked of him was no more than he'd always asked of himself: lots of hard work and the willingness to take on more. "This place," as Seth Shein put it to him one afternoon, in one of their increasingly frequent chats, "is the last true meritocracy. Like God, the ACF helps those who help themselves."

The routine into which he'd settled may have been the standard one for junior associates: three days a week working the hospital; the other two in the clinic, dealing with protocol patients on an outpatient basis; between the cracks evaluating new candidates for possible acceptance into ACF protocols in the Screening Clinic. Yet, almost alone among the junior associates, Logan's work had never been singled out for criticism.

Quite simply, he took the protocols as a sacred trust—eliciting consistent cooperation from even the most difficult patients and making himself so familiar with his patients' medical histories, so alert to subtle changes in their appearance or test results, that already he'd headed off several potential crises.

His superiors had been equally struck by his work in the Screening Clinic. For a protocol to yield the best possible results, every patient on it must perfectly match the profile established by its creator. Working with biopsy slides of promising candidates forwarded by their local pathologists, Logan actually came upon more than one misdiagnosis.

It was as if all his years of training—hell, his entire existence—had been preparation for his work here. A skeptic by temperament and experience, he never accepted the seemingly obvious at face value; questioning all assumptions, carefully scrutinizing even routine incoming data. Yet, unlike most of his contemporaries, he could also make the creative leaps so essential to problem solving.

Under the circumstances, he had little trouble understanding that some of his peers took his success personally; in their place, he might have felt the same way. At the ACF, more than at any other institution he'd known, another's rising status could feel alarmingly like one's own failure. So he tried to accept the inevitable sniping with relative good humor.

"Hey," as Barbara Lukas nodded in greeting one early morning, "got your Chap Stick ready? We're going on rounds with Larsen."

"So?"

"So who knows how many asses you're going to have to kiss?"

Smiling, Logan patted his breast pocket. "No problem, I always keep some handy."

"What is it with you, Logan? Don't you even have the self-respect to be insulted?"

"Not if that's the best you can throw at me."

For all the trouble she gave him, Logan liked Lukas. Insecure, easily provoked to anger, far too outspoken, she herself had proven completely inept at the gamesmanship that seemed so vital to success at the ACF. In fact, this tiny, combative Duke grad had already been pegged by their superiors as a headache likely to blossom into a migraine.

But Logan was perceptive enough to know it was the toughness that had gotten her here; and to recognize the vulnerability behind it.

Then too—and this always counted heavily with him—he was aware that she was a truly gifted doctor.

"Look," he tweaked her now, "if you're looking for personality guidance, just ask. For starters, Barbara, you gotta start smiling more."

"Can it, Logan."

"Hey, and maybe you oughta consider wearing a real short skirt every once in a while. That's *guaranteed* to win these guys over."

"*Not* funny," she said, suppressing a smile.

He shrugged. "Just trying to help."

"Thanks," she said, turning on her heel. "And you should start smiling a lot less."

In brief, Logan was starting to feel he was one of the chosen. Lukas had it right: somehow, remarkably, thus far he had managed to remain on good terms with everyone who mattered. Either directly or by inference, half a dozen of the senior men had indicated that, when the time came, he would be welcome as a member of their team.

Indeed, he'd already begun viewing the day when he'd have to actually make such a choice with apprehension. The consequences—possibly on the entire course of his career—were incalculable: the implacable enemies it would create, the doors it would forever slam shut.

Just now, even Larsen seemed to be nurturing newfound regard for him. Logan figured this out the day Larsen unexpectedly took a seat beside him in the hospital cafeteria and began making his own tortured version of small talk.

"So," began Larsen, "you come to us from Claremont Hospital. . . ."

Given that they'd been over this territory months before at his initial interview—and Larsen had been singularly disinterested in the fact then—Logan was at a loss. "Yessir, that's true. . . ."

Larsen nodded. "Very good, very good. . . ."

"Thank you." Logan bit into his burger, to keep his mouth occupied.

"I understand they have a lot of wealthy Arab patients up there."

Logan nodded; in fact, at one time or another, the place had played host to half the Saudi royal family. "Yessir, that's true."

Astonishingly—for it was the first time the younger man had ever heard such a thing—Larsen laughed: a dry, reedy sound, more like the clearing of the throat than anything suggesting joy. "I guess they know the score. When the chips are down, they run right to those Jewish doctors."

He laughed again and, rising to his feet, clapped a hand on Logan's shoulder. "Keep up the good work, young man. Perhaps we'll have a chance to work together more closely one of these days."

"I'd like that, sir."

Not that he trusted Larsen for a minute. He knew how quickly the volatile chief of the Department of Medicine was liable to turn on him; and how, once incurred, his displeasure seemed to grow ever more dangerous.

He was reminded of this the very morning of his exchange with Barbara Lukas. Less than an hour afterward he and Lukas were among the five first-year associates escorted by Larsen on their weekly teaching rounds. The group had visited four or five patients, Larsen holding forth after each visit in the corridor outside the patient's room, when they entered the room of Congressman Al Marino.

Marino was in for colon cancer. A ranking member of the House Science and Technology Committee, he was one of the handful of patients on the premises who enjoyed nonprotocol status.

"Al, my friend, how are we doing today?" boomed Larsen, with a sudden ingratiating smile. The junior associates exchanged furtive looks; with every one of the patients they'd seen earlier, he'd been coolly impersonal to the point of rudeness.

The congressman, sitting up in bed before a pile of documents, bifocals perched on the end of a bulbous nose, hardly moved. "I'm doing shitty. How are you doing?"

Larsen moved over beside him. "I know that last course of chemo was a little rough. I'm sorry."

"Yeah," he said disinterestedly.

"Carol's okay? I had a nice phone conversation with her a couple of days ago."

"She's fine."

His reserve of happy chat exhausted, the doctor pulled out his stethoscope and got to work. "You know the drill, Al," he said, summoning up a last bit of good cheer, "—heart, lungs, and abdomen. Nothing to it."

Running through the rote procedure in less than a minute, he called for the congressman's progress chart. As he read it, his brow darkened. "Dr. Lukas," he suddenly spoke up sharply, "are you responsible for this?"

She hesitated, a doe caught in headlights. "Yes, sir." But, characteristically, she instantly drew herself up straight, determined not to appear intimidated.

"Would you mind telling me why these lab values are written in *pencil?*" The throbbing vein in his left temple was a familiar sign of building rage. "Were those lab values *temporary?* Was it your intention to go back and *change* them?"

"No, sir. It was my understanding that—"

"Excuse me, Doctor? WHAT was your understanding—that we encourage *incompetence* at this institution?"

"No, sir, if you'll allow me to finish?"

"No! I will not allow you to waste Congressman Marino's time or mine!"

Suddenly the chart was flying across the room in her direction. "This kind of sloppy work will NOT be tolerated, Dr. Lukas. I strongly suggest you learn proper procedure by studying one of Dr. Logan's charts!"

He turned to the patient, who seemed disinterested in the whole thing. "I'm sorry, Congressman. I hope you won't take it as the way things are done around here."

"Forget it, she's just a kid." He gave a wave of his hand and added the words that this day would spare the young doctor further torment. "Why don't you lay off? She's kinda cute."

Lukas stared straight ahead, unblinking, but Logan caught the stricken look in her eyes. He wanted to let her know how mortified he was to have been made part of her torment.

But too, at that moment, on some level, his thoughts were on his own future. Like it or not, Larsen was not a force to be slighted, let alone ignored. Shortly, in spite of everything, when faced with the decision of which of the top guys to go with, he would have to consider that fact very, very carefully.

Fortunately for Logan, there was one other junior associate who was an even more tempting target of scorn than he was. Allen Atlas, the junior associate out of Vanderbilt, had shown himself to be so nakedly ambitious that the others joked of forming a 'suck-up watch,' to monitor his obsequiousness toward superiors.

What was infuriating was how well it seemed to work. Indeed, lately he seemed to have made himself all but indispensible to Peter Kratsas, spending virtually every evening in the senior man's lab, tabulating protocol data.

"I *really* can't stand that guy Atlas," Reston put it to Logan one evening in his Dupont Circle apartment. "You notice how he's started to parrot Kratsas on every damn subject?"

Logan took a sip of red wine and smiled. "Why do I have the impression Kratsas encourages that?"

"I'm not kidding, yesterday he actually starts talking to me about how much he loves Alfred Hitchcock movies."

"Look at it this way, he's picking up as many enemies as friends."

"You know that from experience, right?"

"Hey, I don't need that from you. I get enough of it from Barbara Lukas!"

"The difference is I don't mean it as an insult. I'd change places with you in a second."

Logan laughed uncomfortably. Reston was right: talented as he was, no one who counted at the ACF seemed to have noticed, and the fact was becoming a matter of some awkwardness between them. Logan wished he could say something to ease his friend's distress; or, even better, help him to shine. Instead, he was reduced to offering the kind of reassurance that sounded hollow even to him. "You're just biding your time, that's all," he said now. He smiled. "And at least you've got a terrific woman."

In fact, under the circumstances Dan was almost grateful for his own dismal social life; at least it balanced things out a little. "Anyway," he added, "don't exaggerate. It's not as if I run the place."

"Not yet. Thank God."

The exchange was typical of the friendship that had blossomed between Logan and Reston since their arrival at the ACF. Both, seemingly easy to read—one the dutiful subordinate, the other all cocky charm—were in fact intensely private. But with one another, using banter as camouflage, each was able to drop his guard.

"Nah," replied Logan now, with mock solicitude, "I'd be perfectly happy just to be director of research. You can run the place."

"That's better."

"See, I know all about your ego needs."

"You're right." He laughed. "And I'd also be able to fire your ass if you started letting other people in on the secret."

Reston's girlfriend, Amy, emerged from the kitchen, holding a knife and a couple of tomatoes. "Hey, John, aren't *you* supposed to be doing dinner?"

"Yeah, yeah."

As she wheeled and retreated back toward the kitchen, Reston and Logan rose to follow.

"Hey, Amy," said Reston, "we gotta set Logan up with someone. He's trying to use our relationship to get me to feel sorry for *him*."

She stopped and smiled at Dan. "Are you kidding, there're a thousand women on the Hill who'd love a guy like you." Amy's FCC office was in the heart of the government district. "What do you like? Congressional aides with great legs? Busty number-crunchers? Sharp lawyers ready to give it all up for Mr. Right?"

"Could I get a combination of all three?"

She tossed a tomato from hand to hand and laughed. "So we're talking great sex *and* lifetime commitment."

Reston picked up a tomato and began expertly slicing it. "Nah, I think with Danny boy we better focus on the sex. Commitment's not a big part of his resume."

Logan shot him a look. "That's not true."

"Don't worry, Amy's not gonna give you crap about it. She knows how it is."

"You mean about guys being jerks?" She laughed. "Absolutely, I learn more every day at the feet of the master."

"Anyway," added Reston, "I think Danny here's already got someone in mind."

"C'mon, John, let's drop it."

"Who?" asked Amy."

"Why don't you let me do surgery on one of those?" Logan held out a hand, indicating Reston should toss him a tomato.

"*Whoa*," mocked his friend, "talk about a *smooooth* change of subject." He paused. "Sabrina Como."

"Ohh, the Italian bombshell." She nodded at Logan. "You've got good taste."

Logan smiled uneasily. "I really don't know where he comes up with this crap." Actually, he knew perfectly well: Reston had been around more than once when Sabrina's very presence turned him into a bumbling, awkward parody of his normal self. He was only grateful his friend hadn't been with them on rounds the morning Logan caught the Italian, in quiet conversation with an anxious patient, leaning forward to daub the woman's face with a washcloth; the quick flash of full breast in flimsy, lacy bra had haunted him since. "Look," he added lamely, "I don't know a thing about the woman, except that she's a terrific doctor."

"Oh, right. Forgive me. You respect her as a peer, is all. My mistake."

Amy snorted. "John wouldn't *understand* that. He has to respect a woman's body before he'll even notice she has a mind."

Reston popped a bit of tomato in his mouth. "Yum, yum, yum. So, what d'you think she thinks of you?"

"I have no idea. For all I know she's involved with someone."

"No, she's not. I assume you like lots of garlic on your pasta?"

"How do you know that?"

"I checked it out with Sylvia"—the hospital pharmacist, also the hospital's foremost gossip-monger.

Logan shook his head. "I tell you, Amy, if this guy put half the energy into science he does into being a wiseass, he *would* be running the ACF."

Two hours later, they were sitting in the living room sipping Amaretto, still savoring the splendid northern Italian dinner Reston had whipped up.

"See," said Amy, snuggling up against him, "he's good for something after all."

The wine had left Logan even more acutely conscious of being odd man out. He managed a laugh. "Oh, I'd say he makes a pretty good doctor."

"I'm a *terrific* doctor," agreed Reston, slightly drunk. "The bastards just don't know it."

Logan smiled. "Maybe his problem is humility."

"Right," said Amy. "Let's see him convince a shrink of that."

"I'll tell you what my problem is," said Reston. "The crap they have us doing at that place! Why don't they take advantage of what we have to offer?"

"It's called paying dues."

"I thought we paid 'em at Claremont. We're back to doing rectals, for Chrissakes!"

There was a long pause. "You want some advice?" asked Logan seriously.

"It depends."

"Cut out the griping. That's the best way to insure you never get on their good side."

"So what am I supposed to do? Pretend I enjoy this treatment?"

Logan's heart went out to his friend. "Exactly," he said soberly, "pretend to enjoy it so much you'll never be able to thank them *enough*."

"Great. Like you do."

"Face it, that's the game. The only chance guys like us have to get some real clout." He hesitated. "Enough to maybe run a protocol of our own."

Reston cast him a morose glance. "What are you talking about— we're just first-year associates."

"There's no rule against it. I looked it up."

"*Right.* Even you couldn't make that happen."

"You ever hear of Ray Coopersmith?"

Reston hesitated. "Vaguely."

"Don't BS me, why don't you just say no?"

"Because that'd be giving you the upper hand," smiled Amy.

"So . . . ?" pressed Reston.

"He was a first-year associate at the ACF four years ago—and he got a protocol through."

"Like hell. That's impossible."

"I've seen the paperwork. Both the proposal itself and the Institutional Review Board's approval form signing off on it."

The documents were in the antique wooden filing cabinet outside Larsen's office with hundreds of others like them. A seldom-used Foundation resource, in theory they were available to all junior associates interested in the genesis of earlier protocols. Larsen's secretary, Elaine, had grown so accustomed to the ever-curious young Logan studying these protocols that she'd scarcely noticed him, one recent lunch hour, systematically searching the files from three and four years back: going directly to the C's.

"Coopersmith?" asked Reston. "What kind of protocol?"

"What difference does it make? What matters is he made it happen."

"In other words, it was a bust."

"Actually, I don't know. I found the record of the proposal but not the results." As they both knew, this was not unusual; protocol data could run hundreds of pages and were generally filed away on computer discs. "Anyway, it was something about shooting radio-labeled antibodies directly into the bloodstream to go after prostate tumors directly instead of relying on standard chemo. Interesting idea."

"Prostate? Who'd he get to sponsor this, Larsen?" The very idea was almost beyond imagination.

Logan shook his head. "A genitourinary guy, someone named Locke. I think he's now in private practice."

"So—what are you saying?—now you want to go off and do something on your own? *You?*"

"*Us.* Maybe. Why not?"

"Why not? Because, frankly, I don't even register on their radar around here. And—don't take this the wrong way, Danny boy—but you're not exactly known for your guts." Reston stopped, drawing it out; on some level he was enjoying this. "So just don't pull my chain, all right?"

Stunned, Logan was momentarily silent, then came back with surprising heat. "I'm just trying to . . . What the hell do you think gives you the right to—"

"Look," Reston cut him off. "I'm just saying I don't need your pipe dreams right now. I've got my own problems."

"Fine," snapped Logan, his face flushed. "Forget it."

Reston smiled. "Hey, don't go away mad. I'm perfectly willing to talk—as soon as you've got something serious on the drawing board."

I n fact, Logan had been toying with the beginnings of an idea for weeks—ever since the morning Larry Tilley had stepped into his examining room.

For Tilley was potentially one of Gregory Stillman's famous secret-bearers: a patient in whom disease so defies expected patterns that his case forces a competent researcher to rethink old assumptions.

A Kansas City lawyer, thirty-four and gay, Tilley was on a Phase Two AIDS protocol for a drug called Compound J designed to interfere with viral reproduction—a protocol that seemed to be going nowhere. To date, Compound J appeared to be totally inactive.

No real news there. The AIDS virus had long been a particular source of frustration to ACF researchers, on a par with the most baffling cancers in its sinister complexity. AIDS protocols were notoriously ineffective in yielding practical results, and as Shein one day put it, with characteristic gallows humor, "when one of those mothers bites the dust, it takes a lot of people with it."

As a protocol patient, Tilley was unaware of this, of course. He had come in from Kansas City for a series of tests. His numbers, like those of most on the protocol, were not good.

But within minutes of the start of the examination, he casually mentioned something that got Logan's full attention: Though he'd been feeling dizzy and weak a lot lately, it had nothing to do with overactivity. "In fact, it usually happens when I've been resting. I get up from a chair and I feel like I'm going to faint."

Logan, who'd been checking his lymph nodes, paused—what could *that* be about?—and momentarily excused himself. In the adjoining room he looked more closely at the paperwork forwarded by Tilley's local hospital.

Unable to pinpoint a cause for the unusual course of events, his private physician had first put forth a likely diagnosis of pancreatitis—a simple inflammation of the pancreas. After a couple of days in the hospital, feeling better, Tilley had been sent home. But, literally within hours, the problem was back.

Logan returned to the patient. "You seem to have stumped your doctors back there."

Tilley smiled. "They kind of threw up their hands and said I should come here to let you guys figure it out."

Logan liked Tilley immediately. No self-pity, lots of fight.

"All right, let's figure it out. Why don't we start with an easy one? How do you feel when you stand up?"

Sure enough, Logan noted that every time Tilley rose to his feet, his blood pressure dropped precipitously and his heart rate increased.

"Well, we've established that the problem isn't your imagination."

"Great. Even the boobs out in K.C. knew that."

Logan laughed. "Did the boobs ask if you've been thirsty a lot lately?"—worth asking, but just barely. From his days at Claremont, Logan recalled that such simultaneous changes in blood pressure and heart rate can be symptomatic of extreme dehydration; though on this cool fall day, it seemed almost impossible that a man not engaged in vigorous physical activity could become so seriously dehydrated.

To his surprise, Tilley nodded. "But that's just something that comes from taking the drug, isn't it?"

"Well, let's see if this boob can clarify that a bit further. I'm going to want to run some tests."

"Does that mean I have to go back in the hospital?"

"I don't think that's necessary. We have contracts with a number of hotels in the D.C. area. Why don't we just have the ACF give you a free vacation?"

Tilley smiled. "Thanks, Doctor."

"I'll have someone make a reservation for you at the Madison Arms. Be here tomorrow at eight-thirty and we'll get started."

"How long am I gonna have to stay?"

It was part of Logan's job to allay apprehension, but he would never intentionally mislead a patient. "I really can't tell you, Larry. Probably no more than a few days. In the meantime, I'm going to give you a couple of liters of intravenous fluids and see if that helps."

Briefly, it looked like a miracle cure. By the following day, Tilley reported he was feeling better than he had in months.

But the day after that, the dizziness was as bad as ever.

As test after test came up dry, the patient's few days in Washington became almost two weeks. Disappointed as he was on Tilley's behalf, Logan's curiosity continued to mount. Every second day Tilley arrived at the ACF clinic to be examined and pumped full of salt water. Sure enough, he would feel better; yet, just as surely, within two days he was dizzy again, his blood pressure dropping sharply.

Finally, at long last, the tests yielded up the reason for Tilley's persistent dehydration. His adrenal cortex had ceased to produce the hormones that enable the kidneys to retain salt and water. To Logan, the reason seemed apparent: the protocol drug was somehow blocking the normal function of the organ.

And yet, going over the lengthy proposal that had led to the Compound J test, he found nothing to indicate that the drug might have so alarming a side effect. Nor, as far as he knew, had it so affected even one other patient on the protocol.

The afternoon the test data came in, Logan could focus on nothing else. It simply didn't make any sense: what was it in the makeup of this patient—or in the specifics of his condition, or in some heretofore unrecognized aspect of the drug itself—that could have produced such a result?

Yet already he had begun to formulate an even more pertinent question: Could such a discovery have some meaningful practical application?

The day's events crystallized in Logan's mind an intention that had earlier been only a vague thought: he saw Shein's secretary and picked up a ticket in the ACF box for that evening's ball game. His favorite team, the California Angels, was in town, and since boyhood he had done some of his best thinking at the ballpark.

Arriving at Baltimore's Camden Yards early for batting practice, he was not surprised to find himself alone in the box—he'd heard it was seldom used.

The box was on the mezzanine level, slightly to the first-base side of home plate, and Logan had a commanding view of the stunning new stadium. He bought himself a hot dog and beer and settled in, reveling in the feel of the place.

It wasn't until the fourth inning, with the Angels already enjoying a three-run lead, that he reached into his briefcase and withdrew Larry Tilley's case history. His plan was to review it from the beginning, prior even to the diagnosis of the disease; looking for some clue in Tilley's past, anything that might—

"Dan?"

He looked up and there, to his astonishment, a cardboard food tray in her hands, stood Sabrina Como.

She smiled uncertainly. "I hope you do not mind to be bothered."

Hurriedly, he replaced the papers in his briefcase. "No, of course not. I'm just . . . surprised."

"Most times no one else is here." She took a seat beside him.

"Aha . . . " He stared at her wonderingly. "You like baseball?"

She nodded. "It is a game of numbers. I like numbers, my mother teaches statistics." She pointed at the scoreboard in right field. "The Orioles, they are not doing so very well. Only three hits and two errors already."

He nodded. "Tim Salmon hit a home run for the Angels." This was *crazy*; no way she could know who Tim Salmon was.

"And Bo Jackson? That is a big reason I came—to see a man with a hip replacement run around on the bases." She smiled. "That is a *real* medical miracle, no? Better than our little tricks."

He smiled uncertainly. "I know. Unfortunately, he's not playing."

"No . . . I know he is hitting only .233, not so high." She was staring down at her scorecard, matching the numbers listed on the board in centerfield with those in print. "Tonight instead they use this other man, Davis."

Logan was overwhelmed. He couldn't have dreamt up such a woman. He strained to think of something to say. "So . . . what are you eating?"—then instantly berated himself. *Why was it that every time this woman spoke to him forty points seemed to drop from his IQ?*

She picked up the hamburger from her tray. "Not the best."

"Well, at least it beats the food at the ACF." He hesitated. "Is hospital food any better in Italy?"

"No, maybe even not so good. What could be worse than days-old pasta? But there the doctors may bring their own food to eat. Sometimes I do the same here—Italian pastries and chocolates."

Reaching into her pocket, she withdrew a piece of candy wrapped in gold foil. The label read *Maracini*. "Would you like?"

He unwrapped it and popped it in his mouth. "It's delicious."

"They are not to be eaten so fast, Logan," she said, smiling. "They are not Hershey's Kisses."

"Oh. Sorry."

"I give them sometimes to my patients in the hospital."

"You do?" Fleetingly, Logan wondered if that might violate some regulation.

She shrugged. "I started this practice back home. In the hospital there we had many children."

"A pediatric ward?"

She nodded. "But it is good with adults too. Such a small thing, but it helps create good relations with patients."

"I find it pretty hard working with kids."

"Pardon?" He'd said it so softly, she actually hadn't heard.

"I don't know, when I go into a children's ward and see those little tables and chairs . . ." He hunched his shoulders slightly. "I have trouble even reading the literature about kids and cancer."

Though her gaze didn't waver, she studied Logan with new interest. "Well, you are very lucky then we do not treat children at the ACF."

"No." He hesitated, struck by the change in her manner. An explanation seemed in order, if not an apology. "I know it's not very professional . . ."

She turned away to stare out at the field. "Ah, Mr. Ripken is coming to bat."

He felt a rising sense of alarm. "So," he picked up, "are you enjoying your work at the ACF?"

"Enjoying?" She turned back to him, seemingly baffled by the word. "It is like a medieval Italian city-state, I think. It makes me go back and read Machiavelli."

Gratefully, Logan burst out laughing. "That's true."

"Some of the people there . . . just *horrible*!" She paused. "You are not friends with them, I hope."

"No. It's strictly professional."

"Like this Larsen and Stillman. Among the greatest experts in ovarian cancer and breast cancer—no?—and they do not like women. Not at all. How could such a thing happen?"

On the field, the Orioles were rallying, and the crowd let out a roar as a ball shot between a pair of infielders into left field. Logan shook his head. "I really don't know."

The crowd noise died down. "Even the work—it really is not so interesting as I expected."

"I think a lot of us feel that way."

"Back in Florence—this is where I did my training—I had a year of specialization in endocrinology. You see? But here"—she offered a help-less shrug to indicate the immensity of her frustration—"here what is the use of such a specialization?"

"I didn't know you were an endocrinologist,"

"Yes, and very good too." She laughed. "No good hiding it under a bush."

Her laugh was a lovely sound. He leaned forward. "Listen, I've got something you might be interested in. . . ."

He withdrew the pages from his briefcase; then, in broad strokes, he outlined the Tilley case, stressing his continuing confusion over what appeared to be the patient's bizarre reaction to the protocol drug.

Eyes fixed on the field, Sabrina listened intently. "You are sure in the protocol proposal there is nothing at all about such side effects?"

He shook his head. "Absolutely not. Who knows, maybe it has nothing to do with Compound J. Maybe it's a result of the disease itself."

"You know," she said, "I have several patients also on the Com-pound J protocol. One of them, she has similar symptoms."

"Weakness? Dizziness? Dramatic change of blood pressure?"

She nodded. "Only not so severe. Her doctor in New Jersey, he is handling it." She paused. "You have been to the library at the Founda-tion? You have checked for information on Compound J?"

"I've just made a start." In fact, the ACF archives had the vastest collection of data on cancer and related diseases anywhere in the world;

and most of what it didn't have was retrievable electronically. The only real limits on a dedicated researcher were those he imposed on himself. "Unfortunately," Logan confessed, "I'm not strong in languages. Only English and some German."

Sabrina shook her head. "This is truly a disgraceful thing about you Americans"—then, worried that she might be offending him, "I don't mean this in a bad way."

He couldn't keep from laughing. "I can see that."

"Anyway, my English is not so perfect also."

"Just drop it, Sabrina, you're in too deep.'

"Anyway," she added, her green eyes luminous, "this is why I went into medicine—the fun of the hunt."

"That's a nice way of putting it."

"And you?"

He thought a moment. "The same. But I guess I'd also have to tell you about my father."

"He is a doctor also?"

He shook his head. "He owns a stationery store."

"He wanted for you to be a doctor? This was his dream for you?"

"Actually, what he mainly wants is for me to make a lot of money. I speak with my family every few weeks. He never fails to remind me that I'm not."

She laughed. "This story has *no* connection."

"He was someone who could've done just about anything. He was smart enough. Only, his father died when he was in high school and he had to help out the family. So he got a job, and never really got back on track." He shrugged. "That's it, nothing dramatic. A lot of people have the same story."

"I am sure he is proud of you."

Logan managed a pained smile. "Actually, no. He resents me." He paused, feeling terribly awkward; he'd probably told this woman too much already. All this wimpy self-revelatory stuff would only scare her off. "Do you play any sports yourself?"

She noted the change of subject and respected it. "In Italy, in the high school, I ran. The four hundred and the eight hundred meters. But now I do not even walk fast."

"Well"—he hesitated—"maybe one day we could go out and throw a ball around."

She nodded. "Yes."

He glanced at his watch and reluctantly he rose to his feet. "Will you be all right here? I'm afraid I have an early flight to New York tomorrow."

"Why New York?"

"That's where I did my internship and residency. At Claremont Hospital."

"Ah, and you maybe have a friend there?"

Incredibly—or was it just his hopeful imagination?—Logan thought he detected a note of jealousy. "Well, yeah. That's one of the reasons I'm going up . . . he's getting divorced."

"Ah," she said, her tone betraying nothing. "You are a good friend."

He smiled. "Nah. Just a guy looking for an excuse to get away from the ACF for a day. But this lets me rack up a few good-guy points."

"Well"—she rose to her feet and extended a hand—"I am pleased to know you at last. You seem to me like not such a bad guy after all."

Her smile was so disarming, Logan entirely missed the faintness of the praise. "Thank you, Sabrina. That's nice of you to say."

Catching the 8:00 A.M. shuttle out of National Airport, Logan made it into midtown Manhattan before 10:00. Not scheduled to meet Perez till half past twelve—his only appointment—he viewed the day before him as an almost sinful indulgence, and he was determined to take full advantage. He had the cab drop him off at the Metropolitan Museum, and spent the next hour in his favorite sections—Egyptian art and medieval armaments; then headed over to another old haunt, the small, quirky Museum of the City of New York, with its current exhibit on New York sports history. Hurrying down to Fifty-ninth Street, he still had a little time to wander through F.A.O. Schwarz, examining new toys and gadgets that struck his fancy.

Ruben Perez was on time, waiting across the street, in front of the Plaza. As Logan approached he held up a deli bag.

"I figured we'd eat in the park."

"Some things never change." Logan grinned as they shook hands. "Why do I keep imagining you have class?"

"Hey, not all of us make doctors' dough."

"*I* don't make doctors' dough. I'm at the ACF, remember?"

"That's why I didn't suggest a restaurant. Didn't want to embarrass you."

Having established nothing had changed between them, they began almost instantly comparing notes on their respective institutions.

"You're not gonna believe this," said Logan, as they walked toward Central Park, "but a lot of people'd say the ACF's as bad a work environment as Claremont. Maybe even worse."

"I had the impression you liked the place."

"I do, personally. But I'm a scientist, I'm giving you objective data."

His friend shook his head vigorously. "Oh, c'mon, man. You *forget* what Claremont was like. Assholetown, U.S.A."

"I'm telling you, some of these guys at the ACF are just unbeliev-able bullies. Cross 'em, even by accident, and you can kiss your career good-bye."

"So how you handling it?" Perez took a seat on an empty bench.

The simple question seemed to hit a raw nerve. "There's no *han-dling* it. You just work hard and try like hell to stay out of harm's way."

"Right."

"Problem is, you get known as a kiss-ass for the trouble. What the hell am I supposed to do, do crappy work? *That* makes me a hero?"

His friend was taken aback by Logan's intensity. "Hey, man, *I'm* not accusing you of sucking up to anyone. Sounds like they're working you *too* hard down there." He patted the bench. "Sit down."

Logan did so. "Sorry. I only wish the work came without all the other crap."

"Dream on, pal. Just don't get me worried about your mental state. I got my hands full worrying about my own."

"Yeah, I know."

"How'd we even get started on *your* problems? I mean, it's so typi-cal."

Logan couldn't help but smile. "Fine. Your turn." He extended his hand. "Give me my sandwich and talk to me."

But as Perez launched into his story, the tenor of the encounter quickly changed. In fact, his impending divorce was far messier than Logan had realized. It seemed his estranged wife was drinking heavily. Increasingly bitter, she'd been denying him access to their young daugh-ter. He'd begun to feel he had no alternative but to consider a custody fight.

Having zero firsthand experience with such a nightmarish scenario, knowing nothing about the emotional needs of children beyond what he'd picked up in a month-long mental-health course he'd had to take as a medical student, Logan understood he was in no position to offer advice. He mainly listened. But this seemed to be fine with Perez.

"It's so damn hard," he softly concluded. "Just because I want out, everyone thinks I'm the bad guy." He stopped and brushed a sleeve over suddenly damp eyes.

Awkwardly, Logan threw an arm over his friend's shoulder. "You know I'll do everything I can." He'd almost forgotten—perhaps only now fully grasped—the depth of his feelings for this man.

"I mean, no one knows what really goes on inside a family. How people treat each other. I'm trying to save my kid, man. I'm working three extra shifts a week just to finance this."

Looking to ease the tension, Logan went for a laugh. "Eighteen more hours a week at Claremont? Now, *that's* depressing."

He was immediately sorry. But, typically, Perez offered him a smile. "I know, man. You ain't kidding."

Half an hour later, as Perez hurried off in the general direction of Claremont Hospital, Logan found himself at a loss. What to do now? He tended to see life as a series of firm commitments and he'd set aside this as a leisurely day of R and R. Still, the idea of spending the afternoon alone suddenly seemed immensely less appealing.

He considered heading home immediately. As always, there was work to be done. Patients who'd be delighted to see him. Slides to study in the Screening Clinic. Data to be input into the computer system—including Tilley's, which, in his preoccupation with their significance the night before, he'd neglected to enter.

Doggedly, Logan headed off to the movies, where he spent the rest of the afternoon. Afterward, feeling better, he decided to stay for dinner at his favorite Thai restaurant. Needing something to read, he made it over to the bookstore at Sloan-Kettering just before closing and picked up the latest edition of Vincent DeVita's authoritative *Principles and Practice of Oncology*.

He found the book so absorbing that it was only after ordering coffee that he thought to call in and check his messages.

The first several were routine: a hospital secretary with word of a protocol patient who'd checked back in; an old college friend planning to be in Washington over Christmas. But the third caught him entirely by surprise.

"*Hello, Dr. Logan. Or perhaps I now know you well enough to say Danny? Anyway, never mind. This is Sabrina Como calling and I am eager to talk with you as soon as possible. I think I have found something important. So if you will please call me as soon as you can. (703) 555-4103. Ciaò."*

Logan checked his watch—it was eight-sixteen. Hurriedly dialing Sabrina's number, he got her machine and left a message: he was hoping to make the nine o'clock shuttle. He'd try her again when he reached home.

It wasn't until he was in the cab, speeding toward the airport, that he realized he'd left his book on the table.

abrina was waiting for him at the gate.

Even if he'd expected her, it might've taken him an instant to recognize her. Her long dark hair was pulled back in a ponytail; instead of one of the stylish suits to which he'd grown accustomed, she wore jeans and a sweatshirt.

He stood there, stunned, suddenly aware that his heart was racing.

"I hope there is no one else to meet you," she said simply.

"No. I was going to take a cab."

"I have brought my car." She hesitated, seemingly embarrassed by her own brazenness. "Perhaps I should not have come. But I have some news."

"What kind of news?"

"Today was my day of not working. . . ."

"Your day off?"

They started walking.

She nodded. "And so I went to the library. I want to show you what I have found."

"The library's closed, Sabrina."

"The references are on the computer at my home. If it is not too late . . . ?"

As they headed toward the parking garage, she began telling the story of her discovery: how, poring over documents in the archives all morning long and well into the afternoon—reports and articles and internal memos, in French, Italian, German, and Dutch—she'd come upon an editorial in a vintage German chemicals periodical called *Ange-*

wandte Chemie on what appeared to be a fairly close relative of Compound J.

"What's the name of this compound?" he asked.

"They do not give the name. But they talk about the structure. And they talk of polynaphthalene sulfonic acids, as in Compound J."

"And . . . ?"

"And what it says in this paper is *tremendous* interesting."

Sabrina switched on the light. Glancing around the small apartment, Logan couldn't help but note how clearly it mirrored Sabrina's personality—no-nonsense yet quietly tasteful; such a vivid contrast with his own place, still barely furnished after all these months.

She walked over to her computer and switched it on. "This paper was published in 1924."

"Nineteen twenty-four?" He could scarcely believe it; she was bringing him back to the Dark Ages. Back then almost no one had even the vaguest understanding of the nature of cancer. But he kept his skepticism in check. "What exactly does it say?"

Sabrina inserted the disc and soon the screen was filled with text. "You told me you speak some German, no?"

In fact, he didn't know it quite as well as he'd led her to believe. Logan pulled up a chair and, leaning close, set about trying decipher it. It took formidable powers of concentration not to be distracted by Sabrina sitting a few feet away on the floor, eyes incredibly alive with anticipation.

What instantly struck him about the brief article was its tone. Written in the aftermath of the German defeat in World War I and the devastating inflation that followed, its aim was apparently not scientific at all, but political. Its point was that Germany's scientists, for all their lack of financial resources, remained vastly superior to their detested counterparts in England and France. The mention of the compound—"the work of a researcher from the former laboratory of the great Paul Ehrlich"—was very much secondary; its alleged cancer-fighting properties were merely cited, without substantiation, as another example of German brilliance. "May this work continue to prosper," it loftily concluded. "May these compounds always be a credit to German science!"

Logan turned from the screen. "I don't know, Sabrina. There are claims made here, but there's not even a shred of evidence."

"Don't you see, Dan, they talk of cancer! This is important."

He shook his head slowly. "It's so little to go on."

"It is a clue. I was looking for clues."

"I know. But"—he hesitated—"I've got to tell you, it's hard to imagine those people would even have recognized an anticancer agent."

Unexpectedly, she flashed sharp irritation. "You are very arrogant, Logan, for an American living in the 1990s."

"Sorry." He shrugged. "I'd like to believe, but I just don't. Anyway, Compound J has already been eliminated as an anticancer agent by cell line tests."

Such tests, in which drugs are tried against malignant cell growths in petrie dishes, are a shorthand method of determining which compounds merit further trials. There exist cell lines for many cancers: this compound had failed against them all.

"A cell line is not human," she said heatedly. "A human being, a human environment, how cancer cells interact with healthy cells, these things cannot be seen in a test tube."

She was right and he knew it. "Still . . ."

"It is a pity you do not know French," she added sharply.

"Why is that?"

But she was already calling up another document on the screen. This one was longer, three or four pages. "This is from the Pasteur Institute in Paris. You maybe have respect for them?"

He peered at the screen. Though he spoke scarcely a word of French, what he was after was the date. There it was: 1937. "What does it say?"

"It is a paper . . . observations of one of their researchers who visited in Africa."

"Case reports?"

She nodded. "From one of the French colonies. Guinea. This researcher worked in a clinic there, he tells of the interesting things he saw."

"And . . . ?"

She indicated a passage she'd highlighted in boldface. "Twice the same thing. Two different women. They had infections, from spiro-chetes—"

"Syphilis? Yaws?"

"It does not tell exactly."

"It doesn't say?" Logan was incredulous.

"The point is something else. These women had breast malignan-cies also. And after three injections for the infections—a big surprise!—the *tumors* began to shrink."

"What are you saying? Some relative of Compound J was active against breast cancer?" It was so farfetched as to defy belief.

She nodded. "Perhaps. From what it says."

"What, exactly, does it say about the compound? Does it give any details of its structure?"

She scrolled slowly down till she found what she was looking for. "Based on organic dyes . . . Consisting of fused polycyclic sulfonates." She smiled at him. "This sounds a little familiar, no?"

Despite himself, he was starting to share her excitement. "Any-thing else? Any names attached?"

She indicated a footnote in minuscule print at the bottom of the final page. Amid the foreign words, Logan noted what appeared to be a name: "M. Nakano."

"It talks of an unpublished paper this person wrote about the com-pound," she noted. "The name is Japanese, no?"

It rang only the faintest of bells. "Nakano . . . Didn't Paul Ehr-lich like to use Japanese chemists in his lab?" In fact, if memory served, the great man's key assistant in the development of the antisyphilis agent that insured his reputation was a Japanese named Hata. "From what I've read, he had enormous respect for their work ethic."

Sabrina shrugged. "This is history, not science." She stopped, abruptly realizing what he was getting at. "Ah . . . because in the other article . . . ?"

He nodded. "Ehrlich died around the beginning of World War One. Who's to say this Nakano character wasn't the one from his lab who continued work on this compound after the war?" Logan stopped, look-ing at her closely. "Or is that too farfetched?"

"I do not know the meaning of this word."

"Do you think these two articles could be referring to the same research? The same person?"

She stared back. "Yes."

For a long moment he said nothing. "But let's not get carried away. We don't know anything about the Frenchman who reported these findings. Was he qualified to make these judgments? Did he even examine these women himself? For all we know, it might've been nothing more than chronic mastitis or some other routine inflammation of the breast."

But, in fact, he could no longer hide his own mounting enthusiasm. This is what he'd been hoping for. Hadn't the Tilley case already impressed on him that the compound could be enormously active? If, in certain circumstances, it inhibited the growth of healthy cells, who was to say it couldn't also block the growth of malignant ones?

They talked for the next two hours; discussing the many, many ways such a theory could go awry; if anyone else should be trusted with their secret; above all, given the realities of the ACF, whether it made real sense to pursue such a project at all. Logan, in particular, was torn between his enthusiasm and his qualms; one moment drawn by the challenge, the next sobered by the certainty that their involvement with such an enterprise, should it come to nothing, could only do them harm.

Not that they would make any final decisions now. When Sabrina yawned, Logan suddenly thought of the time—and for the first time all night, he found himself feeling self-conscious. "It's late, I guess I should be heading home."

Slowly, he rose to his feet.

She looked at him directly. "Is this what you want to do?"

Logan was taken aback. Could this be a proposition? No, he immediately chided himself, far more likely Sabrina's English had fallen short, leading him to misinterpret the question. "Do I want to?" he repeated.

Sabrina rose from her chair and walked over beside him. "Do you want me to drive you home, or perhaps stay tonight with me here?" She gently stroked his cheek. "I would like you to stay," she added. "It will disappoint me if you do not."

In reaction to his startled silence, she kissed him lightly on the cheek—then began undoing his shirt buttons.

"I guess I don't want to disappoint you," he said finally, smiling.

* * *

"When did you decide we were going to sleep together?" he asked an hour later, as they lay side by side in the darkness.

She laughed. "I do not know. But if I waited for you to try first, we would never be here right now."

"I wanted to for a while, you know."

"I know."

"The only reason I hesitated . . . I mean, we're colleagues. It can be tricky getting involved with someone you work with, you know that."

Sabrina reached out and drew him close. "Please, Logan. Stop the analyzing for once." She kissed him tenderly. "You have to understand—this is sex, not science."

Unchecked, the malignancy has begun to work at her lumbar verte-
brae. With every sharp twist or turn, the tension comes to bear on
the weakened bone. Some tumor cells have moved to within millimeters of
the nerve roots leading to the spinal canal.

Her personal physician is comforting but perplexed. Finding nothing
but a slight tenderness over her lower back, he prescribes a nonsteroidal
antiinflammatory and orders her to slow down.

Though she denies it, even to herself, the condition is starting to
impact her daily routine. Normally able to get by on four or five hours sleep
a night, now, as her body searches desperately for the resources to fight off
the relentless invader, she is often exhausted before nine. Usually alert and
remarkably perceptive, now she more and more lacks focus.

In his office, her physician won't let it rest. His training and instincts
tell him, even in the absence of hard evidence, that something is terribly
wrong. He calls and informs her that he has scheduled a series of tests at
Bethesda Naval Hospital.

"Impossible." She laughs, though completely in earnest. "Un-
schedule them."

She has fourteen months to live.

Logan arrived at the hospital ward the following morning a half hour later than he'd originally intended; he hadn't figured on having to catch a cab to his own place for a change of clothes. Still, it wasn't yet seven o'clock: if he hurried, he still had time to input the Tilley data before preparing for morning rounds.

Making a sharp right off the lobby, he headed to the small room at the end of the corridor that served as the junior associates' computer station.

The hospital was silent, not uncommon at this hour. But shortly after he sat down at the terminal, he was aware of someone hurrying down the hallway. A moment later, Lennox, the night nurse, stuck her head in the doorway.

"Excuse me, Doctor."

He looked up from the terminal.

"I'm afraid we have an emergency."

"I'm not on duty."

She nodded briskly. "I know that. But I can't find Dr. Lukas anywhere."

"*Great.*" But instantly he was on his feet. "Who is it?"

"Congressman Marino."

"Jesus H. Christ!" Flying from the room, he reached the congressman's bed in fifteen seconds. Though it had been less than three days since he'd last seen him, the deterioration was dramatic. Marino was comatose, his color ashen, his breathing agonal, the shallow, raspy breaths coming no more than once every seven or eight seconds. Had he been less familiar with the sudden turns for the worse so common among advanced cancer patients, Logan wouldn't have believed it.

Logan leaned close and spoke softly. "Congressman? Congressman Marino?"

No response. Just another labored breath passing over a parched throat, what used to be known as a death rattle.

Logan looked up at the nurse. "He's DNR, right?" Code for "Do Not Rescusitate."

"Yes, Doctor."

Not that it mattered; he was beyond that.

"Has the family been contacted?"

She shook her head.

"Well, do it. *Now.*"

As she moved briskly off, he placed his index finger on the patient's carotid artery. The pulse was barely detectable.

Thanks a lot, Lukas, he reflected miserably. *Now guess who's gonna have to take shit for this?*

But, looking down at the dying man's face, he was suddenly ashamed. *Jesus, were these his priorities? Look what this place was doing to him!*

In silent contrition, he took Marino's cool hand in his own and, staring out the window at the early morning mist, held it till he heard the nurse returning.

"They're on their way," she offered. "I also reached his administrative assistant at home." She hesitated. "Is he gone?"

Logan nodded. "A couple of minutes ago."

"Anything you want me to do?"

"Just stay here. I'm gonna go find Lukas!"

"Give her an earful for me."

He had a pretty good idea where she might be. Late at night, when junior associates wanted to make themselves other than readily available, they often retreated to a tiny room on the other side of the building, near the ventilation ducts; formerly an on-call room, it still contained a cot. He'd spent time there himself—but never without letting someone know where he was going.

The room was at the end of a long hall, but approaching he saw a crack of light beneath the door. His knock was intentionally sharp.

"Lukas? Hey, you damn slacker, you in there?"

He turned the knob and slowly pushed it open. "Hey, I have some news for—"

The sight was so completely unexpected, it took him an instant to grasp its meaning. She was hanging limply from an overhead pipe by a length of plastic intravenous tubing.

But now he clicked onto automatic pilot, years of training kicking in.

Christ, I've gotta resuscitate her!

Fumbling in his breast pocket for his bandage scissors, he cut the tubing at the nape of her neck and gently lowered her to the floor. No carotid pulse; the skin was far cooler to the touch than the body he'd felt only minutes before.

C'mon, Lukas, you bitch, don't do this to me!

Pinching her nose, he took a deep breath and placed his open mouth upon hers. There was no taste, only a sudden, sickening sensation of cold, like kissing half-thawed meat.

This time he said it aloud. "Come on, Lukas! Come ON!"

He gave her chest a sharp thump; then began repeatedly thrusting an open palm onto her sternum, compressing her heart with his full body weight.

Desperately, he lunged for the phone, punching in the emergency code—5-0-5-0. "We got a code blue in room two twelve!"

Within moments, people started rushing in: the on-call anesthesiologist, thrusting an endotracheal tube down her throat; two nurses with the EKG machine; the rest of the code team.

But they were only going through the motions.

Only now did Logan notice the line of thick computer printouts leading from the spot beneath which the body had been suspended; *that* was how she'd done it, stood on the stacked printouts and kicked them out from under her.

It took ten minutes before a couple of men from the ACF's private security force appeared on the scene, followed closely by local police.

Pad in hand, one uniformed young man, strapping and blond, took Logan's statement.

When they finished, Logan was told he was free to go. Wearily, he began toward the door. But, sensing someone watching him, he stopped and turned.

Stillman.

"It's a sad thing," Stillman observed, breaking the silence.

Logan nodded gravely.

"And I'm sure it was terrible for you. I'm sorry."

"I can't understand it," said Logan softly. "Why would she have done something like this?"

"People do strange things. We're all under a lot of pressure here."

"I thought I knew her. I keep wondering if there's something I should have picked up on."

"Yes, well"—he motioned toward the door—"there's no sense hanging around here. It's still a workday."

Logan remained rooted to the spot. "I just can't understand it," he repeated.

"Dammit, Logan," Stillman erupted in sudden exasperation, "enough hearts and flowers."

The younger man stared at him, bewildered.

"*I just can't understand it,*" parroted Stillman sarcastically. "You think you've had it hard this morning? I've just come from seeing Congressman Marino's family—*that* was hard." He paused. "Learn this, Logan: What happens to some junior associate means squat. It's the Foundation that counts."

Logan hesitated. He couldn't mean it the way it sounded. "I guess she was under a lot of stress," he said.

"*Stress?* Dr. Lukas's problem was guts. She fucked up and she couldn't face the music."

Logan was aghast. It had of course crossed his mind that the possibility of being scapegoated for Marino's death was what had pushed Lukas over the edge—but he'd dismissed the thought. "I don't think there's much she could've done for him," he replied, with a mildness even he recognized as repugnant.

"You're right, she was hardly the most creative doctor around here."

Before them, the horrific scene was nearing its conclusion; the body, placed on a gurney and swathed in sheets, was being strapped into place.

"I don't think that's fair, sir. It's a terrible loss. She was an excellent physician and a good person."

Unexpectedly, Stillman flashed a small, indulgent smile. "A terrible loss? Let's not exaggerate, Logan. She wasn't going anywhere."

Logan didn't connect with Sabrina until that evening, nearly twelve hours later. This was by prearrangement; they'd decided to keep what had happened between them to themselves; dealing with one another on the ACF grounds, if at all, with strict professional detachment. It was a precaution born of intimate knowledge of the place—surely, someone would find a way to use it against them.

But for a while, after this day's ghastly events, it was as if the previously evening hadn't happened at all.

"It is late, no?" she demurred, when Logan called to ask if he could stop by.

He hesitated—it was barely nine. "Well . . . I just wanted to talk. I'm sorry."

"Logan, listen to me. Please do not take what happened last night so seriously. We are colleagues, that's fine. But I do not wish to be the person you call up late at night."

"No problem," he replied dully. "Of course." *Huh? In the past, those had always been his lines.* "Look, maybe we'll talk some other time."

She sighed deeply. "But you are right, it has been a terrible day. All day long everyone talks about it, and no one really says anything."

At his pay phone, Logan felt a surge of hope. "That's because no one knew how to react. No one's been through anything like this before."

"No, I think it was something else. Everyone was sad—but were afraid to let the senior people see. Especially Larsen and Stillman."

Instantly, he knew she was right. "Well, screw 'em," he replied, with sudden bravura, "we're not gonna let that affect our project."

There was a long silence. "Tell me, Logan, how long will it take you to come here?"

As soon as she closed the door behind him, she gave him a passionate kiss.

He pulled back in surprise. "I guess I said something you wanted to hear."

She pointed to a chair. "First we must talk. The lovemaking is for after."

"You're not an easy person to figure out, Sabrina, you know that?"

Ignoring this, she took the seat opposite and leaned intently forward. "You knew her well, this Lukas?"

"Not really. You?"

"No. I don't think she liked me very much."

"She did have that way about her, didn't she?"

"Tell me everything that happened. All the details."

He took a deep breath and did so.

After taking it in, she sat expressionless for a full fifteen seconds. "You didn't see a note?" she asked finally.

He shook his head. "My guess is it was spontaneous. She was already in trouble with the brass—and with Marino about to die on her, it must've felt like a career killer. You know as much as I do about clinical depression."

"Do you know Rachel Meigs?"

Rachel Meigs was another junior associate, a mousy, studious type out of San Francisco General. Logan shrugged. "She seems nice enough."

"You see, Logan, this is the problem with being a man. Rachel, she was best friends with Barbara Lukas. And today she talked to me—just because I am a woman."

"And . . . ?"

"She went into details. All the things they were doing to Lukas. How every day in some way they insulted her, belittled her. Just yesterday, Kratsas told her she was not good enough even to be a candy striper."

"I know, they were making her life a living hell."

"No, it is more than that. *Why* did they do this to her?"

He shrugged. "Let's face it, Lukas was no one's idea of a charmboat. Call it chemistry. She rubbed them the wrong way."

She shook her head adamantly. "No, what you must see is the sickness at this place, Logan. It is pathological. Even more than I realized. What you said on the telephone . . ." She paused. "I love your passion for this work, it's the same as mine. But if we go ahead—"

"*If?*"

"—we must understand how dangerous these people can be."

"Of course," he said blithely. *"Obviously."* He gave a consoling smile. "But just let's not get paranoid about it."

"This is wrong, we *must* become paranoid. And you especially, Logan."

"Oh? Why's that."

"Because you like to trust. And you care very much about pleasing people."

This was starting to get on his nerves. "There's nothing wrong with that, Sabrina."

She rose to her feet and extended her hand. "Come."

Instantly, he was beside her. Drawing her toward him, he smiled. "All right, all right, I'll be careful."

"This is not something to laugh about, Logan. Science you know well—but people, I think, hardly at all."

Their first sharp disagreement involved John Reston. Sabrina strongly resisted letting him in on their secret.

On a purely pragmatic basis, Dan Logan recognized she had a point. He knew as well as she did that, at its current stage of development, the hypothesis might well strike even a sympathetic outsider as preposterous. It still required buttressing by solid supporting evidence, at least some of it of a clinical nature.

But Sabrina's objections to Reston had to do with more than just science. They reflected her own guarded and fiercely independent nature.

"Why?" she demanded. "What is the use of having another person anyhow?"

"Look, Sabrina, we have to be realistic—we can't do this alone. If we're going to have a shot at getting a protocol accepted, we'll have to come at them with a team in place. Reston's a terrific doc. And I trust him."

"I do not. There's something about this man I have never liked."

"Who, then? We have to trust *someone*!"

The argument exasperated Logan. This is why he preferred conflicts about pure science: in the end, those could usually be resolved by a clearheaded assessment of data. The ones about human beings were always so much messier.

Yes, of course, in the best of all worlds, he, too, would prefer to lock others out—for personal as well as professional reasons. Already, between them, there existed the kind of mutual respect lovers can take years trying to achieve; and day by day, as they warily revealed themselves, it was being matched by genuine trust. Why tamper with that? Never had Logan dreamed he could find a woman like this: someone to whom he was not just wildly attracted, but whose passion for this extraordinarily specialized work equaled his own. Once, on hospital rounds, he actually found himself chuckling: he'd been trying to decide which thought got him more excited, of the sex he'd have that evening, or of the conversation that would follow.

In fact, Logan even found himself growing attached to the cloak-and-dagger aspect of the relationship. If most days held far too few hours for all he needed to do—work, research, unwind with Sabrina—the distance they placed between themselves and the rest of the world only heightened their growing reliance on each other.

Sometimes, lying beside her at night, it was almost possible to believe they could pull it off: that, as she argued, the possibilities of success might actually be enhanced if they kept the project to themselves. Certainly, they'd be able to exercise tighter control over the standard of work and the handling of data.

But his pragmatic side told him otherwise. For all his regard for Sabrina's scientific acumen, he had far less faith than she did in the power of her intuition about human beings. The simple truth was, her endless suspicion of others' characters and motives—much as she insisted on seeing it as a virtue—could sink them before they even got started.

His own view of his colleagues seemed to him not so much generous as realistic. Sure, some of them were jerks—petty, erratic, narcissistic, even cruel. That had been more than amply demonstrated. But in the end, who could doubt they all shared the same goal?

It all came to a head one late night when Logan reported on the conversation he'd had that day with Steven Locke, the former ACF senior researcher whom he'd finally tracked down at Southwestern Medical School in Dallas. Admittedly, it had been a bit unsettling. In fact, at first Locke hadn't wanted to talk at all.

"Look," he said, "I'm sorry, but nothing I say about the ACF's going to do me any good."

"I just want to ask about a protocol. It was by a first-year associate named Ray Coopersmith?" He filled the silence that followed with a hasty "I'm a first-year associate myself. It piqued my interest."

"Coopersmith was bad news, okay? That's all I have to say."

"Why? I don't understand."

The other sighed. "He faked his data and he brought other people down with him. End of story. Look, I've got patient rounds to make."

Logan was momentarily speechless. "You don't have any idea where I can find him, do you?"

He laughed hoarsely. "Why in the world would I know a thing like that?" And a moment later he was off.

But now, hours later, Logan felt he had the exchange in perspective. "Look," he told Sabrina, "it was a bit of a scandal, it left some casualties. But that has zero to do with us."

"Maybe you are right," she replied with unexpected mildness. "But this Coopersmith was also a first-year associate, no? This will give them another reason not to let us try a protocol."

"Look, it happened how long ago?" he asked reasonably. "Four years? Four and a half? Have you heard a single word about it since we've been at the ACF?"

Still, before long, she was using it as further reason not to include Reston in the project.

"This Reston, you must stop looking at him only with the eyes of a friend."

"I'm sorry, he *is* a friend. But I knew him as a scientist first—and *that's* why I want him. He has skills we need."

"What skills? To be a wiseguy? Because that is mainly what I see."

"That's not fair, Sabrina."

What, then? What are these special skills?"

Looking at her perched on the edge of his sofa in leggings and a clingy silk shirt, Logan momentarily had trouble concentrating. Once again, fleetingly, he wished this were an ordinary conversation with an esteemed colleague, free of all other factors.

"You have a problem with my question, Logan?"

"Look, Sabrina, please, let's just stop kidding ourselves about what's involved here. We're talking about a mammoth undertaking: designing the protocol, putting together the right patient pool, tracking them, assembling and analyzing data. We're novices, we haven't even been here six months. This whole thing could fall apart for lack of enough competent hands and heads. It's happened many, many times before. Who knows, *that* might've been that guy Coopersmith's problem."

He wasn't sure, but he thought he could sense Sabrina starting to waver. She indicated a six-inch stack of research on the adjoining table, some of the material they'd assembled to review. "Let's get to work. I have only three hours before I must go back to the hospital."

Logan slipped an arm over her shoulder. "You're even good at changing the subject."

She removed it. "Not now, we haven't the time."

"Well . . . I guess I should get started on the introduction to the proposal. . . ."

"Good." She gave him a chaste kiss on the cheek. "You always say the just right things to a girl, Logan."

"Though writing has never exactly been my strong suit."

"At least it's your own language. I'm sorry, I cannot be much of a help in this."

"You know"—he grinned—"Reston's a *helluva* writer. . . ."

"Compound J?" repeated Reston, three evenings later, in the trendy Georgetown restaurant to which Logan had unexpectedly invited him. *"Compound J? For breast* cancer?"

Logan nodded uneasily. He had expected surprise but not incredulity. "Sabrina Como and I have been doing some research. We have what we think is a pretty sound theory."

"Sabrina?" He grinned. "Hey, good for you."

"She's an incredible doctor."

"Right. I know. What some guys'll say to get a woman into the sack."

"That's not funny."

"Ooooh, don't tell me there actually is something going on with the bombshell."

"Look, that's not what we're here to talk about."

He shook his head. "Now, there's a *real* miracle of modern medicine."

"We're here to talk about Compound J."

Reston snorted. "Compound J is a bust. Every doctor at the ACF knows that. Hell, even the janitors know it!"

"Maybe they've just been using it the wrong way. Against the wrong disease."

"I think we should order something." Reston picked up the menu and flipped it open. "Jeez, this place isn't cheap. Let's not forget who's buying."

"Look," said Logan, "I understand your reaction. It's a lot to digest."

He snorted. "I'd say it's indigestible."

The truth was, Logan saw his friend as a kind of test; the objections he raised were precisely those he knew they would face trying to sell the idea within the ACF. It was simply common wisdom that Compound J's anticancer properties were nonexistent.

Given how the discussion had started, neither man pressed it. Only with the arrival of their food did it resume. "All right," picked up Reston suddenly, "tell me what you have that makes any kind of dent in that evidence."

"Where is it written that cell lines are reliable models for what goes on in a living, breathing patient? There are hundreds of exceptions to that rule."

"It's still the rule. Or do you plan to start rewriting those?"

"Making a judgment based on cell line is like looking at an elephant's toenail and thinking you see the whole elephant."

Reston looked up from his cassoulet. "Okay, I agree with that. So what?"

"So if you discount the cell-line results, you can start to look again at this compound's possibilities—with a more open mind."

"Fine. Let's hear some evidence."

"Listen, I hardly even know where to start. Because I really think this stuff is a lot more interesting than anyone realizes. You just can't think about it the way you think of other anticancer compounds."

"*Evidence.* I'm waiting."

Logan raised the Larry Tilley case. "If a drug seems to be that active against a healthy gland, you've got to at least wonder if it won't be active against a diseased gland."

"That's reasonable speculation—but why does that lead to cancer?"

Logan told him about Sabrina's finds in the archives.

Again, Reston was dismissive. "You're giving me stuff from the twenties and thirties?" He shook his head. "Man, that woman must have some hold on you!"

Logan glared at him. "This isn't a joke to me, John. No more sarcasm, okay?"

Reston raised his hands in mock surrender. "Sorry. I thought you wanted an honest reaction."

Logan pulled a folded sheath of photocopied pages from his inside pocket and handed them across the table. "Try telling me *this* is ancient history."

Examining the pages, Reston was immediately impressed by the origin of the document: The *Journal of Molecular Biochemistry*, one of the most highly regarded biomedical scientific publications in the world.

"What's this?"

"You probably missed it. It's a paper presented at one of the seminars they were always holding when we were third-year residents at Claremont. Look at page four."

Reston flipped ahead, noting that Logan had highlighted the key passages: the paper's author, a Professor Engel of the University of Minnesota, was an expert on the proteins called growth factors, produced by all cells, normal and otherwise. What he had shown was that some tumors, especially those of the female breast, develop the ability to secrete growth factors into surrounding tissue where they interact with receptors on the surface of neighboring cancer cells—signaling these cells, in turn, to reproduce. Thus is created an endless circle of secretion and growth as the tumor grows unchecked.

Yet, along the way, almost incidentally, Engel had noted a curious phenomenon: sometimes, inexplicably, drugs containing polynaphthalene sulfonic acids—like Compound J and its relatives—appeared to block the binding of the tumor growth factors to the tumor cells.

"How's that for evidence?" asked Logan. "If we can show this stuff screws up a cancer cell just a little bit more than it does normal surrounding cells, we have ourselves an anticancer drug."

Reston burst out laughing. "Logan, you're crazy. You're a fuckin' megalo. Finding a drug that works among all the millions of compounds out there is like hitting the lottery on your first try. People a lot smarter than you or me work their entire lives and never get anywhere close to testing on human beings." He shook his head. "You might as well suggest pouring hydrochloric acid into patients' veins—you know for sure that'd kill their tumors."

"I'm not saying anyone's going to hand us anything on a platter." Logan paused. "Come on, John, you know as well as I do that this is enough evidence for a protocol. This thesis is entirely plausible. Cancer cells are like sharks—without forward movement they die. Interrupt the growth process and you kill the tumor!"

Reston fell silent. "Who else knows about this?"

"Only you, me, and Sabrina."

He nodded. "Tell me something—what does your friend Sabrina think of me?"

A miserable liar, Logan feigned nonchalance. "What do you mean?"

"She thinks I'm an asshole, right?"

"I don't think so. She knows I'm talking to you about this."

"Because if I've got one talent, it's reading the looks I get from good-looking women. And this one shoots lasers."

"Trust me, that's not true." He took a sip of water. "Anyway, what difference does it make? You're not going to spend your life with her."

"Right, you are."

Despite himself, Logan smiled.

Reston put his hands behind his head and leaned back, staring at the ceiling. "Jesus H. Christ, I thought this was just gonna be a pleasant dinner."

"Sorry."

He leaned forward again, and spoke softly. "You're gonna get massacred on this, Logan. Breast cancer belongs to Stillman! He's about to launch *his* trial."

Logan was more aware of it than his friend could ever know. Nor, at this point, did he have the heart to bring up what he'd learned of Coopersmith. "So"—he managed with what felt like a cocky grin—"we'll go head to head with him. For the good of humanity."

"If this thing is going to have any chance at all, you're going to have to get one of the other top guys behind it."

"I know that."

"And by a process of elimination . . ."

"There's only Shein."

The implications were clear to both. For all his spirited noncon-formity, indeed, largely because of it, Shein wielded far less power at the ACF than most of the others.

Logan leaned forward. "So you with us, or what?"

Reston shook his head with resignation. "Ah, what the hell. I guess we've gotta give it a try, right?" He paused. "I'm gonna order another bottle of wine and get drunk. You'd better start thinking of how you're gonna suck up to Shein."

As it happened, Shein made things easy for him. Two days later, at the end of another long workday, the senior man called Logan into his office and closed the door.

"You speak German, don't you, Logan?" Noting the other's confu-sion, he added, "I checked out your resume. How well?"

"Enough to get by."

"Getting by doesn't impress me. Getting by I can do with my Yid-dish."

"Actually, I've been working on it a lot lately."

Shein nodded. "I know. I see you've taken a lot of material out of the archives."

Logan just stared: was there *anything* this guy didn't know? "May I ask what this is about?"

" 'May I ask what this is about?' " echoed Shein, mockingly. "What is this, a church social? Sure you can. I'm going to the Tenth Interna-tional Chemotherapy Conference next month in Germany. Frankfurt. And I'm gonna want a junior associate to come along for the ride. There's a lot of panel discussions and poster presentations, and I'm gonna need another set of eyes and ears." He nodded at Logan. "Yours."

"Seriously?"

"Write it down, December fifteenth through the eighteenth. Or you worried that'll fuck up your Christmas shopping?"

Logan shook his head no.

"It'll give us a chance to get to know each other a little better, maybe talk about things that have nothing to do with this place. Chess. Women. Barbecue."

Only now did Logan let himself get excited. "That's wonderful, Dr. Shein. Really, I can't tell you how much I appreciate it."

"Yeah, yeah, yeah." Shein dismissed this with a wave of his hand. "My pleasure, I'm sure."

"Say, Logan," hissed Shein, eyeing a tall blonde in an elegantly tailored suit, "get a load of that."

They were standing by the carousel at the airport in Frankfurt, waiting for their luggage. The woman, seemingly harried and slightly severe, the very definition of the no-nonsense executive, was distinctly not Logan's type. He nodded. "I noticed her on the plane. She was in first class."

Shein cast her a look that would have been inappropriate even in a bordello. "Wouldn't you just love to do her? Boy, *that'd* make you feel young again."

"Dr. Shein, I *am* young."

Ignoring this, Shein turned back toward the carousel. "Trust me, Logan, we're going to enjoy ourselves here. If the goddamn luggage ever comes."

Already, after only eight hours together, Logan was starting to have second thoughts about this entire venture. If part of the point was to get to better know his superior, he suddenly found himself knowing more about him than he'd ever wanted to. Even before the flight had left the ground at Dulles, the change had begun. "Okay, Logan, now you're gonna see my fun side."

"I think of you as a fun guy already," said Logan, in what seemed to be the spirit of the moment.

"Naah," came the reply, "wait'll you see. I live for these trips."

Over the next several hours as the plane moved over the North Atlantic, most of the other passengers dozed in the darkened cabin. But the flight attendants kept Shein supplied with a steady supply of Bloody

Marys and the tales of his exploits on the road came one after the other. Dead tired but wide awake, Logan could scarcely believe what he was hearing: the research assistant Shein met at the conference in Rome; the English physician with whom he'd found himself deeply smitten in Tokyo; the sultry prostitute with whom he'd spent most of his waking hours in Rio.

There was, to be sure, a large element of braggadocio in this. More than once, Shein caught his colleague's eye and broke into a broad grin. "That surprise you, Logan?"

But, too, listening, Logan could hardly miss the desperation behind it; the sense that this man, so widely admired and envied, had a void in the center of his life that could not be filled. Even in his own telling, not all of the trysts had gone well. After the first night, he'd been unable to perform with the English doctor. It turned out that a woman who'd been excessively friendly at a meeting in Seattle just wanted to use him for her own professional ends. The Brazilian prostitute took him to the hovel where she lived on the outskirts of the city and, showing him her two young children, exacted a promise that he'd send her cash from the States. He did so for more than a year.

Late in the flight, as Logan finally began to doze, he was aware of Shein's elbow gently nudging him back toward consciousness.

"Dr. Shein?" he asked. "Is there something you want?"

"I'll bet you think I'm an asshole, don't you?" came the soft reply.

Logan hesitated. "No, you're not. Just human."

"Don't kiss my ass, Logan, you don't know a damn thing about it. Alice—when I think of all she's done for me. Working at some goddamn bookkeeping job to help me through med school, dealing with my moods. I don't even know why she puts up with me."

Momentarily, Logan felt not only sorry but slightly embarrassed for the guy. It seemed someone with Shein's brains and experience should have a less mundane lament, something more *interesting*.

But, never one to disappoint, an instant later Shein forgot all about self-pity. In its place there came controlled rage. "The bastards'd use it against me, of course. I know that!" he hissed.

Logan did not have to ask who he was talking about. The ACF was probably one of the last remaining institutions in America where a charge of infidelity might still do someone's career serious harm; a circumstance born of its reliance on the whims of powerful politicians, some of whom continued to make a public fetish of personal morality. Thus it was that, at least on the campus itself, the kind of casual sexual adventurism so common elsewhere was all but unknown.

"As if they don't do it themselves, the cocksuckers," Shein added suddenly. "Every chance they get. Every damn one of 'em!"

Logan silently checked his watch, not yet set ahead: twelve forty-eight. Already early morning Frankfurt time. In little more than an hour they'd be on the ground. "Dr. Shein, maybe we should try to get some sleep."

"Well, maybe not Larsen. He's too stupid to figure out how to get away with it."

There was no way Logan was going to get any sleep now, of course. His head was spinning. Suddenly he felt himself to be less a colleague—a very junior colleague, at that—than a chaperone. Hell, a keeper. This guy was more unstable than he'd ever suspected. A few hours before, Logan had viewed this trip as an immense opportunity, his primary concern choosing the right moment for the delicate task of trying to enlist Shein's support for their trial of Compound J. Now he had to worry about the esteemed scientist embarrassing the ACF; and, hardly incidentally, taking him down with him.

For an instant, by the carousel, Logan was afraid Shein might have in mind following the blond businesswoman. But when their luggage finally arrived, he allowed himself to be led toward the taxi stand, and half an hour later they were checking in at the Hotel International.

Before the younger man's eyes, Shein now underwent another metamorphosis. Relaxed and bright eyed, he stood in the large, tastefully appointed lobby, greeting colleagues from around the world; seeming to effortlessly recall not just their names but minute details of the research in which each was involved.

Dead on his feet, wanting nothing more than to collapse on something soft, Logan quietly excused himself and went to his room. In less than five minutes he was out.

When his eyes at last fluttered open, he was momentarily disoriented. The numbers on the digital clock in the TV read 3:08. Sunlight streamed in from the window opposite. Midafternoon. Groggily, he picked up the phone and asked for Shein's room. No answer.

"But there is a message for you, Dr. Logan," said the voice in heavily accented English. "Shall I have it fetched to your room?"

The note was in Shein's slapdash hand, the one he used when writing prescriptions: *Papa's gone a-hunting. Don't wait up.*

Sitting alone at dinner that night in the hotel restaurant, Logan once again reassured himself there was no reason for concern. The three-day conference would not officially open until the morning. Shein was not due to speak until the following evening. Surely by morning . . .

But Shein was not at breakfast the next day; nor, Logan discovered, had he even picked up his credentials at the front desk. Attending the conference's opening ceremony on his own, watching from the back of the vast auditorium as the elderly head of the Joachim Brysch Stiftung der Deutschen Krebshilfe welcomed the delegates, he could not shake a sense of dread. What should he do? Summon someone back at the ACF? But who—and what would be the consequences of *that?* Alert the Frankfurt police? That might prove even more disastrous. Seth Shein was among the world's most eminent cancer researchers. Who knew, maybe he was just contentedly camped out in the city's red light district.

In the end, Logan decided to do nothing at all. This seemed not just the best choice for him personally but as close as he could come to following the instructions Shein himself had left in his note. Besides, he also had an obligation to pay attention to the conference itself. In Shein's absence, wasn't it more vital than ever that he serve as the senior man's eyes and ears?

Nor was this just a convenient rationale. The work being discussed and evaluated here was of immense importance. Never before, not even at the ACF, had Logan seen so much talent in one place: preeminent cancer specialists from almost every research institution of any significance in the world. Sitting in the auditorium, leafing through the program schedule, he was actually able to briefly put his problem out of mind. This was like being an eight-year-old at Disney World, with a free pass to every ride. Lectures on everything from common basal-cell carcinoma to oligodendroglioma of the brain, workshops running the gamut from garden-variety chemotherapies to cutting-edge research. So many cancers, so little time.

Then, again, the sheer variety of choices only made his own easier: he'd focus on malignancies of the breast.

On the second page, his eye fixed upon a talk to be held immediately after this ceremony in a lecture hall a floor above: "Prognostic Factors in Early Stage Breast Cancer." The listed speaker was Sergio Ferrati of Milan's Instituto Nazionale di Tumori, a name Logan had been liberally dropping since he first came across it during his second year at Claremont. Obliged to speak in English, the international language of science, Dr. Ferrati proved nearly impenetrable, but Logan didn't care. The treat was seeing him at all. So what if his notes were useless, Reston would bust a gut with envy!

After a break for lunch at the cafeteria, Logan headed straight for "Novel Chemotherapeutic Agents for Advanced Breast Cancer" by Arthur McGee of Houston's M. D. Anderson Cancer Center; then, as a change of pace, dropped by for the last third of a seminar on "Cell Cycle Progression in Malignant Breast MCF-7 Cells."

By the time the question and answer segment ended, it was nearly five o'clock. Shein was scheduled to speak at eight, immediately after dinner. The sense of impending disaster returned with a rush. Where could the guy be? What was wrong with him? Throughout the day, Logan had exchanged scarcely a word with anyone on the premises. This he didn't mind; young and without a big-time reputation in a gathering of some of the most ambitious souls on earth, he was grateful to be able to distance himself from the ego-driven scene. But now he felt not so much apart as deeply, harrowingly alone.

The formal sessions concluded for the day, intent on somehow keeping his mind off his problem, Logan made his way down to the large room off the lobby given over to "poster sessions."

The atmosphere here was reminiscent of nothing so much as a high school science fair, confidence commingling with just a touch of desperation. Lining the aisles, edge to edge, were easels, each about six feet high and four feet long. This room was open to even the most modestly credentialed, from ambitious postgraduate students, to young researchers of recognized promise, to older midlevel academics hoping against hope to stay in the game. Anyone with data to display or even a product to hawk was welcome; he or she had merely to scrawl a shorthand description of his wares on a poster, paste on a bit of supporting data, and stand there, awaiting interested customers.

Though poster sessions were the low-rent neighborhood of every such convention—senior scientists tending to wander through only in protective packs, like socialites slumming in Harlem for soul food— Logan had heard that they often featured innovative work. Now he slowly made his way past the exhibits: "The Role of p53 in Retinoblastoma" by Edinoff and Bender of New York's Memorial Sloan-Kettering Cancer Center; "Mutated H-ras Sequences in Pancreatic Cancer" by a researcher from Madrid; "K-Balb Cells Efficiently Internalize Antisense Oligonucleotides" by . . . no affiliation was listed. But the young woman whose work it apparently was stood at the ready.

More out of politeness than genuine interest, Logan paused, reading her poster.

"Affiliation?" she suddenly spoke up.

"Pardon?" said Logan, startled.

"What is your affiliation, please?" She had some vaguely mid-European accent. Maybe Czech.

"The American Cancer Foundation."

Her eyes brightened. "Excellent. This will interest you, then." And, without awaiting a reply, she launched into her presentation. "You see, what we are trying to establish is that antisense oligonucleotide constructs can be used in these cells to sequence-specifically inhibit gene expression. This could be a whole new way of treating patients."

Forget it, thought Logan, *it'll never work.* "Actually," he said, "my specialty is breast cancer."

"Oh." Glumly, she nodded to her right. "Over there."

The next aisle was entirely devoted to breast research, no fewer than fifteen displays.

As he began strolling down it, one exhibit immediately seized his interest: "Inhibitors of Growth Factor Binding to MCF-7 Breast Cancer Cells."

Logan stopped short. Even as he tried to feign nonchalance, he was aware of his heart starting to pound. This was precisely the claim he intended to make for Compound J! Had someone else already done *his* research? Had they been scooped?

He and the man beside the poster, identified as Willem Van Meter,

Ph.D., of the University of Antwerp, looked one another over. Obviously unimpressed, Van Meter resumed scanning the crowd for more likely prospects.

Logan moved in closer. A cursory glance at the accompanying display cards confirmed his fear that this was indeed real science, not quackery. He began reading the cards one by one, weighing the hypotheses, critiquing the experimental technique, trying to decide whether the thesis could hold water in its entirety.

Glumly, he concluded it might.

"Interesting work," he ventured, with studied neutrality.

Van Meter looked at him—"Thank you"—then turned his attention back to the room.

"It reminds me of the study done by Professor Engel at the University of Minnesota."

"Yes, I am aware of that."

Logan waited for some elaboration. When none came, it struck him that the other knew nothing at all of the study in question.

But Van Meter became considerably more animated a moment later when an older, far more distinguished scientist happened by: Dr. Vickers of the Royal Marsden Hospital in London.

"So what have we here?" asked Vickers.

"It's a red-colored polycarboxylate polymer," the other readily explained. "We think it's quite interesting."

"Ah, a polymer, is it . . . ?"

"We are trying to establish activity in metastatic breast cancer. . . ."

"But," repeated Vickers, fixing on the key detail, "you say it's a polymer . . . ?"

"Yes, sir."

"What a shame. All these fascinating results, and no one will ever treat a patient with it."

A polymer, which is composed of linked repeating units with the number of units differing from molecule to molecule, has by definition erratic behavior. Nor, because it is produced by a chemical reaction that ends unpredictably, can uniformity ever be achieved. In the same batch will be found molecules varying dramatically in size and weight, some active, some inactive, some perhaps even toxic.

"No," conceded Van Meter. "What we have is far too . . . *ill defined* for practical use."

"I should say so. The American FDA will never approve the stuff! They tend to be such sticklers about knowing what you put into patients." The Englishman laughed. "Well, I suppose you'll at least have your bit of fun with it."

"Naturally, for the moment, I'm concerned only with the principle," returned Van Meter defensively. "Down the road, we will certainly need better compounds, but for now . . ."

But Logan had already heard more than he needed to know. Nodding pleasantly, he turned and resumed moving up the aisle.

"Where the hell *you* been?"

Logan would know that voice anywhere—and *never* had he been so glad to hear it. He had to resist the impulse to take Shein in his arms.

Though red eyed, unshaven, and still wearing the same clothes in which he'd arrived, Shein appeared just fine.

"I've just been attending the conference, Dr. Shein." He paused. "I was worried about you."

"About *me*? Didn't you get my note?" Suddenly he leaned in close. "I gotta get changed for my damn speech. Come up with me, I'll tell you everything."

Shein was fairly bursting with the news.

"Remember the woman at the airport?" he blurted out suddenly, as they rode up in the elevator.

Logan glanced uneasily at the only other passenger, a bellboy with a food cart. "The blonde?" he replied softly.

"She has a name, for Chrissakes. Christina. Logan, your problem's you got no respect for women."

The door opened and Logan gratefully stepped out. "You were with *her*? How'd you find her?"

Shein smiled with pride. "You're not as smart as you look—I read her luggage tag. Turned out she's a translator, can you believe that? Talks better than you and me put together."

As they headed down the corridor, Logan glanced at his watch. The speech was in less than twenty-five minutes.

"Only one hitch—she won't sleep with me!"

Though some sort of response seemed called for, Logan was at a loss as to what it might be. "That's too bad," he ventured.

"Wants me to have an AIDS test. *Me?* Can you believe that?"

Fifteen minutes later, standing in his underwear before the sink, face covered with foam, Shein was still on the subject. "I try to explain to her the statistical probabilities, right? A guy my age, my background, number of sexual partners. But it's like talking to the Berlin Wall!" He laughed. "That's what I call her, my little Berlin Wall. She loves it."

"Dr. Shein, I'm getting a little concerned about the time." That, and the fact that his colleague evidently hadn't given his talk so much as a moment's thought.

"I tell you, Logan," he said, shaking his head ruefully, "this really hits home how much goddamn ignorance and hysteria there is out there about this disease!"

Not that Logan need to have worried. Shein was brilliant. Speaking without notes on the granulocyte colony stimulating factor—a genetically engineered protein that enables bone marrow to quickly regenerate, thus rendering tolerable extremely high doses of chemotherapy—he kept the overflow audience in the main auditorium mesmerized. In the question-and-answer session that followed, completely in his element, he described his own research experience with the compound in ways almost unheard of at such gatherings; discussing not only the technical aspects, but his interactions with patients and their families; along the way getting laughs from this gathering of senior scientists that would have delighted a veteran Borscht Belt comic.

"That was amazing," enthused Logan, greeting him at the podium afterward. "I don't know how you do it."

But to his surprise, Shein looked almost crestfallen. "Christ, it's too easy. From these people you think you'd get a little more skepticism."

Logan just stared at him.

"C'mon, Logan, you know it as well as me—it's all bullshit. The survival rate for metastatic breast cancer hasn't changed in twenty years. And all the goddamn colony stimulating factors on the planet aren't gonna raise it one bit."

L ike almost everyone else of her generation, she still felt young. Was it possible it had been eighteen years since she was back in Sacramento, writing on local politics for the Bee? Sometimes, closing her eyes, she could see herself, hair still shoulder length, wearing one of those ridiculous pants suits, working away at her heavy old Underwood, struggling to meet a deadline.

But the regrets rarely lingered. The choice to set aside a promising career had been hers alone, prompted not only by altered circumstances but by a changed sense of herself. Fourteen years ago, when Charlie was born, she had wanted to stay home—and considered herself immensely fortunate to be in a position to do so. She wanted to watch her children grow up, to be there when they needed her. Seven years later, by the time her second child, Allison, was old enough for school, her old life no longer seemed feasible. Now, unavoidably, John's career came first. Sacramento was only pleasant memories, the house where they'd lived then replaced by a larger one, before they'd ended up here. When she entered a newspaper office now—struck by the silence, computers having replaced clattering typewriters—it was always at her husband's side.

True enough, over the years she'd sometimes resented this. It wasn't easy living in the shadow of a rising political star. Always, the moment he entered a public place, he changed, his eyes turning hard even as his cheek muscles fixed in a grin. His frequent absences were especially hard on the children.

Still, she told people theirs was a good marriage, and unlike most *political spouses, she meant it. Maybe it wasn't so rock solid as that her parents had made, but what else was new? These were changed times, difficult times. If John was ambitious, well, wasn't that part of the reason she'd married him?*

Above all, she respected him. She alone knew how much he agonized over the compromises he felt bound to make; and how often, under fire, he struggled to remain true to his best self. She saw herself as an essential part of that process, a partner in far more than name only. He trusted her absolutely.

Perhaps even more, she realized now, than she trusted him. For almost a week after the gnawing ache in her lower back returned, she failed to mention it to him. After all, the doctor was still reassuring. He said he was suggesting a biopsy only as a precaution. (As a precaution for whom? she thought, with reflexive irreverence. Whose future was he REALLY worried about?)

She finally agreed because it was easier than fighting it. Anyway, it would put her own mind at ease.

Still, she decided not to tell John. It just wasn't a good time, he had so much on his mind. She'd let him know afterward, when the results came in, when she was free and clear.

The biopsy was set for day after tomorrow. Looking in the mirror, she again succeeded in quieting the doubts. This was not a sick woman staring back at her. This was a woman who looked exactly as she felt—unbelievably young.

The following morning, Shein was gone again. But Logan no longer saw this as his concern. Never mind appearances, this guy was obviously as capable of fending for himself as anyone he'd ever known.

Anyway, he had other things on his mind. This was the day he was to visit the building in which Paul Ehrlich had conquered syphilis, now a cancer research center. Its directors had taken advantage of their proximity to the conference to arrange a tour and various sessions.

Logan didn't have much interest in the topics to be discussed, but he had another reason for coming. This was a pilgrimage. He was coming to this place as a wide-eyed tourist and unembarrassed fan, the way others, back home, visited Elvis's home at Graceland; imagining, like them, that he might pick up some small sense of what made the great man tick.

The chartered bus from the convention center deposited Logan and two dozen others before the building shortly before eleven. Instantly, he was disappointed. From the outside it was curiously unimpressive; a massive, ivy-covered cube of gray stone fronting a narrow street (renamed the Paul Ehrlich Allee after the war) and adjoined on either side by buildings of nearly identical size and shape. The only sign of its remarkable history was a tiny metal marker in the corner.

Entering, Logan was further disheartened to note that the interior seemed to have been lately refurbished; incongruously, the large reception area was filled with the kind of ultramodern furniture Logan had come to associate with eager-to-impress Park Avenue physicians like Sidney Karpe. Now it was the few remaining traditional touches that seemed out of place: A pair of large, ornate Oriental vases, filled with peacock feathers. A stately portrait of an elderly woman in turn-of-the-century attire—identified as the wife of the home's original owner and Ehrlich's benefactress. An alabaster bust of the scientist himself on a marble plinth, his name and the dates 1854–1915 inscribed on the base.

The visiting doctors and researchers were greeted by an earnest young researcher who identified himself as the assistant to their host, the center's director. In impeccable English, he gave a brief rundown of the kinds of work being conducted here. As they would shortly see on their tour, the Institute's labs were state of the art; less than two years before, the upper floors had been gutted and rebuilt. Lunch would be served at the conclusion of the tour, with the featured speaker, the center's research director, speaking over dessert and coffee. He and his colleagues were, of course, very much looking forward to questions, remarks, and observations from the distinguished guests.

Inwardly, Logan shuddered. This had nothing to do with the magical place that had stirred his imagination all those years before. From the sound of it, even those who worked here had little appreciation of the extraordinary things that had once been said and done within the walls; no sense that they were inheritors of one of the most remarkable research legacies in the history of science.

Perhaps it would have been wiser not to come; leaving the illusion, at least, intact.

By the time, half an hour later, they were midway through the tour, he was sure. Logan was ready to bolt the place—and would have, if he'd had any idea where, in this quiet, dull neighborhood, he could grab a cab. The labs the young researcher was showing off were identical to those Logan had worked in himself: in fact, the flow cytometer of which he seemed so proud—a machine that shoots cells into the path of a laser beam so they can be studied individually—was the model the ACF was about to retire.

As the group moved en masse up the stairs toward the top floor, housing yet another set of labs, Logan slipped down the stairs, heading for the reception area. He'd been sipping coffee throughout and it had caught up with him.

"Pardon me, do you speak English?"

The receptionist cast him an impatient look. "Yes, of course."

"Can you tell me where the bathroom would be?"

She nodded in the general direction of the front hallway. "Go through there and down the stairs. Then straight on to the next room. Turn left. And turn left again. You will see it on the right."

He was certain he'd done precisely as told—which is why he was confused to suddenly find himself in a narrow corridor that dead-ended against a wooden door.

Was this what he was looking for?

Tentatively, he pushed the door open—and instantly knew he should close it again. Wooden stairs led downward into the basement. But, after a moment's hesitation, he flicked on the light instead. Moving quietly, feeling an almost perverse sense of exhilaration, he moved down a few steps and bent low to peer beneath an overhang.

What he saw convinced him to go the rest of the way down: vintage lab equipment, the kind he'd seen before only in photographs, neatly arranged within old glass-fronted oak cabinets lining the walls.

Moving closer, he was as baffled as he was intrigued. These were museum pieces, as useless to contemporary researchers as mortars and pestles. Oversized bronze microscopes. A polished steel balance. Hand-blown glass condensers with beautiful spiral cooling coils. More prosaic Bunsen burners and ring stands. Over it all lay a thick cover of dust, as if no one had even laid eyes on this magnificent junk in decades.

A skeptic by nature as well as training, Logan nonetheless could not wholly suppress the thought: Was it remotely possible these had once been used by Paul Ehrlich himself?

Now, in the corner, he noticed a stack of wooden crates. Gingerly, he lifted off the top one and set it on the floor. Within were exquisite old bottles that had once contained chemicals, each protectively wrapped in a single sheet of yellowed newspaper. Though their contents had long since vanished, the raised lettering on several indicated what they'd held: concentrated HCl, H_2SO_4, ammonium hydroxide. Other bottles bore glued labels, now brown with age, the spindly handwriting faded almost to invisibility.

Keenly aware that he'd already been down here too long—lunch might already have started—Logan began hastily rewrapping the bottles. But he paused to note the date on the newspaper—7 Juli 1916—and, despite himself, was soon caught up trying to decipher that long-ago day's events. A terrible battle was in full swing—could it have been the infamous Battle of the Somme?—and the German people were being urged to even greater sacrifices on behalf of their Kaiser and his glorious troops.

Logan picked up another discarded page to look for more. But his eye was quickly drawn to something else: a crumpled sheet of lined notebook paper, wedged in the corner. He picked it up and smoothed out the page. In pencil—difficult to read in the dim light—was the date 25 November 1916, followed by a line of tight script. But what seized his interest was the sketch beneath: twin hexagons sharing a common side and, protruding from the end of each hexagon, additional sulfonate molecules. He took a deep breath, sucking in the musty air. What he held in his hands defied all logic. A primitive version of Compound J!

Carefully, he folded the page, stuck it in his pocket, and resumed putting the bottles back in the crate. Five minute later, heart racing, he rejoined the group.

Sabrina had always been good at keeping her feelings under wraps and she gave John Reston no reason to suspect she'd opposed his involvement with the project. Her philosophy on human relations was simple: Don't go looking for problems, resist the impulse to make them. In scientific collaboration, especially, team harmony is essential—even, if as is often the case, it is forced or artificial.

"Give him the benefit of the doubt, can't you?" Logan had urged. "Give *me* the benefit of the doubt." And that, finally, was what she'd decided to do.

By now, even she was sure that was the right course. In the couple of days since Logan's departure, her ill will had completely dissipated. Working with Reston on the protocol proposal, spending much of that Saturday hunched together over her computer, she found him every bit as bright as advertised; and what she had before taken as self-centeredness increasingly seemed nothing more than garden-variety masculine insecurity; the kind that, taken in the right frame of mind, can actually be endearing.

What mattered was they were so obviously on the same wavelength. Given the severe handicaps under which the team would be operating—their youth, the fact that Compound J had failed so dismally in AIDS trials, the likelihood of serious opposition—the proposal had to be close to flawless. The distinctions between this protocol and all that had come before had to be meticulously spelled out, the case for its likely success vigorously and creatively argued.

Like Logan, Sabrina had had the basic arguments for Compound J down pat for weeks. But it was only now, with Reston manning the keyboard, that she saw them being marshaled for maximum effect. He was a gifted editor—and in a field where such a skill is rare. Sabrina knew that Logan had been right: Reston's presence could be crucial to the eventual outcome.

By midafternoon they had completed a rough draft of the introduction to the proposal, six pages' worth.

"You are excellent with words, Reston," she said, reading it over. "You make everything so clear."

He smiled up at her. "Coming from you, I appreciate that."

"From the way it sounds, who would not wish to support such a protocol?"

"It's called piling on the bull. Now we get to the hard part—the particulars." He paused. "Say, got any liquor around here?"

She nodded. "But I do prefer not drinking and working at the same time."

"I figured maybe it was time for a break."

"Why? The sooner we start, the faster we will end, no?"

Reston laughed. "I swear, sometimes you talk like someone in a spaghetti western."

"I do not know what this is."

"Don't worry about it, it's great." He smiled. "C'mon, just a glass of wine?"

She shook her head. "After."

"Look, I gotta tell you, I've got an agenda. There's a good chance we're going to have a serious argument in a few minutes, and I was hoping to dull your mind so you won't win quite so easily."

She suppressed a smile. "Oh, yes? What kind of argument?"

"Before we go much further, we're going to have to discuss patient eligibility for this protocol. I have a pretty good idea where both you and Logan stand on this."

Sabrina was taken aback. The question of how relatively sick or well a patient ought to be to qualify for such a protocol was absolutely fundamental. She'd simply taken it for granted that it was something on which they'd all see eye to eye.

To the outsider a seemingly straightforward medical question, in fact the matter of patient eligibility is also a political, even a *moral,* decision. Like edgy speculators in real estate or finance, many ambitious researchers will try to secure an edge in advance, limiting their treatment protocols to patients whose relative good health going in vastly increases the odds of a high success rate.

Sabrina paused a moment before responding. "Where *do* I stand?" she asked, betraying nothing. "This is something I have not even decided."

"I'd guess you'd want patients at fifty to sixty percent on the Karnovsky Scale." The reference was to the standard shorthand measure of a cancer patient's condition. Ninety percent or above means close to fully functional; thirty percent, bed bound; ten percent, moribund. At fifty to sixty percent, a patient would most likely be in decline; still ambulatory, but easily fatigued and steadily losing weight.

She couldn't argue. That was precisely the sample that would accurately gauge Compound J's effectiveness. "And you would want something higher? Sixty to seventy?"

"Eighty-five and above."

She snorted. "These people are almost well already. These people you can take out dancing. Or"—she strained to come up with something appropriately outrageous—"watch them play American football!"

"What's wrong with that? Damn good game."

Sabrina felt herself flushing. Eminently reasonable herself, she was always at a loss in the face of what she took to be lunacy. "Listen to me, Reston, do you not believe in this compound? Logan and me, we do. Very much."

"You understand all our careers are on the line here? You DO understand that?"

"And a trial with such a bias? This will help your career?"

"Don't exaggerate, these women are sick with breast cancer."

Her rising contempt was hard to hide. "Such a proposal"—she shook her head—"when the data comes out they will laugh. And they will be right."

"Think of it as a negotiating position. We can drop down to eighty percent, maybe even a little lower."

"We should not discuss this now. We will all talk when Logan has returned."

Turning her back to him, she worked to regain control.

"What should we talk about, then?"

"I do not know."

"Is there an Italian version of the expression *beautiful when mad?*"

"What?"

"There should be."

Suddenly, incomprehensibly, she felt his arms around her waist, his breath against her neck.

"John, what are you doing?"

He didn't move. "I guess this isn't the greatest time to try this, huh?"

"You STOP. Right now!"

"But you look so good, I can't resist. I've been thinking about it all day."

She twisted her upper body, trying to pull away.

"Hey, take it easy." He kissed her neck. She could feel his crotch pressing against her. "C'mon, Sabrina, what's Logan got that I don't?"

"Bastardo! Figlio di puttana!"

With a violent lurch, she wrenched herself free.

He held up his hands in a gesture of uncomprehending innocence, like a basketball player unjustly charged with a foul. "You're not interested, fine. It was worth a try."

"You get out, Reston. Right now!"

"C'mon. don't be stupid. Let's get back to work."

"You get out NOW."

Never had he heard any words spoken more coldly.

"Look, I'm only human. It won't happen again." But already he was reaching to a nearby chair for his down jacket. "I really mean it, Sabrina, I'm sorry."

He zipped the jacket closed and took a few steps toward the door. "Please, let's just keep this in perspective, all right? And to ourselves."

Before the conference was half over, Logan had decided it was impossible to compete with Shein's private life. He would save the subject of Compound J—and the forthcoming protocol proposal—for the trip home.

Yet two hours into the return flight, he was still trying to find an opening. To his frustration, if not his surprise, once again *he* was the captive audience, forced to listen to the particulars of Shein's latest escapade. It seemed things had worked out well with Christina after all. Though she had persisted in refusing to listen to reason on the probabilities of HIV transmission, she'd revealed a delightful and unexpected kinky streak: they'd spent most of their last afternoon together reading aloud pornographic letters from back issues of *Penthouse*. "A *terrific* young woman!"

Now, his tale complete, the scientist appeared to be dozing contentedly.

"Dr. Shein, is there any particular aspect of the conference you'd like to discuss? I took extensive notes."

"Later."

He hesitated. "I had quite a particularly interesting experience when I went to the place where Paul Ehrlich once worked."

Shein didn't so much as open an eye. "I know about that lab. They're not doing anything worth wasting your breath on."

"It has nothing to do with that. I went into the basement and ran across some equipment. Ancient stuff. I have a pretty good idea it's from Paul Ehrlich's own lab."

He sat up and looked at Logan in genuine surprise. "What the hell were you doing in the goddamn basement?"

"Well, see—"

"Take anything? Get any *souvenirs?*"

Flustered, Logan reached into his inside jacket pocket for the sheet of paper. "This."

"Thattaboy." He reached out a hand for it. "Schmuck, don't you know I could have you arrested?"

Putting on his reading glasses, Shein looked it over quickly.

"I found it in a crate of old chemical bottles. As packing."

"And?"

"Well, I thought it was pretty interesting."

"Why? Some scribbling on an old scrap of paper?"

"You're right. But if you look at it closely . . ."

Shein shot him a hard look. "Logan, when the hell you gonna come clean? You and I both know this is an early version of the chemical structure you and the Italian babe have been looking at."

Now that the moment had presented itself, Logan found himself completely unprepared for it. "That's right," he acknowledged.

"What do the words say?"

"The words?" He looked at the page as if for the first time. "You want a translation?"

"Yes, Logan, I believe that's what they call it."

"Well"—he hesitated. "Basically, it just describes the compound in the picture."

"A polysulfonated aromatic."

"But the language is strange, a bit stilted. I was thinking it might've been written by one of Ehrlich's Japanese researchers as part of some kind of journal—"

Shein brushed this aside. "Deal in facts, Logan. What does this little find of yours *mean?*" He waved the paper aloft. "If anything."

"Well"—he paused—"I think it's pretty meaningful. I mean, we'd read that this compound may have originated in Germany, way back when. It's fun to find what seems like direct confirmation."

"So which is it, Logan—meaningful or fun? You're a scientist, they're not the same."

Logan looked crestfallen. "No, I suppose it doesn't mean much— not in scientific terms."

"All right. You want fun, go body surfing. Or go fuck something." He paused. "Now, we got time to kill: I want the whole story of what the hell you've been up to. Every detail."

So over the next couple of hours he told it, starting with Larry Tilley's appearance in the examining room. Shein sometimes seemed impatient—cutting into the narrative with a sharp comment or a challenging question—but his interest never wavered.

"Compound J for breast cancer?" he said at the end. "Well, it's a novel notion, I gotta give you that. Where do you stand now?"

"I'm hoping Sabrina and Reston will have something on paper when we get back."

"So it's just you three?" His tone was ominously noncommittal.

"So far."

Closing his eyes again, he settled back in his seat. "Sounds like a pretty involved way to set up a ménage à trois, if that's what you're after."

Logan's reaction was sharper than he intended. "Look, Dr. Shein, I don't need to hear that. We've put a lot of time into this project. We think it has real potential."

Surprised, Shein opened his eyes and shrugged—as close as he knew how to come to an apology. "Oh, excuse me, you didn't say you were *shtup*ping her. Why the hell are you always less open with me than the other way around?"

"I'm just trying to tell you how much—"

But Shein cut him off with a consoling squeeze on his arm. "It's a good idea. I'm impressed. Of course, I'll wanna see your data. I'll wanna see your proposal."

"So you're interested? You'll help us?" asked Logan, flabbergasted.

"Why do you think I took you along on this goddamn trip?"

21 September 1919
Frankfurt

An anniversary of sorts—six years exactly since we began working on the compound in the laboratory of Professor Ehrlich. How long ago it seems! How naive I was to think answers could be found quickly! Many days now I despair that they will ever come.

Near the end of the war we thought things could not get worse. Now we know how wrong we were! Everyone is hungry. Beggars everywhere! Naturally, some work supplies impossible to come by. We joke of catching rats for laboratory use in the cellar—only, seeing the larder empty, they have all fled.

Still, I press on. This morning, finished latest variation of the compound: #74—beautiful white crystals, darkening slightly upon exposure to sunlight. Am hopeful of increased activity. Perhaps answer is in the length of molecule!

More than ever, I miss Dr. Ehrlich's strength and counsel!

Staring at the page, bone tired, Reston suddenly began to laugh. Across the room, Logan and Sabrina simultaneously looked up from the pages they'd been reading.

"I don't know about you guys," explained Reston, "but I've read this damn proposal so many times, it doesn't even register anymore. It might as well be in ancient Greek."

"We are all tired, Reston," snapped Sabrina. "That's no reason to stop working."

"I mean," added Reston, ignoring this, "I just read *providing a meaningful cure* as *procuring a meaningful whore*. I didn't *think* we'd put in anything so interesting."

"I'll bet *that* would catch their interest," said Logan.

"Especially Shein's," agreed his friend.

Logan laughed; he'd naturally passed on every detail of his remarkable conversations with the senior man.

"This is nothing to joke about," said Sabrina sharply. "I do not think Shein wants a protocol to laugh at. Or the review committee either."

Once again, Logan found himself caught short: What was going on with her? Why these sudden lapses into humorlessness? And the constant low-level hostility toward Reston?

It had begun the very day he returned from Germany. That evening, over dinner, Sabrina told him of their seemingly irreconcilable differences on the issue of patient eligibility.

"This is a big conflict," she put it. "I know you like Reston, but I really do not think we can let this man work with us."

Logan, too, recognized the argument as a source of serious concern. Yet he found that when it down came to it, Reston proved eminently—even uncharacteristically—reasonable. True, he forcefully made his case at their first joint meeting after the holidays, producing statistics on the success rates of similar protocols over the years to buttress the arguments he'd made to Sabrina. But once it became clear he was not going to win, he made no attempt drag out the battle.

"So," Logan asked, "I take it you still want to be part of this? Even though we can't *guarantee* success?"

"Hey, what else have I got going? I mean, it's not as if I didn't expect it. If this thing's gonna work, I guess we'll all have to get used to majority rule"—he smirked—"even when the majority's wrong." And, opening up his briefcase, he produced a split of champagne. "I think a toast's in order." He looked meaningfully at Sabrina. "Something along the lines of 'All for one and one for all!' "

In the weeks since, the scientific disagreements among the three of them had been minimal. Yet Sabrina's attitude toward Reston seemed unchanged. Nor did Logan find himself able to discuss it with her. The couple of times he tried, she flatly refused to acknowledge there was even a problem.

"Look," Logan said now, "we're all nervous about Shein's reaction to the draft. Why don't we try and relax?"

"Bet I'm not as nervous as you," offered Reston. "Shein expects nothing of *me*."

"Thanks a lot," said Logan, conceding the point. "It's so great to know you're always there with a reassuring word."

In fact, since he was one who'd recruited Shein as senior advisor to the project—and the senior man so obviously saw him as a comer—Logan had infinitely more at risk than his colleagues. So far, Shein had kept his distance, choosing to let the three junior associates work out the draft of the protocol proposal on their own. It was a courtesy that was also a challenge: only now, having studied it, would he let them know whether he'd give them his full backing.

"Well," said Logan, sighing, "we'll know in"—he glanced at his watch—"anytime. How do you like that, the son of a bitch is late!"

"Me, I am not worried," reassured Sabrina. "It is good work."

Sighing, Logan flipped his copy of the protocol proposal shut; at fifty-five pages, plus reprints of six articles and other supporting data, it had the solid feel of a corporate annual report.

That was part of the point, of course. Even with Shein's support, the task before them would be daunting: to impress upon a skeptical review board that, though young and woefully inexperienced, they were dedicated and resourceful researchers, working on something with genuine promise. Yet—this is what made the balancing act so exceptionally complex—neither could they risk appearing unrealistic about their goals, or more than modestly hopeful about their chances for success.

In fact, starting with the title, "A Phase Two Clinical Trial of Compound J in Metastatic Breast Cancer," they'd lent the proposal a tone of calculated blandness; as if it had been written by a trio of old, knowing souls, certain only that the world almost never surrenders its secrets.

Too, they'd paid unusual attention to the Informed Consent Document that made up the proposal's concluding section. Since Compound J had no clinical history as an anticancer agent, they could only speculate on how patients treated with it in such a trial might react. But this they made a point of doing at considerable length, listing possible toxicities that other researchers might have readily discounted.

They'd given the same care to almost every aspect of the proposed trial. The toughest decisions after the one on patient eligibility had been essentially technical. They involved the dosing schedule and—since Compound J cannot be absorbed if taken orally—the choice of which intravenous delivery system would prove more effective: a continuous drip or more concentrated doses in sporadic bursts, via a large slug known as a bolus.

After several long evenings of largely fruitless back and forth, they'd opted for the drip. After all, like so much else, such a choice finally involves little more than guesswork. Were cancer cells more likely to be worn down by a steady level of medication in the bloodstream? Or would they be destroyed only if overwhelmed by toxins—a course that obviously could also place healthy cells at greater risk?

In the end, it was this possibility that determined their decision. The drip was clearly the more conservative choice; and, determined to come off as responsible, they decided, after hours of discussion, that made it the sounder one.

"Sorry," offered Shein, when he finally turned up at Logan's apartment, forty minutes late, "a guy from Health and Human Services came by my office and I couldn't get rid of him."

"That's okay, Dr. Shein."

"Those bureaucratic bastards never rest. Now they want summaries of every damn clinical trial going on at the ACF. Can you believe that? It's not like they'd even understand what they were reading!"

Logan nodded, impatient. "Right." *How long did Shein plan to string them along?*

"Well, glad to see you're all here." Shein laughed. "I love this cloak-and-dagger stuff. I trust you were all careful you weren't followed."

"May I take your coat, Dr. Shein?" asked Logan.

"It's *Seth*, Logan. How many times you gonna make me tell you that?"

Logan naturally took this as an encouraging sign. He smiled. "Sorry. May I take your coat, *Seth?*"

"No, Alice expects me home—I gotta spend a little time with her, too, for Chrissakes. What I have to say won't take long."

It felt like a blow to the solar plexus, but Logan showed nothing.

"Not a bad place," observed Shein, glancing around the room.

"Thank you."

"So—what?—you furnish it totally through the Salvation Army or did you step up to Goodwill?"

"Actually, Dr. Shein—excuse me, Seth—I went to Ikea."

"What's wrong with you, Logan, losing your sense of humor?"

"He does that a lot," piped up Reston. "Not one of his better traits."

"I think," said Sabrina evenly, "that we all are concerned to hear what you think of the proposal."

Shein beamed her way. "See that. At least one person here's got the balls to say it straight out." Unbuttoning his coat, he tossed it on an empty chair. From the inside pocket of his rumpled tweed jacket he removed a folded copy of the protocol proposal. It appeared to have been well read. "You got something to drink in this place?"

"Please, Dr. Shein."

Shein cast Logan a baleful glance. "Okay. It's good. It's very good."

Logan could breathe again. He waited an instant. "You really think so?"

Shein looked from Reston to Sabrina, the pleasure—or was it just relief?—apparent on both faces. "Wait a minute. Not that I don't got some serious criticism."

And an instant later, as if rankled at having even briefly delivered unambiguous pleasure, he was into it: "I don't like the drip. You gotta go with the bolus."

"We of course gave that a lot of thought," ventured Logan. "Why would you say—"

"Because taking risks is supposed to be your business," he was cut off impatiently. "Not stupid risks, for Chrissakes, but, yeah, appropriate ones! Otherwise what kind of impact are you gonna make?"

"Very little," said Reston, softly.

"Don't just gimme the answer I wanna hear, Reston. Tell me something I don't already know. Under the best of circumstances, what kinda toxicity you gonna get with this drug?"

Reston visibly reddened. "A lot."

"Damn right. The stuff made your friend Tilley's goddamn adrenal glands *fall out*! So why're you pussyfooting around? The cancer's gonna eventually kill 'em anyhow—why not hit the cancer cells *hard* and get out?"

"We were trying to minimize damage," offered Logan. "We'd like to end up with a living patient."

"Screw that. You do a trial like this, you face that there might be fatalities. Because basically what you're doing is poisoning people within an inch of their lives. You can't make omelettes without breaking eggs."

There was a long silence in the room.

It was Sabrina who broke it. "Dr. Shein, we are talking about the therapeutic window, no? The dose that will be toxic to cancer cells but not toxic for healthy cells."

He nodded. "You got it."

"And this is a tiny, tiny margin . . . even for the best drugs."

"The trick is finding it. That's what separates great cancer docs from the chaff—the willingness to go right to the edge and not flinch. It's a helluva lot easier saying it than doing it."

Shein studied his listeners. Sabrina clearly had a handle on this; she'd go his way. So would Reston, if only to stay on his good side. But Logan seemed unconvinced.

"Listen," he added, directing his words Logan's way, "it's not like I don't understand the impulse. You give a patient an intravenous drip with a subtoxic dose and she'll love you to pieces. She'll tell everybody, 'My doctor's a genius, he's giving me chemotherapy and there are almost no side effects!' " He paused meaningfully. "But you know what you're doing? You're killing that patient with kindness."

He paused, as serious as Logan had ever seen him. "Your job is to come up with a treatment! Do that and—never mind if you're a saint or an asshole—you'll never have to worry about being popular again."

Logan could not argue with any of it. The fact was, hearing the man lay it out so starkly, his respect for him only increased: the guy had not only a high-tech, microchip-driven brain but, just as vitally, old-fashioned brass balls to go with it.

Still, he hesitated—because he was also aware of something else. No mattered how well intentioned Shein's advice was, and no matter how ultimately sound, the senior man was in a no-lose position. Logan and the Compound J team could not proceed without his blessing. And yet, if things went wrong, he would not be the one to take the fall.

"How about the adrenal problem?" pressed Logan. "With the dosage you're suggesting, every patient in this trial could have her adrenal glands"—he hesitated—"*fall out*. Like Tilley's."

Shein shrugged. "You'll prophylax them with hydrocortisone. That'll neutralize the toxic effects of the drug—provide the same hormone in pill form normally produced by the gland."

Logan considered this. "But that could be just the beginning. I mean, that's what we were trying to get at with our Informed Consent provision. Who knows how many other problems you're going to have to fix along the way?" He paused. "Well, I guess those are bridges that have to get crossed."

Shein smiled: he knew he had him. "Fortunately, you'll have me to help devise solutions."

"We can count on that?"

"Absolutely." He stood up and reached for his coat. "By the way, when you rewrite the proposal, I want you to tone down that goddamn

Informed Consent provision. You don't have to go out of your way to imagine every possible side effect."

"We just wanted to be candid. And responsible."

"Listen, what you had there scared the hell outta *me*. The committee knows all that anyway."

"I suppose you're right."

"Don't forget, Logan, we're all on the same side here."

That night, when Reston had gone, Logan produced a bottle of champagne of his own. Roederer Cristal—a hundred and forty bucks it had cost him.

Yet, though he'd planned this moment for weeks, it was astonishing how soon it began to feel like an anticlimax.

"Is there something wrong?" he asked Sabrina as they sipped their second glass. But, quietly exasperated, within he phrased it differently. *What the hell's wrong now?*

"I am just a little tired."

He slipped his arm around her. "Get used to it. The *real* work hasn't even started yet."

"This Shein," she said, with a forced smile, "he has the morals of a cabbage. But he is not dull."

"No—anything but that. Get him an organ grinder and a little suit and he'd do handstands in the street." He paused. "I only wish he'd stop making nasty cracks all the time."

She looked at him closely. At the beginning his face had struck her merely as conventionally handsome; now she was equally taken by the deepening worry lines—evidence of what she knew to be character. "He doesn't mean it. It is a sign he likes you."

"Right. Much more of his friendship and I'll put a gun to my head."

For all his seeming self-assurance, Logan was, she'd come to know, deeply vulnerable; the product of an unsettled homelife she couldn't pretend to understand. She sympathized with this—but it also left her ill at ease. Every bit as committed to career as he was, she'd long been

equally disinclined to waste time and energy on complex romantic en-
tanglements. She cared for this guy—more than for anyone in a long
time. But increasingly, she couldn't help thinking he'd been right from
the start: this confusion of the personal and professional could be a
terrible mistake.

"I'm sorry, Logan," she said, "this is a time we should be happy."

"Who says I'm not happy?" He smiled. "Are you kidding? All I'd
need to make my life *perfect* at this moment is a great Havana cigar!"

She laughed, but he knew he hadn't begun to bridge the distance
between them. "Look at it this way, Shein's just my cross to bear. You've
got Reston."

Reston! He, of course, was the crux of the matter. Could she open
up to Logan? More than once she'd come close. But always it came down
to the same pragmatic question: What kind of havoc would that wreak?
What mattered now—*all* that mattered—was the well-being of the protocol. And for the foreseeable future, that seemed to mean making the
best of life with Reston.

"Well," he suddenly spoke up, brightly enough that if she demurred
it would come off as kidding around, "I think it's time we did some real
celebrating around here." He nodded toward the bedroom.

"Not yet, Logan. This is so nice."

Still, she was torn. For it was increasingly apparent the awkward
personal situation might itself threaten the work. She simply could not
trust Reston. Logan did, absolutely. As a result, she now sometimes
found herself hesitant to confide in her lover/colleague even on scientific
matters.

She reached for the champagne. "If I show you something," she
spoke up suddenly, "can we keep it just for ourselves?"

What now? "Animal, vegetable, or mineral?"

"I'm serious, Logan. An article I found. About Nakano. Nothing so
important—but I do not want John Reston involved."

"Ahh." *Christ, when's she gonna get off this obsession with Reston?*
"What the hell, I guess so. John doesn't care about any of the background stuff anyway. He thinks it's all pointless."

"This is a promise?"

"If you want."

She rose, crossed the room, and retrieved a sheet of paper from her briefcase. "Here," she said, handing it to him. "Not much—but it has some new details."

It was a Xerox copy of a newspaper clipping, dated August 18, 1924, and a mere three paragraphs in length, from the German daily *Frankfurter Allgemeine Zeitung*. Studying it, Logan quickly understood it was a sort of social announcement. Dr. Mikio Nakano, associate director of the Medicinal Chemistry Division of the I. G. Farben Company, was to speak the following day at the Frankfurt League of War Wives. His subject: *I. G. Farben Wissenschaftler erzielen Fortschritte im Kampf gegen die Krankheiten der Menschheit* (Advances made by I. G. Farben scientists against human disease). The item identified the speaker as a native Japanese, formerly an assistant to the great Paul Ehrlich. His age was listed as thirty-four.

"Where did you get this?" asked Logan, looking up.

"I contacted all the important German chemical firms. I asked if they had any information on this man."

"But I. G. Farben no longer exists. . . ."

As they both knew, the lesson left by the giant chemical firm about the potential misuses of science was among the most shockingly savage on record: having enthusiastically participated in the program of genocide instituted by the Third Reich—even to the point of operating a slave labor camp within Auschwitz—the company had been dismantled by the Allies immediately after the war, its directors convicted as war criminals.

"No. It came from one of the successor companies, Hoechst. It was in their files, all they had on this man." She smiled. "I think the Germans do not throw much away."

"So we were right about this guy—he was with Ehrlich." He looked at her. "You're unbelievable, you know that?"

"No, just curious. Same as you. We still know very little of his work."

But he could see she was her old self; her sense of intense preoccupation replaced, at least for the moment, by an openness appealing beyond description. "You're also very beautiful," he added, spontaneously. "I think you've definitely earned some more champagne."

"No, thank you." She took his hand and kissed it gently. "I think now is the time to do the rest of our celebrating."

18 August 1924
Leverkusen

Why did I accept work at Farben? They use me like a trained monkey! Had to waste whole afternoon giving a speech. Me—with my German! Surely as painful for audience as for me.

More proof Farben has little interest in project. Herr Direktor Ambros, once a supporter, says too much lab time spent on compound—questions its commercial potential. Harder than ever to get time in the laboratory for the work.

Last night could not sleep. What would be worse—losing job or keeping it?

Compound #157 useless. Unstable at room temperature and poorly soluble in aqueous media.

Begin tomorrow on #158.

L ogan was a bit shaky when he arrived at the hospital the next day for his morning rounds—and even less inclined than usual to deal with Rochelle Boudin.

Over the months, Rochelle had grown ever more difficult. Much as Logan prided himself on his skill with tough patients, with her it could be a physical effort to maintain his usual bedside manner of cheerful calm. Almost daily—even on those days when he was not charged with hospital duty—Logan received word Rochelle needed to see him. If it wasn't about her dosing schedule, it might be the quality of the hospital food; or perhaps even a program on cancer research she'd seen the night before on PBS that she imagined had some bearing on her treatment.

Logan recognized, belatedly, that he'd help bring this on himself. Because he'd made an effort to show her special consideration at the start, she'd come to take it as her due; now feeling entitled to make demands she wouldn't make on any other doctor at the ACF.

The truth, of course, was that what she mainly wanted was a friend —and never had it been more true than in recent weeks. Rochelle's husband, Roger, who'd earlier made such a point of his devotion, had all but disappeared from view, and Logan noted that there was less and less conviction in her claim that he was just away on business.

Obviously, such a scenario is always poignant. A severe illness is the ultimate test of the human bond, tending to point up moral bankruptcy in loved ones nearly as often as character; and had it been someone else, someone less manipulative or even slightly more considerate of others, Logan might have found her circumstance more touching.

As it was, his dealings with Rochelle were governed only by a sense of obligation to the protocol of which she was a part. Which, finally—because the protocol in question was the volatile and unpredictable Larsen's—was nothing more than a sense of obligation to his own future.

Now, as he scrubbed down, splashing cold water on his face to wash some of the bleariness from his eyes, he was suddenly aware of someone waiting off to the side. Nurse Lennox.

He turned and stared at her balefully. This woman was not in the business of giving him good news.

"What?"

"I hate to bother you with this, Doctor."

"Boudin?"

She nodded. "She started asking for you yesterday afternoon, and began again as soon as she woke up this morning. Her latest white cell count is in."

"Oh, God." In general, he had no problem with the ethical guideline giving patients full access to their medical records. But Boudin made a habit of abusing it, seeking test results before they'd even been seen by her doctors, often interpreting them in ways that had only the most tenuous link to medical reality. "What is it?"

"Forty-two hundred. I have it right here."

She handed Logan the sheet and he briefly studied it.

"So . . . I guess she wants to cut down on her dosage again, right?"

She nodded. "That's what she wants, all right."

"Jeez, what a pain . . . !"

"Good luck."

"Yeah. I wish luck were all it took."

Resignedly, he started moving down the corridor toward her room, the challenge at hand all too familiar: *How to keep this conversation down to five or ten minutes? How to get through it with minimal emotional fallout?*

"Dr. Logan?"

Logan was so preoccupied, he momentarily failed to respond to the voice addressing him from behind—or maybe it was just that it was so uncharacteristically moderate.

"Dr. Logan."

He wheeled, and was startled to see . . . Stillman!

"D-Dr. Stillman," he stammered, "I'm sorry, I didn't hear you."

The senior man approached him, hand extended, smiling. "No problem. I was just wondering if you might have a couple of minutes to talk."

Logan hesitated. "Actually, I'm on my way to see a patient. But if it'll only take—"

"Who?"

"Rochelle Boudin."

"Lucky you. No, you'd better take care of it, you don't want Larsen on your ass." Another smile, this one full of comradely understanding. "Come see me in my office afterward."

A moment later, stepping into Rochelle Boudin's room, it was all he could do to mask his reaction—curiosity, tinged with anxiety—to what had just occurred.

"Good morning, Rochelle," he said with brisk efficiency. "I'm told you want to see me."

She was propped up in bed, *Good Morning America* showing on the mini-TV suspended at eye level. "Where were you yesterday?"

"Rochelle," he said, with exaggerated patience, "you know I'm not on hospital duty Wednesdays, I'm in the Screening Clinic."

"I mean yesterday evening. You used to come in the evenings."

He couldn't deny it. Earlier in his tenure at the ACF, he'd often spent time with patients after-hours; a bit of apple-polishing for higher-ups that could also actually be a nice change of pace. But since beginning work on the Compound J project, that had been out of the question. "Look, Rochelle, I'm sorry, it's been a busy time." He cleared his throat. "I'm told there's something you want to discuss."

"Have you seen my white cell count?"

"I have it right here." He assumed his best sympathetic air. "I know it seems low. But I can assure you, we're not close to the danger zone yet."

In fact, after seven months of having her bone marrow pulverized by chemo, Boudin was holding up remarkably well.

"I want to cut the dose. I *insist* on it."

"Rochelle, you know perfectly well that according to the terms of the protocol—"

"I'm so sick already," she interrupted, "why can't you just give me a break . . . ?"

"Please, Rochelle, you know that I—all of us—have only your best interest at heart."

"Do you?" she asked, suddenly girlish. "Sometimes I can't tell."

"Listen, have you given any thought to what we talked about the last time?"

The reference was to the implanting in her upper chest of a subclavian intravenous line. As often happened with long-term chemo patients, the veins closest to the surface had narrowed and virtually disappeared from sight, making the insertion of an intravenous drip a dicey and sometimes painful procedure. Such a line would make it as easy as inserting a plug into a socket.

"I don't know," she said. "Would it hurt?"

"Rochelle, we've been through this. Any pain would be minimal. The surgeon can do it in fifteen minutes, with a local anesthetic. When you're finished with chemo, it's just as easily removed."

"Do you think I should?"

Under other circumstances, it might have been a reasonable question. Now it merely annoyed him. "Yes, I certainly do."

"Then I will. If you say so."

"Good, I think that's the right decision. I'll have the surgeon, Dr. Dawkins, come by." Logan glanced at his watch. "Listen, Rochelle, I've got a very busy morning. Perhaps you can take this up with one of the other doctors."

"I don't want to talk about it with anyone else."

"Well, I'm sorry, I really do have to go." And he turned, heading for the door.

"Will you be back to see me later?"

But he pretended not to hear, not stopping until he reached Stillman's office.

"How'd it go?" asked the senior man, as unsettlingly pleasant as before.

Logan shook his head. "The woman's a nightmare."

Stillman laughed. "Well, sit down, relax." He indicated the chair facing his desk. "Who knows, maybe we can arrange it so you don't have to do that sort of thing anymore."

Logan sat down and returned his smile. *What the hell was this about?* "That would be nice."

"I haven't seen much of you lately. What have you been up to?"

Logan offered a stiff shrug. "Nothing much. This and that."

"This and that? Sounds like you could put your time to better use." He paused, leaning forward. "No sense beating around the bush. I'd like you to join my team."

"Your clinical research team?" Logan was stunned. "Really?"

"That drug I talked about to you and what's his name about . . . ?"

"John Reston."

He nodded. ". . . I'm almost ready to bring it to trial. We're putting together the protocol right now, and I'm going to have to beef up on support staff."

"My God! That's incredible."

If Stillman had sensed there was less than full enthusiasm in his tone, he didn't let on. "I know I don't have to try and sell you on this, Logan," he said. "But I can tell you this could be a big drug. And big for everyone close to it."

"It's incredibly flattering. Thank you."

Stillman waved this away. "Forget that, I want you because you're good. I've seen your work in the Clinic and on the inpatient wards. Patient accrual is going to be a very important aspect of this trial."

He waited for a response. When Logan merely nodded, he pressed on. "Needless to say, assuming things work out satisfactorily, at the end you'll get your name on the paper." He laughed. "Not as a lead researcher, but it'll be there somewhere."

Logan knew how unusual such an offer was. He appreciated what, under other circumstances, it would mean to his career.

He also knew that he had to find a reason not to accept.

Logan nodded again, then decided to take the risk. "Sir, could you possibly tell me a bit more about the drug?"

Such a question from a junior researcher might have been seen as highly presumptuous. But Stillman, utterly confident, took it with good grace. "Well, as I told you before, it's an anti-growth factor strategy. I'm really not ready to go into more detail than that."

Still *not ready*, Logan wondered, *with the thing almost set to go before the Review Board?* Something odd was going on here. "Sir, it's just that, well, if I'm going to commit to work on the project, I'd really love to know just a little more about it."

"You would, huh?" Stillman leaned back in his chair. "Well, start by knowing this. This is the sexiest drug to come down through the pipeline in a while. It's new and it's different and the press is going to eat it up."

"That's great."

"And," he added, "you'd be a fucking fool not to leap at this chance."

Suddenly, sitting there, it hit him, a gut feeling so powerful he'd have bet his life on it: Stillman had *zero* faith in this drug! It was just another variation of the same old stuff. *That's* why he wouldn't come clean.

This protocol posed no threat at all to Compound J. Stillman was thinking only short term—the hype, and the funding it would bring in.

"Can I just think about it a little while?" Logan waffled. "I mean, it's such a huge decision."

Stillman's eyes flickered with annoyance, but he held it in check. "Certainly," he said. *"Of course."* He got to his feet and extended his hand. "Like I tell people, that's one of the things I like about you, Logan. Not an impetuous bone in your body."

Logan and his associates had been aware from the start of a great irony: that before their protocol could go before the Review Board, they would have to get the man who'd be most unhappy about such a project to sign off on it. Raymond Larsen.

Quite simply, as chief of the Department of Medicine, Larsen ran the system into which any new protocol had to be made to fit. He assigned beds and clinical time, determined the availability of the Outpatient Clinic, and, when scut work needed getting done, controlled access to first-year associates.

Yet what might have appeared to outsiders a major potential obstacle, Logan recognized as merely an inconvenience. In his view, there was no chance Larsen would hold up the project: no responsible research scientist can afford to put himself in the public position of trying to block a reasonable idea. Too, vitally, Compound J had the backing of Seth Shein; and, Shein enjoyed the support of Kenneth Markell, the powerful head of the ACF.

If nothing else, Larsen understood the realities of institutional politics.

Which is hardly to suggest that Logan was comfortable putting the senior man in such a position—or that he imagined for a second that Larsen would take it with good grace. Sometime before, Shein had offered what seemed like the definitive take on the man: "You know why Larsen has to resort to mugging people? Because he doesn't have the talent to make it on his own."

For the chief of the Department of Medicine, the Compound J

protocol would represent a double humiliation; proof positive not merely that this first-year associate, this *nothing*, had rejected his overtures, but that he'd gone with his nemesis Shein instead.

Clearly, Logan would have to make at least some attempt at damage control. Walking across the campus toward Larsen's office in the Administration building, clutching the twelve-by-fourteen manila envelope bearing the final draft of the protocol, Logan again rehearsed how he would lay it before the older man: that he'd been working on this idea for quite a while now; that along the way, Shein had become interested in the project; but that he very much hoped he—Larsen—would now also offer a critique of the proposal.

He was pleased to find that the senior man was not in.

"May I leave this with you?" he asked Elaine, Larsen's secretary.

She looked at him with sudden curiosity. "What is it?"

During his long sessions in the outer office, studying protocols from years past, they'd developed a relationship that sometimes actually bordered on cordiality. He decided to tell her the truth. "Actually, it's a new protocol."

"By *you?*" She gave him a look that registered either bemusement or contempt. Logan couldn't tell which. "*Really . . . ?*"

"Me and a couple of others." He paused, smiling. "I was going to bring you some flowers so you'd be favorably disposed to our cause. But I thought it'd be a little obvious."

"You should've."

"When do you think Dr. Larsen might be in?"

"Why, are you planning to bring him flowers?"

Logan knew his smile was growing pinched. "I just wanted to talk to him, tell him a little bit about it in my own words. . . ."

"I'm sure," she said dismissively, "that he'll enjoy that." She pointedly laid the envelope to the side and went back to work.

When Logan returned toward the end of the day, Larsen was back —and when he saw his face, he knew he'd read the proposal.

But the man was a model of control.

"Dr. Logan," he said with a crisp nod, emerging from his office.

"Dr. Larsen," he returned. There was a momentary silence: wasn't the reason for his being here obvious? "Sir, I was hoping you might have a few minutes to talk."

Larsen glanced at his watch. "I'm afraid that's quite impossible, I'm due at the lab in five minutes."

"I see."

The senior man shuffled through some papers on his secretary's desk, then suddenly looked up. "We're doing some very interesting work on the development of the malignant phenotype. Some very exciting work."

Logan was speechless. Never before—not once—had he heard Larsen talk of his research; or, for that matter, express enthusiasm about *anything*. "That's wonderful, sir," he offered finally.

"Yes, well . . . if you'll excuse me."

Logan followed him out into the corridor. "Dr. Larsen . . ."

Larsen, quickening his pace, made no reply.

"Sir, is there another time I might see you?"

"I'm very busy just now, young man."

"I just wanted a couple of words about—"

Abruptly, Larsen stopped and faced him. *"What?"*

The unmistakable note of anger made Logan flinch. But there was no turning back now.

"I was wondering if you've had a chance to read what I left for you earlier."

"Yes, I looked through it. What exactly would you like me to say?"

Logan had tried to persuade himself this would not sound unctuous. "Actually, sir, I'd appreciate any comments as to how it might be improved."

"My *comments?*" Larsen smiled, a sudden maliciousness in his eyes. "Very nice job, Logan. My compliments to you and your little friends. And Dr. Shein, of course."

"Well . . . would you have any specific recommendations?"

He stood there a long moment, staring at him coolly. "I'm late, Logan." And, turning on his heel, he strode away.

By the next morning, word of the proposed protocol was already making its way through the ACF, a piece of gossip juicier than any love affair. *Who WERE these three? How'd they gotten so tight with Shein? Could this thing actually have a shot at success?*

At least to his face, most of the peers Logan ran into in the hospital that day were supportive, managing to mask whatever envy they felt by good cheer. "Is this as good for *all* us little guys as it sounds?" asked one fellow first-year associate. "Or should I forget about that and get right down to hating you?"

But the reaction Logan was most worried about was Stillman's. It was not long in coming. Late in the afternoon, as he was about to call it a day, he saw the senior man heading his way.

"So," said Stillman sharply, before Logan could say a word, "I guess I've got your answer to my invitation."

"Dr. Stillman—"

"Shut your mouth, you little shit! I have no interest in your explanation!"

Logan nodded and stared at the floor.

"Just know that I can make your life hell, Logan. You stuck a fucking pickax in my back, and now you'd damn well better watch yours!"

"Well," sighed Reston that evening, "it could've been a lot worse."

"How?"

"He could have told you what he *really* thinks."

Logan returned Reston's smile. He knew his friend was as shaken as he was. "Thanks. That's reassuring."

"Look, Logan"—Sabrina's tone was less consoling than practical—"what does it matter? We knew Stillman would not be so happy, right? Larsen also. And maybe others. But what can they do to us?"

Logan shrugged. "I guess not much—once we get the proposal through."

"Exactly. This is my meaning."

"I'm just worried they'll try to hurt the proposal with the committee. They've got almost six weeks to try and sabotage us."

"Remember what you say to me before, that maybe I am a little paranoid? Now it is my turn to say the same to you." She looked from one to the other. "Our protocol is strong. The Institutional Review Board will see so. After that"—she gave a distinctly Italian gesture of acceptance; eyes heavenward, palms moving in the same direction—"it is not in your hands or my hands."

"She's right," concurred Reston eagerly. He looked at Sabrina. "You're absolutely right."

"Yes," she allowed, barely acknowledging him. "I am right."

"Well," said Logan, "nothing we can do about it now anyway—except try and watch our step. Who knows what kinds of crap they could pull."

In fact, the petty annoyances began almost immediately. Suddenly various functionaries around the hospital and labs—a head nurse, the pharmacist in the Outpatient Clinic—were cooler than before, and slower to cooperate with routine requests for administrative assistance. Reston one day found that for no apparent reason his dial-out number—the code he needed to make long-distance calls—had been changed, and a new one was not readily available. Soon afterward he was reprimanded by a second-year associate for, of all things, taking a drink of water from a pitcher in a patient's room; every patient's water intake was closely monitored, he was sharply reminded—as though a few sips could make a meaningful statistical difference.

As if to top this, a week later Sabrina was called into Peter Kratsas's office and ordered to desist from giving her patients occasional pieces of chocolate.

"He tells me these diets must be strict," she reported late that evening. "He tells me this is a research institution, only research materials can be allowed. Even food! And, even while he tells me this, he is smiling, like it is a big joke!"

"That's exactly what it is," concurred Logan. "Patients' families bring them stuff to eat all the time."

Drawing her closer, he could feel the tenseness in her shoulders. They were a matched set; he'd left work with a killer headache of his own. "What'd you say to him?"

"What can one say? He is the boss, no?"

More than any other, this episode seemed to sum up the character of their foes. The reprimand had been intended to wound her on the deepest possible level; it was her talent as a nurturer they'd attacked, one of her real gifts as a physician. "Ignore 'em," said Logan, wishing he'd remembered to pick up some aspirin on the way home, "what else can we do? It's only temporary. Just a couple more weeks till we go before the Review Board."

For, of course, neither for a moment lost sight of the key fact: things were right on track. If their adversaries had real power to get at them, they'd never have had to resort to such pettiness.

"That's very easy for you to say, Logan," she said, with a sudden smile. "Me, I have four pounds of Perugina chocolates in the closet. Soon I will have the mice and roaches."

"Easy? Who had his parking spot given to a visiting fellow from Estonia? Who has to walk half a mile every day from general parking?" He paused, his head throbbing, but managed to smile back. "I haven't even told you the latest. Guess who just discovered he now needs clearance to get a Tylenol from the hospital pharmacy?"

Ten days later—a Sunday, five days before the long-awaited Review Board session—they were awakened by the jangling of the telephone.

It was Reston. "Do you have the *Post* delivered?"

"Yeah," replied Logan.

"Go get it. Page six of the second news section. Call me back."

On the face of it, the story, headlined "Cancer Funding at Risk," was just another piece bemoaning the effects of the budget crunch on high-level medical research. But to the trained eye it was immediately recognizable for what it was: a Stillman plant. Stillman himself was prominently featured, identified as "one of the world's leading experts in breast cancer"—and, more to the point, as "the man behind what is said to be a new drug with 'breakthrough potential.' " If, that is, it could get adequate funding. The problem was that other drugs, including "some said to have virtually no chance of practical application," were diverting monies from Stillman's miracle cure.

"I'm concerned with saving the lives of real women," Stillman told the pliant reporter. "Too often these days government invests in fantasy. And then we wonder why we don't get results."

He called his friend back. "I don't think we have anything to worry about. The bastard's just blowing off steam."

"Really?" asked Reston, desperate to be reassured but not quite trusting what he heard. "You think so?"

"Read it again, John. Carefully."

For what Logan had immediately focused on was that the clear target of the attack—Compound J—was never cited by name; nor was it even suggested that any of the drugs eliciting Stillman's displeasure might be linked to the ACF.

In fact, what seemed to Logan most clear was that Stillman's hands were tied: he simply could not risk shattering the carefully nurtured illusion that the ACF was above petty politics, a bastion of inspiration and hope staffed by men and women intent only upon doing God's work. Ultimately, it was this that kept the Foundation so well funded— and all of them in business.

A s the Compound J team waited outside the Administration Building's third-floor conference room, Logan's confidence soared. Exchanging greetings as the Board members filed in, the junior associates felt themselves to be among peers.

He was aware he even *looked* good. At Sabrina's direction, both he and Reston had bought new suits for the occasion, conservative and far from the least expensive on the rack; almost as classy as the charcoal-gray Italian pinstripe suit she wore.

Logan, having been chosen to represent the team, had a twofold task: to summarize for the Board members the key points in the document they'd all already read, while conveying that they had what it took to see the project through.

Of the seven, Logan was already on a first-name basis with four: Dr. Lauren Rostoker, representing Surgical Oncology; Dr. Brendan Herlihy of the Department of Medicine; Dr. Myra Manello of Radiation Oncology; and, of all people, on behalf of Nursing Services, Marilyn Lennox. The remaining three had backgrounds not in traditional medicine, but in realms with which modern institutions must nonetheless concern themselves. They included a bioethicist based at Georgetown University; an Episcopal minister from nearby Annandale, Virginia; and someone from Patient Services named Marion Winston, a sort of ombudsperson for those receiving treatment at the ACF. But—yet another good omen—this last, a pleasant-looking, heavyset woman, took the time to introduce herself, shaking hands with each of them and wishing them luck.

The Board stayed behind closed doors for no more than fifteen minutes, presumably discussing the protocol in very general terms. Then the three junior associates were invited to join them.

"Well," began the Department of Medicine's Herlihy, chairing the meeting from the head of the conference table, "right off the bat, I must say a lot of solid thinking went into this idea." He paused, waiting for those pleasant words to register. "However, as you know, we are able to approve only a very small number of protocol plans. Only those that meet the strictest criteria, not just for scientific merit but ethical accountability." He nodded their way. "Now, I gather you, Dr. Logan, are speaking on behalf of the team?"

"Yessir."

Logan rose and took a seat in the empty chair at the opposite end of the table. He smiled. "Ladies and gentlemen, on behalf of my colleagues and myself, I want to thank you for your time and consideration. I'm sure I have little to tell you today that you don't already know. We are proposing a Phase Two pilot trial of the compound known as Compound J for metastatic breast cancer. In order for the trial to have appropriate statistical power, we feel we need to accrue forty patients over the next twelve months. . . ."

And he began to lead them through the case for Compound J; emphasizing, particularly to the lay people on the Board, the significance of the various reports of the drug's activity spanning decades and great distances. "I will not pretend to you that we know more about this drug than we do," he wound up, with what he hoped was just the right note of deference and candor. "But what we have already observed is compelling: clear evidence that this drug is capable of binding growth factors to their cell-surface receptors. The truly astonishing thing is that, as long as this drug has been around, it has *never* undergone a rigorous and closely monitored clinical trial for activity against this disease. That is a situation that, with your help, we now hope to rectify. Thank you."

And nodding once again to the board members, he sat down.

"What about your Informed Consent Document?"

It was Winston, the patient care rep.

"Pardon?"

"Is it your position that this document displays sensitivity to the needs of the women you would enlist for such a trial? That it serves *them* well?"

Logan hesitated. What could she be getting at? "We think the Informed Consent Document does what it is supposed to do," he offered finally. "Which is present all the most likely problematic scenarios."

"Oh, does it? Dr. Logan. As you've acknowledged yourself, this is a very toxic drug. I am not a physician, but I have it on the very best authority that you do not come close to covering all likely eventualities. For example, you never even address the possibility of cerebral hemorrhage. Or heart attack."

In fact, the woman was only confirming her ignorance—of all the possible calamitous effects of Compound J, the chances these were among them were infinitesimal. Still, Logan worried she might be scoring points with the others; following Shein's instructions to the letter, in the final draft of the proposal, they *had* passed lightly over the unsettling matter of side effects. He was suddenly aware that the room seemed to be overheated.

"Ms. Winston, I really don't think the possibilities you raise merit serious consideration."

"The point, Doctor," spoke up the bioethicist, "is that some of us feel that a less than thorough investigation has been made as to the downside of this drug. Some of us feel that rather strongly."

There was a superior note to the guy's tone that drove Logan crazy. What the hell did *he,* who'd never in his life so much as touched a patient, know about the thoroughness of their investigation? He felt like diving across the table and taking him by the throat.

"Well," he said evenly, "all I can tell you is that we've spent a great deal of time on this. Certainly, if we'd been completely exhaustive, other possible eventualities might have been listed. I acknowledge that. But it would have been pure speculation. That's the point: we need to know more about this drug."

"I see"—Winston again—"and you're planning to use these patients as human guinea pigs."

"I didn't say that. That's not fair." He stopped, collected himself. "Isn't it fair to say there's a certain degree of uncertainty in a test of any new compound?"

He looked hopefully at the medical personnel around the table: the surgeon, the radiologist, the nurse. Surely, they were with him on this.

But no one gave a word of support.

"Dr. Logan," said Winston, her voice taking on a dangerously hard edge, "we are not raising these questions in a vacuum. We must all be aware of the fact that the public's confidence in breast cancer trials has been badly shaken in recent years by doctors more concerned with their own reputations than with the well-being of patients. Frankly, in your case, we would find such questions less troubling if certain other aspects of your history had not been brought to our attention."

He tried to smile. "Ms. Winston, I really have no idea what you mean."

"Are you aware of a patient at the ACF named Rochelle Boudin?"

Logan felt his stomach rising, the beginnings of nausea. He stole a glance at Lennox, but she was looking down, making notes on a legal pad. "Yes, I've been one of the doctors who's helped care for Rochelle Boudin."

"I gather from that response that you feel your care has been adequate."

"Yes. I would say very much so. She appears to be in complete remission from her disease."

"It is fair to say that the patient does not share that assessment. I have interviewed Ms. Boudin personally." She held aloft a notebook in grim triumph. "Perhaps you'd be interested in some of what she has to say." She opened the book. "She describes you as—this is a quote—'the most insensitive doctor I've been exposed to at the ACF.' She says you are chronically indifferent to her needs. She says—again I quote—she feels 'you look for ways to take advantage' of her, and she feels you rarely if ever tell her the full truth." She closed the notebook. "I could go on."

Never in his life had Logan been faced with such a thing. By temperament, he simply was not equipped to deal with it. "I could probably say a few things about Rochelle Boudin too," he offered lamely.

"She is not the one asking for authority to conduct a protocol."

"So," he added, "could almost everyone at this place who's had to deal with her." He looked toward Lennox. "I think Nurse Lennox might confirm that."

Lennox looked up from her pad, her face going red. "Sometimes she can be difficult."

"You are aware that Ms. Boudin is a patient on one of Dr. Larsen's protocols?"

"I am aware of that, yes."

"Well, I must tell you that Dr. Larsen fully shares her view of the situation. Are you now going to tell us that Dr. Larsen is incompetent to make such a judgment?"

So that was it? Larsen! Abruptly, Logan was overwhelmed by a sense of helplessness. It was over. There was no way to fight this.

"Ms. Winston, I don't know what you expect me to say. I've done my very best with Rochelle Boudin, as I have with all my patients. I—"

"Look," he was interrupted, "this is *absurd*. We're talking about the *wrong* things here."

The voice was unmistakable, but Logan jerked around to see for himself. Shein was standing just inside the door. There was no way to know how long he'd been in the room.

"You want to talk about the Informed Consent Document?" he picked up. "Fine, blame me. I'm the one who told 'em to make it short and sweet. But, Christ, you don't throw out the goddamn baby with the bathwater!"

Shein's intrusion, as everyone in the room knew, was highly unorthodox. But they also knew—and Shein better than anyone else—that no one was about to stop him. Now he moved to the table and stood beside Logan.

"What the hell are we really here for?" he picked up. "I don't mean just in this room but at this institution. We have a major problem in this country with cancer, and an especially major one with breast cancer, okay? And don't think we're making such strides against this disease. The mortality rate is the same as it was twenty years ago. Nobody wants it that way. But the bottom line is, we still don't know what the hell is going on.

"Now, our friends here have come up with an idea that seems— that *may*—attack this thing at its roots. In my considered view, based on twenty years in the business, this is a novel and rational idea that has been thought through very carefully. And as such it represents a not irrational hope for women who otherwise have no hope."

Pausing to look around the table, he drove the point home. "So I'm asking you now to put aside the politics. Put aside the bullshit and the arguments about things that don't matter. Because we all know that no one who's terminally ill gives a damn about anything but trying to get well. Those people have only one question. They look their doctor in the eye and say, 'Should I go on this protocol?' And if the doctor believes in his or her heart it's the right thing, then that patient will go on that protocol. That's reality. It may not fit the textbook theories, but that's the way it is."

He paused. "And I'll tell you one other thing. If, God forbid, it were my wife, I'd sure as hell want her on this protocol—even if I don't know every one of the goddamned toxicities."

It took the Review Board, meeting in private, little more than a half hour to reach its decision. The Compound J team was granted a modified protocol—a smaller and more closely monitored version of the one they'd proposed.

The note on the bottle of champagne that arrived at Seth Shein's door that evening didn't even try to be clever. The words, in Logan's hand, appeared above the three signatures: *All the gratitude we can ever express will never be enough.*

According to the guidelines imposed by the Review Board, the Compound J team had to have a "hit"—a demonstrably positive result—within the first fifteen patients. That meant tumor mass had to be reduced by at least fifty percent.

It was a daunting task. Still, for days after the meeting, Logan was flying. Finally, he and the others had their opportunity—and if it came in a slightly revised package, this is what they'd bargained for all along: a shot at making the case that the drug was both active and relatively safe.

Already, they knew they were most vulnerable on the toxicity issue. If patients failed to respond to the drug, that would be taken as unfortunate, an unhappy outcome to a worthy effort. But if the drug made patients dramatically sicker, or, God forbid, started killing them, it would be a catastrophe—nearly as much for the doctors involved as for the patients. Since before Hippocrates, medical science has dictated that the life of a patient is a sacred trust. To be perceived as abusing that trust, even with the best of intentions, is to raise questions about one's very fitness for the profession.

Going in, they were determined to take every possible precaution to avoid such a disaster.

That placed even greater than normal importance on their most immediate order of business, putting together a patient roster. "It's easy," as Shein pointed out, "to kill a good drug with a bad trial." And the easiest way to screw up a trial is to stock it with patients whose chances of doing well are already compromised going in.

Unfortunately, almost every potential candidate for this protocol would likely fall into that category since, upon diagnosis, they'd have been treated by either chemotherapy or radiation; and it is a given that anyone who's already proven resistant to one therapy is likely to be resistant to others.

Thus, the best they could reasonably hope to do was locate fifteen women whose exposure to such treatments had, for whatever reason, been minimal.

The process of accruing protocol candidates was made far more cumbersome by Larsen's refusal to grant the Compound J team a private office. This meant they'd be unable to field incoming calls directly, having to rely on their beepers to stay abreast of those that held promise; and make outgoing calls from the phone bank in the communal room—half work-space, half lounge—they'd shared with other first-year fellows from the start.

But Larsen could not prevent those calls from coming. For he could not deny them access to the ACF's Community Outreach System—its link to the world of oncology beyond its borders. Like every other protocol being conducted at the ACF, a summary of the Compound J test was duly recorded in the system, available in printout to any physician calling the Foundation hotline.

The description of the protocol was followed by an appeal for likely candidates. At the urging of Reston, the wordsmith among the trio, this last they made short and sweet: *This test requires a small pool of women with metastatic breast cancer; minimum performance status of seventy percent; must have no history of bleeding disorder or heart attack. Contact: Dr. Daniel Logan, Dept. of Medicine, ACF. 1-800-555-2002.*

"It's a trick I learned writing personal ads," explained Reston, smirking. "Trust me, the more exclusive you make yourself sound, the more bites you'll get."

In fact, they expected a rush of calls—and so were concerned when the first several days produced only one inquiry. Alerted to the call via his beeper while on his rounds, Logan managed to make it down to the junior associates' room within ten minutes to return it.

He found himself talking to a physician named Gillette, in Brownsville, Texas. From the sound of his voice and his courtly manner, he seemed to be well up in years. Gillette's patient was a Mrs. Mary Brady.

"She's just a lovely lady," he explained, in a gentle drawl, "it's just a shame what's happening to her."

Never having fielded such a call before, Logan wasn't quite sure of the etiquette. How hard to push for the vital information he needed? How encouraging to sound about the protocol itself? "I'm very sorry to hear that," he said. "Can you tell me a little something about the case?"

"Well, she's forty-eight years old. Got two teenage boys that play on the football team—nice boys, not the sort that cause anyone trouble. We just want to do whatever we can to help her."

"Uh-huh."

"And this morning I just happened to dial up the ACF and I noticed this new protocol you've got going."

"Yes. I see."

"Can you tell me a little something about it?"

How, Logan wondered, had he suddenly become the interviewee? "Uh, well, it involves a drug called Compound J. We have reason to hope it will show activity against metastatic breast cancer. But I must stress this is a highly experimental treatment. We're actually just getting started."

"Well, frankly, I'm at the end of my rope down here. We've been through just about everything with this woman. At this point I don't know what to do with her."

"Can you tell me how long ago she was diagnosed?"

"Certainly . . . I've got the records right here in front of me." He paused. "Mary first found the lump fourteen years ago—that would make her thirty-four. I recall it was during her second pregnancy."

"Uh-huh."

"So we waited. But after the birth, she had a modified radical. She got an axillary lymph node dissection at the same time."

"But it recurred . . . ?"

"I'm afraid so—five years ago. Since then we've been trying to handle it with standard chemotherapeutic agents. But, as I say, things are looking pretty desperate now."

Logan had already heard more than he needed. Still, he didn't quite know how to break the bad news to the man on the other end. "I presume the tumor is estrogen-receptor negative," he pressed on, hoping the other would pick up the hint. The absence of the protein necessary to bind estrogen to cells is a devastating prognostic factor in such cases.

"Yes, I'm afraid so." Dr. Gillette paused. "We even tried giving her taxol, that stuff from Pacific yew tree bark. Her family insisted, after the newspapers made such a fuss over it and all. But it didn't do a bit of good."

"I'm sorry. That's unfortunate."

"So, Dr. Logan, what's the next step? Would you like me to send you her records?"

Logan hesitated. "Listen, Dr. Gillette, I'm afraid the truth is we're not going to be able to help her." He explained about the need for patients with a comparatively clear treatment history.

"Please, Doctor," came the reply, now almost a plea, "I'm not going to tell you how to run your business. But I'm sure there's more you can do for her up there than we can here. You have fourteen other spots, what would you have to lose? What would *she* have to lose?"

"I'm truly sorry" was all he could say. "Please understand that we must include only patients who fit the profile. To begin doing otherwise would put the entire test at risk."

The call put Logan in a funk for the rest of the day. This was one of the aspects of the process to which he'd frankly given almost no thought: the degree of ruthlessness the accrual process demanded of him. Almost as bad, he'd be regularly reminded of the fact by other doctors, decent men and women, earnest and uncomprehending, pleading on their patients' behalf.

Over the next few weeks, as the calls slowly began to pick up, Logan noted a strikingly high percentage of those doctors making referrals to the protocol turned out to be in their sixties and seventies; people whose sense of values seemed rooted in a time as alien to most at the ACF as the nineteenth century.

Because, finally, for a doctor to refer a patient to a trial such as this was not merely a leap of faith—an acknowledgment that an untested treatment was likely of more value than anything he could offer—but an act of self-denial. It meant punting away easy money—in those cases where the patient was still in the relatively early stages of the disease, potentially a very great deal of it.

As the days passed, promising candidates got no easier to come by.

Three weeks into the process, only a handful of women were being closely considered, their written records, X rays, and pathology slides having arrived for study; but not a single one had yet been accepted into the protocol.

The ice was finally broken late one Friday afternoon. Sabrina was preparing to head home when a nurse gave her word that Rachel Meigs, on duty in the Screening Clinic, needed to see her immediately. Meigs was one of their few peers who seemed sincerely interested in the success of the protocol.

Pragmatic as she was by nature, Sabrina allowed herself some hope as she made her way to the clinic.

"I think I've got a live one for you," confirmed Meigs. She nodded toward the waiting room. "I finished the exam about half an hour ago."

Sabrina looked through the glass partition. Except for a young woman, evidently very pregnant, the room was empty.

"That one?" she asked, incredulous. *What was this? Did Meigs imagine a pregnant woman could even be considered for the program? Or was she merely having a joke at her expense?*

Meigs nodded. "That one. I think you'll like her."

Entering the room, Sabrina extended her hand. "Hello, I am Dr. Como."

The woman struggled to her feet. "Hi. I'm Judy Novick."

Only now was it apparent: Aside from her bloated midsection, the woman was emaciated; instead of a robust pink, her skin was sallow.

She wasn't pregnant at all, her abdomen was full of tumor!

It took just a moment to compute. Of *course*, a week or so earlier Sabrina had studied this woman's X rays and the slides indicating a breast tumor that had metastasized to the liver. Novick was among those she and her colleagues had okayed for further investigation. It crossed Sabrina's mind as she looked at her that once, not long ago, this woman had been very pretty.

"You must be tired, no?"

In fact, the procedures the patient had already undergone this afternoon hardly qualified as rigorous: a chest X ray, an EKG, drawing a little blood, some manual probing of the tumors. But her condition was such, Sabrina knew, she felt as if she'd just done a dozen rounds with the heavyweight champion. Rocking unsteadily on her feet, she appeared scarcely able to keep her balance.

"Actually, yes, I am. *Very.*" Judy Novick smiled gratefully. "It's been a long day."

"Come," said Sabrina, leading her toward an examining room, "let's go to a more comfortable place."

The numbers in the patient's paperwork confirmed the visual evidence: the cancer was laying waste to her body at an awful rate. Yet, at least from the perspective of the protocol, there was also some good news. To date, the only treatment Novick had undergone was a single course of adjuvant therapy. She'd been referred to the program after the most active drugs available had proven useless.

And she lived in Bedford, Pennsylvania, little more than two hours from the ACF.

"Now," offered Sabrina, as the patient stretched out on an examining table, "I am sure you have some questions, no? And I have some questions for you also."

"Well . . ." Novick began, then stopped. "I really don't even know what all this involves. I'm only here because my doctor wanted me to come. And my family."

Sabrina nodded, showing nothing. According to the guidelines, candidate selections could not be made on the basis of criteria as vague or subjective as "morale" or "attitude"; yet she knew that once a patient has given up, her chances of doing well decreased markedly.

"The first thing I will tell you," replied Sabrina, "is that this is an outpatient trial. We might need you here in the hospital at the beginning, but afterward you would live at home."

"But what does it do? What kind of—" She stopped in midsentence. "I don't even know exactly what I'm asking—I was never any good at science."

"What the trial will do?" Sabrina moved closer and made eye contact. Her tone was at once straightforward and sympathetic. "I can only tell you of our hopes. This is a new treatment—it is something some of us believe in very much. But I cannot say it will be easy."

"What kind of success have you had with it so far?"

"I must tell you, this protocol is just now beginning. This is a very new idea."

"How many patients has it been tried on?"

Sabrina hesitated. "You will be the first—number one." She smiled. "This is kind of an honor, no?"

The woman looked away. "I don't know whether to be flattered or horrified."

Like Logan, Sabrina had never imagined this part of it would be so tricky. Suddenly she found herself having to sell the protocol—and to a patient she wasn't even sure she wanted. "I understand," she allowed. "I wish I could tell you for certain. . . ."

"What you're telling me instead is this is the only chance I've got."

That was something no reputable doctor would ever say to a patient, even if, as now, she believed it to be the case; playing God was not part of the job description. "You are possibly a good candidate for this treatment," she offered simply. "And this is not a thing we can say to very many."

For a long moment, Novick said nothing.

"Judy . . . ? May I call you that?"

"I was just thinking. It's not an easy decision."

"I, too, would like to ask some things."

"Okay."

"You talk of your family. You are married?"

As Sabrina well knew, a strong family—a devoted spouse, or sister, or parents—could provide crucial support in such a situation, logistical as well as emotional. It had to be anticipated that there'd be times when a protocol patient would be unable to feed herself, let alone, if it came to that, make it on her own to the ACF emergency room.

"Yes, I'm married. He's been wonderful."

"Good, this is so important."

"But I wouldn't be doing this just for him," she cut in, with sudden spirit. "I don't want you to think that."

"No. I do not think that."

I'm doing it because *I* think it's the right thing."

"Of course."

Sabrina betrayed nothing; but the excitement was building within: hadn't she just agreed to participate in the test?

"Because it really is my only shot, isn't it? I'm not one of those people who lie to themselves."

That put to rest Sabrina's last lingering apprehension. Morale wouldn't be a problem, after all.

"Still," Sabrina said evenly, "before we agree, you must think about it a little. I want you to look carefully at the Informed Consent Document. And talk with your family and with your doctor. And I must talk with my colleagues."

She nodded. "Fine. But if we're doing this, I'd like to get started." Perhaps unconsciously, she passed a hand over her distended belly. "The sooner the better."

3 October, 1927
Frankfurt

Such a glorious afternoon! Took long lunch with Emma in the park. Still cannot believe my good fortune—her family does not disapprove! Not an endorsement, but one would have been a fool to expect such a thing. Surely warmth will come later, with understanding. I am proud, but must also be realistic. A Japanese son-in-law cannot be easy for any German family to accept.

Reality is something I learn more about each day in the laboratory. Yet versions #284, 285, and (especially) 286 of compound continue to give hope. Melting point sharp, composition successfully determined by elemental analysis. When it works, nothing is more beautiful than chemistry.

Except Emma.

Must now write my family in Japan. How will they take idea of a German-Jewish daughter-in-law?

It soon became clear to the Compound J team that Judy Novick's attitude—wariness and skepticism mingled with hope—would be the norm among those drawn to the protocol. Most metastatic cancer patients tend to put up a brave front for a time. But eventually, physically debilitated and emotionally drained, they begin making peace with the apparently inevitable. Only a modest percentage, aware of the risks involved and the odds against long-term success, are ready to subject themselves to the hazards of experimental treatment.

Yet, for precisely that reason, as the roster pool began filling out—with five women having signed on the bottom line by late March, the end of the second month—Logan was already looking upon the Compound J patients with admiration and gratitude. As word of the protocol spread, the patient accrual phase began clicking along surprisingly smoothly. Some days now there were as many as a half dozen serious inquiries; sometimes producing three or four legitimate prospects at the Screening Clinic a week.

In fact, a greater concern now became the screening evaluations themselves—especially after Logan learned that Allen Atlas, while on clinic duty, had tried to disqualify a woman from the Compound J test who, in most respects, seemed an excellent candidate.

"Get out of my face," shot back Atlas, when Logan called him on it, "the woman has high blood pressure."

"Don't fuck with me, Atlas," he told him. "We both know what you're trying to do."

"Right, asshole, my job. So let me do it."

"Uh-uh. You were doing a job, all right. For Larsen and Stillman."

Atlas's face reddened, and for a moment Logan thought he might've gone too far; for all the viciousness of ACF politics, the junior associates pretended, at least, to be collegial. Such a charge, implying as it did deliberate sabotage of a protocol, was extremely serious. If brought to higher authorities, it could land one or the other of them in very hot water.

But Atlas, enraged, didn't even bother with the formality of a denial. "At least," he spat back, "those guys know what the hell they're doing."

When he calmed down, Logan was warier than ever. He and his colleagues decided that from now on, when any of their adversaries was slotted to screen a Compound J candidate, one of them would drop by the Clinic to oversee the exam. The silent, smoldering looks they had to endure were small cost for the certainty that no likely prospects would fall through the cracks.

That is why Logan happened to be in the Screening Clinic when he was alerted by the beeper on his waist to an incoming call. The woman with whom he was talking, one Sally Kober, was missing a kidney as a result of an auto accident in her teens; since she was sixty-six, this was of little consequence—but under other circumstances, it might have been used to keep her out of the program.

When the beeper sounded, Logan switched it off and smiled at the patient. "I'll get that in a few minutes."

"Don't you have to get it now? It might be an emergency."

"No emergency. Just a doctor calling about someone else who might be interested in this protocol. *You're* already here."

"And immensely good company," she observed, laughing.

Though he tried always to keep a professional distance, Logan couldn't help but be struck by this woman. A veteran of a radical mastectomy twenty years before, she seemed to be taking the appearance of the new node above the clavicle—an exceptionally ominous development—with amazing calm.

"Now, just so I know where I stand," she said, "—this thing I've got is pretty desperate, isn't it?"

"I wish the news were better," he replied evenly.

"Well, then, you seem to be in the majority."

Unconsciously, she passed a hand over her steel-gray hair. "Are you a football fan?"

He nodded, confused. "The Dallas Cowboys."

"Oh, please, you struck me as someone with common sense!" She smiled. "I love the Giants."

"You're excused—you live in New Jersey."

"I will bet you, right now, on the first game the Giants and Cowboys play next season."

"Why'd you want to do that? It wouldn't be right taking your money."

She laughed. "It's called faith. It's a convenient way of betting on myself to still be here."

"I've only known you fifteen minutes, but *that's* a bet I'll take."

She waved her hand. "Please, enough flattery. Go return that call."

"Mrs. Kober, how much do you know about this protocol? Have you read the Informed Consent Document?"

"My doctor recommended it, and you seem all right. I can't see any good reason not to do it."

"I'm afraid that's not good enough. I'm going to want you to read it over very carefully."

She thrust out her hand. "Hand it over. I'll read it while you make your call."

As he dialed, still chuckling, he noted approvingly that the area code—804—was central and southern Virginia; little likelihood of transportation problems with this one.

"Hello," answered a male voice.

Logan was momentarily taken aback. At a hospital or clinic, he generally got a receptionist. "Yes. I hope I have the right number. This is Dr. Daniel Logan at the American Cancer Foundation—I was given this number but no name."

"Yes, Dr. Logan. You've got the right number."

"Did you call? Are you a doctor?"

"Yes, I'm a doctor. But I'm afraid I don't have a patient to refer to you. My name is Ray Coopersmith."

* * *

As soon as Logan walked into the Hotel Jefferson in Richmond, he knew why Coopersmith had chosen it for their meeting. A vestige of the antebellum South, all potted plants and faded upholstery, this was as distant from the high-tech, high-pressure world of the ACF as one could get. Logan, jumpy throughout the two-hour drive south, was instantly heartened; their chances of being spotted here were roughly the same as coming up with a cure for cancer in a bathroom sink.

Though it was early on a Saturday evening, the lobby was nearly deserted. Logan was about to take a seat in one of the overstuffed chairs beyond the imposing main staircase when he happened to look up. There he was: at a table behind a wrought-iron railing on the second floor, a man was nodding at him!

"Nice place, don't you think?" said Coopersmith, when Logan reached the top of the stairs. "I thought for a second you wouldn't see me." He extended his hand. "Ray Coopersmith."

"Dan Logan. Yes, very nice."

Logan didn't know what he'd expected, but this wasn't it. Though probably no more than a few years older than himself, Coopersmith looked middle aged. Tall and rail thin, with dark hollows beneath penetrating eyes and thinning hair in need of a trim, he had the same edgy, unfocused quality Logan had noted in gamblers and junkies.

As they took their seats at the small wicker table, Logan noticed, with a rush of sympathy, that the worn suit jacket the other man wore didn't quite match the pants.

"You want a drink?"

"Sure. Thanks."

"Me too." Coopersmith motioned for a waiter.

Coopersmith ordered a gin and tonic, Logan a beer.

They stared at one another for a long moment. Logan had no idea how to proceed and Coopersmith didn't seem inclined to help.

"You come here a lot?" Logan finally spoke up, lamely.

"No."

"Do you live in Richmond?"

"No."

"Where?"

"Place called Hopewell. About twenty miles from here."

"So what are you doing with yourself these days?"

"I'm getting by," he said, with sudden, unmistakable rancor. "Don't worry about me, I'm practicing medicine."

"Where's that?"

"At a clinic. In Petersburg. Why, you gonna check me out?"

Logan chose to ignore this. "I read your protocol. It was very impressive."

The waiter brought the drinks, and they momentarily fell silent.

"You're obviously a gifted researcher," picked up Logan.

Incomprehensibly, Coopersmith snickered. "Maybe I'll read yours sometime." He tapped the side of his head and smiled. "Breast cancer. Smart. A glamour disease."

Logan didn't know whether to be amused or offended. The remark was obviously intended as a put-down, but the man making it was more worthy of pity than scorn. "That isn't why we're doing it."

"No, of *course* not. Me—genius!—I go after prostate—try to get funding for *that*."

This was the opening Logan had been looking for. "I heard it wasn't lack of funding that got you in trouble."

Spasmodically, Coopersmith's head jerked left, then right. "Who said that?"

"Steven Locke. He said you faked your data."

"Bullshit! They wouldn't give me the resources I needed. The people. The money."

"That doesn't sound—"

"What am I supposed to do? There was too much damn data, I couldn't monitor it all. But I'm a scientist! I didn't *make up* anything!"

Logan nodded. *What was the point in arguing with the guy?*

"The data was good data," he insisted. "But they said it was uninterpretable."

"Who's that?"

"Larsen. Stillman. Kratsas. That whole bunch. They're scum, they were against me from the start. What I'd give to ream out those fuckers!"

Logan stared at him. *That's* why this guy had gotten him down here? "Look, Ray, I appreciate the warning, but it's not news about these guys. They're already making all the problems for us they can."

"You don't know what you're talking about, you don't know the half of it."

"Really, I understand what you're saying. But we're not in the same position you were. There are three of us. And ours is just a mini-test—fifteen patients."

"You're such an arrogant SOB. You fit right in at that place!"

Logan was caught short by the savagery of the attack. "What's that supposed to mean?" he snapped.

"Arrogant, complacent, and dumb as shit." He shot him a malicious grin. "Bet you don't like hearing that, do you?"

Logan glanced at his watch. "Look, I've gotta be getting back."

"Before someone sees you with me?"

"Because I don't think this is doing either of us any good."

"It's done me lots of good. I found out what disgusting little ass-kissers that place is turning out these days."

Unsettling as this was, Logan found it useful too—even reassuring. Who could doubt that this guy was wildly unstable? Or that—for all his accusations and complaints—that fact had been at the very heart of his problems?

"Wait a minute," said Coopersmith with sudden contrition, "don't go yet. I don't get to talk serious science much anymore."

"Sorry, I really can't."

"C'mon, just one more beer."

Logan held up his glass, still more than half full. "No. I've got to drive back home."

"You're being careful?" The other's sudden, strangled laugh caught him by surprise. "You're such a fucking jerk, Logan!"

Well, the doctor said, in at least one sense she was already lucky. They wouldn't have to put her under complete anesthetic for the biopsy. She'd get a local and be back home by afternoon.

"Why?" she asked, relieved. "I thought it would be a lot more complicated than that."

Her questions, she recognized, standing back, always sounded weirdly dispassionate, as if this were happening to someone else. She figured it was probably her training as a reporter. But maybe it was just a defense.

Well, came the explanation, during the preliminary exam the CAT scan had picked up a slightly enlarged lymph node near the spine, directly above the area of concern. They would be able to take a tissue sample from there instead of having to go into the bone; a far more dramatic procedure that would have required the participation of an orthopedic surgeon. In any case, soft tissue is always easier to work with than bone—easier to process and more readily converted into microscope slides.

New questions came immediately to mind: Could an enlarged lymph node really be taken as a positive sign? Was the point here merely the ease of this procedure or her long-term health?

But this time she let them pass.

There were three others in the room, in addition to her private physician: an anesthesiologist, his assistant, and a nurse. All seemed pleasant enough and she had been assured they were trustworthy. The room itself was in a secluded wing of the facility; she could hear none of the usual hospital noises in the corridor outside, not even the sound of footfalls.

The first shot of Xylocaine, delivered with a small needle, was designed to anesthetize the skin. It made possible the second—a three-inch needle from hell that went directly into the muscle.

The talk in the room was about, of all things, TV. She admitted she had always been a big fan of medical shows, St. Elsewhere in particular, and wondered how accurate they thought it was. Not very, they said— except the nurse, who found the show's depiction of doctor-nurse relations right on target. Which led to a discussion of differences in the way women and men see the world. And that, in turn, led her to her son and daughter.

Anything but the matter at hand.

She had to wait five minutes—to be certain the anesthetic had kicked in—before she was helped into the CAT scanner and carefully positioned by the doctors.

She was aware that many other patients hated this enclosed cylinder, finding it claustrophobic. But she didn't. "You know, I'm actually getting to like it in here," she told them. "It's like being in the womb."

But now she had to stop talking: the procedure demanded absolute stillness.

The screen the doctors watched so intently showed everything—her internal organs, her skeletal structure. But their total focus was on the long needle, moving slowly toward the node. It took several minutes for the needle to travel the six centimeters.

"Got it," said her personal physician softly.

He pulled back on the syringe attached to the needle and sucked in a tiny bit of tissue. The sample they needed was no larger than the head of a pin.

Five minutes later she was out of the machine and in bed. They made her stay there two hours for observation and would have kept her longer, if she'd let them. "Listen," she insisted, "I got lots of better things to do."

In fact, the anesthetic had done wonders for her disposition. She was in less pain than she'd been in weeks.

The results would not be in for another twenty-four hours.

Logan liked Faith Byrne the instant he met her.

"So, Doctor," she greeted him as he walked into the examining room to conduct her exam, "who does a girl have to suck up to around here to get well?"

"You mean to get into the program?" He laughed. "I'm afraid sucking up won't do it."

"Ah. In other words, it's you."

This sixty-two-year-old widow from the Boston suburb of Brookline —slightly overweight, with lively blue eyes beneath a halo of white hair —was obviously going to keep him on his toes.

"All right, a *little* sucking up won't hurt. But, sorry, I'm still going to have to do the exam."

Still, from that moment on, Logan wanted her on the protocol. After all, where was it written that he shouldn't look forward to seeing a patient?

What he appreciated about Byrne as much as her good humor was her directness—for in Logan's experience, invariably it was patients' reluctance to say what was on their minds that caused problems.

"I want to tell you it was my own decision to come down here and see you people," she told him five minutes into their session. "My doctor wanted to give me the same old stuff. But I told him 'no dice.'"

"Why's that?" Logan asked.

"Look, I'm not an idiot, the cancer hasn't hit my *brain* yet. I've read up on my chances." She looked directly at the young doctor. "You'll find I'm a strong, independent woman, not a babe in the woods."

Logan smiled. "I wouldn't guess many people think otherwise."

"And"—she smiled back—"I've always got plenty to say."

In fact, during the initial session in the examining room, Logan learned more about Faith Byrne than he knew about some people he'd known all his life. He discovered that her husband, Ben, a salesman, had died of heart disease almost five years before; and that, though they'd had their problems—"Who doesn't?"—the marriage had been a good one. Still, it was only since his death, working as a part-time copy editor at a local weekly newspaper, that she felt she'd really come into her own. She had two daughters. One, a married schoolteacher, lived in Minneapolis. The other, a social worker, was gay and lived in New York.

"Actually, if you want to know the truth," she confided, "I prefer the woman Ellen lives with to my son-in-law. If I'm ever gonna be a grandma, I really think it'll be Ellen and Francine who make it happen, not Joyce and Ron out in Minnesota."

Fortunately, Logan was equally intrigued by the particulars of Byrne's disease. The physical manifestation of her malignancy was unusual: hundreds of tiny pink nodules cutting an angry swath across the chest wall and extending around to the back, scattered tumors having reappeared at precisely the spot where she'd had a mastectomy some fifteen years ago.

"I look at it," she observed during the exam, "and it just seems unstoppable. When I get depressed, I feel like running out and trying every kind of acne cream I can find."

Though in that sense the case was atypical, the young doctor saw this as no impediment to her inclusion in the trial. The key fact was that Byrne's malignancy had not yet invaded vital viscera. Too, she had been exposed to only minimal levels of adjuvant therapy; and that had been quite a while back, at the time of her mastectomy.

Then there was something else: Faith was an irresistible chance to stick it to Stillman. For he found in her paperwork that this patient had had the chance to go with the senior man's protocol—and rejected it.

"Why's that?" he soon felt comfortable enough to ask. For a patient seeking innovative treatment to turn down a doctor with Stillman's reputation was almost unheard of.

"*Why?* You're kidding me, right? I *met* the guy. Call me weird, but I like to feel I'm gonna get more consideration than a slab of beef."

Despite himself, Logan burst out laughing.

"I don't think you're supposed to do that, Doctor. He's a colleague."

"You're right. Sorry."

"But I guess you can't help yourself—you've met him too."

The exam was all but over. "Well," he pronounced, "I'll want to look more closely at your case. And naturally talk it over with my colleagues. But I think I can tell you I'll probably have good news for you."

She beamed. "Good. I knew this was going to work out."

Logan felt a momentary twinge of unease. *Was she expecting too much? Did she fully grasp how remote were the chances of success of such an experimental trial? Had he, in brief, been as straight with her as the other way around?*

"Faith," he gently launched into his standard litany, "it's important that you know exactly what you'd be getting into. This is an unproven drug and there's a real possibility of side effects. I want you to read the Informed Consent forms very carefully. And talk it over with your doctor. And come back to me with any questions you have."

"Of course, of course." Nodding briskly, still smiling, she rose to her feet. "Just do me a favor. Tell your colleagues not to worry, we're all going to have a wonderful relationship."

When she was formally accepted five days later, Faith became the eighth woman attached on the protocol. A half dozen other likely prospects waited to be seen. Having begun in February, by now—the first week in April—the patient accrual process could be judged a success.

The time had arrived to begin administering the drug.

By custom and simple fairness, patients in such a test receive treatment in the order in which they've signed up. That meant Judith Novick leading off.

Logan was keenly aware this was not ideal. The progress of the early patients—and especially that of the first—would be watched closely by their more senior colleagues; and of all the patients on their growing roster, Judith was in the worst shape.

But, given the range of considerations involved, he kept his misgivings to himself.

It was Reston, at a meeting one rainy Sunday morning at Logan's place, who raised the issue. "Look," he said, "this is something we've been avoiding. But I say we launch this thing with someone else."

"No!" Sabrina brought her hand down on the glass tabletop. "This is not tolerable! This is something we should not even talk of!"

"Why not?" said Reston, turning on her. "We can do whatever we please. It's our protocol—and it's also our asses. *That's* what we oughta be thinking about."

"This woman needs this treatment. She is counting on it."

"To begin with Novick is to compromise the whole program."

"John," cut in Logan, "let's not overstate things."

"Judith Novick is just too far gone," he said flatly. "She was far gone when we accepted her and she's deteriorated since. We can't become too attached to individual patients."

Sabrina stared at him murderously. "We made a contract with Judith Novick. This cannot be changed now."

"Frankly, I was never crazy about giving her a spot in the first place."

"That is another lie! She was our first, we were happy to find her!" Sabrina looked toward Logan. "Anyway, what does it matter who is sicker or less sick? Our big concern is toxicity. Compound J can be just as toxic to a person with a small tumor as a large."

She had a point. At least in the early stages, their main goal was to prove that the drug wasn't *hastening* anyone's demise. If the cancer killed a patient—particularly one as advanced as Judith Novick—that would hardly be taken as a definitive judgment against the drug.

"In fact," added Sabrina, warming to the theme, "if Judith does well, it would look even better for us, no?"

"Sabrina . . ." Reston smiled indulgently. "Look, I admire your compassion. Probably I could use more of it myself. But all I can see right now is that when Judith Novick goes, she's gonna take one of our fifteen slots with her. And you damn well know as well as I do that, because she's weak, the toxicity is likely to be heightened."

He waited for a response, but there was none. Reston almost dared believe he'd won the point. Turning to Logan, he spread wide his hands, a picture of sweet reason. "Look, Dan, why can't we just drop her back a few slots? What difference would it make? We could substitute one of those hardy old dames of yours. Kober. Or Byrne."

"John, Mrs. Kober is number five on the list. Byrne's eight."

He shrugged. "Fine, I respect your scruples. Let's go with number two, Mrs. Sutton."

Logan looked toward Sabrina, then back to Reston. "So it's up to me, right?"

Neither of them felt it necessary to reply.

"Well, then, we're going to go ahead the way we planned."

Abruptly Reston was on his feet, the wooden dining room chair in which he'd been sitting crashing onto the floor behind him. "Shit, what kind of power does she have over you, anyway?"

"What you say makes a lot of sense," Logan replied calmly. "I'm just afraid that to change now would be to draw the wrong kind of attention to ourselves. We can't afford to look insecure. Either we believe in Compound J or we don't."

But already Reston had grabbed his coat and was heading for the door. "Screw you both! Screw this whole project!"

For a long moment, Logan and Sabrina sat in silence.

"He will be back," she said finally, "the bastard."

"Why do you hate him so much?"

She looked at him intently. "He's just not my idea of a good scientist, Logan. You will see."

Two weeks later, on the morning of Judith Novick's first treatment, Reston was by her hospital bedside with the others. If he was still smarting, he was keeping it to himself.

An intense seriousness of purpose marked the occasion. This technically modest procedure was their Olympic debut, their Broadway opening; a time, if ever there was one, to look beyond petty squabbles.

The patient, slightly propped up in bed, was pale, her grossly distended midsection appearing larger than ever beneath the flimsy hospital gown. Before Compound J could be administered, she had been scanned to measure the tumor site so a comparison could be made as treatment proceeded. Novick's tumor measured an astounding ten by ten centimeters, and it was surrounded by fully ten liters of the malignant sewage known as ascites fluid.

Novick hadn't been allowed any solids since noon the previous day and she looked like she hadn't slept much the night before. "You're sure this isn't going to hurt?" she asked, looking to Sabrina.

"The procedure itself? I promise you, no." She took the patient's hand. "About the rest, we are being extremely careful. That is why we are all here."

"My husband wanted to know if he could be here while I'm getting it." She indicated with her head. "He's downstairs in the waiting area."

"Really, darlin', I think that wouldn't be the best idea," spoke up Sadie McCorvey, the Irish research nurse who'd actually be performing the procedure. "You know as well as I how men can get in the way."

"I resent that," laughed Logan.

"Be my guest, Doctor, resent it all you wish—as long as you stay off to the side."

Logan wasn't yet sure how he felt about McCorvey, allocated to the team on a part-time basis by Shein. She was new to the ACF, having worked for almost two decades in endocrinology at nearby George Washington Hospital, and he worried about whether she was up to the technical demands of this kind of work. On the other hand, her no-nonsense manner came with the kind of mordant, take-no-prisoners humor with which he himself was most comfortable; and, obviously, she was good with patients.

"Don't you worry, dear," she added now, leaning over the bed toward Novick, "it'll be over sooner than you know." In a couple of quick moves, she inserted the IV line into the patient's arm and taped it in place. "Now we'll begin the drug in just a few minutes. We'll be starting you off with just a tiny dose to make sure you're not allergic."

But the items that were wheeled into the room a moment later could not have been reassuring: an EKG machine, lights glowing; then the paddles, prejudiced to 300 watt-seconds, so as to be ready to go if her heart stopped beating; followed by the mobile crisis center known as the "crash cart," each of its drawers bearing a different drug in a hypodermic for ready administration. Isoproterenol for hypotension. Atropine to stimulate the heart rate. Epinephrine, to increase its contractility.

Novick was so focused on these that she failed even to notice that McCorvey had removed the clamp on the IV sleeve. The Compound J team watched in silence, their gazes moving from the small overhead bottle bearing the clear liquid to the patient's face, and then back again.

If she was to have a negative reaction, it would come within the first five minutes.

They waited eight.

"Well," spoke up Judith Novick finally, "when are you going to give it to me?"

Sabrina laughed and pointed toward the bottle, the liquid flowing from it visible through the clear tubing. "You see. No problems.

"I think perhaps her husband can come in now, no?" said Sabrina.

McCorvey shrugged. "Fine by me."

"Let's continue the slow drip for another ten minutes, just to be sure," instructed Logan. "Then we can speed up the dose."

If it hadn't been so unprofessional, he might've grabbed Sabrina and kissed her full on the lips. Instead, he turned from one to the other, grinning. "Let's hear it for anticlimaxes, right?"

A dozen times that day, as he went about his daily routine, the thought seized Logan's consciousness: *We're really doing this thing! Soon, one way or another, we'll know!*

He made three visits to Novick's room during the next six hours. Sabrina made four. Even Reston stopped by a couple of times. Always she was resting comfortably, watching TV or reading; and by the end of the day, the doctors' repeated appearances seemed to baffle her as much as they pleased her.

"Are you looking for something?" she asked Logan finally as he hovered above her with a stethoscope. "Is something wrong?"

"Not at all," he exclaimed, feeling just slightly foolish. "Just making sure you're okay."

In fact, they were all hoping to find the same thing: evidence of a miracle. Generally, under the best of circumstances, a drug may take several weeks to show its effects. But once in a very great while, the impact on the tumor will be almost immediate.

Logan was back the next morning, and again late that afternoon—though, like the others, he made a point of being less intrusive. By staggering their visits, the three of them were still able to guarantee she was seen every couple of hours.

By the third day, she was ready to go home, and there was no plausible reason to keep her.

"Fine," agreed Logan, "tell your husband he can pick you up tomorrow morning."

"Great. I'm ready."

Gingerly, he felt the tumor. By now, he knew it intimately—not only its size, but its *feel*, its distinctive contours. "As long as you're back here a week from Tuesday for your next treatment."

"Of course."

Could the tumor really be slightly softer than before? No, that had to be his imagination; he knew from experience that he could be as suggestible as anyone else.

"So everything's status quo? No pain?"

"Same as this morning. Just fine."

"Good, that's what we like to hear—"

Abruptly, there came a knock at the door.

"What is it?"

"I'm sorry, Doctor," said a nurse-trainee, opening the door a crack. "Mrs. Byrne is on the phone and she says it's very important."

"Okay, we're almost done here anyhow." He smiled at Judy Novick. "Just keep on keeping on. We'll see you on Tuesday."

A moment later, abruptly switching gears, he picked up the phone at the reception desk. "Faith?" he said, with concern. "This is Dr. Logan. Is something the matter?"

"With me, nothing. Except the cancer. What I want to know is what's wrong with you."

"I don't understand." There was a hardness to the voice that had nothing to do with the woman he'd seen here just a couple of weeks before.

"You told me I have to wait a month and a half to get my treatment."

"Yes."

"So how come someone else has already gotten hers? What do you do, play favorites?"

"Who told you that?" For precisely this reason, the ACF made a policy of not keeping protocol patients abreast of the status of others in their tests. This wasn't a competition; in the final analysis, the order rarely had any bearing on patient performance.

"Never mind who told me. That isn't the point."

"Faith, listen to me, we've got a schedule we must abide by. The drug is administered according to when patients joined the protocol."

"I don't give a damn about that," she shot back. "I've got cancer! I've got to look out for me."

"Faith," he said, with exaggerated calm, "we'll have to discuss this later. I'm very busy right now."

"When?"

"*Later.*"

As he headed for home a few minutes later, he felt confused, exasperated, *betrayed*. Unavoidably, the most disheartening question any doctor must face loomed increasingly large: how in the world could he have been so wrong? Could he no longer trust his own instincts?

It wasn't hard to pinpoint Faith's most likely source: Marion Winston, the patient care representative. As Logan well knew, Winston made it policy to contact every patient accepted onto the protocol. Her purpose was to let them know that, as she put it, she "was available to mediate in the event of misunderstandings with medical personnel."

When Logan stopped by her office the next morning intending to raise the subject of Faith Byrne's call, Winston stopped him short with her opening words.

"I heard from Mrs. Byrne at home last night. Apparently, you are not being very responsive to her needs."

Logan was determined to keep this civil; he knew more than enough about this woman's readiness to cause trouble.

"Listen, Ms. Winston, our job is to be fair to all the women on the protocol."

"Good. Well, just so we're clear: I see it as *my* job to empower these women. So that they can also help decide what's"—she made quote marks with her fingers—" 'fair.' "

"I see. So you suggested that Faith call?"

"She was troubled, I let her know it was up to her to let you know that."

"I see," he repeated, with practiced calm. *How the hell to neutralize this nut case?* "Look, Ms. Winston . . ." he began again, "there's no sense pretending. We both know you weren't crazy about this protocol at the start. That's all right. I'm just hoping we can work together now to minimize friction."

"Of course." She eyed him coolly. "That's always my intention. This has certainly never been personal."

He nodded; she said it with such certainty, he thought it was likely she actually believed it. "Well, I just want you to be aware that it can create problems for us when certain kinds of information are passed on to patients."

"Dr. Logan, I know many doctors prefer to keep patients in the dark. It gives them more power. For *your* information, it's my policy to let in the light wherever and whenever possible,"

"I'm just saying that Mrs. Byrne was made needlessly upset. There's nothing we can do to help her."

"Why not?"

"Because there's a logical system to how these things are done. Anyway, it doesn't even *matter* what order she goes in."

"Perhaps not to you."

"To *her.* To her chances."

"Well, then, if it doesn't matter, why don't you just move her up? We both know there are others on this protocol who truly don't care what order they go in."

"Because that wouldn't be right."

"Why? If it doesn't matter." Her eyes narrowed. "You see what I'm saying? Your own position doesn't make sense. Just switch her with someone else and be done with it."

Logan's head was starting to spin. He sighed. "I don't know. Maybe. I'll have to give it some thought."

"Sorry, I'm afraid I have another appointment," she said, abruptly rising to her feet. She offered what under other circumstances would pass as a friendly smile. "But I'm sure you know how much Faith and I would appreciate that."

When Judith Novick showed up at the hospital the following Tuesday for her second treatment, the change was unmistakable. Though she was still unsteady on her feet—and, to the naked eye, her tumor appeared undiminished in size—her color was dramatically better, and so was her disposition.

"I've been feeling great," she confirmed. "Less tired than anytime I can remember."

Standing beside her in the examining room, Logan and Sabrina exchanged a quick glance, sharing their pleasure.

But Sabrina deliberately understated it to the patient. "This is good," she said evenly, "a very good sign."

For, of course, both doctors knew that such a reaction—if, indeed, what they were seeing was even a reaction to the drug—could prove fleeting.

Still, checking the tumor, there was no question it was slightly more yielding to the touch: more like a tennis ball than a hardball. And when they measured it, they found that it had even shrunk three quarters of a centimeter—not statistically significant, but still a very encouraging development.

In any case, Novick wasn't waiting for the doctors' authorization to celebrate her sudden new vigor. "This past week has been so wonderful," she announced. "I've been seeing people again. My husband took me to the movies. The other day I even went out shopping."

"That's terrific, Judy," agreed Logan. "Just wonderful." He hesitated, not wanting to play the ogre. "Just remember: Go slow, take it easy. We're still very early in this process."

"Of course. I know that. I don't have any illusions." Suddenly she smiled and her face looked nothing short of radiant. "But, I'll tell you, I almost don't care. I never thought I'd ever feel this good again—not even for a day."

_____

15 May 1929
Frankfurt

Improved results on latest series of experiments. Version #337 showing heightened activity in laboratory rats. Some tumors shrinking twenty-five percent! Could this be a breakthrough? Must guard against overoptimism. Sixteen years on the project already, and toxicity as great a problem as ever.

Was definitely the right decision to come to Christian Thomas Company. Herr Thomas follows work closely. Very interested in progress, yet also recognizes synthetic biological problems.

Emma an even greater source of comfort. She keeps me balanced, listens to my frustrations and complaints. Wish I could be as good a husband to her. If it ever comes, my success will be her success.

As she lay in bed, waiting for her treatment to begin, Faith Byrne appeared as calm as could be expected. "That's our girl," encouraged Nurse McCorvey, inserting the IV line into her arm. "You're not gonna feel a blessed thing."

Since Faith had assumed the fourth slot—it had previously belonged to a certain Hannah Dietz, who welcomed the delay—they'd been through the procedure three times by now; it was starting to feel routine. In fact, standing off to the side, Logan was the lone representative of the Compound J team on hand. They'd decided that "witness duty" would revolve among the three of them.

"That's right," echoed Marion Winston, "easy as pie." The patient care representative placed her hand lightly on the patient's arm. "I wish I were as comfortable as you look in that bed."

"Hey," said Faith, through a tight smile, "feel free to change places. And I mean *anytime*."

Though they'd had their first face-to-face meeting only the evening before, on Faith's arrival at the ACF, the rapport between Winston and Byrne was obvious. Watching, even Logan had to agree that Winston had a special touch with patients in need of reassurance.

"How long will it be?" Faith strained to get a look at the overhead bottle bearing the Compound J.

"Just a minute now," said McCorvey. "You want me to tell you when it starts?"

"Of *course*. It's my life."

"Then just hold on, dear. I'll let you know." McCorvey waited a few seconds and gingerly removed the clamp. "Now."

The patient exhaled deeply and, staring up at the ceiling, lay perfectly still, working at trying to relax. Logan snuck a peek at his watch. Nine thirty-eight. At, say, ten of, he'd be able to think about leaving.

Two minutes went by. Then a third.

"Something's not right," spoke up Faith suddenly. "I feel strange."

Instantly, Logan was at her bedside.

"What, Faith? What is it?"

"Stop the medicine! Please!"

"What is it? Tell me." Logan looked over at McCorvey. Her face reflected his own intense concern.

"I feel chilled all over! I'm getting nauseous!"

Reflexively, Logan weighed the data before him, focusing on the worst-case scenario: She could be undergoing anaphylaxis—a severe toxic reaction, similar to that produced by a beesting in someone with an extreme allergic sensitivity.

But, no, he discounted the possibility almost at once. The symptoms of anaphylactic shock hit immediately after administration; within seconds, the patient will start wheezing, then usually black out. Faith's breathing was not labored, and her color was good.

"What's her pressure?" he asked McCorvey.

She checked the monitor. "One twenty-five over eighty."

"Heart rate?"

"Seventy-five." Also normal.

The problem, he could only conclude, was nothing more than acute anxiety.

Logan nodded toward the crash cart. "Prepare a milligram intravenous of lorazepam." A Valium analog.

He leaned in close to the patient and spoke soothingly. "Faith, I'm almost certain it's nothing serious. We're going to give you something to help you relax."

"No! What I need is epinephrine!"

Under other circumstances, Logan might have laughed: talk about a little knowledge leading to big-time lunacy! Epinephrine is more commonly known as adrenaline; by speeding up the heart rate by forcing the muscle to contract spasmodically, it can to lead to angina, especially in someone of Faith Byrne's age.

"I really don't think that's necessary," he reassured. "Let's just see how you do over the next few minutes."

"Doctor, the woman is telling you she's in crisis!"

Startled, Logan looked across the bed at Winston. "Please, Ms. Winston, the situation is in hand."

"I'm not sure it is! I would like you to call for backup!"

Goddamn it! What was it with this bitch?

"I assure you that isn't necessary," he replied calmly. "What Mrs. Byrne is describing is not life threatening."

If he could just hold things together another a couple of minutes, he knew, matters would resolve themselves. It would become *obvious* there'd been no reason for concern.

"Listen," he added, "I just think we have to be careful not to overreact. Nurse McCorvey . . . ?"

He saw McCorvey glance Winston's way before responding. "Yes, Doctor?"

Christ, was she going to be a problem too?

"You've been through a number of these treatments. Perhaps if you would reassure—"

"Never mind your reassurance, Doctor! What Faith needs is help!"

"Ms. Winston," he said evenly, buying time, "we've been through this procedure several times already. There've been no adverse effects."

Momentarily, this seemed to defuse the crisis. But with a sudden wail, Faith Byrne again commanded all eyes. "Oh, God, *please*, don't let them kill me."

Winston took her hand. "I promise you, that's NOT going to happen. Dr. Logan, I must insist that—"

"No, it's not," he cut her off. By now he had to make a physical effort to maintain the surface calm he needed to do his job. "But if it'll set your mind at ease . . ."

He picked up the phone and punched in the nurses' station. "This is Dr. Logan in room three fourteen. I'd like some backup here, please, stat."

As he hung up, he glanced at his watch; then, to be sure, waited another thirty seconds. "I just want to tell you, we're already past the danger point. And, as you see, Mrs. Byrne has had no adverse reaction to this drug."

He half expected an apology. Instead, Winston only squeezed Faith's hand a little tighter. "See that. Nothing to worry about."

Now that all concern had passed, Logan eyed the patient care rep with cool disdain. "Ms. Winston, you are not medical personnel. I would *really* appreciate it if you would stand back now."

"*That's* your response, Doctor, to what's just happened here? I happen to be doing my job."

"Yes? Well, you're going to have to learn that the rest of us have jobs to do also. You're going to have to learn it and respect it."

"What is this about? What is this problem?"

And there, in the doorway, stood Sabrina.

"Dr. Como," exclaimed Winston. "Thank God!"

Logan nodded Sabrina's way. "I'm afraid we've had a bit of a misunderstanding. But I think it's fair to say everything's under control now." He looked down at the patient. "Are you feeling better, Faith?"

"I don't know. I guess so."

"Nonetheless," said the patient care rep, "I believe Mrs. Byrne would feel a lot more comfortable if Dr. Como took over now."

Logan just stared at her. *Go fuck yourself, lady! You can go straight to hell!* "Is that true, Faith? Is that what you want?"

Byrne didn't hesitate. "Yes. It is."

"Well, then, that's that." *Fuck you too!* "Dr. Como," he said, with a brittle smile, "I guess it's all yours."

"Yes," she said, a portrait in studied neutrality. "Thank you, Dr. Logan."

And Logan strode from the room, leaving the woman he loved to supervise what had, in fact, from the beginning, been an entirely routine procedure.

Over the days that followed, Logan couldn't stop replaying the incident in his head. This woman had done nothing less than challenge his very credibility as a doctor. And on his own protocol!

Still, the best policy was to play it cool. He hoped against hope that word of what had happened would not get around the ACF. After a week, he'd almost begun to believe it was possible.

Then, late one afternoon, Allen Atlas sidled up beside him in the otherwise deserted junior associates' lounge. "So, I hear you've been rejected by one of your protocol patients."

Logan turned to face him. The bastard was grinning broadly.

"Say, Logan, isn't it supposed to work the other way around? I know in Dr. Stillman's protocol, it's the doctor who's in charge."

"Don't worry about me. Or our protocol." He paused; then, despite himself, the words came rushing out. "The results have been very encouraging so far."

"You're completely full of shit, Logan."

But for all his ostentatious contempt, Atlas couldn't entirely disguise his interest.

"*Very* encouraging," repeated Logan, in too deep to pull back now. "We've already had a partial response. Some tumor shrinkage."

"*Some tumor shrinkage?* Big fucking deal."

"Correct me if I'm wrong, Atlas, but you didn't used to have such a filthy mouth. What's with you, you even have to imitate the way these guys talk?"

"Talk to me when you have a serious response. Anything less than fifty percent shrinkage in a big tumor means shit, Logan, and you know it."

He did know it. "I'll take it," he said blithely. "As a start. I haven't heard anything better coming from your man Stillman's trial."

"Don't worry about Dr. Stillman, he's doing fine." A sudden grin. "He also sends you his regrets about Mrs. Byrne. He knows her, you know."

"I heard. She turned you guys down flat."

"Is that what she told you, *she* turned *us* down?"

Logan looked at him.

"Logan, you're even more gullible than I thought. The woman has a borderline personality disorder. It was in her file. Stillman took one look at it and sent her packing."

"I don't believe that."

"Have it your way."

But of *course* he did—it explained everything. Classically, a borderline sees others in the starkest of terms—good or bad, black or white; and when such an individual's expectations go unmet, no matter how wildly unrealistic they are, good can turn into bad in a nanosecond. The way Faith Byrne had transformed him from hero to villain.

No one would ever knowingly include a borderline in a drug trial. Almost by definition, she'll create havoc in a medical setting; dividing staff, playing one off against the other.

"I didn't see any report like that in her file," Logan tried again, lamely.

"Oh, no?" Atlas smiled, even more broadly. "Maybe that part of it didn't get sent along. These things happen."

If he'd expected any sympathy from Shein, coming across the senior man in the cafeteria the next afternoon quickly put that notion to rest.

"The bastards slipped a poison pill into your protocol?!" exclaimed Shein, wide eyed.

Logan nodded. "I guess you could put it that way."

"How much damage you think she can do?"

He'd been thinking about that himself. "To the protocol data? None—she's still a viable candidate. My only concern is that—"

Suddenly Shein burst out laughing. "That's not bad, I gotta try it myself sometime!" He took off his glasses and wiped his eyes with his sleeve. "God, Logan, you must feel like a fuckin' jerk!"

"There was no way I could've caught it, they didn't send the paperwork."

"You examined her, didn't you? You got eyes and ears, don't you?" He laughed again. "Ah, it's no big deal. Learn from it."

"Learn what—that people'll screw around with your work?"

"In small ways? Sure, all the time." He picked up his fork and held it, poised in midair. "Lighten up, Logan. This is a tough business, get used to it."

"Do you hear me complaining?"

"I don't have to hear the words." He jabbed a forkful of macaroni and cheese into his mouth. "In my book, this falls into the 'acceptable' category. They pushed you into a rookie's mistake—but there's no lasting damage."

Logan, insides churning, hoped he looked half as calm as Shein. *Mistake? What the hell was he talking about now?*

"You were just a little too eager to stick it to Stillman, weren't you?" noted Shein. "So maybe you let down your guard a little with Mrs. . . . what's her name?"

"Faith Byrne."

"In your mind, she became a prize catch. You wanted her so bad, you were ready to suspend good judgment." He paused, took another bite. "Stillman can't read people like I can, but he'll beat an amateur any day of the week."

Logan had entertained the vague hope that Shein would help him find a way out of this; maybe tell him a way he might have Byrne replaced on the protocol by a less troublesome patient; or, at the very least, arrange to have Marion Winston kept at a greater distance from the program. But it was clear now that none of that was going to happen.

"Well," he said blithely, turning away, "just thought you'd want to know."

"Hey, Logan, wait a sec."

The younger man turned, surprised by the new note in Shein's tone —something uncannily like sympathy. "Yes?"

"I just wanna tell you: Hang in there, you're a good man."

As he walked off, Logan, once again, didn't know whether he'd just been flattered or humiliated.

The surest solace, of course, was in the work, and fortunately there was more than enough of it to keep Logan from dwelling on very much else. The next ten days proved particularly arduous. New patients were now being eased onto the protocol at the accelerated rate of three per week, which meant that in short order fifteen women would be receiving Compound J. Already, half the protocol patients were reporting to the ACF semiweekly on an outpatient basis, arriving after lunch and remaining until early evening. Though the actual administration of the drug took less than an hour, each visit also included a thorough examination (including the taking of blood samples and X rays) and a consultation with one of the three young physicians supervising the protocol.

On top of which, Logan, Sabrina, and Reston had their obligations at the hospital.

Under the circumstances, their workdays often continued past midnight—with conversations about the protocol usually left for last. Thus it was that one Thursday night the phone rang in Logan's place just as he was turning off David Letterman: Sabrina needed to compare notes on a patient named Sharon Williams. A black schoolteacher from Baltimore, thirty-eight and married, Williams seemed a promising candidate. But there was something about the case that bothered Sabrina. Her cancer had been diagnosed following a long siege of back pain, tests having revealed a malignant lesion in the fourth lumbar vertebra.

"It is a very interesting case," noted Sabrina. "The problem is that it's in the bone—she has no lumps. This will make it hard for us to measure changes in the tumor."

"That's true," he agreed. In fact, in such a malignancy, tumors are seen only as shadows on a bone scan—and these can remain for months even if a drug is working.

"One must ask: What is the point to have a patient on the protocol if we can't see the results?"

It was a valid question, and hearing Sabrina raise it, Logan realized how much more pragmatic she'd grown in the several months they'd been at this. "You're right. Especially since we have only one place left."

She hesitated. "Still, I found her a lovely woman."

"I know," he conceded. "So did I."

"Who knows," she began arguing with herself, "maybe it is wrong to see the bone malignancy just as a problem. Why not look at it as an opportunity? This is a different form of breast malignancy, a different kind of test for the drug."

"That could be. I think—"

Abruptly, there came a beep on her end of the line—call waiting.

"Who could it be at this hour?" she wondered. "Hold a second, Logan."

A moment later she was back. "I must take this. It is Marion Winston. Something has happened to Judith Novick. I will call you back."

Logan's wait was probably less than three minutes, but it felt like a decade.

"What is it?" he demanded, snatching up the phone before the end of the first ring.

"It is terrible news. She had a bad fall."

"*How* bad?"

"A fractured skull. She is in a coma."

"Where is she?"

"At Bedford General Hospital. In Pennsylvania, where she lives."

Logan was numb. "What's Winston doing in the middle of it?"

Sabrina knew better than anyone how sensitive the topic was. "She is the patient care representative, Dan," she said gently. "Her family gave the hospital her name."

But beyond shock, concern, and empathy, both of them were already starting to think about something else: the impact on the protocol. Which was only part of why Logan found himself irked that Winston hadn't seen fit to notify him, the head of the Compound J team.

"I think I should call her husband," said Sabrina suddenly.

"At this hour?"

"Winston says she just talked to him. He is at the hospital."

"Tell him how much we're all pulling for her."

"Yes. Of course."

Thirty seconds later, Logan had Winston on the line.

He could almost see her stiffen at the sound of his voice. "Dr. Logan, it's late. I've already passed on all the pertinent information to Dr. Como."

"Please bear with me, I just have a few more questions. Can you tell me exactly what happened?"

"She fell. That's all we know."

"At home?"

"No, it was at a mall."

"A mall?"

"On some steps by the parking lot."

"Jesus," he exclaimed softly. *What the hell was WRONG with her, shopping at that hour? Her balance was off! Shit, I WARNED her to take it easy!*

"Is that all, Doctor? Think you'll be able to save your protocol?"

Logan ignored the unmistakable note of contempt. "Ms. Winston, my primary concern is her condition."

"No, I think your primary concern is keeping her on the protocol. But, obviously, that is now out of the question."

"Of course." Even if such a thing were plausible medically, it would be unthinkable to continue dosing a comatose patient. "I'll be keeping close tabs on her condition. Perhaps if she recovers soon enough—"

"I meant *permanently* out of the question."

Since the matter was almost entirely theoretical, Logan was surprised by the adamant nature of the response. "Why? She seems to have had some response to the drug already."

"Because, Doctor, some of us don't take those kinds of risks. We don't know what happened to Mrs. Novick—but it could be your drug caused her to black out." She paused, letting it sink in. "In my view, this must be regarded as a possible drug-related toxicity."

The next morning, in Shein's office, Logan didn't bother with the niceties. "Something has to be done about Marion Winston," he announced flatly. "The woman's hostility toward this protocol is pathological."

Shein stared at him evenly across his cluttered desk. "Toward the protocol or toward you?"

"Both. It doesn't matter, the result's the same. Can you believe it, she's going to try to pass this off as a toxicity problem?"

When Shein made no response, he pressed on. "That's bullshit and you know it! The odds are one in a thousand that the drug had anything to do with it. *Ten* thousand."

"Forget it, Logan," spoke up Shein. "I'm not gonna buy a piece of that problem. No way I'm gonna put restrictions on her."

"Look," pressed Logan, "all I want is enforcement of the existing regulations limiting laypersons' access to—"

"I told you, Logan, enough!" Shein's hand came crashing down, sending papers flying. "What the hell's wrong with you, whining at me like some kid starting med school? You think you're the first doctor who ever had some nasty little bureaucrat up his ass? Deal with it!"

Logan was bristling, but he tried hard not to let it show. "Don't worry. I will."

"Good. Now get out. If there's one thing I can't stand it's a whiner."

The younger man was stunned. Erratic as he was, Shein had never before addressed with him such frank contempt. He turned to leave, then stopped at the door. "I really don't know what your problem is."

"My problem? Lemme tell you something, Logan. You show me some results—then maybe you can ask me for favors."

"What are you talking about? We only started administering the drug five weeks ago! Judy Novick was—"

"Forget her, the woman's a goner! What're you gonna do, haul her corpse around to show what a great job you're doing?"

"Dr. Shein, that's not—"

"How much time you think you got? In case you haven't heard, people around this place aren't known for their patience. A lotta drugs, they would've shown activity by now. *Convincing* activity."

"We're exactly at the same stage as Stillman's protocol."

"You think you're Stillman? You think you got his options? Or his friends?"

Logan stared at him. So that was it—Shein wanted it both ways: credit if Compound J succeeded, but an escape hatch if it bombed out. He'd of course always known that, much as he relished the role of unbridled maverick, Shein was nearly as political as the rest. Yet never before had the fact been so nakedly obvious.

Shein picked up the disillusionment in the younger man's look and caught himself. "Look, Logan, it's not that I don't understand your problem. Sure, Winston's out to get you. It's a good bet every vicious little thought that crosses her brain goes straight to the bad guys."

"I'll bet," Logan concurred, although, in fact, the thought had never before occurred to him.

"But what I'm telling you—and there's no better advice I can give —is stay focused on the big picture. Get results and *no* one'll be able to fuckin' touch you!"

"I'll bear it in mind. We cure cancer and we're home free."

"Screw that self-pitying crap! You'd better pick up a lot more arrogance if you're gonna make it in this business."

"Don't worry," replied Logan. "Whatever has to be done to protect this protocol, I'll do myself."

"Oh, yeah?" Shein was suddenly interested. "Like what?"

"I've already arranged that from now on all our contacts with Winston's office will be through Dr. Como. Neither Reston nor I will be dealing at all with any patient in the program with whom that maniac has any influence."

"How many is that?"

"At least half of them."

Going in, he'd hoped this would force the senior man's hand; since, in leaving Sabrina with a far heavier workload than either of her associates, such an arrangement could disrupt the mechanics of a protocol in which Shein too—or so he'd thought—had a proprietary interest.

But Shein only smiled. "That's what really gets to you, isn't it? That she shows you up in front of that hot little number of yours."

Abruptly, Logan forgot about concealing his anger. "You know something, Dr. Shein—"

"Seth."

"—*Dr. Shein.* Sometimes you're as big an asshole as anyone around here!"

"Well, so much for all that famous gratitude of yours." He grinned. "If I were you, Logan, I'd worry about keeping me *your* asshole."

2 October 1930
Frankfurt

Version #452 of compound a terrible disappointment. A gray mass, unable to recrystallize. All modifications in length of molecule have also failed! Deeply frustrated. Fear Herr Thomas is losing patience with this work.

Could it be after all this time that synthetic approach is incorrect? Almost too horrifying to consider!

Emma supportive as ever, but my moods cannot be easy. So many detractors! So much pettiness among rivals! Where is the love of pure science?

Begin work tomorrow on version #453.

Logan chose not to share with his colleagues the specifics of his exchange with Shein. What would be the point? Wouldn't it only threatened the stability of an already fractured team? Anyway, he reassured himself, it was clear the senior man was exaggerating his qualms about Compound J for dramatic effect. Wasn't overstatement—hell, shock value—the very essence of Shein's style? The truth seemed self-evident: Shein had committed himself to the protocol publicly—and his senior colleagues would never let him forget it even if he wanted to.

But why would he want to? It was still early. The drug's promise, at least in Logan's own willful estimation, was undiminished.

Still, he knew he was suddenly reduced to dealing in hunches and feelings and odds—for they were stuck with a sponsor whose behavior was as unpredictable as that of the most volatile compound. Is this what being in the big leagues was all about? Operating in a state of chronic insecurity, never sure that even a friend won't give it to you in the back?

He knew he couldn't entirely hide his growing anxiety, at least not from Sabrina. He only hoped she would write it off to more mundane daily pressures, or to fatigue, or to a continuing reaction to the Judy Novick situation. After all, she had more than enough problems of her own. Suddenly saddled with exclusive responsibility for nearly half the protocol roster, Sabrina was overwhelmed with work.

For her part, Sabrina did not ask questions. But she sensed something was seriously wrong; and, more than that, regarded Logan's clear unwillingness—or inability—to confide in her as potentially menacing as anything their enemies could throw at them. The fact was, their relationship, both in the personal and the professional realm, had always been an act of faith. Two strong personalities blessed with the good fortune to have different yet complementary strengths, they both had to overcome parts of themselves to fully trust each other. That's what made their bond at once so precious and so fragile. And now, in her view, their private balancing act seemed at risk.

"Listen, Logan," she put it to him late one Wednesday afternoon, "perhaps we can go away for this weekend. No Compound J—just Sabrina and Dan."

"Have I told you lately I love the way you put things? But I'm on duty Sunday afternoon."

"I know. I thought to leave on Friday and come back Sunday morning. Almost two days."

"Where?"

"Do you know a place called Cooperstown? Near Albany, New York? There is a museum of baseball there."

He smiled. "Yes, Sabrina, it's called the Hall of Fame." He paused, intrigued; after an endless winter, spring had never been more welcome —and being alone with Sabrina beyond the ACF orbit was virtually a revolutionary thought. "Let's do it."

The place itself helped put Logan at ease; less a traditional tourist town than an unspoiled nineteenth-century village on a lake. The first morning, after the obligatory visit to the baseball museum, they silently strolled hand in hand down a broad, tree-lined street, gazing at the gingerbread-trim houses, soaking up atmosphere.

"I was here once before," said Logan suddenly. "I didn't remember it being so beautiful."

Sabrina turned to him, flabbergasted. "You were here before? Why didn't you tell me before now?"

"I don't know." He offered his best helpless-little-boy shrug. "Look, it was a long time ago, with my family. It wasn't much fun."

"Why?"

"My mother and my sister didn't want to be here. They didn't even go with my father and me to the museum."

She shook her head. "This is hard for me to understand. It is so interesting."

"And my father . . . You know the plaques honoring the great ballplayers? He spent half our time there quizzing me on the stats: birth dates, ERAs, career batting averages. He saw it as a chance to test me. I must've been all of eight years old."

"So it was more fun now?"

"I'd say so."

She took his hand and they walked in silence for thirty seconds. "Tell me more about your father, Logan."

He shook his head. "Sabrina, some things are hard to talk about, okay? Even to you."

"When he calls, what does he say to you?" More than once she had noted that, after taking one of his father's calls, he'd reenter the room deflated.

"I don't know. It's not the words, it's the attitude. Everything's sarcastic, everything's a put-down."

"Really?" Despite herself, she smiled. "This sounds to me like someone else."

He looked at her quizzically—then it hit him. "Seth Shein." But immediately, he started shaking his head. "No way. C'mon, don't play amateur psychiatrist."

"I am not, I am just listening to what you say."

He managed a smile. "Anyway, it's the coward's way out, blaming my problems on my father. I'll bet Stillman and Larsen do the same thing."

"No. People like this do not even let themselves think about such things. But, yes, it is certain they were not well loved when they were little. Otherwise why today would they always need others to say how great they are? It's only because there is nothing within that tells them."

"I'm sure you're right." He exhaled deeply, wondering the extent to which the observation might also apply to him.

She squeezed his hand. "But there is a big difference—you also have a good heart."

"You think so?"

"A beautiful heart. I know it well." She paused. "Maybe you get this from the same father, do you ever think of this?"

* * *

Later that afternoon, they were sitting on the terrace of the magnificent Otesaga Hotel, sipping wine and staring at a vista out of an Impressionist painting: distant sailboats, sails billowing, upon a shimmering lake. "How about *your* father?" he asked.

She looked at him, surprised; it was the first time he'd ever shown more than a perfunctory interest in her past. "My father? Him I love very much."

"Tell me about him. I know that he teaches anthropology—"

"It is also my mother's hobby," she noted.

"But what made him so special? Call it research—in case I ever have kids myself."

Sipping her wine, she thought about it a moment. "He made sure to always let me know I was a serious person," she said. "Nothing to a girl is more important from a father."

"To anyone."

She nodded. "But I think especially a girl. Without it, it is almost impossible for a girl to feel . . . *strong* in the world, to feel she can do what she wishes."

"Sabrina, there's no difference between men and women that way. Believe me, feeling insecure—or powerless—isn't exclusive to either gender."

She placed a hand lightly on his shoulder. "I understand what you say. You Americans are nice to believe the sexes are always the same—but it is also naive." She paused. "You see how this Winston talks always of power?"

"That's such a crock."

"Yes and no."

"What's that supposed to mean?"

She considered. "Let me ask you something else: Do you think there will soon be a woman president of the United States?"

"Absolutely," he replied readily, pleased she was making the point for him. "The way things are changing, probably within the next twenty years."

"Ah, but you see, if we ask the same thing of almost any woman— even the most successful—she will say no, it is a fantasy."

"That's crazy, you only have to look at the facts, these days women are—"

"No," she cut in, "that's what I am saying: it is NOT only facts—it is also how women *feel*. This cannot be changed by insisting." She paused. "And it is something that is important to know for our protocol."

He looked at her closely. "How so?"

"No man, even the best, can really know how frightful this disease is for women. It is impossible. Or how vulnerable it makes a woman feel."

"Sabrina, I do understand that."

"Yes, perhaps, in your head. But I am telling you why many patients will be less trusting with a man that with another woman."

He waited a long time before answering. "Winston—"

"I am not supporting what she does," she said quickly. "She does not understand our protocol, she does not understand *you*. But we must be honest: she does understand the fears of these patients. And these are real also."

When he made no reply, staring off into the middle distance, she thought she'd gone too far. Her intention was to be constructive—to open up lines of communication—not to be hurtful.

"Do you think a lot about Judy Novick?" he asked suddenly. In the three weeks since her accident, she'd remained comatose. Suffering a subdural hematoma and brain stem compression, she was given only the remotest chance of survival.

"Sometimes."

"I really think some of those guys are *glad* about it." He hesitated. "I keep wondering how it happened."

"That's crazy, Logan. There is no mystery, she fell." Brushing the back of her hand lightly over his cheek, aware of the extent to which they'd switched roles, Sabrina didn't try to hide her smile. "I know I told you to be paranoid. But sometimes we must remind ourselves, *caro*, cancer is our biggest enemy, not other doctors."

"I keep telling myself that."

"Truly, I do not think Stillman or Larsen even worry about our little protocol. They don't believe it has real possibilities."

"I know that." He paused. "Even Shein seems to have some pretty serious doubts."

"Shein? He has said something to you?" She looked at him closely, tensing: so that was it! "When?"

"A couple of weeks ago. He made it pretty clear he's trying to cut his losses."

"Why didn't you tell me this? This is my life also, Logan."

"I didn't want to worry you."

"Do not do that to me, Logan. Ever again."

"Look, I made a mistake. I agree with you. I'm sorry."

"Tell me now. Everything."

He did so, down to Shein's appalling remarks about Judith Novick; yet, even as he noted Sabrina's rising agitation, he felt a sudden sense of relief. No question, this was a burden he should never have tried to bear alone.

"Well, then," she said when he was finished, her voice taking on a steely edge, "it is now up to us. We will just have to show his doubts are wrong."

He nodded. "Better than that, let's force an apology out of him. That's a sight I'd pay money to see."

"It's true, Logan. So many of the people at the ACF, they lack a soul. I will not mind at all when it's time to get out of there." She looked out over the lake. "Would you like to work here? I am told there is an excellent teaching hospital right outside of this town."

"I didn't know that."

"It would be nice—no?—to just be done with all the nonsense."

He smiled. "Let's be honest, we'd probably also go stir crazy." Reflexively, he glanced at his watch. "I'll tell you the truth, I'm just about ready to head back there now."

Following his brushes with Marion Winston, Logan had made one other self-protective move. It became policy of the Compound J team that visits by protocol patients to the ACF be scheduled with a minimum of overlap, with particular care taken that those likely to have the loudest complaints have as little direct contact with the others as possible.

Generally, the arrangement functioned smoothly. But, of course, it is never feasible—nor, finally, even necessarily desirable—to isolate patients entirely. Most of the Compound J patients were independent and resourceful women, many wanted every scrap of information they could get their hands on; so the sense that things were being kept from them could only heighten their apprehension.

Inevitably, after a time, they started recognizing one another in the waiting room or the parking lot—standing out from others by dress or demeanor, by their labored breathing or chalky skin—and began talking.

They compared notes; their conclusions were mixed. No one, it seemed, was being made sick by Compound J, and obviously that was good. None of the dire possibilities of which they'd read in the Informed Consent Document—from debilitating headaches to loss of appetite—had yet occurred.

Yet none had signed up merely *not* to be made ill by the drug. Though the doctors had been at pains to explain that this was a highly experimental procedure and they shouldn't expect miracles, on some level, like patients on every such protocol, that is precisely what each was looking for: a miracle.

And the truth seemed to be that this stuff was doing *nothing at all!*

Unavoidably, there was another dimension to the concern. From the start, the relative youth of the doctors running the program had been much remarked upon by patients, usually with bemusement. But now it gave rise to an increasingly insistent question: Did they know what they were doing? Did they have the experience—the *wisdom*—to handle such awesome responsibility?

What they couldn't know was that Dan Logan and his colleagues were as troubled as they were by the drug's baffling nonperformance. Going in, they wouldn't have been at all surprised to discover unforeseen side effects; that was Compound J's clinical history. But they were certain it would demonstrate *some* kind of activity. And now that they weren't seeing any, tensions for some time held in check began to show themselves.

Early one Monday morning, busy with their respective hospital duties, Logan and Sabrina heard themselves paged over the intercom. They were to report immediately to the Outpatient Clinic.

There they found Reston, as sober as Logan had ever seen him.

"This is it," he said. "We can kiss our careers good-bye."

"What are you talking about?" demanded Logan.

"I've been doing an exam on one of the ladies. We've got a toxicity problem."

"Which patient?"

He indicated the examining room off to his right. "Hannah Dietz. I swear, I didn't know what to tell her."

"Stop worrying about yourself," snapped Sabrina. "What is her problem?" Dietz, a feisty, headstrong refugee from Hitler's Germany, was the patient who'd so willingly switched places with Faith Byrne. She was a particular favorite of Sabrina's.

"Profuse bleeding from the gums," said Reston. "Every time she brushes her teeth."

There was a momentary silence. Under other circumstances, such a complaint would merit little concern. But Logan and Sabrina realized immediately Reston had a point. "All signs point to Compound J," he added. "What else could it be?"

Sabrina led the way into the examining room. "Hello, Hannah," she said to the heavyset woman with steel-gray hair—and then spotted the man sitting in the corner. Balding, with a seedy, unkempt mustache, he appeared in his early sixties, a few years younger than the patient. "Hello, Phil."

Phil, her "companion," had accompanied her on both her previous visits to the ACF.

"Hello," he said, barely looking up.

"Dr. Como," said Hannah pleasantly, her German accent evident within two words. "Well, well, the gang is all here."

"Yes," said Logan, "Dr. Reston's told us about your problem."

"I really don't think it is *that* big a problem. Do you, Phil?"

The way he looked at her was almost worshipful. "I hope not."

"Just some bleeding when I brush." She glanced at her friend. "But Phil gets upset. The sink gets all red."

"Not you?"

"I am upset that he's upset."

"Have you noticed if you've been brusing more easily than usual?" asked Logan. The obvious thought: The drug was playing havoc with the proteins responsible for coagulation.

She shrugged. "No. I have not noticed."

"And otherwise," noted Sabrina, "you are feeling not so bad?"

Dietz smiled, showing a mouthful of caps. "Not so bad for a woman with cancer."

"Well," said Logan, "I think the first thing we have to do is take a little blood. That should give us a better idea of what's going on. And we might have to keep you a couple of days for observation."

He turned to Phil. "I'm afraid now you will have to wait outside. This shouldn't take too long."

He stood, and Logan saw his eyes had suddenly gone moist. Bending down, he took Hannah's hand like a medieval courtier, and kissed it tenderly. "I will be close by."

The blood test was back late that afternoon. It showed what they'd expected: the prothrombin time—a measure of the speed with which blood clots—had been drastically elevated. At least one of the proteins in the coagulation cascade was seriously malfunctioning.

It had to be Compound J.

When the results came in, the three of them retreated to the deserted junior associates' lounge.

"Shit!" erupted Reston. He kicked a chair violently, sending it crashing to the floor. *"What now?"*

"You are a child, Reston," said Sabrina disgustedly. "A selfish baby." Turning to Logan, she added, "We treat Mrs. Dietz, *this* is what we do now. It is a simple matter. Vitamin K should bring the prothrombin time down in a few days and with little risk."

"That's not the point!" raged Reston. "That woman down there is the *least* of our problems. You realize this is going to have to be reported to the Institutional Review Board—"

"Don't overreact," Logan cut him off. "I don't see that this is a terrible setback. If we can tune up Mrs. Dietz quickly, we're just about back to where we were."

"Hold on a *fucking second!*" Reston held up both hands. "No *way* she stays on this protocol. The next time the bleeding could be internal —and fatal."

"You know as well as I do, she doesn't have a chance otherwise."

"Not my problem! Is that clear? Not my *fucking* problem!"

Logan cast Sabrina a glance. She returned it fleetingly, then looked away. She was going to let Logan handle this.

"Listen, Reston," he said, "this woman was there for us. She didn't gripe when we needed her to give up her treatment slot."

"What the hell does that matter?" Reston was so apoplectic, he could hardly get the words out. "What are you, Logan, suicidal?"

"You can just forget it, I'm not going to cut her loose. We've already lost Judy Novick, we're down to fourteen as it is."

"I was against keeping Novick too! That was another mistake!" He shook his head violently. "What's wrong with you?"

"Just trying to be fair, John. And human."

"I will arrange for the Vitamin K treatment," said Sabrina, walking briskly from the room. "And I will give the news of what is going on. To both of them."

"Anything new on Compound BS?" sneered Reston, when Logan took a seat across from him the next afternoon in the cafeteria.

"Cut it out, John," snapped Logan, eyeing a pair of fellow junior associates within earshot.

"Don't you even want to know what it stands for?"

"I *know* what it stands for."

"Oh, but it also has another meaning." He paused. "Boffing Sabrina. 'Cause that's the only purpose this damn drug seems to serve."

"Screw you, Reston!" Logan glanced quickly at their colleagues down the table; thankfully, they seemed not to have been listening. "I've just about had it with you."

"Oh, you have a problem with that? Well, you know what—I'm getting pretty damn sick of you two ganging up on me."

"Bullshit! We're just doing what we think is best for the protocol."

"What, you honestly still think this drug's gonna work?"

"That's exactly what I think." Logan picked up his tray and stood up. This was pointless—and there was a chance it could escalate into something serious.

But Reston rose to follow him. "Oh, right." He erupted in a transparently phony grin. "I almost forgot the great life lesson you've learned from the bombshell: Keep smilin'!"

Logan started toward a deserted corner of the room. "You think that's funny?"

"I don't know. At least I get some honesty points—that's more than you can say."

"All I'm asking you is not to sabotage us. Goddamn it, John, we've got to hang tough. Now more than ever!"

"When this drug of yours goes bust, it's really not going to matter how tough we hung."

"Fine. Good. I just hope when things start looking up, it'll still be *'this drug of yours.'* " Logan closed his eyes for a moment. "In the meantime, I'm asking you as a friend: Please keep your mouth shut. Think you can do that?"

"Sure," said Reston breezily, "I can do that. But tell Sabrina—it's gonna cost you two your firstborn."

"**W**hat're you reading?"

Startled, Logan looked up at Seth Shein. He'd deliberately chosen this spot—a bench in a quiet nook behind the Institute library—to avoid being bothered; and there was no one he wanted to see less than Shein. They'd scarcely exchanged a word in the several weeks since the unpleasantness in Shein's office. "Just a letter."

"Who from?"

"Just something to do with the protocol," he evaded. "It's nothing."

"From a doc?"

"A researcher, retired. An old guy. It's nothing."

"They really come out've the woodwork, don't they?" he said pleasantly. "You should see some of the kooks I hear from after starting a trial. All these losers with something to say."

"Oh, yeah?" For the life of him, Logan couldn't figure out why Shein was being so damn friendly. *Was he ever going to figure out where he stood with this guy?*

"The old ones, they're the worst. Either they're bored and want you to amuse them with details of the work, or they have advice to give you based on hundred-year-old science. Which one's this one?"

Logan smiled. "He wants to hear about the work." *Worse, was he ever going to get past this need for Shein's approval? Sabrina was right, it was like his father all over again!*

"Lemme see it," said Shein, sitting beside him on the bench.

"It's a personal letter."

"C'mon, will you?" He held out his hand. "I'll show you mine if you'll show me yours."

Reluctantly, Logan handed it over—then, as the senior man started to read, watched for a reaction.

> My dear Dr. Logan:
> Greetings and best wishes. My name Rudolf Kistner. I live now in the city of Köln, as a pensioner. I write to you in the English that I learned years past in the Gymnasium in the time of the First War.

Shein looked up. "You didn't say he was German. Stop holding out on me, Logan."

"Holding out on you?"

"I'm *joking*, Logan. Jeez, when'd you get so damn sensitive?"

> Formerly I am an organic chemist. I write you because I learn from my readings of the protocol you conduct at the American Cancer Foundation. This is interesting to me, because many years ago I worked also with compounds of sulfonate derivatives against cancer. In those times, we had many hopes for such drugs.
> Surely, you are a busy man. But it would be a great favor if perhaps you could take a moment to tell me of your labors. I am old now, but I have much time to think and wonder. For this, one is never too old.
>
> With very sincere regards,
> Rudolf Kistner

Shein handed back the letter. "Christ, the guy's gotta be ninety years old. Straight outta the Dark Ages."

"What do you think I should write him back?" For, in fact, given the letter's place of origin, Logan's curiosity was piqued.

"Tell him to go fuck himself." Shein grinned. "Nicely—you've got the ACF's reputation to consider." He paused, turned more serious. "Sorry to hear about that woman's prothrombin time problem. You got it under control?"

Logan hesitated, acutely aware that Hannah Dietz's toxic reaction, mild as it was, could be used to slight the protocol. "Absolutely. The Vitamin K tuned her right up."

"Good, that's good."

"We're just going to have to keep a close watch on her."

"Uh-huh."

What now? Far from concerning Shein, the Dietz problem barely seemed to hold his interest.

A moment later he found out why.

"Listen, Logan," he said, turning to face him, "I gotta tell you something. You really got that sick fuck going!"

It took a couple of seconds for Logan figure it out. "Stillman?"

Shein laughed. "He's scared to death he's gonna be shown up by a bunch of punk kids!"

"Us?" asked Logan, reasonably. "Why?"

"Why?" Shein's voice dropped. "Because Stillman's finally faced the fact that *his* protocol's gonna be a total disaster, that's why. He has the evidence in hand. He knows the stuff's just gonna keep laying there and pretty soon everyone else will too." He laughed again. "Poor son of a bitch!"

Logan didn't need to ask how Shein knew—the guy had sources everywhere.

Anyway, just as meaningful to him at the moment was the revived sense of intimacy between the older man and himself.

"That's great," he said, uncertainly. "Are congratulations in order?"

Shein clapped him on the back. "Damn right they are, Logan. The bigger his failure, the bigger my success." He stood up. "Now what I need from you is not to let up. Wring some activity outta that stuff of yours and it'll be the stake through his heart!"

Sabrina, when she reached Logan that night from the hospital, was not amused by any of this. "This Shein cannot be listened to. Every minute he will change what he says."

"I know that, Sabrina," he said—though, in fact, he could not help but view the senior man's latest attitude change more hopefully. "I'm the one he keeps jerking around."

"Yes—but then you jerk me." He could hear the exhaustion in her voice. It was the end of another very long day—one even longer than most. A couple of hours earlier word had come in that Judith Novick had died.

"You I don't mind jerking," he tried to lighten things up, "as long as you jerk me back."

"Anyway, on the subject of Stillman, I have heard something today also. About Reston . . ."

"From who?"

"Rachel Meigs." Her friend who was assisting on the Stillman protocol. "She says Reston makes fun of Compound J right in front of them. Even Atlas."

Silence. What was there to say?

"He talks about the Hannah Dietz case. He makes these bleeding gums sound like, I don't know, a massive coronary."

Logan had no trouble at all imagining the scene. "He's trying to protect his own miserable ass," he said bitterly.

"I despise this guy."

"You're not gonna hear me argue, Sabrina. You were right all along."

"It isn't why I tell you this, to be right. But it is important to face. Because it is something we must to deal with."

"Unless the protocol pans out. I know this guy. Believe me, if things start going better, Reston'll be right back with the program."

She was in her private office, meeting with two associates, when she was told her doctor had been waiting some time to see her. It wasn't exactly that she'd forgotten he was due, just that she'd been so determined to carry on business as usual.

"We're going to need some privacy," she said, dismissing both women with a curt nod. "I hope this won't take too long. Why don't we plan on resuming around five?"

The younger of the women, fairly new to the job and eager to impress, quickly gathered up her things and headed for the door. But the other, Beverly, her chief of staff, lingered a moment and gave her hand a squeeze. "Good luck."

Having given up smoking nearly fifteen years ago, she rarely even craved a cigarette anymore. But suddenly, now, she did.

There was a knock at the door.

"It's open."

As soon as she saw his face, she knew the news was bad.

"So," she said, forcing a smile, "they got it done in less than twenty-four hours. Tell them I'm impressed."

"I will." He offered a small smile of his own—a doctor's smile, not nearly so sincere as a competent politician's. "Mrs. Rivers, I hope you'll forgive me, I've taken the liberty of—"

Abruptly, John entered the room. He was ashen faced—not a politician now, but an ordinary husband. My God, she thought, he knows too!

Wordlessly, he took a perch on the arm of her chair and kissed her cheek. "I love you, Elizabeth," he said.

"That bad?" she said, glaring at the doctor. *Lord help me,* she thought, *I'm not prepared for this! Why didn't I prepare?*

"I'm afraid that the biopsy shows there is a malignancy present."

There it was: the death sentence.

"Could you be a little more specific?"

But as he launched into a jumble of medical jargon, she scarcely even listened.

"So you're saying this is bone cancer?" asked John.

"No, sir. Based on what we see, the disease originated in the breast and metastasized to the bone."

"Then what are we talking about"—he hesitated—"breast surgery? I don't understand."

The doctor shook his head sympathetically, secretly surprised that a man renowned for his wide-ranging knowledge could know so little about something that in his own circle was regarded as elementary. "I'm afraid, sir, that at this point surgery on the breast would only eliminate a small portion of the disease."

"I see." *Briefly, he glanced out the window at the vast expanse of lawn.* "I take it this is certain? No chance of a mistake?"

"No, sir. I'm afraid not."

He placed a reassuring hand on her shoulder. "What is the next step? Can you give us any kind of realistic prognosis?"

"Look, we've come a long, long way. There are some very effective treatments. I recommend the first thing we do is call in Dr. Markell from the ACF."

"How dare you?" *she suddenly erupted.*

They both turned to her in surprise. She was in a rage, glaring at the doctor.

"This is MY life! What in hell do you think gives you the right to supersede my wishes?"

"Mrs. Rivers, I'm sorry, it just seemed to me that your husband had the right—"

"Well, that's not your call to make! How DARE you!"

"—that your husband had the right—"

"That's crap, you were worried about your own ass!"

"Elizabeth, please, you're upset."

"Damn right I'm upset! I've got cancer! And his only thought is how he's going to look in front of the President!"

"Mrs. Rivers, I assure you that's not true. I'm sorry, perhaps I did use poor judgment." He looked to her husband, then back at her. "I can only tell you I've known many patients with metastatic breast cancer who have done very well. That's what you must focus on now."

But her fury was spent. Suddenly, there were tears in her eyes, and a moment later she was sobbing. "I don't understand it, I've done everything I'm supposed to. Self-examinations. Mammograms."

Her husband took her in his arms. "It's not your fault, darling, it's nobody's fault. The doctor's right—what we've got to think about now is fighting it."

With his free hand, he snatched up a phone from the table and punched in three numbers. "Diane, cancel my appointments for the next couple of hours. I'll be reachable upstairs in the private quarters."

The doctor shifted uneasily. "I understand you want to be alone. You've got a lot to talk about."

"Yes, well . . ." President Rivers rose to his feet and extended his hand to his wife. Slowly, wearily, she drew herself from the chair. "We should probably talk tomorrow."

"I just want to say in the strongest possible terms that there is every reason for optimism." He nodded out the window, in the general direction of the ACF, across the river in Virginia. "They're doing remarkable things there, just remarkable."

T heir first year at the American Cancer Foundation came to an end the second week in June. That weekend, Shein held his annual party to welcome the new crop of raw rookies.

Logan elected to miss it. That was all he needed just now—to spend an entire afternoon making nice to Larsen and Stillman and their assorted underlings.

For, increasingly, he was aware that the Hannah Dietz case had left Compound J riper than ever for ridicule. True enough, in a strictly medical sense the protocol was not fundamentally compromised: Dietz's toxicity having been minimal and eminently treatable.

But—especially coming as it did within weeks of Novick's fall—there was also the *psychological* factor. Like it or not, the Compound J protocol was now regarded at the ACF as being in some trouble. Before, its opponents had merely been able to say it was a harebrained idea that amounted to nothing. Now they could say something else—and it made Logan almost physically ill to think of the pleasure they got saying it: It was a harebrained idea *that makes people even sicker*.

More than ever, Logan knew, time was working against them.

The great irony—at least if Shein could be believed—was that Stillman's own protocol was already, demonstrably, a complete bust.

Then, again, *could* Shein be believed? Certainly Stillman gave no sign that his protocol was in trouble. His public posture was that it was proceeding exactly as planned; the drug's lack of activity described as anticipated, his sole aim at this early stage being to establish nontoxicity.

As much to the point, Shein had said not another word about it. In fact, the next time they saw each other, the conversation might as well never have happened.

"Hey," the senior man greeted him, "you're looking good. Good color. Looks like you've been getting some sun."

"Thanks."

"Don't reach for compliments, Logan. Maybe if you worked a little harder you'd get some results."

Shein's return to humiliation mode could not have come at a worse time. With the rookies coming in to take over the hospital scut work, the second-year associates were now moving up to lab work—which, for both Logan and Sabrina, meant going to work directly under Seth Shein.

And, as if his opening put-down hadn't been enough, ten minutes later, facing his entire flock of second-year associates, the senior man gave an introductory talk that registered as a personal message to the Compound J team.

"Well, boy and girls," he began, "I know you and you know me, so we can save all kinds of time. The work we're gonna do here won't always be fun. And there won't be a helluva lot of glory." He glanced at Logan and Sabrina. "Sorry, it's back to real life."

That brought smirks from several others in the room. "But here's the upside," he continued. "As you all know—as some of you *especially* know—I do play favorites. So work hard to stay on my good side. And never, ever make me look bad."

The worst part was that Logan was no longer sure he could blame him. If Compound J failed to pan out, he, Sabrina, and Reston would of course take the hardest hit. Pegged as arrogant kids whose ambition had proven greater than their judgment or skill, they'd be unceremoniously hustled off the fast track, and kept off it for the forseeable future. But as their most ardent supporter, Shein would be in for his share of grief too. Surely it was his prerogative, now, to think about cutting his losses.

The pity, for Logan, was that there'd never been a time when favoritism would have been more welcome. While most other junior associates, including Sabrina, had little experience in organic chemistry beyond a few basic undergraduate courses, he not only held an advanced degree in the field but had trained under a renowned Nobelist; where the others found the routine lab work doled out by Shein instructive, he found it as mind numbing as anything they'd left behind at the hospital.

Not that the project to which Shein assigned them wasn't ambitious: determining the base sequence of the gene that encodes a protein involved in transforming healthy prostate cells to malignant ones. It was just that he found himself the scientific equivalent of a laborer on the Great Wall of China; doing grunt work on a tiny section of a project so large that its importance to the big picture was almost beyond imagination.

The second-year associates' role was simply to clone and sequence this gene so that other, more senior people would have material to work with. For Logan, day after day it was like following directions in a cookbook: *Add three lambdas of the restriction enzyme Xba to DNA; spin for fifteen minutes; cool at four degrees Celsius; add 300 microliters of chloroform and 150 microliters of phenol; spin for five minutes; remove phenol and chloroform; add 300 microliters of one molar sodium chloride and one milliliter ethanol; keep at minus twenty degrees overnight.*

Under the circumstances, he soon began regarding the routine sessions with the protocol patients as a relief; a chance, if only fleetingly, to exercise a little control. Now, even the hours perusing accumulated protocol data became less a chore than a pleasing change of pace. Studying the numbers, trying to discern the significance of modest fluctuations from week to week, was the only creative challenge he had left.

Thus it was that he and Sabrina happened to be in the chart reading room—the librarylike chamber in the hospital basement—when Logan started going over the numbers of a patient named Marjorie Rhome. By the luck of the draw, he hadn't seen Mrs. Rhome, a forty-eight-year-old dental assistant from Dover, Delaware, in over a month; on each of her last three visits, Reston had handled her.

Her file, like that of every other patient in the protocol, was now massive: over a hundred pages of printouts, nurses' notes, and comments by the examining physician in the outpatient clinic. Every medicine she had ever taken was listed here, as well as the result of every test; for blood work alone, that meant thirty-three individual results for each semiweekly visit.

For fifteen minutes, sitting in a wooden carrel, he scanned the file. Then, on the fourth to last page, listing the results of her blood work

from three weeks before, something caught his eye: the woman's creatinine level, a measure of kidney function, was at 1.7. Immediately, he
skipped ahead to the final page, listing the results of last week's visit.
The level had jumped to 1.8. Normal is 1.4.

"Sabrina!"

Sitting five feet away at the adjacent carrel, she was startled. "What
is it, Logan?"

"Look at this."

She, too, immediately grasped its significance. "My God," she said
softly.

An elevation of the blood creatinine level meant the kidneys were
not clearing it properly. Which meant that in all probability they were
not clearing far more dangerous substances; particularly potassium,
which can make the human heart flutter chaotically or even come to a
dead standstill.

"That idiot must've missed it," said Logan bitterly. As far as Logan
was concerned, the final straw on Reston—the definitive proof that he'd
turned his back on the protocol—had been his erstwhile friend's decision to do his lab work under Larsen's associate, Kratsas. "He didn't give
a damn. For him it was just busywork."

"No," countered Sabrina who, now that Logan had adopted her
own view of Reston, was prepared to be fair. "There were hundreds of
lab values. It could have been any of us."

They spent the next hour going over the files of all of the other
patients on the protocol, looking for the same syndrome. They found it
in one: Faith Byrne was also at 1.8.

"This is a problem, Dan," said Sabrina intently. "A *real* one."

"Yep," he grimly agreed.

"If the level goes to two point zero or two point one . . ."

"They'll have to leave the protocol. And if the creatinine level
continues to rise, we may be talking a worst-case scenario of chronic
renal failure, or even permanent hemodialysis." He shook his head.
"Kidney failure—not one of your better outcomes."

"And this time there are no magic solutions."

Looking at her, he was struck by how weary she looked; and, worse,
how uncharacteristically discouraged.

"Come," he said, "we have to go somewhere to talk."

* * *

The fact was, Logan had been turning the idea over in his mind for a while—since Hannah Dietz's toxicity. Only now, suddenly, it began to look less like just an intriguing possibility than like an imperative.

They retreated to a small restaurant in Alexandria. A classic Yuppie hangout down to the single flower vases on marble-topped tables, it was the sort of place that no one they knew at the ACF would ever go near.

"I really don't think that we can be surprised by this," he began deliberately. "There'll always be unexpected toxicities with new therapeutic agents."

A waitress came by and they ordered a couple of beers.

"Please, Logan," she picked up, "I *know* that. Yes or no, do you have a way to treat this creatinine problem?"

"Uh-uh." He hesitated; it sounded crazy even to him. "What I'm thinking is we should take this drug back to the lab."

"Try to *change* Compound J?"

"Not entirely. Take it apart, look at it in new ways. Try to find some way to cut down on its damn toxicity!"

She looked at him quizzically; he was talking high-level chemistry, far beyond anything in her experience. "How does one even start?"

"It's not as tough as it sounds. I'm not talking anything drastic, just a slight adjustment in the molecule. I've got some ideas."

"But what is the point?" she asked. "The drug we are using—*that* Compound J—by the terms of the protocol, it's the one we must stay with. Even if we make something better, we cannot use it."

They fell silent as the waitress placed their beers before them.

"You're right," he said when she was gone, "but I'm trying to think beyond that. Look, the fundamental idea is sound—we know that, right?"

She nodded.

"There's just something about this molecule that makes it toxic. We've *got* to redesign the molecule."

"Can you do this all by yourself?"

He gave her a look.

"Logan, you know I cannot help with this."

"*You?* Don't you dare give me the helpless bit, it won't wash. You got a pen?"

She handed him one.

"Now, then," said Logan, sketching on a cocktail napkin, "this is the Compound J we've got, right?" He produced an awkward rendering of two spheres, with three spikes protruding from each, connected by a long, thick tube. "Basically, we've got three parts that more or less fit together: two naphthalene rings, each bound to three sulfonate groups—those are the spikes; and connected to one another by an organic polymer. Think of it as a modular couch thing, with the larger section in the middle."

He looked up and she nodded. "To me it looks more like a lobster."

He laughed. "You should see me try to draw a female nude." He paused. "Anyway, to simplify things, what I'm thinking—what I think our problem is—is that the bridge between the two outer modules might be too long. If we could shorten it . . ."

For five more minutes he went on, explaining how, in scientific terms, what he proposed to try was quite elementary; how, in fact, under the right circumstances, it could be achieved in a matter of days.

"And what about lab space?" came her typically pragmatic question.

"First things first. Are you with me?"

She gave a wan smile. "Yes, of course."

"Well, we're *working* in a lab, that's not a bad start." He paused uncertainly. "I guess I'll feel Shein out tomorrow."

Logan waited till a little past noon, when most of the others had departed for lunch, to approach the senior man.

"What the hell do you wanna hang around the lab for after hours?" he demanded. "Don't I give you enough shit work around here?"

When Logan explained that his intent was to look more closely at the Compound J molecule, the senior man was a picture of consternation. "What's wrong with you, Logan? Hasn't your little life been screwed up by this thing enough?"

Logan blanched. "Well, then, what does it matter if I screw it up a little more?"

He was startled to see Shein's face erupt in a grin. "Thattaboy, I was waitin' for you to ask."

"You were?"

"No initiative—that's what makes me despair for so many of you damn kids. You think I like coddling you every step of the way?"

They got the lab to themselves the following Friday evening—by happy coincidence, the start of the three-day Independence Day weekend. Logan figured they would need at least that much time to do the necessary tinkering on the molecule.

All was in readiness, including a dozen lab rabbits bearing tumors induced by a carcinogen and waiting to be dosed with the new drug. All that remained was to create it.

Now that the moment was at hand, Logan found himself considerably less certain. The procedure he had in mind required no fewer than six chemical reactions in a preset sequence. If they were to succeed in concocting the slightly altered compound—Compound J-lite, as they'd begun referring to it—each step had to go flawlessly.

"Part one," he noted at the start, feeling oddly professorial, "basically involves creating the two modules. Each is made up of aminonaphthalenetrisulfonic acid. To do it, we combine naphthalene and—"

"This is what I hate," she interrupted, "these words . . . !"

"Relax, Sabrina, don't let that scare you. This part is nineteenth-century chemistry. The Victorians used to do it before breakfast—probably instead of making love. Trust me, it's idiot proof."

"Do not patronize me, Logan, this is not a lesson. I don't *have* to know the words. Just tell me what to pour and what to mix and what to heat."

And that, essentially, was the basis on which they proceeded. It was intense and grueling work—punctuated by long, frustrating breaks as they waited for one or another chemical reaction to reach completion.

In fact, the first evening they decided to break for dinner and a movie: the mix they'd concocted needed to heat for four and a half hours.

Returning close to 1:00 A.M., Logan noted approvingly the brown gelatinous liquid bubbling away in the heating mantle. "You want to take a break, go ahead." He indicated a small room off the lab; inside was a cot, precisely for times like these. "I'll do the next part myself."

"But you are tired also, no?"

He threw back his head in a maniacal laugh, Dr. Frankenstein at play. "Me? Nah! This is fun!"

She moved beside him and gave him a quick kiss on the lips. "Good. Thank you. I will take this nap."

He kept at it through the night. By the time this aspect of the procedure was complete it was early Saturday morning, and he was out on his feet.

"Good morning, Logan," she announced, sauntering back into the lab. "How is the work?"

She looked completely fresh. He'd had no idea she'd brought along a change of clothes.

"Terrific." He held aloft a beaker bearing yellowish liquid. "My turn. I've written down instructions for you for the next step. It's simple as pie, but you know where to find me."

Six hours later she gently jostled him awake. "I have finished," she said softly.

It took him an instant to get his bearings. *Right—Saturday afternoon, still in the lab.* "It worked out okay?"

She nodded uncertainly. "Come see."

The container of liquid she held aloft seemed to be of precisely the right hue.

He beamed. "See that? You're a natural."

"Thank you," she said, genuinely flattered.

"After we boil off the liquid and recrystallize the residue, we'll be left with a nice, high pile of white powder. That's the material that will make up the modules."

"What now?" she asked.

He stretched. "Now we start on the material that will make up that damn bridge. Here's where we get to work with thiophosgene. You know what that is?"

"Another name."

"It's the liquid version of a poison gas they used in the First World War. We're going to have to be extremely careful here."

But to his surprise, she only smiled. "You're right, Logan, this work is interesting. Why did I not know this earlier?"

The procedure that followed took most of the next two days. Basically, as Logan told it, the various elements they were fitting together were analogous to pieces in a Tinkertoy set. "We may not be able to see the pieces, but essentially the same rules apply. Certain pieces fit neatly together and others never will. You can't make an amide out of a carboxylic acid and a tertiary amine. Yet under the right conditions, a carboxylic acid and a primary amine will fit together as neatly as a key in a lock."

By the end, they were left with a second batch of white powder, identical, at least in appearance, to the first. It was seventy-five hours after they'd started. Outside, on this early Monday evening—the Fourth of July!—the sun was starting to set.

Logan, exhausted, gazed at Sabrina and allowed himself a small smile. "Just one more step. Combining them to make the Compound J-lite molecule."

"How do we do this?"

"It's the simplest part. Just mix it all together with a condensing agent. It'll only take an hour." He paused. "Any interest in celebrating?"

"Very much. Only, Logan . . ."

"Yes?"

"You need a shave. Badly."

He ran his hand over the stubble on his cheek. "That's part of what I have in mind. . . ."

Taking her hand, he led her from the lab into the dimly lit corridor.

"Where are we going?"

Logan just looked at her and smiled.

They turned a corner, passed down another corridor, then made a sharp right into a narrower, more private hallway. At its end stood an imposing door. Affixed to it on a copper plate was a single word: DIRECTOR.

"Logan," she hissed, "this is Dr. Markell's office!" But even in the dim light, he could see that her eyes were alive with excitement.

He tried the door—and was not surprised to find it locked. But directly to the right was another. It was open.

Markell's private bathroom!

Only now did Logan begin to have qualms. Over this long weekend they had spotted only one other person on the premises, and then only once—the night watchman, two evenings before.

But now Sabrina was urging him within. "Come . . ." she said, tugging his hand, ". . . darling."

She turned on the light and quickly locked the door behind them. By *Fortune* 500 standards the facility might not have been considered extraordinary—no sauna, no gold plating on the fixtures, not even a phone alongside the toilet—but it was top-of-the-line institutional issue. Everything was in marble, and there were a separate tub and shower; the latter featuring heads on three sides in addition to the one overhead. Whipping off her clothes, Sabrina turned on the shower and stepped inside. Ten seconds later, Logan was with her, arms around her, pressing her tight, totally aroused.

She brushed her lips lightly against his, the evidence of her own excitement clear in her heavily lidded eyes, the hardness of her nipples, her lower body grinding into his. But now she pulled back slightly. "Shhh," she said, her voice low. "Slowly, my love."

From the raised ledge she produced a bar of soap and began deliberately lathering his body. His chest. His sides. His penis.

"Oh, God, I needed this," he managed. "I'm feeling so *dirty*."

"Shhh." Now she was soaping his face, her long fingers massaging his beard, his temples, his hair. And, now, with a disposable razor from a cupful on the ledge, she began giving him the shave of his life.

Only when she finished did they finally let loose. For a full twenty minutes they went at each other, forgetting everything else. Where they were. How they sounded. Even the extraordinary achievement that had brought them to this moment, to these extremes of passion and love.

It was only when they were done, cradled in one another's arms, the warm water still coming from all sides, that they finally took stock. Turning off the water, Sabrina peered from the shower stall. Amazingly, there was almost no water on the floor. Laughing, they ran their hands over one another's bodies, trying to run off excess water; then settled for tamping it off with his cotton shirt.

They were still damp when they made it back to the lab, Logan carrying in his pocket the one item that might have made for incriminating evidence: a used Bic razor.

"Okay," he said, "where were we?"

She nodded at the twin beakers of white powder, side by side on the lab table. "Now they are going to mate also, I think."

"Right."

The process didn't even require an outside heat source. Logan merely mixed the two powders in a two-liter flask with a condensing agent and the reaction generated its own power. Within two minutes, the flask was so hot that he had to stick it in ice to cool it down.

Now it was only a matter of purifying the stuff, separating the various products of the reaction by means of a long glass vessel, and discarding the chaff. It took less than two hours.

They were done. Compound J-lite was a reality. On the table before them was fully one hundred grams of it.

"Well," Logan said, "if nothing else, we probably set some kind of speed record."

He picked up the phone and called down to the animal holding facility in the basement. He was not surprised when it was answered on the first ring; there was a veritable menagerie down there—monkeys, goats, sheep, even a couple of llamas, in addition to the mice, rats, rabbits, and dogs that are stocked in most such facilities—and *they* didn't know it was a national holiday.

"Good evening," said Logan, "this is Dr. Daniel Logan in Dr. Shein's lab. . . ."

"Yessir. How may I help you, sir?" It was the young Bangladeshi guy, part of a crew of four or five that ran the place.

"It doesn't sound like you've had much of a holiday."

"Yessir," he answered seriously. "Do not worry, I have a TV down here. How may I help you, Doctor?"

"My colleague Dr. Como and I will be down shortly. I believe we have twelve rabbits with induced tumors . . . ?"

"Yessir. Please, just one moment, sir. I must check the book."

Usually Logan found obsequiousness both unnerving and counterproductive. But given that the experiment at hand was rather unorthodox, especially for a couple of junior associates, he was not sorry to be dealing with someone more eager to please than to ask questions.

"Yessir," he came back an instant later, "I have found it. Twelve rabbits. Would you like me to prepare them for you, sir?"

"Yes, please. I'd appreciate that."

By the time they made it down to the basement, the animals had been moved from the holding area to an adjacent lab space for treatment. The young Bangladeshi—he introduced himself as Mr. Hassan—gestured toward it. "Please, sir, let me know if I can be of further assistance."

The rabbits, each in its own cage, were a sorry-looking bunch, grotesque versions of the adorable creatures found in pet shops every Easter. There was an ineffable sadness about them, their eyes not shiny bright but dead, like crocodile eyes. How could it be otherwise? For the fur of each was pocked with pink tumors—rough to the touch and rock hard. Untreated, none would live longer than three weeks.

Logan turned to Sabrina. "Which one first?"

She gazed dolefully at the miserable creatures. "Look at them, Logan. It always makes me so sad."

"Well, pick out a favorite. It helps to have a rooting interest."

He was sorry he'd said it. Though he'd never regarded lab animals with anything more than academic interest, she clearly did.

"That one," she said after a moment, pointing at the miserable-looking specimen in the first cage.

"Okay. Get it out."

Logan drew a syringeful of the new compound and shot it directly into the animal's peritoneum.

Quickly, now, they repeated the process eleven times; then summoned Hassan. "You can put these back now."

"Yessir." He nodded. "Tell me, do you have any special instructions for their care? Any dietary supplements you wish or the like?"

Logan looked at Sabrina and shrugged. "I don't think so."

"Only to let us know if there is anything unusual in their behavior," she noted.

"Yes. I will write it in the book."

"Listen, Mr. Hassan, just one more thing." He smiled, as if making a joke of it. "This experiment we're working on is kind of offbeat. Not too many of our colleagues know about it."

At this, the other winked knowingly. "Yessir. I understand."

"Good. I was hoping you would."

Unexpectedly, Mr. Hassan laughed. "You would be surprised, Doctor, how many of you people make such requests."

A s an additional precaution, the meeting was set not for the White House but across the street in the Old Executive Office Building. Though few in the President's circle regarded the press as particularly astute, one of the key participants—Kenneth Markell, Director of the ACF—was marginally recognizable, since his picture had appeared from time to time in the newsweeklies. So had that of the somewhat younger man at his side: the renowned breast cancer specialist, Gregory Stillman.

The three others in the small meeting room stood to greet the doctors as they entered. Stillman knew only one personally.

"Hello, Paul," he said, shaking the hand of the President's personal physician.

Dr. Paul Burke nodded crisply. "Greg. Good of you to come."

Burke introduced the other two: Charles Malcolm, special assistant to the President for domestic affairs; and Roger Downes, identified as the First Family's private counsel.

Stillman maintained a careful reserve. Clearly, these people were in no mood to banter. Markell had told him nothing in advance—not the identities of the participants, nor even where it was to be held—a sure sign of the meeting's importance. But only now was he starting to gauge *how* important.

They took their places around the table.

"Well," began Malcolm, evidently presiding, "Dr. Markell assures me you're the top man in your field. The very best in the world."

Stillman stared at him levelly. "I try."

"Dr. Stillman is being uncharacteristically modest," noted Markell quickly, and his colleague cast him a glance; it was Markell who was being uncharacteristically deferential. These guys really had him cowed.

"I take it you have not yet been made aware of the reason we've asked to see you today?" asked Malcolm.

"Of course not," reassured Markell. "The instructions were explicit on that point."

Malcolm looked at Dr. Burke, who picked up the cue. "It's about the First Lady, Greg. She's got breast cancer—with widespread metastases to bone."

Stillman nodded soberly. "I see. I'm terribly sorry." But inside the contradictory emotions were already stirring. This was unbelievable, a potential career capper, a wide-open shot at superstar status! But, on the face of it, it could also be a bitch of a case. "How widespread?"

Burke handed him a large manila envelope across the table. Wordlessly, he opened it and withdrew the contents. He held a CAT scan up to the light, then handed it to Markell.

"I've seen it," he said.

Now Stillman turned to the thick file of reports, skipping to those, in pink, bearing blood-test results. Almost immediately he spotted two negative prognostic factors: the tumor was estrogen-receptor negative; and the tumor cells were undergoing an extremely high rate of DNA synthesis and mitosis.

"How old a woman is Mrs. Rivers?" he asked. "Fifty? Fifty-one?"

"Forty-nine." Malcolm shook his head sadly. "Just a wonderful woman, extremely vital. As you know, she's been a major asset to us."

"Obviously," picked up Burke, "I—we—are hoping you will take the case."

"I don't think there's any question about that," interjected Markell. "Personal considerations aside, we are aware of our duty."

"Of course," concurred Stillman.

Involuntarily, Malcolm made a face. A top-notch player of political hardball, he had an extremely low tolerance for everyone's bullshit but his own. "Good. I don't know much about these things, but I assume you'll want to start immediately."

"Yes."

"I'll talk to Mrs. Rivers today," said Burke. "Perhaps you could set aside Friday morning?"

It was less a question than an order.

"Yes, of course."

"Obviously, this is highly privileged information. You are to discuss it with no one. That includes family members."

"I understand." Though, in fact, this extraordinary degree of secrecy struck him as extreme. The First Lady was human, after all, and human beings get sick.

"I'm sure you will appreciate the political ramifications should this information emerge prematurely," added Malcolm, as if reading his thoughts. "The President is very devoted to the First Lady—but he must also run for reelection next year. There are those, even in his own party, who'd be only too happy to use President Rivers's long absences during his wife's illness to their own advantage. There might even be suggestions in the press that a caring husband would not run at all."

Of *course* Stillman understood. No one at the entire ACF was prepared, by experience or temperament, to better understand such thinking. He smiled. "You can count on my total discretion."

"I know we can." It was Downes, the lawyer, speaking for the first time. "We've had the FBI check you out." He looked at Markell. "No names—but not all of your colleagues fared so well."

Stillman looked quickly at his boss. *So he'd considered letting Shein in on this too!* Yet almost instantly his annoyance gave way to quiet elation: the little bastard, his extracurricular antics and big mouth had finally caught up with him!

"There is no question in my mind that, if we all play our part, we can make it through this very difficult period," said Malcolm. "I don't know if you're aware of it, but there happens to be a precedent for such a situation. A very encouraging one."

"Oh, yes?" Stillman's interest was not feigned. He was actually starting to get caught up in the intrigue.

"Early in his second term, President Grover Cleveland was diagnosed with cancer of the mouth. The country was in an economic crisis and had the President's illness become public knowledge, the financial markets might've collapsed. So they handled it. They got him to New York on some pretext, and had surgery performed during Independence Day weekend on a boat in the East River. Pretended it was an outing. Then they pretty much kept him out of sight until Labor Day."

"July 1893," said Markell helpfully. "The boat was called the *Oneida*. I looked it up after you mentioned it at our first meeting."

"Of course, that was over a hundred years ago," continued Malcolm. "No radio, never mind TV. But he was the President, we've only got a First Lady to hide."

"We won't have to hide her," said Stillman. "With luck, the treatment shouldn't be too drastic. I ought to at least be able to buy you a year. That'll get you past the convention."

"Excellent. But you know what? The President would be even happier if you got her well." He looked again at Markell and his voice grew cold. "Let's not forget something else I mentioned the other day—all the resources we've pumped into the ACF over the last thirty years. Now we're going to find out if we've been getting our money's worth."

Within minutes of reentering Shein's lab the next morning, Logan crashed back to reality, the remarkable weekend light-years away. Posted on the bulletin board, his assigned task for the day was even more tedious than usual: "cell splitting"—a fancy name for garbage duty. Waiting in the tissue-culture hood, like so many filthy dishes piled up before a GI consigned to KP, were twelve flasks of over-grown cell cultures that had to be cleaned up. From sterilization to laying down new medium, it would take him, minimum, a half hour per flask.

Yet in contrast to what was in store later this morning, he almost welcomed the assignment. At noon Faith Byrne was due at the Outpatient Clinic for her weekly exam.

In the five days since he and Sabrina had come upon her creatinine problem in the reading room, they had kept it to themselves; and their preoccupation with the new compound had enabled them to effectively put off facing its implications. But this morning Byrne would have additional blood tests—and no longer could they avoid it: the results could jeopardize the future of the protocol.

"I just love watchin' you work, Logan."

He looked up from a flask into the amused eyes of Seth Shein.

"Right," he said sourly, wishing that for once he could hit the guy with a decent comeback.

"Who says I don't give my associates great job training? You could probably get work in a pet shop right now, cleaning out cages—"

"I'd take it, it probably beats this—"

"Or down in our very own animal theme park."

"Where?" asked Logan.

"Downstairs." He indicated with a nod. "Don't you have some rabbits down there? I heard you shot up a dozen of them."

"Oh, right." As always with this guy, Logan was unsure how much to volunteer.

Shein smiled. "So you really did it—reconfigured the molecular structure in one weekend?"

"Yeah, I guess we did."

He shook his head wonderingly. "Every experiment clicked? No screw-ups?"

"I don't think so. We were pretty lucky."

"Find any time to fuck her? Here in my lab?"

"Nope," he noted, grateful it was the truth. "Sorry."

"You should be." Shein paused. "Well, I'm impressed."

Then, as Shein turned away, "Listen, I was wondering if I could spring loose from here around noon. There's something I want to check up on at the Outpatient Clinic."

Shein stopped. "Oh, yes, that woman is coming in this morning, isn't she?"

Logan looked at him uncertainly. "Mrs. Byrne."

"Right, your best friend." He paused. "Some sorta problem?"

"No. Just routine." He had no idea if Shein bought it. "Dr. Como will be seeing her."

"Good. No need for you to rush over there, then. I'll expect you to finish your work here first."

It was past twelve-thirty by the time Logan made it to the Outpatient Clinic. He had just settled into a chair in the physicians' lounge when Sabrina walked in. Reading her face, he knew the news was not good.

"Logan, I have been looking for you."

"You got the results of her blood work?"

She held aloft the computer printout. "Her creatinine is at two point zero."

He closed his eyes and shook his head. "Well, there it is." He looked up. "Does she know?"

"No. She is still in the examining room. I wished to talk first with you."

"I think we've just got to be straight with her. At this point keeping her on the protocol will endanger her health." Logan rose to his feet. "I'll be glad to go in with you."

"No, Logan," said Sabrina, as he knew she would. "That could be more trouble for us all. By myself is best."

"Of course," he said, resuming his seat.

He was still sitting there fifteen minutes later when Sabrina returned, flushed. "Logan, you should come. This situation, it is impossible."

"What?" he said, though he already had a pretty good idea what she meant.

"This woman, all she does is argue with me. Such anger."

"Where is she?"

She nodded in the general direction of the examining room. "She wanted to make calls to her family."

He exhaled deeply. "Look, Sabrina, maybe I shouldn't get in the middle of this. My relationship with Faith Byrne—"

"Logan, please, she hates me now also. But this is a job that must be done."

Reluctantly, he followed her down the corridor and into the examining room. Byrne was perched on the edge of the examining table in a hospital gown.

"Hello, Faith," he began, as pleasantly as he could manage.

She made no response, just stared back defiantly.

"Dr. Como tells me you have some questions about your blood-test results."

"Is *that* what she tells you? Well, *I'm* telling you your results are bullshit. I feel fine."

He nodded. "I understand. We plan to run a second series of tests to check those results." For the hundredth time, there came the bitter thought: *Byrne should never have even gotten on this protocol!* But now, suddenly, he was struck by a new one: *Could it be—was it possible?—that Stillman also had known in advance about a looming creatinine crisis?*

"You listen to me," snapped Byrne. "I have been coming down here for almost three months and no one's said a single word to me about this so-called problem until today."

But, no, that made no sense: How could he have? There was nothing on her chart, nothing in her medical history. . . . Anyway, what about the other woman with the same problem . . . ?

"Are you listening to me, Logan?"

"Of course." The scowling face at once yanked him back to reality.

"You damn well better. 'Cause you're going to have to come up with something better than this before I let you kick me out of this protocol."

Reflexively, Logan gave his best doctor's smile. He hadn't believed anything this woman might say or do could surprise him. But the suggestion that the test results had somehow been rigged as part of a personal vendetta left him at a loss. "Look," he said, "perhaps I can give you a clearer idea of what the problem is. You see, the creatinine level—"

"I'm sorry, Faith, I got here as soon as I could."

And there, stepping into the small room, not entirely to the doctors' surprise, was Marion Winston.

"Ms. Winston," said Logan, "I'm not sure you're up to speed on what's going on here—"

"I have some idea."

"Perhaps, then, you can help Mrs. Byrne understand that, for all our past differences, we're really all on the same side here."

"Are we? Would *you* have called me—as Faith did?"

Logan intended his smile to be self-effacing. "Well, no. But actually, I'm glad you're here. I know how much respect you have for the integrity of the Informed Consent Document."

"You see," added Sabrina reasonably, "this is set in the terms of the protocol. If a patient's creatinine level rises above two point zero, then she *must* leave the protocol. It is too dangerous to continue."

"No," cut in Byrne, "you've got it backward. It's too dangerous for me *not* to continue. I'm going to *die* if I don't continue."

Winston gave a decisive nod. "Frankly, I don't know anything about this little experiment of yours. And frankly, I don't really care. My concern is that you are attempting to break faith with this patient." She turned directly to Logan. "*Again.* Only, this time you've got Dr. Como fronting for you."

Astonished, Logan threw up his arms, looking toward Sabrina. Her mouth had literally fallen open.

"Not, I suppose, that I should be surprised," continued Winston. "Given the nature of your relationship."

"This is just completely uncalled for," sputtered Logan.

Interrupting, Winston addressed herself directly to Sabrina. "I'd have thought that as a woman, you'd have a bit more understanding. Obviously, I was wrong."

"This is not a question of men or women," came the reply. "Why would you say this? What is gained?"

"No, you're right, Doctor. It is about honesty. And competence."

"*You* are the one who is not honest!" countered Sabrina; the very first time Logan had ever seen her so furious. "YOU! We are trying only to do what is best."

"Look," cut in Logan, "we are going to double-check the blood tests. We'll triple-check them if you like. But the bottom line is that we cannot in good conscience continue to administer this drug to a patient who manifests this kind of reaction."

He waited for a response. There was none.

"Now, Faith, as far as we're concerned this examination is over. You may get dressed."

Winston put a hand on the patient's shoulder. "Go ahead," she said gently. "You and I will talk in my office."

As Byrne walked slowly toward the adjoining changing room, Winston, not unexpectedly, lingered behind.

"Are you waiting to have the last word?" asked Logan evenly.

"I just want you both to know that we are not going to let this stand. I'm not through with you."

In an odd way, it was as if the pressure was off—at any rate, the pressure to be civil. Logan smiled. "You know, I've got an almost irresistible urge to tell you what I think of you—"

"Go ahead," she replied too eagerly, chin forward. An invitation, it suddenly struck him, that could lead to a whole raft of new charges against him.

"But"—he turned to Sabrina, seemingly on the verge of an outburst of her own—"unfortunately, we've got better things to do."

* * *

Arriving on campus the next morning, Logan was not surprised to find a note in his box instructing him to report to the office of Dr. Raymond Larsen.

"You've done it now, Logan," began the head of the Department of Medicine. "I suppose I don't have to tell you that."

"How exactly do you mean, sir?" The fact that the senior man was so clearly enjoying this scene only reinforced his intention to play it as cool as humanly possible.

"I don't appreciate that attitude, young man! Show me the respect of not insulting my intelligence!"

"Yessir. That wasn't my intention, Dr. Larsen."

"Let me come straight to the point. It has been five months since this protocol was approved, and I've heard nothing but bad news. Nothing! All you have established is that this drug is highly toxic."

"I'm aware of that, sir. But it is still relatively early."

"And," he continued, brushing this aside, "it's hard to imagine the reports of your personal conduct being any worse. You just do not seem to know how to get along with patients."

Logan simply stared at him. *This, from a man with the bedside manner of a serial killer.* "Sir, I really don't think that's fair," he replied. "Aside from Ms. Winston, with whom I've had a conflict almost from the start, there's no one—"

"I am not interested in your opinion."

"And I really don't think the news on Compound J has been all that bad. Dr. Shein—"

"Or in *his*. Dr. Shein is not the principal investigator on this study, you are."

"Of course. I'm just trying to point out that we haven't done much worse than other protocols at a comparable stage. Even at the moment, we're not the only trial of this kind that's failed to show significant early results."

Though he'd been careful not to name names, the implication could hardly have been any clearer. Immediately, the vein in the older man's temple began to throb. "I should not have to remind you that you are not Dr. Stillman! Nor do you have the standing to speak in such a manner of Dr. Stillman's work!"

"I was just trying to—"

"Dr. Stillman knows enough not to cavalierly place his patients in jeopardy. He has never once placed the reputation of this institution at risk! Which, young man, whether or not you are aware of it, is precisely what your conduct has done! Do you understand what I am telling you?"

Logan started to respond, then stopped himself. It was no good. This guy didn't even know how to pretend to be interested in a dialogue. "Yessir, Dr. Larsen," he said. "I'm sorry. What would you suggest we do now?"

"I don't *suggest* anything. You *will* do the following. How many patients remain on this protocol?"

"With Mrs. Byrne off—I assume she is off . . . ?" When the other only continued to stare at him, he pressed on. "That leaves thirteen."

"And they are continuing to come here to be examined on a regular basis, are they?"

"Yessir."

He leaned forward in his desk chair. "Dr. Logan, it is not within my authority to close down this protocol completely. But it is to take those steps necessary to safeguard the integrity of the Department of Medicine." He paused. "I expect you to inform each of those patients, on her next visit to the ACF, of the extraordinary risks we now know to be associated with this compound. Each shall then be given the option of leaving the protocol." He shook his head, as if in consternation. "And I wish I were in a position to offer each of them my personal apologies."

Logan stood there, dumbstruck. In effect, he was killing the program. *Was this the way it was going to end? Without his even making a coherent argument on its behalf?*

But he also knew that words were not going to mean a thing. And none came.

"That will be all, Logan," said Larsen suddenly, a military commander dismissing a contemptible underling. "Some of us do have work to do around here, you know."

10 August 1936
Frankfurt

The heat unbearable these last days. Still, dare not leave the apartment. Much trouble in this part of city—beatings, broken shop windows, etc.

Must concentrate on financial outlook. By new laws, Emma can give piano lessons only to other Jews. Her father fears he will lose store. Some friends trying to get out.

Since reduced to two days a week by Herr Thomas, have set up alternate facility in basement. So work uninterrupted. Early tests on version #531 of compound, new synthetic modification, show excellent potential. But laboratory supplies getting harder to come by, like everything else.

To date, Logan's firsthand experience with Marjorie Rhome had been limited to a brief introductory meeting. Sabrina had conducted the woman's initial interview and shepherded her onto the program; subsequently, as these things went, her exams at the Outpatient Clinic had been covered by either Sabrina or Reston.

Both confirmed Logan's own first impression: that this woman was genuinely *nice*. Courteous. Cooperative. Above all—for, as he'd learned the hard way, this was the quality often hardest to come by in such a situation—possessed of real balance.

"Mrs. Rhome is not a whiner," as Sabrina had described it. "She—what is the expression?—sees things from others' shoes. She knows that when the news is bad, it doesn't always mean it is somebody's fault."

Logan recalled this by way of reassurance. For Marjorie Rhome, the other patient with a creatinine problem, was due in for her exam this very morning—and it was Logan's luck that he was going to have to conduct it.

Even before his conversation with Larsen, that prospect had loomed as gruesome; after all, there was every reason to suppose that her creatinine level, too, had edged beyond the acceptable range and she would be obliged to leave the program. But now, even the slim possibility that her level would be encouraging offered no hope. For here he was, under orders to trash his own program!

More than an hour later, sitting on a bench in the quad, watching the passersby on this brilliant summer morning, Logan could still scarcely believe it. He found himself trying to figure out exactly what he felt. Could it really be . . . *nothing?* But, no, retreating into his intellect, he recognized the reaction after all: shock. This was interesting, a whole different level of self-protection. Perhaps, if he was lucky, he would *never* feel its full effect.

Sabrina was different; that was why he would wait to call her. No need to hit her with it yet. That would be selfish, self-indulgent. She was stuck all morning in Shein's lab. She would need time to absorb the calamitous news, and also space—sanctuary from the inquiring gazes of their fellow junior associates and, even more, from the bully himself. It wasn't so much (as in his case) the blow to career prospects that Sabrina would take as devastating, or even the affront to her pride. It would be the magnitude of the offense to her powerful sense of justice.

Logan glanced at his watch: nearly noon. Where had the time gone? Slowly, as if the burden had been transformed into something physical, he bestirred himself and began making his way toward the Outpatient Clinic.

Marjorie Rhome was waiting for him in an examining room, ready in her hospital gown.

"Sorry I'm late," he said, extending his hand, offering his customary version of a reassuring smile.

"No problem, Doctor, really." A heavyset woman with a pleasantly round face and sharp blue eyes, she seemed just as concerned with reassuring him. "I think we just finished up here a little early."

In fact, she'd already been on campus for some time, having blood drawn and posing for her monthly X ray.

"Well, I hope they haven't made things too unpleasant for you." He realized as he said it that the words were coming by rote. He was on automatic pilot.

"Oh, no, everyone's been very nice. As always."

"And you've been feeling all right? No new special aches or pains?"

"No, actually I've been feeling pretty darn well."

"Good."

Even as he continued to grin his idiot grin, he knew that soon he'd have to begin working toward the subject at hand: her future with the protocol—and the near certainty that there would be none. But, no, the results of her blood work should be in anytime now. He'd wait for those.

"So," he said, "if you'll just take a seat on the edge of the examining table, we'll try and make this as short and sweet as possible."

"Okay."

Before he began, Logan picked up her chart and scanned it. Yes, he was reminded, of course: Mrs. Rhome's problem was intraparenchymal lung nodules—a dozen or so BB-sized growths in each lung field. Her prognosis could hardly be worse.

He flipped to the page on her personal history.

"So," he said, "how are your kids?"

Her face lit up. "Oh, fine, thank you." She laughed. "But keeping me busy. You know teens."

"Actually, only by reputation."

"Of course, you're hardly older than that yourself."

He smiled; imagining, in fact, the incredible degree of will this woman must possess to maintain even a semblance of a normal daily life. "It's a boy and a girl, isn't it?"

"You got it. Jen, my daughter, just found out she'll be the captain of the high-school soccer team next season, isn't that a kick?" She laughed. "That's the big event at our house. I guess it doesn't compare to what goes on around here."

"Yes, it does. It compares favorably." He moved over beside her. "Now, I want you to relax. Breathe normally."

He placed his fingertips on either side of her neck and began working down, feeling for supraclavicular nodes.

"That's good," he concluded. "Still clear."

"Can I talk now?"

"I really don't think I could stop you."

"Well, I just wanted to put in a good word about my son also. He's pretty sensitive, so I like to give him equal time, even when he's not around to hear it."

Logan smiled. He'd been trying to think who this woman reminded him of, and suddenly it hit him: Jane Withers, the onetime child star who'd grown up to be TV's Josephine the Plumber. The physical resemblance was only part of it; even more so, there was the same relentless aw-shucks brand of optimism. "Go ahead, I'd love to hear about your son."

"Well, his name's Peter. . . ."

"Uh-huh. Mrs. Rhome, would you mind getting to your feet now?"

She slipped off the examining table. "He's fourteen. And you'll never guess what he announced the other day he wants to be. . . ."

Logan knew the answer; he'd heard this one before. "I have no idea."

"A doctor! It's ever since I've been coming here."

Oh, God, he thought, *she's going to make this even harder than it is already.*

"I don't know whether to be flattered or send him a warning."

She laughed. "Oh, I don't think even you'd be able to discourage him."

"Now hold still a moment. Breathe in."

Gently, he felt her abdomen for the liver edge. He couldn't feel it. Also good—the organ wasn't yet distended.

He was interrupted by a knock on the door. "Doctor?"

This is what he'd dreaded: a nurse bearing the results of Rhome's tests. He opened the door and took them.

"Excuse me, Mrs. Rhome, just a moment."

"Take your time, Doctor." She resumed her perch on the examining table and, to his surprise, began *humming.*

There were three pages, but his eye went right for the line that mattered. "Creatinine: 1.9."

He didn't know whether to be pleased or despondent. On the one hand, she was still below the cutoff; technically, she could remain with the protocol. On the other hand, he'd just been robbed of his easy out. Now he would have to discuss the overall ineffectiveness—no, he'd have to be more forthcoming than that—the *dangers* of this trial.

She stopped humming. "What's the word, Doctor? Good news?"

"Status quo."

"Well, where I come from, no news *is* good news."

Talk about a dream patient! If only they could manufacture them to these specifications!

Distractedly, he laid aside the blood results and slid the X ray from its envelope. "Mrs. Rhome, there's something I've got to discuss with you. . . ."

"Shoot." But he could detect a trace of concern through the breeziness.

"Do you know what creatinine is? Has anyone explained that to you?"

"Not exactly."

He stuck the X ray onto the view box and snapped on the light.

"Well, it's a measure of kidney function." He turned and faced her. "It's one of the things we're able to track through the blood tests."

"Is there some problem with mine? Because, frankly, I feel great."

"Well, yes and no. I'm sorry to say that we've had to take one woman off the drug because her creatinine rose to dangerous levels. Yours is not quite that high yet. . . ."

He paused. *That was strange.* He was staring at her chest X ray. The lungs appeared clean.

"But you're saying there's a danger of that?"

"It's something we have to watch. . . ." His voice trailed off as he examined the film more closely. "Excuse me, Mrs. Rhome, you did have a chest X ray taken this morning, right?"

"Of course. Just a little while ago."

"And how long ago was the last one taken?"

She shrugged. "Oh, I don't know, two or three weeks ago."

"Excuse me just a moment, will you?"

Taking the X ray from the view box, he held it sideways and read the name: RHOME. Putting it back in place, he looked at it once again.

No way, someone must've mislabeled this thing!

"What is it, Doctor?," she asked, with sudden trepidation. "Nothing too serious, I hope."

"No, no . . . I'm just looking at something. Nothing to worry about."

He stepped across the room and picked up her file. He located her previous X rays—four of them, in chronological order. Taking up the most recent one, he read the date—"You're right, the last one was exactly two weeks ago today"—and stuck it on the screen, alongside the other.

No question about it.

The X rays were Rhome's. Both lacked a breast shadow on the right side, where she'd had her mastectomy. But one showed nodules, clear as day. While on this new one . . .

Only now was Logan aware of his heart beginning to pound.

"Doctor, can you tell me what's going on? I feel a little like I'm in the dark here."

He turned to her with shining eyes, trying desperately to maintain a professional bearing.

"Mrs. Rhome, Marjorie, I think I'm seeing something interesting on your X rays. Potentially very interesting."

"Good news?" Despite himself, enthusiasm was coming through, and this was not a woman who had trouble catching it.

"I think so. Maybe. What I would like to do, if it's all right with you, is have another X ray taken, just to be on the safe side."

"All right."

"And also call in my colleague, Dr. Como."

"Oh, of course! I like her."

"Excuse me for just a moment, please."

He picked up the phone and dialed the nurses' station. "This is Dr. Logan in Examining Room C," he said evenly. "I'm going to need another chest X ray on Mrs. Rhome. If you could get someone in here, stat. . . ."

Hanging up, he turned to the patient. "A nurse will be in here soon. If you'll excuse me just a few minutes . . ."

As soon as he was out of the room, Logan dashed down the corridor. He grabbed the in-house phone in the doctors' lounge.

"Logan?" asked Sabrina, concerned. "Why are you calling me here?" Before he had a chance to respond, she suggested an answer to her own question—the one she had been dreading all morning. "This is about your meeting with Larsen?"

In fact, the session with the head of the Department of Medicine— which only minutes before had been the central fact of his world—now seemed completely beside the point. "No, no. I'm at the Outpatient Clinic, can you get right over here?"

"What for?"

"Please, Sabrina, tell them anything. Just get over here."

She was there in ten minutes. "What, Logan? What did Larsen say to you?"

"Look at this."

He handed her the two X rays and watched as she held them up to the window. "These are of Mrs. Rhome. . . ."

"Yes. And so . . . ?"

But now, as she looked from one to the other and back again, he saw her expression begin to change; her eyes suddenly alive as the significance of the evidence before her became clearer. "These are the correct X rays? You checked?"

"Absolutely. No question."

"I must see them in a light box!"

"You won't see anything different." He paused, then, softly: "I tell you, Sabrina, it's a miracle."

She'd never have believed she would hear Dan Logan say such a thing; like herself, like all dedicated researchers everywhere, he'd always defined himself, above all, as a skeptic. There *were* no miracles in medicine. *Everything* had a plausible explanation.

But now she only nodded in mute agreement.

"The question is what to tell her. She's still waiting in the examining room."

"She doesn't know?"

"I wanted to talk it over with you first."

She sat down on the window ledge and again held the latest X ray to the light. "I think we must take another picture, no? To be sure."

"I did already. Sabrina, this *is* the second X ray."

She nodded soberly. "Still, we must not give false hope."

"No. Of course not."

Such conservatism came with the territory. The fact is drilled into those who fight cancer from day one: Perspective is everything. While the lows may be as low as they seem, the highs are never as high. For, in the final analysis, there *are* no definitive cures for cancer, just more or less effective ways of keeping the killer cells at bay for greater or lesser periods of time. Even if the story suggested by Marjorie Rhome's X ray held up—indeed, if on further investigation ninety-nine and nine-tenths percent of her tumor mass had disappeared—that meant there still lurked within her millions of malignant cells; any one of which could set in motion the process that would lead to her death.

Still, even as they conscientiously went for dispassion, neither could long deny what they were feeling. Complete and utter elation.

"So," pressed Sabrina, "what should we tell her?"

Logan erupted in a smile. "That's the problem, isn't it? Words don't do the job."

Ultimately, they elected to let the patient make the discovery for herself. When they returned to the room, Sabrina again put the X rays side by side on the light box.

"Would you like to see what Dr. Logan was seeing?" she offered.

Rhome shrugged and walked over. "I don't think it'll mean heads or tails to me."

But as Sabrina indicated the nodules in the first picture, then indicated the same area in the second, entirely clear of tumor, Rhome turned to her with a sense of wonder that was almost childlike. "Does that mean what I think it does?"

"It's a very hopeful sign," agreed Logan. *"Extremely* hopeful."

"This drug? It's . . . working?"

Neither Logan or Sabrina had yet dared to say it aloud, but suddenly here it was. "We have real reason to be encouraged," said Logan.

All at once there were tears in Marjorie Rhome's eyes. "Oh, God! Oh, dear God!" And opening her arms wide, she drew Sabrina into a long embrace.

"Hey," said Logan, laughing, "I had something to do with this too."

Wiping away the tears with the sleeve of her gown, Rhome pulled away long enough to invite him into their embrace.

"I have to call home," she said. "I have to tell my family."

"Of course. Let me get you an outside line. Then we'll give you some privacy."

As soon as Logan and Sabrina were alone again, back in the doctors' lounge, he smiled sheepishly. "It got a little sentimental in there, didn't it?"

Sabrina turned to gaze out the window. A moment later, when she turned back, he was not surprised to see that her eyes were moist also. "Oh, Logan," she said, throwing her arms wide, "I can hardly believe this."

He took her in his arms and held her tight. Suddenly, now, she began crying in earnest; and, within moments, her body was racked by sobs.

"Shhh," he comforted her, squeezing her even tighter. He managed a small laugh. "What's going on here? This is *good* news, Sabrina."

But as she continued on, he fell silent, his face buried in her hair. He didn't want her to see that he was crying too.

Gregory Stillman was waiting when the First Lady's car—a late-model Chevy Caprice—pulled up to the ACF's Radiation Therapy Center.

"Right on time," he said, helping her from the car.

"With all you're doing for me," she replied, "it's the very least I can do."

"Wait around the corner," he instructed the driver, and ushered her into the nondescript brick building.

As in all such facilities, the floors aboveground were superfluous. For safety's sake, the radiation equipment is housed deep underground. They proceeded directly to the elevator that would carry them five stories down.

Mrs. Rivers was operating under no illusions. At their first, extended meeting, Dr. Stillman had explained that, in cases like hers, radiation is almost always the treatment of choice; the conservative one that, for all horror stories told about it, actually carries relatively few side effects. She'd likely experience some diarrhea, he noted, "because there'll be some scatter into the GI tract," and perhaps fatigue. But even during the ten-day period she'd be receiving her daily dosage of three hundred rads, she'd be able to carry on almost as normal.

And if such treatment proved unsuccessful in eradicating the cancer? she'd asked.

Stillman had frowned, as if this was a bit of unpleasantness there was no need at this juncture to even consider. Well, he'd replied, there are a whole range of chemotherapeutic options to be considered—plus

some exciting experimental options working their way through the pipeline.

"So," he asked her now, as they slowly descended in the elevator,
"how are your children?"

"Well, thank you. Of course, they don't know about this."

"No, I would guess not."

"I've talked it over with John. We agree there's no point telling
them now."

"No."

She glanced at him, his eyes on the ceiling. She'd always been
perceptive about people—far more so, really, than her husband—but it
hardly required insight to see that this guy couldn't have cared less about
her kids.

"Do you have children, Doctor?"

"Umm. Actually, I do, yes."

"Boys? Girls?"

"Two boys."

"Ages?"

He actually hesitated. "Fourteen and twelve, I think. They live
with their mother."

He *thinks*? After their first meeting, she'd been prepared to give him
the benefit of the doubt and assume that his manner was a matter of
shyness or discomfort due to her position; heaven knows, she'd made
that mistake often enough in recent years. But, no, it was the real thing.
Gregory Stillman might be as gifted a cancer specialist as advertised, but
he was hardly someone she'd ever choose as a friend.

They emerged from the elevator into a large, well-lit reception area.
Today it was deserted.

"Where's the receptionist?" she asked.

"Almost everyone in this facility has been given the next ten days
off. They've been told we're doing repairs on the equipment."

"I hope no one is being denied treatment on my account."

"I don't think so. I would suppose they've been diverted to other
facilities."

Abruptly, a door at the far end of the room swung open and a short,
dark man in a lab coat walked toward them, smiling broadly, hand

extended. "Forgive me, please," he said, in an accent she took to be Greek, "I was not expecting you quite so soon."

"Mrs. Rivers," said Stillman, "this is Dr. Andriadis, our director of radiation therapy."

He took her hand, still smiling. "I am a great admirer of both yourself and your husband."

"Thank you."

"Dr. Stillman has explained the procedure here? Everything is clear?"

"Yes, he has." It wasn't complicated, after all. The idea was to kill cancer cells by zapping them with a radiation beam. The specifics—that the radioactivity source was cobalt-60, producing a beam composed of energized photons—didn't really interest her. She only knew that it destroyed everything in its path, healthy tissue as well as diseased.

"Now, the first thing we shall have to do," he was saying, "is to draw some red-purple lines on your skin. I'm afraid these will be indelible for about two weeks. But they are necessary, so that each day we aim the beam in precisely the same place."

She was reassured by his own obvious assurance. "I understand. I'll just live with it."

"I tell patients it is not so bad, as long as they stay away from the beach." He smiled again. "But maybe with this heat, that's not so easy."

He led them from the reception area into a spacious room bearing four imposing machines, each set apart from the others by a concrete partition. Waiting here to assist in the procedure were two nurses, one male and one female. "This is where we will do our work," said Andriadis. "But first I will ask you to put on a gown. The changing room is right over here."

Only once she was in the room, the door shut behind her, was she aware of the full extent of her terror. She was about to put her life in these people's hands! To allow her body to be attacked by a device out of a 1950s Japanese sci-fi film! She couldn't pretend to be brave any longer. Why, oh why, hadn't she insisted that John come with her?

But, no, of course not. That was impossible.

"I'm ready," she said a moment later, emerging from the room.

Dr. Andriadis seemed to sense what she was going through. "No need to worry," he said, "you will do just fine. We are here to help."

As she followed him toward the cobalt-60 device, she looked at Dr. Stillman standing off to the side in seeming detatchment. Once again, more strongly than ever, she found herself wishing he were a different kind of man.

When Sabrina answered her door that evening, Logan was standing there with an armful of sunflowers. "Just so you won't forget who's the sunshine in your life," he announced. "To Marjorie Rhome I sent roses."

She laughed. "So did I." From behind her back she withdrew two giant packs of Chunkys. "So you will remember who is the sweetness in yours."

He tossed the flowers onto her living-room floor and took her in his arms. "As usual, I got the better deal."

She kicked the door closed behind her as they kissed.

"I tell you, Sabrina," he said, pulling back, "I've been flying all day. I can hardly stop myself from telling people!"

"I know."

He laughed. "Or, rather, throwing it in their faces."

"When are you seeing Reston?" she was reminded.

"Nine, at his place." He glanced at his watch. "Bet you'd like to be a little Italian fly on that wall."

"That way I could see him through a fly's little prism eyes. Maybe he would look better."

Something suddenly hit him. "Oh, I got something to show you." From his breast pocket he withdrew a folded letter. "Talk about fate."

"What is it?"

"It was in my box this afternoon."

He handed to her. After a moment, she recognized the envelope, identical to the one bearing the first communication from the elderly

German chemist two months earlier. This letter was longer than the first, almost a full page of labored old-fashioned script.

> My dear Doctor Logan:
> Greetings and best wishes. I am pleased to hear from you in your letter of 31 May. The work you do on your protocol sounds interesting indeed. Please let me know of your results, or of publications where I might find such things.
> You ask me about the work we did long ago. It was under a Japanese named Mikio Nakano.

Sabrina looked up at Logan. "Nakano?"

He beamed. "Pretty neat, huh?"

> Nakano came to our country as a young man and worked for the great Dr. Paul Ehrlich. It was Ehrlich who put him to work on this problem of cancer of the human breast.
> I came to know Nakano in 1927, when he arrived to work in the Christian Thomas Company in Frankfurt. He was the chief chemist and of course I was only a young assistant. But we got on well.
> I can still see him before me now, very clever and full of energy. Our main work at Thomas was with petrochemicals, but Herr Nakano was most interested still in the cancer experiments with sulfonate derivatives. He was certain he could find a cure!
> Herr Thomas at first believed also. But the compounds were highly toxic. Some rabbits became blind and some died. So after a time, Nakano left Thomas.
> But I know he did not stop working on this problem. He was a determined man. After all, Paul Ehrlich spent twenty years on the problem of toxicity in his treatment for syphilis. Six hundred six compounds Ehrlich synthesized! And in the end even he found only one solution!
> Please, sir, write me more of your work. I am interested in all details. Now I have so much time in my hands, and am so easily bored.
> With very sincere regards,
> Rudolf Kistner

Sabrina carefully replaced the letter in the envelope. "You see," she said softly, "it does not all begin with us. This man, he had the same ideas."

"I wish he could have seen what we saw today."

She looked at him quizzically. "How do we know that he did not?"

* * *

Entering Reston's front door an hour later, the first time he'd visited the place in months, Logan's feelings were extremely mixed. Obviously, as a member of the team, John Reston had a right to the extraordinary news; in fact, he should have been told of it hours earlier. On the other hand, it had been Reston who distanced himself from the project. The thought of Reston now sharing in the glory, if, in fact, there was to be any, was almost too much to swallow.

Even tonight, Reston's first impulse was to trash the protocol.

"So, Danny boy, what's so important that it couldn't wait till to-morrow?" he asked, while they were still in the entryway. "As if I didn't know. . . ."

"Can we sit down, John? This is pretty important."

"That bad, huh?" said Reston, leading the way within. "Christ, I'm starting to think of you as Mr. Bad News."

He took a seat in the cluttered living room. "What is it, another goddamn toxicity?"

"Actually no. It's about Marjorie Rhome."

"What about her?"

Logan held up the X rays. "We had pictures taken today. She's clean."

Reston sat up. "What are you talking about?"

"Take a look."

Reston didn't move. *"Clean?* As in *nothing there?"*

"Not that we can see."

A smile began to bloom on Reston's face. "Really? You're not bull-shittin' me?" He got to his feet. "Lemme see those."

He studied them only momentarily. "Amy!" he shouted. "Amy, get in here!"

"What?" she called from another part of the apartment.

"Baby, hurry!"

A moment later she came rushing in, wearing a terry-cloth robe, a towel around her hair. "What!" Then, spotting Logan, "Oh, Dan, I didn't know you were—"

But already Reston had her in his arms, dancing her around the room. "We've had a hit, Amy! The drug actually works!"

"What?"

"We did it, Amy! Compound J's for real!"

She stopped and turned to Logan, what she was hearing apparently striking her as flatly impossible; clearly, she'd heard nothing but negative talk about the drug for months. "Is that really true? After all the problems you've had?"

He shrugged and smiled. "It looks good so far. Of course, it's pretty early to—"

"Get dressed," said Reston, "you and I are gonna go out and celebrate. And I mean big time!" He turned to Logan. "You coming along, too, Dan?"

He smiled. "No thanks, I've never been any good as a third wheel. Anyway, I've got to be somewhere."

Reston walked over and extended his hand. "Look, buddy, I want to thank you. I guess all the rough times were worth it, right?"

"Hey, we all did our part."

"Right." Reston laughed. "And don't you forget it."

The next morning, Logan was both pleased and surprised to discover that Seth Shein had not already gotten his hands on the information.

"Well," said Logan, grinning, "this looks like a first. I get to tell you something important you don't already know."

Shein was actually irritated. "And what might that be? Don't tell me you've found yet another way of poisoning patients."

By now Logan had come to regard Marjorie Rhome's X rays as a kind of totem. Their effect on others was magical. "Take a look at these," he said now, sliding them across the desk.

Shein did so—but his face remained disappointingly impassive. "This is your second creatinine patient?" he asked finally.

Logan nodded. "Actually, that was my concern when she came in yesterday morning."

"And what was her creatinine level? Or were you so swept away by this triumph that you forgot to check?"

"One point nine. Not good, but still eligible to stay on the program."

"Good." He paused thoughtfully. "This is an excellent development, Logan, you obviously know that."

"Yessir." *What was going on here?* Logan wondered. *Why the hell was he so sober about it?*

"My concern," continued Shein, as if reading his mind, "is that something like this could get you carried away. We don't know if this result is going to stick, do we?"

"No, we don't."

"Nor have you come close to licking your toxicity problem."

"No."

"What I'm saying is that one response is nice, but it does not a successful protocol make."

"Of course not, I know that." *Something was going on here. Could it be that Shein resented this success?*

Shein suddenly grinned and threw out his hands. "That said, I am bowled over! Congratulations, Logan, I'll tell you the truth, I was startin' to think you were gonna make me look bad."

Logan laughed. "I kind of got the idea that's what you were thinking. Never. Not a chance."

"This is gonna kill that bastard Stillman. *Kill* him." He actually cackled. "Have you thought about how to break the news?"

He shrugged. "No, not really."

"Let me handle that." He rubbed his hands together. "Start it out as a rumor—you know, some interesting results on the Compound J trial, that sorta thing. Then leak it out in dribs and drabs over two or three days. Make 'em *suffer*."

"Shouldn't we maybe wait a little while? Keep a close eye on Mrs. Rhome—and see if we find activity in any other patients?"

Shein nodded sagely, the cat who'd swallowed an entire nestful of canaries. "I have a pretty good idea you're going to be seeing other results."

"Really!" Logan sat up in his seat. "Why?"

"You haven't paid much attention to your bunnies lately, have you, Logan? Too busy playing the big man over at the Outpatient Clinic."

"The rabbits? Not since yesterday morning when I gave 'em their second dose."

"Better take a look, then, don't you think?"

A moment later, Shein was leading him down the hall toward the bank of elevators.

Stepping into the animal holding facility, Logan spotted the change even from across the room. At least half the animals looked healthier, their fur less ragged, their movements brisker and more assured. But it was only when he was beside the cages that he recognized the extent of the transformation: on almost every animal, the tumors were markedly smaller.

"My God!" exclaimed Logan. "Look at that."

"Look almost good enough to eat, don't they? If you go for that kind of thing."

"But it's so soon. It's only been four days. . . ."

Shein nodded. "Wanna know what I think? I think you and your little girlfriend's playing around with this molecule achieved something quite interesting: you didn't alter the effects of Compound J but you accelerated the process."

"In other words—"

"My hunch is that you're going to see more responses with Compound J. It's just taking longer than you thought."

"Why? What makes you so sure?"

"This stuff you made, what do you call it?"

"Compound J-lite."

He smiled. "Oh, you're such a clever bastard, aren't you, Logan? What seems to be happening is that this new stuff of yours isn't cleared by the body as rapidly as Compound J—which means, since there's more of it working at any given moment, that its effects are enhanced."

"So you think we can expect a *major* response rate?"

Shein gave him that familiar look of contempt. "How the hell do I know? We're dealing with human beings, not rodents." He paused. "But it's a pretty damn good bet you're gonna get a response in more than just one."

For a long moment, Logan stared at the rabbits. "That's good enough," he said finally. "I'm up for that."

It was little more than a week before they had their second response. Reston was the one who first noted it. Back on board with a vengeance, he'd been making a point of seeing virtually every protocol patient in for her regular exam, hoping against hope to come up with a "hit" of his own.

There was considerable irony in the fact that the patient in question turned out to be Hannah Dietz—who, following her toxicity problem, Reston himself had tried so hard to have removed from the protocol. In fact, uncertain as to how much the patient knew about that conflict or his role in it, Reston had come close to letting one of his colleagues deal with her now.

But he was immediately reassured by the warmth of her greeting. "Dr. Reston, it has been far too long."

He smiled back. "Don't you worry, Mrs. Dietz, I've been keeping up with your every move. I see you've licked that bleeding gums problem."

"Yes, yes. No more of that, thank goodness." She nodded. "My Phil is such a good fellow. You know what he tells me all the time now? 'We beat one, we'll beat the other.'"

"That's important," he said. "Any doctor who tells you a patient's attitude doesn't matter hasn't been keeping his eyes open."

"I'm sure." She smiled. "It's just too bad the other is cancer."

Dietz's case was distinct from the others on the protocol in that hers was a palpable tumor: a discrete rocklike mass of five by four centimeters, it was more easily monitored by touch than via X ray or CAT scan. So immediately, when Reston began manipulating the tumor, he was struck by the change. Not only had there been a significant reduction in size, but what remained was now rubbery, blending seamlessly into the surrounding tissue.

Reston made little effort to hide his excitement.

"Mrs. Dietz," he announced, "I think I've got some unbelievable news for you! This tumor of yours seems almost *gone*."

Having grown accustomed to doctors speaking in measured tones, Mrs. Dietz took a moment to react. "Really?" was all she could find to say.

He nodded vigorously. "I swear to God, I can hardly feel the bastard. Pardon my French."

She grinned. "At the moment, I do not mind your French one bit, young man."

"Would you like to call in your friend? What's his name?"

"Phil. Oh, yes, I would like that very much."

"Just for a minute, just to give him the news."

"She's better?" asked Phil a moment later, incredulous. "Is this what it means?"

Reston hesitated. "Let's just say that we're a lot better off than we were yesterday."

In fact, now that he was past his initial euphoria, he was painfully aware that he should never have led them to so definitive a conclusion; a tactile diagnosis can be inexact—and sometimes dangerously misleading. Until he had solid confirming data, it would remain the medical equivalent of hearsay.

"Listen, Phil, I'm afraid you'll have to leave us now. We're going to have to run a couple of tests."

"Will it take very long?"

"Not at all. Maybe forty-five minutes." He began easing him toward the door. "And, please, at least for the time being, don't mention this to anyone."

"Why?"

"It's just a bit premature. It would not be in Hannah's best interest."

"Now, then," said Reston, closing the door behind him and facing Dietz. "What we're going to do now is do a biopsy."

She literally shrank back. "Will it, you know . . . ?"

"Hurt?" He smiled. "Nah, you'll hardly feel it. You won't even have to leave the room."

In fact, the most difficult part of the process was the administration of local anesthetic. The cytologist charged with performing the biopsy itself—a good friend of Reston's—finished his part of the job in less than two minutes; with a modified hypodermic extracting from the tumor site two small specimens of pinkish matter.

Under normal circumstances, it is several days before the results of such a test are available. But before the cytologist headed back toward his lab, Reston called him aside.

"Listen, Roger," he said, dropping his voice, "could you put a big rush on this one? That lady in there's sitting on the bubble. I'd like to be able to give her some good news."

The other considered a moment, then nodded. "I don't get to deliver enough of that myself. And she seems like a nice woman."

The results were back before noon the next day. The material removed from the lower outer quadrant of Hannah Dietz's breast was nothing more than fatty tissue. Not a single malignant cell had been found.

Reading over the data, Reston let out a whoop and dashed across campus. By the time he reached Seth Shein's lab he was breathless, his faced bright pink.

"What the hell happened to you?" asked Logan.

"I got some news," he panted. "Get out here." He turned to Sabrina. "You, too, signorina."

In the hallway, he thrust the page their way.

"Hannah Dietz . . ." began Logan.

"Is *clean*. You're holding her bill of health. We should get Shein out here, he'll wanna know this too."

Logan smiled broadly. "Number two. I can hardly believe it." He stopped. "Wait a minute, when did you examine her?"

"Yesterday," said Sabrina, eyeing the page.

"Why didn't you say something before this?"

"He wants the credit," said Sabrina in a low voice, turning to Reston with disdain. "This Reston, he does not change."

"I wanted to be *sure*," he countered. "I didn't want to waste anyone's time. Including the patient's."

"I presume," said Logan, "that you told her before you came running over here."

He hesitated. "Not yet."

"Where is she?"

"Over at the clinic with that boyfriend of hers."

"Well," said Logan, starting to betray the full extent of his irritation, "don't you think that's something you should do?"

Reston stared at him coolly. "Sure. But I'd like to tell Seth Shein first."

"We can handle that."

"I'm sure you could." He snorted. "I'm sure you'd love to cut me out of this thing entirely, the way you have from the beginning."

Logan shook his head and sighed. "Never mind. I'll tell Hannah."

"I will too," said Sabrina.

Fixing him with a look of unapologetic contempt, Logan bowed low, a musketeer pointing up a rival's utter lack of class. "Go ahead, *Doctor*," he said, gesturing extravagantly toward the door to Shein's lab, "he's all yours."

Of course, it was willful delusion on Reston's part. Everyone at the ACF with any interest in Institute politics knew who was most responsible for the Compound J trial: Logan and Como. It was they who'd done the important groundwork and, equally to the point, they who'd stuck by the protocol through the lean times; publicly defending it in the face of criticism that sometimes bordered on derision. If it now achieved any measure of success, there was no question they'd be the ones getting most of the credit.

Which, the rumor mill at the ACF had it, was suddenly a very distinct possibility. Specifics were lacking; few had followed the trial closely enough to know even how many patients the Compound J team had accrued, let alone the particulars of their treatment.

But all at once the tenor of comment about the protocol underwent a startling shift. Before, conventional wisdom was that the thing was a bust: there were toxicity problems, patients were being dropped from the program. Now the talk was of surprisingly positive results. Word had it that Seth Shein, no less, was talking in terms of "a breakthrough treatment."

True to form, Shein was publicly uncommunicative. A veritable student of the art of rumor-mongering, once he'd leaked just enough to set things in motion, he pulled back, deflecting questions with what was taken as bemused innocence. "Hey, I haven't *seen* any results. What d'you think, I spend my life lookin' over those kids' shoulders?"

But to Logan, he soon made his strategy explicit. "You're doin' great, unbelievable!" he put it to him a couple of days after learning of the second response. "I'd just like to see you build up the case a little bit more before we hit 'em with it."

Logan looked quizzical. " 'Hit 'em'?"

"I've been thinkin'," elaborated Shein, "about settin' you up at Grand Rounds. Think you could handle that?"

Logan looked at him incredulously. The Grand Rounds presentations, held every Tuesday morning in the ACF's cavernous main auditorium, were the most prestigious forum afforded by the Foundation; speakers were generally top scientists, both American and foreign, hoping to draw attention to major research developments.

"I'm thinkin' after Labor Day," added Shein. "They'll be in a good mood from roasting their fat asses in the sun."

"You think I'm ready for Grand Rounds?"

"Ah, bullshit," said Shein, waving this away, "nothin' to it." He paused. "I'm gonna want you to go into detail about some of the responses you've had."

"*Both* of the responses," corrected Logan. "There've been only the two."

"So far. Two outta fourteen ain't bad. And I'm bettin' there'll be some more icing on that cake."

By now, Logan knew enough not to question Shein's uncanny intuition. And, in fact, they had a third response only a couple of days later: sweet old Mrs. Kober, whose supraclavicular node, like the malignancies of Marjorie Rhome and Hannah Dietz, had seemingly vanished.

Sabrina, who conducted the exam, brought Logan the news—along with a note from the patient.

> Dr. Logan,
>   Don't forget . . . we have a bet on the Giants versus the Cowboys next season at the Meadowlands.
>   Sally Kober
> P.S.—Suddenly I am feeling *much* better about my chances of collecting. Thank you.

It was a day after that that Logan was summoned back to Larsen's office.

"I've been expecting to hear from you," began the head of the Department of Medicine, fixing him with a cool stare. "I thought it was understood, in light of our earlier conversation, that I would be kept informed of the status of your protocol."

Logan recalled no such understanding at all. "I'm sorry, sir," he stammered, "there must have been some sort of misunderstanding."

"I'm sure," said the other. "How convenient for you."

"But we've done exactly as instructed."

"You have, have you?" He arched his eyebrows, lending him a sudden resemblance to William F. Buckley. "I suppose you expect me to take your word on that?"

"Dr. Larsen, I assure you that every patient we see is made aware of the toxicities associated with this drug."

It was true, the creatinine problem was now mentioned as a matter of course. But what Logan failed to note was that so, too, was the fact that the drug had begun showing highly impressive results.

"And, as a consequence, how many of these patients have chosen to discontinue treatment?" asked Larsen.

"None, sir."

"*None?!* And you expect me to believe that you've told them the whole truth? What kind of fool do you take me for, Logan?"

"I'm sorry, sir, I don't mean to imply that—"

"You're a *liar,* young man!" he suddenly shouted. "I've known it from the first day I met you. You should never have been accepted into this program!"

But sitting there across from him, Logan felt a remarkable sense of well-being. This was the performance of a desperately insecure man, flailing about for a solution to a problem he knew was beyond his control. Larsen was aware of the growing regard for Compound J—and there wasn't a damn thing he could do about it.

"I'm sorry you feel that way, sir," replied Logan, "I really am."

"Spare me your feelings," spat back Larsen. He hesitated. What most concerned him—the responses the drug had lately elicited—was something he dared not broach. If the rumors had merit, he certainly had no intention of hearing it from this source. "You'd just better pray," he added, "that when all is said and done, everything you've told me holds up."

"Yessir," nodded Logan, far from intimidated. His heart was soaring. *He'd beaten the son of a bitch! Look at him, reduced to firing blanks!*

"And that you have in no way brought disrepute upon this institution. Because there are still some of us who take things like that extremely seriously."

"Yessir."

Abruptly, Larsen stood up. "I really don't think," he said scornfully, "that you and I have anything more to say to one another."

The fourth response came a week later: Sharon Williams, the woman whose tumor had migrated to the bone.

This one, however, was somewhat less definitive. Establishing a response against malignancies in the bone is a dicey proposition, since bone scans can take months to reflect the healing process. Rather, Logan made the judgment about Mrs. Williams based primarily on the testimony of the woman herself.

Showing up at the clinic for her exam, she was positively glowing.

"Something's happening to me," she announced. "It's remarkable."

"How do you know?" asked Logan.

"How do I know?" She put her hand on her hip and replied with exaggerated sauciness. "Honey, I know every inch of this body. I can *feel* it." She paused. "Or, rather, I *can't* feel it."

"You're saying there's been less pain?"

She laughed. "Doctor, the pain is *gone.* For a year and a half, I've had to take codeine regularly every three hours just to keep going. But last week I stopped, and I haven't even thought about it since."

In the absence of the usual confirming data, Logan and Sabrina were at first hesitant to count this as a response. Yet there was another fact that went a long way toward making the case. A marker of the disease, the antigen 1Y-32, present in an overwhelming percentage of breast-cancer patients, was suddenly absent in the blood of Sharon Williams. True enough, the 1Y-32 test was itself experimental—but in this case it jibed so well with other factors that making the leap seemed reasonable.

"Besides which," noted Logan, grinning but meaning it, "it'll be terrific for the Grand Rounds presentation. The more variations of this disease we can claim to be getting at, the better."

The truth was, as the big day approached, Logan's excitement and apprehension grew apace. Some evenings, awake in bed, he saw himself the focal point of a triumph as stirring as the one in his favorite medical movie classic, *The Story of Louis Pasteur*; his stunned audience leaping to their feet in spontaneous tribute. But just as often, the thought of even appearing before so vast and distinguished a throng, most of them highly skeptical and some frankly hostile, filled him with dread.

Shein was naturally keyed into Logan's mindset almost from the start. "Jeez, what the hell's wrong with you?" he put it to him a week before the speech. "I mean, the *crap* you put yourself through!"

As usual, Logan wasn't sure whether Shein's words were meant to taunt or reassure. Probably Shein didn't know himself.

"I know," he conceded. "I guess it's just nerves."

"What're you worried about, Logan? You got it made."

"You keep forgetting, I've never done anything like this before." He paused. "I guess I'm a little concerned that, you know, Dr. Markell is going to be there."

"That's right, he is." Shein nodded thoughtfully. "I see what you're sayin'—you'd better be absolutely fuckin' *brilliant*."

"Thanks. I needed that."

"Christ, Logan, Markell's nothing to worry about. Believe me, I know—no one handles him better."

Logan was well aware of the extraordinary complexity of Shein's relationship with the imperious head of the ACF. Though virtual opposites in manner and style, they were intellectual soulmates, sharing both a respect for talent and a contempt for those who got ahead without it. It made sense that, formerly Shein's mentor, Markell—known in the infighting of institution politics as a stone killer—had turned into his protector; the reason, for all Shein's calculated outrageousness, his enemies couldn't touch him.

But by the same token, free spirit that he fancied himself to be, Shein hated it that others were so aware of the fact. He chafed at being known as Markell's boy, especially among his own people. More than once, Logan had been struck by how, out of the blue, awed and intimidated as he clearly was by Markell, Shein would make a point of slighting him.

"I'll tell you something else," he breezily added now, "Markell's screwed up plenty of times himself."

"So—what?—you're saying he'll understand if I'm a little shaky?"

"Did I say that?" Shein grinned. "He's got plenty of patience for his own fuck-ups—not for yours."

As the morning approached, Logan did what he always had when faced with a difficult challenge: he sought to overwhelm self-doubt through sheer preparation. He spent every available moment retracing the critical steps of the previous eight months; carefully reviewing his notes on the Tilley case and the articles unearthed by Sabrina that had helped them make important connections; returning to the voluminous files on the candidates for the protocol; rereading the case histories of each of the fifteen women who'd eventually been accrued; amassing the slides necessary to illustrate various aspects of the presentation.

His plan was to recount the history of the Compound J protocol as a straightforward chronological saga, explaining as best he could the factors—prior research, new data, and simple intuition—that led to certain key decisions. In this way, he'd let the suspense build. Only in the final quarter hour would he reveal the striking responses the drug had now elicited in four patients.

There was no way to guess how this would be greeted. He knew full well that everyone at the ACF had heard such claims before. Few in that audience would fail to understand that a handful of responses in a protocol setting do not automatically add up to a credible treatment approach, let alone a breakthrough. Still, the responses *had* been dramatic; and, more than that, the drug had apparently performed almost precisely as they'd predicted. At the very least, he felt he could make the case that Compound J was off to a flying start.

To make things easier on himself, Logan wrote out the entire speech on three-by-five cards. No sense risking an extemporaneous slip of the tongue, not with this crowd.

The process was a laborious one, consuming most of the weekend, and it was late Sunday afternoon when he laid aside what felt like a completed draft.

"What the hell," he said aloud, heading into the kitchen for a beer. "It's in the hands of the gods."

Less than thirty-six hours later, he stood on the stage in the vast amphitheater, as a staff member named Follansbee offered a surprisingly breezy introduction.

"Ladies and gentleman," he began, "today we have with us a young doctor from the Department of Medicine who, I understand, is going to address himself to the matter of whether old compounds can be taught new tricks. . . ."

But Logan, looking out over the crowd, heart pounding, hardly heard the words. Only perhaps a third of the plush red seats in the hall were occupied, but that meant at least four hundred people. He recognized dozens of faces—but was most conscious of the three directly in front of him in the second row center: Raymond Larsen, Allen Atlas, and Gregory Stillman.

Shein, hands in pockets, stood in the back. Sabrina, in the first row over on the left, smiled at him, then quickly averted her eyes. *She's almost as nervous as I am,* he thought. And, scanning the room: *At least Markell didn't show.*

"And so," wound up Follansbee, "I give you Dr. Daniel Logan."

Logan stepped to the podium to a smattering of applause. The shakiness he felt in his knees instantly found its way to his voice, his thank-you for the introduction registering as tremulously as that of a high-school candidate for student office.

For the first several minutes, reading from his cards, he scarcely dared to look up at his audience. But gradually, the terror began to lift, and by the time he showed his first slide—a vintage photo of Paul Ehrlich, sitting amid mounds of journals—he'd found his rhythm.

As his confidence increased, he began looking out over his audience. They were gratifyingly attentive. He noticed that Sabrina now seemed entirely at ease, his best measure of how things were going. And —another good sign—Larsen looked ready to leap onstage and disembowel him!

Kenneth Markell entered the hall midway through the presentation, as Logan was discussing a slide showing the structure of the Compound J molecule. A short man, with a fringe of white surrounding a bald pate, he had the bearing of Caesar. He didn't bother to take a seat, merely stood in back, arms folded, listening. Seth Shein, taking his place beside him, unconsciously assumed the same posture.

By the time Logan reached his climax, even the occasional bout of coughing in the hall had ceased. "I want to tell you about one of the patients on the protocol," he said.

He nodded toward the projectionist, and the slide showing Marjorie Rhome's initial X ray appeared on the screen. "This was what we saw when this patient came onto the protocol."

He briefly discussed her case before nodding to the projectionist again. "This is the same patient's chest X ray after eight cycles of treatment with Compound J."

Logan thought—or was it only his willful imagination?—that there was a murmur in the hall. He paused a moment. "That was only our first response. It has been followed by three others."

For presentation purposes, these cases were less dramatic; he had no slides with which to illustrate them. In fact, the final response of which he spoke—Sharon Williams's—might have been considered suspect. But if he'd lost any significant segment of the crowd, Logan, his earlier anxiety forgotten, didn't notice.

When, moments later, he concluded the speech, it was to highly respectful applause.

Logan acknowledged this with a broad, unaffected smile. But when he glanced down at the second row, his apprehension returned with a rush. The three of them were sitting there, arms folded. And when Logan caught his eye, Stillman suddenly extended an arm, pointing.

Stillman mouthed the words so clearly, it was as if Logan could hear them: "Toxicity, asshole! What about toxicity?"

"Well, well, hail the conquering Logan!" greeted Shein, half an hour after the speech, when Logan reported to work at the lab. The several other junior associates within earshot grinned. Logan noted that Sabrina was not among them. "Thank you," he said.

Shein threw an arm over his shoulder and led him to a quiet corner.

"I think you mighta done yourself some real good out there."

"Really?" asked Logan. Still shaken by Stillman's taunts, he was reluctant to believe the evidence of his own eyes and ears; had, in fact, started to think his failure to suggest a plausible approach to the toxicity problem might outweigh all the rest.

"Let's put it this way, a few weeks ago, this thing was dead in the water, right? Now"—Shein paused—"well, let's not exaggerate, it's *alive* in the water. And swimming pretty good."

"Thank you."

"Let me clue you in on something, boychick. In this case, what I think means squat. I'm talkin' about what Markell thought."

"Markell?" he asked, with sudden excitement. "What'd he say?"

"I didn't talk to him about it, I *watched* him."

Logan didn't know quite how to take this. "Ahh."

"Listen, usually he walks out on these things." He paused. "I think if you play it right, you might be able to get your own lab."

Logan was thunderstruck. "Our own lab?"

"A small one. You made some skeptics into believers today."

"Our own lab! I love it!"

"Don't embarrass yourself, Logan, I said it was a *possibility*." He pointed to the door. "I told Dr. Como to take the rest of the day off. You too. You've earned it."

"Thank you, Dr. Shein. . . ."

"Seth."

"Right." Logan began heading for the door.

"Oh, Logan . . ."

He turned.

"There's a message for you from that Indian kid down in animal land."

"Actually," he replied, smiling at Shein's little joke, "he's from Bangladesh."

"Whatever. You'd better get down there."

The pretense of amusement vanished as soon as he was out of the room. *No way this guy would call unless it was serious. Why the hell could nothing ever be simple around here? Why couldn't he have one moment of unambiguous joy?*

But what he found when he reached the animal holding facility exceeded his worst expectations. Every rabbit that had been dosed with Compound J-lite lay dead in its cage!

Every one!

A moment later Sabrina walked in, also summoned by Hassan.

"My God!" she gasped.

Neither had to speak the word that hovered in the air: *toxicity.*

Logan moved slowly down the line of cages, trying to maintain a detatched bearing.

"When did this happen?" he asked Hassan, at a rickety desk across the room.

The other shrugged. "Oh, sir, I cannot say for certain. This is how I found them just this morning."

Logan was reassured by Hassan's nonchalance. "You don't seem all that surprised."

"Oh, sir, I've witnessed such things many times before. You know, these lab animals do not have a very long life expectancy." He smiled, almost apologetically. "I am just sorry if it is a setback to your experiments."

"Don't worry," he lied, "it's not unexpected. Tell me, is anyone else from the Medical Branch aware of this?"

Hassan shrugged. "Oh, I cannot tell you, Dr. Logan." He gestured around him. "There are people in and out of here all the time. Many people like yourself have business with these animals. How many of those would you like me to dispose of for you?"

"Let us give it a little thought."

"Good, good." He rose from the table and walked toward the door. "I must feed the pigs. If you need me I will be in there."

Logan turned to Sabrina. "What now?" he said, in as neutral a tone as he could muster; as if this were not a disaster at all, merely another step in a normal process of scientific inquiry. "We could cut the dose and shoot up a new batch."

But, of course, the implications of the question were now at least as political as scientific. On the one hand, to drop Compound J-lite would be to essentially write it off as a failure; and this after the drug had achieved such spectacular early results. But, too, given the evidence before them, it was likely that continuing to experiment with the new compound would only kill more rabbits. And if word of *that* started getting around, it could be a PR disaster—impacting on the Compound J trial itself.

Sabrina walked to Hassan's desk and picked up the phone. "The first thing, we must see some reports on these animals."

A few minutes later, Dr. Carrie Schneider, a friend of theirs in pathology, sauntered into the room.

"Whew," she said, surveying the carnage, "I see what you mean. What've you been feeding those guys, arsenic?"

Logan shook his head. "I wish I could joke about it."

"Sorry, just a little pathologist humor there." She peered in at one of the cages. "How many of them you want done?"

"I don't know. At least three or four, I guess."

"Four," said Sabrina.

"You want microscopic or gross?"

"Basically, we need to know what killed them. As soon as possible."

She nodded. "I can get you some gross results by the end of the day. Just slit 'em stem to stern and take a look. For the micro, you'll have to wait awhile."

"Okay."

"Hey, Logan?"

The sudden change in her tone made him cast her a quizzical glance. "Yeah?"

"Sorry I missed you at the Grand Rounds. I hear you were damn good."

They were at Sabrina's late that afternoon when Logan called in for the report.

"I can't be too precise here," Carrie Schneider told him, "but you've definitely got a liver problem. That's your cause of death—liver failure."

"Uh-huh."

"I don't have any toxicology reports yet, of course. But I can tell you that all three of the livers I've looked at so far are mottled, congested, and grossly inflamed."

He thanked her, and a moment later was off.

"Well," he said, turning to Sabrina, "at least we've come up with a foolproof way of killing rabbits."

She made no reply.

"Christ, that stuff is *potent*." He paused. "I guess it's pretty clear we've gotta shelve it."

"Yes. Compound J *must* be the focus. How can there be a question, with the results we are getting?"

"Four out of fifteen."

"It would be crazy to worry now about J-lite."

He nodded. "But I just keep thinking about those first results on Compound J-lite. Every *one* of those little fuckers hopping around with a smile on its face! *Something* in that molecule works." He paused. "Ah, well, I guess it was too much to hope for."

The next week, as reaction to the Grand Rounds talk continued to filter in, it became clear that the young doctor's star had never shone more brightly. A dozen senior and mid-level researchers who'd never before so much as acknowledged his existence made a point of introducing themselves, commenting enthusiastically on the talk, suggesting he stop by their offices so they might hear more.

"You just never know the talent they've got buried away in this place," remarked one, a senior staff member named Frank Beckman, with a confidential wink. "Who'd have guessed we had one of Paul Ehrlich's heirs right here at the ACF?"

Far more crucially, Seth Shein pronounced himself ready to back the idea of their getting their own lab.

"But won't you miss working for me?" he kidded Logan, a proud father pushing a favored son from the nest. "Sure you can hack running your own operation?"

"You're right, how could anything be as much fun as doing shit work for you?" he replied, suddenly feeling curiously like an equal. "Don't worry, I think we'll do all right."

"You gonna take Reston?"

Surprised, Logan shook his head. "Why, you think we owe him?"

"Not if he's a disruptive influence."

"He is. It's like I hardly know the guy anymore. And Dr. Como could never stand him."

Shein snapped his fingers. "There's your answer. The work is everything. If it affects that, cut the bastard loose."

Some would take it as heartless, Logan knew. But he also knew it was the truth. "I'm learning, Seth. I've had the master as a teacher."

Shein laughed, delighted. "Don't you forget that. If you hit it big, just keep remembering"—he slapped himself on the chest—"how to spell the name."

There'd been so much good news lately that the morning the phone call came in, it took a while for its gravity to register.

"Dr. Logan?" said the male voice, at once familiar and unplaceable.

"Yes."

"This is Phil Lester." He waited for some sign of recognition. "I met you with Hannah Dietz?" he added, tentatively.

"Oh, yes, of course. What can I help you with?"

"I'm sorry to bother you, Doctor. Hannah asked me not to."

"No problem, that's what we're here for." Though, abruptly, his antennae were up: what was going on here? Hannah was one of their success stories! And why wasn't *she* on the phone?

"I'm a bit worried," he continued. "I think something's not right with her."

"What do you mean, exactly?"

"Last night, in the middle of the night, she started vomiting. And she doesn't look well."

"Has the vomiting been continual?" The guy's tone was so moderate, it was hard to believe anything could be seriously wrong.

"Continual? Yes, I would say so. Six or seven times. I don't think there's anything left to come out now."

Jesus H. Christ! This woman should be in a hospital!

"She's just exhausted, Doctor," he continued, "and she's also sweating a lot. She's like a dishrag."

"You were right to call. I think she should be looked at."

These words of reassurance were all it took to crack Phil's veneer of calm. "I knew it! It's very bad, isn't it?"

"I can't tell you that, Phil," he said. "Probably not."

"But she was getting better! I thought she was well!"

"It's probably nothing to worry about. Just a minor setback."

"Should I take her to the hospital here?"

Where the hell were they?—somewhere in the New Jersey 'burbs! Chances are no one there would even begin to know what to look for!

"Look, if at all possible, I'd like to get her in here." His mind was racing. "I have a thought—can I call you right back?"

A helicopter! That way she could be on site in little more than an hour. The ACF used them occasionally, but only for dire emergencies; and that required clearance by the director's office.

In seconds, he had Shein on the line. Less than a minute after that, Shein called him back with formal authorization. "It's being arranged through the New Jersey National Guard. Call your guy and tell him to sit tight."

"Thank you, Dr. Shein."

"Thank me if it pans out. Otherwise, keep me the hell away from it. We're both spending a lot of capital here, Logan."

It ended up being more like an hour and a half before the copter put down on the quad. Mrs. Dietz was hustled into the hospital on a stretcher.

Logan and Sabrina were waiting for her. Reston had declined an invitation to participate in the treatment.

One sight was all it took to assess the gravity of the patient's condition. She was extremely pale and completely disoriented. Most worrisome, the whites of her eyes had a distinctly yellow cast, evidence that her liver was no longer functioning properly.

By prearrangement, Sabrina took charge of the patient's care while Logan saw to her friend.

Phil, alone in the waiting room, wearing a Hawaiian shirt and pants of Day-Glo orange, was doubled over, head in hands. When Logan touched him gently on the shoulder, he was surprised to find he had not been weeping.

"Phil," he said softly, "I've got to get back in there. I just want you to know we're going to be running a few tests."

"Tests?"

"We need to assess her overall condition. But I want you to know you haven't been forgotten. If you feel you need to speak to me, tell a nurse."

He nodded. "I understand. Thank you, Doctor."

Sabrina, assisted by a nurse and an orderly, already had Mrs. Dietz hooked up to an IV line to counter her dehydration. The monitor over her head revealed that her heart was racing and she was hypotensive. But the greatest concern was the possibility, based on her obvious sense of confusion, that she was encephalopathic—yet another sign of liver failure.

Still, she appeared to be somewhat more alert now. Sabrina was leaning over her bed and talking soothingly. "Hello, Hannah. Do you recognize me?"

There came a smile on the old woman's face. "How are you, Dr. Como?"

"Good. Excellent. Can you tell me how you are feeling, Hannah?"

"I've been better, thank you." She paused, anxious eyes searching the room. "Where's my Phil?"

"Right in the next room."

"He's fine, Hannah," spoke up Logan, moving closer. "He's just concerned about you. Like all of us."

"He's a good man, don't you think?"

"I do," agreed Sabrina. "You are a very lucky woman. Such a man is not easy to find." She paused. "Now I am going to ask you to do something for me."

"Yes?"

"Could you hold your arm out straight?" She demonstrated with her own.

It is the simplest possible test for hepatic encephalopathy. When a patient is suffering the condition, the hand will jerk back and forth spasmodically.

Which is precisely what Mrs. Dietz's now began to do.

Sabrina looked to Logan and their eyes momentarily locked. There was no need for words.

"Can I put my arm down?"

"Yes, of course." Sabrina managed a smile as she stroked her forehead. "See, nothing to it."

"You're a very kind girl, do you know that? Very loving."

"Thank you. From you, I consider this a great compliment."

Dietz opened her gray eyes a little wider. "I'm going to die now."

For an instant, Sabrina thought to protest.

But, no, Mrs. Dietz wasn't looking for reassurance. It was a declaration.

Though it sounds like myth, many doctors who've done serious time in hospitals believe it: when a patient tells you they're dying, even in apparent contradiction of the facts, they usually are.

Neither of the doctors doubted now it was true.

As she drifted off to sleep, Sabrina remained perched on the side of the bed, watching the beautiful old face.

She touched Logan's hand. "You should get Phil."

He was there a few minutes later when she fell into a hepatic coma; and still there early that evening when she peacefully died.

The initial autopsy report came in two days later. As he read through it, Logan physically shuddered.

A congested and grossly distended liver. Fulminent hepatic necrosis. Holy shit! It was almost identical to the one on the damn rabbits!

The speed of the improvement startled her. Three days after she started radiation therapy, the pain in her back had begun to subside; within a week, she no longer felt it at all.

"I'd forgotten what it was like not being constantly aware of it," she delightedly told her husband that night. "I feel like the Tin Man in *The Wizard of Oz*—like someone took an oil can to me and made all the stiffness disappear."

Her husband, the President, took her in his arms. "That's so wonderful, darling. Maybe the worst is over."

"I hope so. They say so much of it is attitude. Well I'm going to test that theory—because no one's going to top my attitude!"

Gregory Stillman knew not to be fooled, of course. They'd killed only a single, localized tumor—just a symptom, not the disease itself. Now it was a crap shoot. The distinctive cancer cells, born in the breast, could resurface almost anywhere, anytime: in thirty years, thirty months, or thirty days.

And this last was by far the most likely. By every indication, this was an exceptionally aggressive tumor.

Still, for the time being, there was no reason to disabuse the patient of her optimism—especially this patient. "Obviously, things are looking pretty good right now," Stillman told her when the ten days of radiation were over. "The treatment's done everything I hoped it would and more."

"And now?"

"I'm going to want to keep a close eye on you, of course. There's still disease there."

"Isn't that what we should be doing now, rooting out what remains of the disease?"

"It's not that simple." He opened his briefcase and withdrew a book —a copy of his own *Basic Principles of Breast Malignancy*. "Read this, I'd be pleased to discuss any questions you have then."

She looked at him, incredulous. If he hadn't just pulled off what she regarded as a minor miracle, she'd have been tempted to fire him on the spot.

"I would suggest an examination every two weeks," he continued. "But, please, call me if you experience unusual physical symptoms of any kind."

The first three exams were uneventful. When she arrived for the fourth, she once again reported nothing unusual. But it was impossible not to notice her cough.

"How long have you had that?" asked Stillman.

"Just a few days. I've always gotten a lot of colds."

But there were no other cold symptoms evident. The cough was dry and rasping.

This was not necessarily cause for concern. Coughs are wildly non-specific, they can be caused by a thousand things, nine hundred and ninety-eight of which are meaningless. And, in fact, when he took a chest X ray, it was clean.

Five days later, he reached her at the White House. "Just checking on that cough."

Before she could respond, he heard it. "It's no big deal," she insisted. "Aside from that, I'm feeling strong as a horse."

"How you're feeling otherwise doesn't interest me. I'd like you to come in tomorrow."

"No!" Tomorrow truly was impossible. She had meetings all day and, with the Irish prime minister in town, a formal dinner scheduled for the evening. But more than that, she resented his peremptory manner. "It will just have to wait until next week. And frankly, Doctor, if we're going to continue, I'd appreciate a bit more courtesy."

That was the right button to push; like most bullies, he responded well to threats. "I'm sorry, Mrs. Rivers," he instantly backed off, "I didn't mean it as it sounded. My only concern is your health."

"Believe me, Doctor, it concerns me also. But surely this can wait a few more days. Till next week."

"Of course."

The cough was still there the following week, perhaps even a bit stronger. But she resisted his suggestion of another X ray. "Look, I just had one last week. I *know* that's not healthy."

He smiled benignly, his mind brimming with contempt: *This fucking moron's just gotten dosed with three thousand rads and now she's worrying about a twelfth of a rad more!* "Mrs. Rivers," he said, in his best, concerned manner, "I really think this is pretty important. Knowing how you feel, I certainly wouldn't suggest it otherwise."

The new X ray showed it clearly: a streaky density, like a cirrus cloud, in the left lung. Studying it in his office while she waited in an adjoining room, he assumed the worst. The tumor was growing within the walls of the lymph vessels inside the lung. Radiation had taken them as far as it could. If this proved out, he'd have to begin a course of chemotherapy—and soon.

"Mrs. Rivers, I'm going to suggest you have a bronchoscopy. Just as a precautionary measure."

"What's that?"

"Well . . ." There was no way to make it sound anything other than gruesome, snaking a tube down the trachea and up into the lungs to take a look—but he tried. "I really think it's something that must be done."

"I'd like to discuss this with Dr. Burke. I value his opinion."

"Absolutely. Of course." He was coming to truly dislike this woman. *He* was the expert, Burke was a nothing! "If you can possibly arrange it, I'd like to schedule it for the day after tomorrow."

"All right," she suddenly relented, pain in her eyes, "since you seem to feel it can't wait."

This was a very sick woman. He knew it—and now she knew it too.

For the time being, at least, he suspected she wouldn't be giving him much trouble.

F or the first few days after Hannah Dietz's death, Logan found reason for hope, if not optimism. Several of his colleagues expressed dismay at the shocking turn of events; wanting to know what he thought had gone wrong and, more to the point, what it would do to a protocol that had seemed so promising.

"I only know what they tell me," he stiff-upper-lipped it. "As far as I can tell, we're still viable. Patients are still coming in to be dosed. And we still have three success stories on our hands."

But, in fact, he was honest enough to recognize that things had begun to change almost before Hannah was cold. His very first act, after spending a quarter hour trying to comfort a sobbing Phil, had been to call Shein's office. Logan needed some bucking up himself. He didn't expect sympathy from this quarter, but hoped for some realistic counsel.

Typically, Shein was already on top of things: he'd gotten a blow-by-blow account of Hannah Dietz's last hours from the head nurse on duty.

"Sorry," he told Logan. "Tough luck."

But his voice was so flat, he might have been a stranger.

"Look," said Logan, "I'd really like to get together—all of us—to talk about the impact this might have on the protocol."

"Yeah, yeah. Of course."

"Good. Thank you. Is there a good time tomorrow?"

"I don't know." He hesitated. "Why don't you call the office?"

After he hung up, it was Shein's detachment that lingered. Logan would have been far more reassured by a barrage of put-downs.

When Logan reached him the next day, Shein no longer saw any reason for such a meeting. "Look," he said, at least sounding like himself. "What the hell am I gonna tell you? Nothing to do now but tough it out."

"I was just wondering if, from a political perspective, there's anything we might do to—"

"Yeah, bring her back to life." He laughed mirthlessly. "Just, whatever you do, don't use a helicopter again. You know how much that cost us? Six grand!"

Logan had no idea how to respond to this. *Under the circumstances, six thousand—half the price of a third-rate car—seemed like pocket change.*

But of course it was really something else he was hearing. It wasn't the money that irked Shein—it was that he'd let himself be persuaded to put through the request to the director's office. And *that* was Logan's doing.

"Look," said Logan, "things were moving pretty fast. I thought we should get her down here as fast as possible."

"Yeah, well, I guess you were wrong." He suddenly coughed. "And look now, I'm comin' down with a damn cold. Good-bye, Logan, I got no time for you this morning."

Only with Sabrina was there relief from the sense of impending disaster. That night, in bed, they held each other tight for two hours without even a thought of making love. She told him about the summers she'd spent as a child in Lugano, and her long-ago best friend Marissa, and her first wild crush on the pop star Joe Dassin. He talked about his undergraduate days at Princeton and, coming cleaner than he ever had before, the assorted peculiarities of his family.

"I love these stories," she said.

"Hearing them's a lot more fun than living them," he assured her. "We're dealing here with *lunatics*."

She snuggled even closer. "Soon it will be light. We should get some sleep."

"Sabrina . . ."

"Yes."

He'd been avoiding the subject all night. "Has anyone said anything to you? About Mrs. Dietz?"

It was possible no one had. As the least combative member of the

Compound J team, Sabrina was generally spared the hostility that came Logan's way as a matter of course.

She paused before answering. "Allen Atlas."

"Oh, Christ. What?"

"He was *happy* at the news. Making jokes. He said to me, 'So, this is one of your success stories?' "

"I love these guys. They don't mind being known as vicious bastards as long as they're not hypocrites!"

"In Italian we have an expression, *'lupo affamato.'* A hungry wolf."

In the dark, Logan nodded grimly. "It's almost the same in English —'licking his chops.' "

Three days later, just past noon, Logan got the call from a Dr. Edward Reed of Holy Name Hospital in Dover, Delaware. Sharon Williams had just been admitted to his care.

"I understand she's part of a protocol you're running there."

"Yes, that's right," said Logan, in his best noncommittal voice.

Sharon Williams! Incomplete as the supporting evidence remained, Logan considered her response against tumor in the bone the protocol's most startling achievement yet!

"What seems to be the problem?"

"Her husband brought her in just a little while ago. I'm afraid she's decompensating."

"Could you be more specific?"

"Apparently, she was at home when she began complaining about not feeling well. By the time she got here she was already becoming encephalopathic. We've got her in the intensive care unit."

Oh, Christ. Another liver failure!

"I don't suppose there's any chance you could put her in an ambulance and get her over here?" From Dover, the trip would be little more than an hour—with no expenses that had to be okayed.

"I don't think that's a good idea. This woman is really too unstable to be moved."

"No, you're probably right," he paused. "I hope you won't mind if I come to you."

Holy Name Hospital featured little of the super-high-tech equipment that by now Logan had come to take for granted, but he quickly noted the place was modern and efficiently run. By community hospital standards, a superior facility.

To facilitate observation, Mrs. Williams's bed was in a room enclosed on three sides by clear glass. A monitor above her registered an EKG reading of 160 and showed her blood pressure at eighty-five over fifty. At her side heaved a ventilator, helping to keep her lungs going. A Swan-Ganz catheter had been threaded through her subclavian vein, through the heart and the pulmonary artery directly into the lung, where it was recording pulmonary capillary pressure.

Literally within seconds, Logan knew all he needed to know. Sharon Williams was dying.

"Dr. Logan?" He turned to face a smallish young man with white-blond hair and and a face so young, he might have been a teenager. "Ed Reed."

They shook hands.

"It's painful to see," said Logan softly. "I saw her less than a week ago. . . ."

"We did some blood work on her. Would you like to see the results?"

"Tell me."

"It's not pretty. Her hepatic transaminases"—enzymes measuring liver function—"are completely out of sight."

"Do you have her on fentanyl?" The drug in question, a highly potent anesthetic, is often used with patients who are obliged to spend prolonged periods immobile.

"There doesn't seem much point, she's not aware anyway."

"No." Logan sighed. "Look, thanks for putting up with me. I know it's not easy having a stranger hanging around."

The other smiled broadly. "My pleasure, really. I'm a big fan of you people at the ACF."

If only you knew, kid, if only you knew. "Thanks. Do you maybe have a library here, somewhere I can kill some time?"

"You're going to wait it out?"

"I'd like to."

Reed pointed down a hallway. "Take the stairs down and then a left through the waiting room. It's not much after what you're used to."

"Actually, I've been so busy lately, I wouldn't mind just catching up with the basic journals."

He was following Reed's directions, heading through the waiting room, when he spotted a large black man, sitting beside a girl of seven or eight. Or, more precisely, they simultaneously spotted one another. It took Logan a moment for the face to register: Sharon Williams's husband. They'd met only once before, at the ACF, the day his wife came in for her first treatment.

He stopped and turned. But already Simon Williams was on his feet, coming his way.

"Mr. Williams," said Logan, extending his hand. "Dan Logan, from the American Cancer Foundation." Up close, he saw the strain Williams was under in his eyes.

"I know who you are," he said softly. Slowly, with seeming reluctance, he shook the doctor's hand.

"I got here as soon as I heard about Sharon."

"Yes."

"She's a strong person. We're all hoping for the best."

He was sorry as soon as the words were out of his mouth. There are people who want to be bullshitted, but this man already knew the truth. He fixed Logan with a hard stare.

"I have just one question."

"Yes."

"I read that consent form of yours. It didn't say anything about something like this."

"Mr. Williams, I'm sorry. We truly had no way of knowing."

"See that little girl over there?" He indicated his daughter. "Why don't you tell that to her? Or to her three-year-old sister?"

To this, Logan made no reply. It was an uncharitable thought, but given Logan's state of mind, it arose all the same: Would this guy be complaining if, as it had seemed such a short time before, the drug's effects had been beneficial? Yes, he understood the man's distress, even his anger. But doctors are also human—and medicine is imperfect.

"I'm deeply, deeply sorry you and your family have to go through this," he said blandly, just wanting to get the hell out of there. "No one should have to. I only hope you understand that we've done the very best we know how. . . ."

* * *

He spent the next several hours in the library—actually, no more than a
normal patient room outfitted with shelves and a couple of chairs as a
reading room—catching up on the *New England Journal of Medicine* and
the *Annals of Modern Medicine*. But he read distractedly, frequently laps-
ing into troubled daydreaming. What he needed to know would never
turn up in any journal. How could a drug that showed such tantalizing
promise simultaneously be so brutally destructive? And why did the
deadly side effects appear to be so pronounced in the very patients it at
first seemed most to benefit?

It was early evening when Logan heard the footsteps in the deserted
hall and Reed appeared in the doorway.

"She's gone," he said. "Just a few minutes ago."

Logan rose to his feet. "Well . . . thanks for letting me know."

"There was nothing we could do. She never had a chance."

"I know that." He glanced at his watch. "I guess I should be heading home."

"Hey, look. If you're up for it, maybe we could grab some dinner."

Caught off guard by the sudden shift in the young doctor's tone,
Logan looked at him quizzically. Reed was smiling. "Maybe it's not the
best time," he added in explanation, "but I thought maybe you could
give me some tips on how I could hook up with the ACF."

Logan could only smile wearily. "Actually, based on what I've seen,
you'd probably do very well there."

When Sabrina opened her front door, Logan knew she had some bad
news of her own.

"What is it, Sabrina? What's wrong."

"There was a call a while ago. From Pennsylvania. Mrs. Rhome
died today."

He hardly reacted at all—the same way she took his news from
Delaware. Whether by training or instinct, they pressed on.

There was, after all, something vital upon which to focus. If Compound J was killing the very women whose cancer it destroyed, there still
remained one such woman unaccounted for.

When there was no answer at Mrs. Kober's home, Logan suspected
the worst.

"Relax, Logan," said Sabrina, though she was thinking the same thing. "Probably she's just not at home. We would surely hear something otherwise."

"At ten o'clock at night? Where would she be?"

"You left a message. When she gets it, she will call."

But when they didn't hear from her, both spent a fitful night; and it was Sabrina who awoke early—before six o'clock—to call again.

"Listen," she repeated, with diminished conviction, "if she's in a hospital, someone would call us. There is no doubt."

"If they knew they should."

"This is what happened with Mrs. Williams and Mrs. Rhome."

"Both of them had family. Mrs. Kober is alone."

1 November 1937
Frankfurt

More and more I see that my own profession is as bad as the rest. Worse! For should not these men be dedicated above all others to truth?

Today I learn Eisenstadt has been arrested in Berlin. One of our greatest chemists. For what? No reasons are needed anymore! Yet not a word of protest.

Best results yet on version #612. Toxicity marginal—diminished energy and slight loss of appetite. Reason for hope? Must get more rabbits somehow!

Emma nearly ill with fear. Cannot blame her. Who will be next?

Thinking back on it later, Logan was most amazed by not how quickly their support melted away, but how unembarrassed some of his co-workers were by their own behavior. But that morning, arriving at the ACF, there it was. He was a pariah.

Individuals who after the Grand Rounds presentation, barely a week before, had embraced him as a close friend and colleague, now hurried by stonefaced. More than simple slights, these were willful acts of negation, meant to instantly dispel any illusion Logan might have that there existed a relationship between them.

Logan knew he shouldn't be surprised. *After fifteen months at this place? What the hell's wrong with me?* But he was, more than he let on.

That afternoon he found the note in his box. He would learn it was identical to the ones Sabrina and Reston found in theirs. Written on the stationery of the director of the Medical Branch, it was vintage Larsen; devious even as it seemed to come right to the point:

> *In light of recent developments surrounding the clinical trial of Compound J in metastatic breast cancer, and because of questions that have arisen about the conduct of this trial, as well as other issues, you are hereby requested to meet with representatives of the Department of Medicine. This meeting will occur tomorrow, Friday, October 14, at 3:00 P.M. in the conference room of the Department office.*

Logan noticed that Larsen had signed his name with an unusually zestful flourish.

* * *

At least the timing was a blessing. As most experienced doctors know, human nature tends toward the morbid; in desperate circumstances, almost anyone with enough time to fret about the possibilities starts dwelling on the worst. More than once, Logan had himself seen patients in for serious surgery, at first upbeat about their chances, then increasingly drained of spirit when the procedure had to be delayed.

Now, with the meeting barely twenty-four hours off, they had far too much to do to let their imaginations run wild. There were patient records to comb through, autopsy findings to be reexamined, a defense of the protocol to be prepared.

After all, reality was more than bad enough. Larsen clearly intended to rake them over the coals; and probably, finally, if he could find a way to circumvent normal procedures, try to shut down the Compound J trial by executive fiat.

Beyond that?

Realistically, what *could* he do? Ten months remained on the two-year contracts they had signed as incoming junior associates. And, in any case, despite everything, who could deny their promise as oncological researchers? Even at the ACF, vindictiveness had its limits. The likeliest scenario was a stern reprimand, a PR move designed to ward off potential embarrassment. Patients on this trial were dying. If the press got wind of it, the ACF had to be seen as having taken some action.

At any rate, this is how Logan evaluated things. Even Sabrina, the ultimate pragmatist, chose to see the positive aspects of what was obviously to be a painful encounter. They would take their shots, but at least there was to be a dialogue; a chance, after all the simmering hostility and silent undercutting, for them to make their case.

And as they worked on it in the library that day and into the evening, that case seemed to them eminently defensible. Yes, of course there had been setbacks, major ones. They were more heartsick about the Compound J–related deaths than anyone. They'd come to know these women, in a couple of cases to admire them deeply.

But, as those who'd be assessing them well knew, developing new cancer treatments was a gruesome business. It must not be forgotten that this had been conceived as a highly experimental trial; initially its object had been nothing more than to establish that this compound was active.

In fact, it was only because they had so dramatically exceeded that goal that it could now be viewed as a disappointment. Suddenly Compound J was being judged by the much more rigorous performance and safety standards normally applied to drugs in Phase Three trials.

Who could doubt, even now, that it would be a mistake to abandon this drug?

The logic seemed so compelling that by late evening, Sabrina wished it were already the next day.

"This night will be hard, I think," she told Logan as he pulled up before her apartment. "Waiting is the hardest."

"Tell me about it. God, I hate those bastards."

She led him inside. "It is late," she said. "Just one glass of wine"— then retreated to the back to check her messages.

"Logan," she said, reappearing a moment later. "Come here."

"What?"

Wordlessly, she took his hand and led him toward the bedroom. Sitting on the edge of the bed, she punched a button on her answering machine. After a brief pause, there came the familiar voice.

"What's all this fuss about?" demanded an obviously perplexed Mrs. Kober. "I get back from my sister's and there are three messages on my machine. Anyhow, if you still need me, I'll be in tonight. If not, I'll be in next week for my regular treatment." She laughed. "Hooray! The last one!"

"That's some good news, no?" said Sabrina. "Maybe an omen."

Logan smiled. "Think we ought to give her a call?"

Snatching up her book, she dialed the number.

It turned out that Mrs. Kober had indeed felt ill briefly several days before. "A little fluish, you know? That's why my sister was looking after me."

"But now it is past?"

"It was the flu—a few chills, a little vomiting, and it went away." There was a questioning tone in her voice. "Why, what's going on?"

"Then you are all right now?"

"Don't hold back on me, Dr. Como. Is there something I should know?"

Logan, listening to her end of the conversation, watched Sabrina shrug. "Some people on the protocol have gotten quite sick, so we are checking. But, no, it sounds like you are fine."

"I *am* fine, you sweet girl. But if that changes, I promise, you'll be the first to know."

When Sabrina got off, she grinned at Logan. "For her, I really think this drug has worked."

"Forget the omens, that's called *ammo.*"

"You're right. We must go in that room tomorrow *aggressive.*"

He reached out for her across the bed. "Why does it do something to me when you talk that way?"

"Because I almost never do." Smiling, she gave his hand a loving squeeze. "Not tonight, Logan, I want you to go home. We must both be alert for tomorrow."

At least there wasn't any suspense. As soon as they walked into the room, it was clear the process was rigged. Larsen sat at the head of the conference table. Around him were a who's who of the protocol's enemies: Stillman, Marion Winston, Peter Kratsas, and, representing their peers, Allen Atlas.

Also present, of course, looking utterly miserable in his seat at the opposite end of the table, was John Reston. As Logan and Sabrina moved to their own places nearby he nodded, but—at least some of the others had to notice—edged his chair a couple of inches in the other direction.

Larsen looked solemnly around the table. "Thank you all for being so prompt," he began. "Courtesy is something I'm afraid we could use a lot more of at this institution. Now then, let us move on to the business that brings us here.

"You are all by now aware of the deaths of several patients on the roster of the trial of so-called Compound J. I am sure you share my sense of the extreme gravity of this situation." He paused, leaning forward slightly, his blue-gray eyes boring in on the Compound J team. "And I must tell you, it is my intention to rectify it."

Only now did Logan see with absolute clarity how bad it was going to be. There would not even be the pretense of allowing them their say. The verdict was already in, it was just a matter of going through the formality of reaching it.

Larsen turned to the patient care rep. "Ms. Winston, I believe you have some preliminary observations."

Logan sneaked a sideways glance at Sabrina. Her expression was absolutely blank, but the rhythmic movement of her jaw muscles let him know her insides were churning as much as his.

"Yes, I do," said Winston evenly. She opened a file folder and stared down at the page. "This is not a pleasant exercise for someone in my position to have to go through. I am interested in helping people, that's why I got into this business. I am not interested in doing harm to anyone's career." Now she looked up and surveyed the table. "But I'm afraid there is considerable evidence that at least one member of this team, its principal investigator, Dr. Logan, has been extremely negligent in regard to patients. I expressed this concern before this protocol was approved, and in light of what's occurred since, I feel it even more strongly today. I would like to bring before this group two women who have had what can only be called emotionally devastating experiences under this doctor's care."

Logan, flushed, raised his hand. "Excuse me—"

"You are speaking out of turn, Doctor," reprimanded Larsen. "Please allow Ms. Winston to continue."

"I was only going to say," pressed Logan, "that I could produce any number of patients who—"

"Perhaps you could," he was cut off. "But this is not a game of numbers. Treating even one patient with contempt is unacceptable."

Logan sunk down in his seat, resigned.

The women, of course, were Rochelle Boudin and Faith Byrne.

Called in first and taking her place at the table, Boudin went through the litany of Logan's supposed abuses. How he'd systematically neglected her needs. How he'd made a point of belittling her concerns. How he'd consistently failed to deliver the treatment her condition demanded. "He just always made me feel," she summed up softly, "that the fact I had cancer was an inconvenience to *him*."

The bitter thought, having crossed Logan's mind, refused to leave: *Funny, isn't it? If I treated you so miserably, how'd you end up cured?*

Byrne, who followed, was even worse. In self-dramatizing detail, she told the story of her initial treatment with Compound J: emphasizing her concern—and his complete absence of same—for what turned out to be the drug's very real dangers. Never mind that she was, at the time, being carefully monitored and showed no danger signs; never mind that the best measure of Logan's performance was the fact that she was sitting here, right now, *alive*; Byrne's fable was accorded serious weight. Around the table, she was met with sympathetic nods.

"The worst of it," chimed in Winston, "was that subsequently, on his own authority and against her will, Dr. Logan removed Mrs. Byrne from the protocol. I personally regard this as an act of petty vindictiveness."

At this, Logan actually came close to smiling. These people would say anything. *Which was it—he was a monster for knowingly subjecting patients to a horribly dangerous drug, or a monster for NOT allowing them to take it?*

But by now, logic seemed the farthest thing from anyone's mind.

"I'd like to say something, if I might," said Allen Atlas, as soon as Byrne left the room. Ever the kiss-ass, he glanced meaningfully toward Stillman and Kratsas. "I don't know if this is the appropriate time to raise this, but one thing that might be considered here is that Drs. Logan and Como developed a second, related drug. They call it Compound J-lite, I believe."

Beside him, Peter Kratsas snorted. "Real clever," he observed, sarcastically.

But Logan was too stunned to notice. *How did Atlas even know about the variant on the original drug?*

"When tested in lab rabbits," continued Atlas, "this compound at first showed a good deal of activity—followed by extreme toxicity."

"I think what Dr. Atlas is driving at," picked up Stillman, speaking for the first time, "is that this is the same pattern observed in the deceased patients. Now, obviously this is speculation. The evidence is only circumstantial." His eyes narrowed and he flashed an odd half-smile. "But it seems the possibility must be considered that these doctors substituted this second drug for the one that had been approved for protocol use."

Instantly, Logan was on his feet. "That's a damn lie! Compound J-lite was a private experiment. We did NOT violate the protocol!"

"Dr. Logan, sit down!" shouted Larsen.

"Logan is right," said Sabrina loudly, pointing a finger Stillman's way. "You know we did not do this thing! Why would you say so?"

It was as close to losing control as anyone had ever seen her, and momentarily Larsen seemed at a loss. "Dr. Como . . . *please.*"

"No, this is not to be smoothed over. To say such things, *that* is wrong—not what we did!"

"All right," said Larsen, decisive again, "we are going to take a break now. And when we come back, I expect both of you"—he stared at Logan and Sabrina—"to control yourselves. You are not doing yourselves any good here."

Leaving the room quickly, they moved down the corridor, turned up another, and retreated to a quiet corner. Both were seething. "I'm going to bring up Mrs. Kober," said Logan quietly. "We've gotta say something on the drug's behalf."

"They will not let you."

"We should've brought her down here, no way they could've stopped us." He shook his head bitterly. "That son of a bitch Atlas. How'd he even know about those fucking rabbits?"

"Oh, here you are!"

And there, to their astonishment, stood Gregory Stillman.

"Sorry to interrupt," said Stillman, ingratiatingly, "I know how it is." He nodded back toward the meeting room. "Tough going in there."

Sabrina eyed him with undisguised loathing. "What kind of man are you, Dr. Stillman?" she said, her voice hard enough to cut glass.

In response, he actually managed a smile. "Look, I understand how you feel. I really do. All I can tell you is that it's not personal. We're competitors, sure, but we share the same goals." He paused. "Dr. Logan understands that, don't you?"

"Me? Not for a second."

"Your friend Reston does." He flashed that smile again. "I've just gotten through talking with him."

Logan and Sabrina exchanged a glance, but made no reply.

"Look," added Stillman, a model of sweet reason, "no one denies you've had some interesting results. But when there are legitimate questions about methodology, we've got an obligation to raise them."

Abruptly, Logan knew what this was about. "You want to take over this drug, don't you?"

"That's a hell of an accusation," said the other, without missing a beat. "Let's just say that, given the history of this protocol, it's pretty obvious it could use an experienced guiding hand." He looked from one to the other. "I'd even say Compound J's finished without it."

"No," said Sabrina flatly. "We don't even want to talk with you!"

Stillman shot her daggers. *"You* don't want to talk to *me?* Perhaps you fail to grasp the position you're in."

"You're doing this to us only because your own protocol has shown no results. Anyone can see that!"

Logan could see the effort it took for the man to retain a semblance of calm. *No one* spoke to the esteemed Gregory Stillman this way. "Well," he said, "why don't we just let your boyfriend, the principle investigator here, answer for himself?"

"So we would still have a major role?" asked Logan evenly.

"Absolutely. This has been your baby. I don't for a second flatter myself that I could pull this off without you."

An astonishing admission. This guy wanted this thing *bad.*

But Logan's interest in the proposition was as counterfeit as his seeming calm. The bastard's intention couldn't have been clearer if he posted it on the bulletin board in the administration building: Compound J was to become a Stillman project. Their dogged work with the compound would earn them nothing more than inclusion among a long list of junior associates—if that. For who could doubt that, once Stillman had his hands on their research, he'd cut them out entirely?

"I take it Reston's already agreed to this?" asked Logan.

"Happily. After all, his bottom line is the same as mine: he only wants to see this drug succeed."

Logan paused thoughtfully. "Well, then, I hope you enjoy working with John Reston as much as we have."

Stillman's face darkened. "That's it? That's what you have to tell me?"

"Yes," said Sabrina, taking Logan's hand, "that is it."

"Fine," snapped the other, turning on his heel. "See you inside."

Whatever satisfaction the exchange with Stillman gave them vanished the moment they reentered the room. At the table, where Boudin and Byrne had been, sat . . . Ray Coopersmith.

He wore the same anxious expression Logan remembered from their meeting at the Hotel Jefferson. How long ago was that? Nine months? Ten? Only, now his hair was neatly trimmed and his suit, gray with muted pinstripes, appeared to be brand-new.

"Dr. Coopersmith," began Larsen, "we understand you met some time ago with Dr. Logan."

"November sixth." He looked around the room and smiled broadly. "A Saturday."

"And this was at your instigation?"

"His."

"That's another lie," said Logan.

"Dr. Logan, I am ready to conduct this hearing without you."

"I'm just supposed to sit here? I don't even get to present my side?"

Larsen's voice grew even colder. " 'Your side?' You had almost a year to inform me that you had met with Dr. Coopersmith. It was your choice not to do so. Unless you deny that such a meeting occurred."

Logan made no response.

"I thought not." He turned to Coopersmith. "I promise you, that won't happen again. Now, perhaps you might fill us in on your background with this institution."

Coopersmith exhaled dramatically. "I was a junior associate here five years ago. And I was good too."

Larsen nodded. "That strikes me as a fair assessment."

"But I screwed up. I was working on a Phase Two prostate cancer trial." He momentarily stared down at the table, downcast. "I altered some data."

There was a silence in the room—a sympathetic silence.

"It was stupid. I'm trying to live it down."

"Why do you think Dr. Logan wanted to see you?"

"I knew it the moment I saw him, he's one of these sons of bitches just out for the glory."

They waited for him to continue, but instead he looked back down at the table.

"Yes . . . ?"

"He wanted to know how to pull the same thing. Just in case."

"He told you that?"

"Sure. How to rework data that wasn't working for him, how to get away with underreporting toxicity, all that shit."

To Logan, it was as if the talk was of someone else. It was so preposterous, under other circumstances he'd have been embarrassed for the guy. *Who in his right mind would ever buy any of this?*

"You talked about underreporting toxicity?"

"I told him it's not that easy. It's a shell game. To do it right, you need a ton of legitimate data so the bad stuff gets lost. You need people."

"And what did Dr. Logan say to that?"

"He said that was no problem."

What could they have offered to get him here? Reinstatement? Right— when Porky Pig becomes the head of the ACF! Probably nothing more than a few kind words.

Coopersmith gave a sudden maniacal grin. "Of course, he also wanted to talk about you, Dr. Larsen. And you, Dr. Stillman."

"About Dr. Stillman and me?"

"He said you screwed him over every chance you got." The grin grew even wider. "He told me he hated your fucking guts. He said you were scum."

Larsen turned to glare at Logan. Despite himself, the moment actually gave him a surge of pleasure.

"He called you assholes." Coopersmith, clearly improvising wildly, couldn't have been enjoying himself more. "*Fucking* assholes. He said he wanted to show you up and I was the man to show him how."

"And how would that happen?" Larsen soberly asked, as if the man before him were something other than a certifiable lunatic.

Logan felt a presence looming behind him. Instinctively, he turned —Seth Shein!

"He said he knew how fucked up you were, he'd play *mind games* with you. Both of you."

Shein had been staring in bewilderment at Coopersmith, but at this last, Logan saw him break into a broad smile. It matched his own.

At last, someone was on their side!

"Did he make any other remarks about senior personnel at the ACF?"

"Yeah," cut in Shein, "he said everyone was an asshole!" He began pointing around the table. "You, you, you, you, and me, assholes! That's just the way we've all heard Dan Logan talk, isn't it?" He eyed Larsen with contempt. "What the hell you think you're doing here?"

But Larsen only smiled. "Dr. Shein, I'm so pleased you could join us. Won't you take a seat?"

"I'm comfortable here."

"Dr. Coopersmith, we thank you. You've been very helpful."

"I should go?" he asked uncertainly.

"Please. Thank you."

Rising from the table, he walked from the room, glancing blankly at Logan as he did so.

"So you found Dr. Coopersmith's presentation enlightening?"

"Come off it, Larsen, it's not *news* you're an asshole! You really think anyone's gonna believe this?"

At this, Larsen began going crimson. Logan felt like leaping from his chair and embracing Shein.

"The p-point," stammered Larsen, "is that these people conspired with a known fraud. Dr. Logan's clear intention was to fabricate data. We have just heard that—"

"We've heard bullshit. That's all you've got, bullshit!"

"Forget that," interrupted Stillman, "none of that matters. Let's cut right to the chase. The real point, as Dr. Shein knows, is that this protocol has become an embarrassment."

"Is that what I know?" shot back Shein.

"Forgive me—as Dr. Shein *should* know." He cast Shein a malevolent glance. "But perhaps, being someone who gave a group of incompetent young doctors the power of life and death over a group of women, he really doesn't know."

Shein just glared at him.

"And the result," continued Stillman, "has been tragic." He stood to face his rival and indicated the empty chair at the table. "My question for you now is simple: Are you ready to go on record continuing to defend these people and their protocol?"

"This protocol has merit, Stillman," he said, but with considerably less fire.

"Is that your answer? You are willing, then, to assume public responsibility for any further patient deaths that result?"

Shein stood there, his face at once showing anger and intense anxiety.

"Well, we're waiting," piled on Larsen, his pleasure at sticking it to his wiseass tormentor all too evident. "I should tell you that we are prepared to bring in Dr. Markell to offer his views."

For a moment longer Shein stood silent. "Fuck it," he announced finally, "the protocol's a goddamn bust."

Stillman beamed. "Would you care to elaborate?"

Shein glared his way. "You wanna hear me say it? All right, this kid Logan got in way over his head." In the bat of an eyelash, his hesitancy gave way to resolve. "Logan's got some talent, but he's arrogant, he doesn't know when to listen. He takes stupid risks."

"Then we all agree," said Stillman evenly. He nodded again at the chair. "I'd appreciate your joining us. *Please.*"

Logan and Sabrina, about to be cast to their fate, exchanged a glance as Shein assumed his place at the table.

"The three of you may leave now," said Larsen, indicating the Compound J team.

The letters Logan and Sabrina received that evening were identical:

> *You are hereby advised that your contract with the American Cancer Foundation has been terminated, effective immediately.*

"You know, we can probably get you out of this," Logan ventured. He watched Sabrina closely, awaiting a reaction. Glancing in the direction of the bar, she appeared not to have even heard. "In some ways, the change will be not bad for me," she said. "At Regina Elena, they do very good work also. Serious oncology."

"It's me they want to stick it to," he pressed. "Stillman, even Larsen—if I take full responsibility for this thing, they'll probably let you stay."

She looked across the table, wide-eyed. "Why? *Why* would I wish to pretend I did not do what I did? Why would I *want* to stay?"

Logan realized, too late, he'd underestimated her. He had been certain, at the very least, she would find the gesture touching. Instead, she remained as frustratingly levelheaded as he, at that moment, was veering toward self-pity.

The worst of it—the part neither of them wanted to discuss, but which Logan's proposal had partly been designed to address—was that they'd no longer have each other. The ACF had always been, literally, their common ground. Stripped of her standing at the Foundation, for Sabrina there was not even the possibility of work at a comparable level outside of Italy.

They would be an ocean apart.

Logan took a sip of his vodka martini; the first time in a year he'd ordered anything stronger than wine. "I don't know," he said, "it seemed like the right thing to say."

"No, it was not the right thing." She reached a hand across the table. "But I understand. *Grazie*."

He could see that already, on some level, she was pulling away in self-protection. Probably he should do the same.

"At least at Regina Elena, they make me feel I am welcome," she said. "Maybe at home we don't have all the resources you have here, but what counts most is people."

"When do they want you?"

"They say at the end of October. But I must go sooner, I think." She momentarily averted her eyes. "The faster to leave, the better."

"You're right."

"And you, Logan?"

He shrugged. "Don't know yet."

"You cannot go back to Claremont?"

"Not a chance. You ever hear the expression 'Out of the frying pan, into the fire'?" He paused. "I'm thinking I might go home for a little while and mull things over."

"To Decatur?" she asked, surprised.

"Just for a week or two. Get organized, sort out my options."

"I see." She sipped her beer. "Your father will welcome you?"

"Who knows? But they say home is the place that, when you go there, they've got to take you in."

"What I mean—he'll understand when you tell what has happened here?"

"Well, it would definitely be better if I were going under other circumstances." He looked at her tenderly. "And with you."

Instantly, her reserve melted away. She gave his hand a tender squeeze. "One day, Logan. I promise."

Logan headed out of town the same morning Sabrina flew out of Dulles for Rome. The trip to Decatur can be made in as little as ten hours, but he didn't press it. He spent the night in a motel, then decided to stop in Chicago for a leisurely lunch. On the phone he'd been vague with his father. He was, he said, planning to take "a hiatus" from his job at the ACF. Would it be okay if he stopped by Decatur for, say, eight or ten days?

He pulled up before the familiar gray clapboard house late afternoon the day after he'd left. Five minutes later, he was still sitting in the car, staring at the house, when the front door swung open and his father came ambling toward him.

It had been almost three years since Logan had laid eyes on him, and he was struck by how much he'd aged. Though he was still rail thin, at close to seventy his long face was deeply furrowed and his unkempt hair had gone completely white.

"Well, you gonna get out, or what?"

"Hi, Dad," he said, emerging. "Great to see you too."

"Don't get smart with me. Is that what they teach you at those places?"

"Actually, yes. You need it in self-defense."

"I'll bet you do, I'll just bet you do."

On his previous visit home, Logan might've laughed. Utterly unconscious of his own behavior, his father never failed to condemn the mean-spiritedness and authoritarianism he saw in others. The difference was that now the older man's take on the world—that invariably it is the ruthless and amoral who succeed—was no longer so easy to dismiss out of hand.

"Yeah. Well, that's one of the reasons I wanted to get away from that place. At least for a while."

"So when you planning to go back?"

"I don't know."

"*Are* you going back?"

He hesitated. "No."

There it was. Logan waited for the inevitable reaction; and, sure enough, the look that attached itself to the older man's face was the one he'd learned in earliest boyhood, disappointment mingling with scorn. "Great, just *great*! What the hell happened?"

"Maybe I can sit down first? Say hello to Mom?"

"You got fired, didn't you? Why the hell didn't you go into private practice like I told you?"

In spite of himself—he'd sworn he wouldn't be drawn into something like this—Logan felt his entire body tensing. "It's a lot more complicated than that."

"It always is."

"Look, I'm pretty tired."

His father snorted. "What'd you do, insult some muckety-muck? Or just screw up?"

The question was actually a comment, but this time Logan didn't let it pass. "I didn't do anything wrong at all, Dad."

His father studied him a moment. "Well, c'mon in and give us the bloody details. I guess it doesn't make a damn bit of difference now."

Billed by his mother as a welcome-home party, dinner that evening quickly degenerated into an even sharper reminder of why, all those years ago, Logan had been so anxious to get away.

"I'm not touching that," announced the fourth family member at the table, his older sister Cathy, as soon as the main course appeared. "You know perfectly well I don't eat meat."

"Oh, darling, I really didn't know that included fowl," fretted his mother, the peacemaker. "Duck is Danny's favorite. Couldn't you this once make an exception?"

"No, mother, no exceptions. This isn't a game, it's my body we're talking about."

"Well, that's the stupidest damn thing I ever heard!" snorted her father.

"C'mon, Dad, it's not as if it's news. Cathy's been a vegetarian for ten years," said Logan.

"Daniel, I prefer to be called Catherine now."

If, as a psychologist would doubtless observe, both the Logan children were living their lives largely in reaction to their father, Cathy's rebellion was probably the more far reaching, an ongoing battle against every attitude and value imposed upon her in that home. Where Logan shared his father's vast respect for traditional learning, Cathy was open to every crackpot notion that came down the pike; where he had always drawn sustenance from the larger world, she was intensely inner directed. She ran a shop that sold locally handmade artifacts. For friends, she chose aging, over-the-hill veterans of the Age of Aquarius. "Pea brains," her father called them.

And yet, in at least one key respect, she was more like the older man than Logan could ever imagine being, for she was as intractable, and every bit as opinionated. It could not have been coincidence that she'd remained so close to home, or that, for all the battling, she stopped by to see their parents at least a couple of times a week.

"Well, Catherine," replied Logan, wondering again how he'd let himself be drawn into this, "I suppose I should insist that you call me *Dr.* Logan."

"Frankly," she said coolly, "I don't know how anyone who professes to know about the human body could put that poison into himself."

"We're all gonna die anyway," observed their father.

"Listen, Catherine," said Logan, "there is absolutely no data to support this thesis of yours that people will drop dead from occasionally eating meat. None. Human physiology is a lot more complicated than that."

"I question the validity of that statement," she sneered.

"What's that supposed to mean?"

"All your alleged data is collected by people whose minds are already made up. Doctors are just in cahoots with the drug companies and you know it."

Their father laughed. "She's got you there."

"What, you're opposed to drugs too?"

"Absolutely. My friend Lucy had breast cancer and they gave her chemotherapy. After every treatment she vomited for hours, and her hair started to fall out. Do you call that natural?"

This was a ludicrous conversation; the equivalent of a big-league ballplayer trying to explain the fine points of sliding technique to someone who doesn't know where the bases are. "I happen to know something about breast cancer," he said. "What would you suggest as an alternative?"

"Native Americans use yucca plants."

"Oh, yes? And do you have any data on *their* cure rate?"

"Catherine made me some yucca plant tea for my arthritis," cut in their mother. "I found it very helpful."

Their father held up his hand to indicate this phase of the conversation was over, a peremptory gesture Logan had seen a thousand times before. "So," he said, turning to his son, "I want to hear about your plans."

Logan blanched; he needed time to prepare for this. "I have a number of options," he equivocated.

"What?"

"Well, I do have one offer."

"Where's that?"

"New York City."

His father looked mildly interested. "In a private practice? With a hospital?"

In fact, the offer wasn't quite firm—and it was from neither a private practice nor a hospital. Among the first people he'd called after the ax fell was his friend Ruben Perez. Perez was now working part-time at a small start-up company in lower Manhattan, a research lab involved in AIDS drug delivery systems—and he was pretty sure the guy in charge could use someone with Logan's credentials.

The job held minimal interest or prestige, and the pay would not be high. Logan would do almost anything to avoid taking it. "I don't want to get into that now. As I say, I want to do some asking around. I plan to make calls all next week." He turned to his father. "Don't worry, I'll reimburse you for the phone bill."

"I'm not worried, I know you will."

"I don't see how you can even begin to defend doctors," said Cathy sharply, "after what they've done to you."

"That's not fair, Catherine. It's really not."

In the silence that followed, Logan poured himself a second glass of wine.

"I've been looking over the latest data on Elizabeth Rivers," said Kenneth Markell, indicating the foot-high pile of folders on his desk. "I've spent the past two hours on it, as a matter of fact."

Distractedly, he picked up the top folder and opened it. Like the others, it was marked "E. Cleveland" on its outside cover; the code name was the one Stillman had decided on right at the start, the afternoon three months before when the case had been tossed into his lap.

"I hear from that son of a bitch at the White House, Malcolm, almost every day. Did you know that?"

"I'm not surprised," said Stillman evenly. "Our problem is also their problem."

"The way they see it, their problem is our problem." Markell paused. "And frankly, Greg, let me put this as bluntly as I can—as far as I'm concerned, our problem is your problem."

Right, thought Stillman, *as if, if the shit really hit the fan and the politicos went head-hunting at the ACF, his would be the one they'd be after*. "I've been aware of that for some time, sir," he said, "and I accept it."

Markell flipped through the folder, as if on further study he might find some reason for encouragement. "Look, the bottom line is this: The standard chemo isn't working."

"It's only been a month, she's only had two cycles. I'd like to try at least one more." In fact, the three drugs involved in the treatment— doxorubicin, cyclophosphamide, and 5-fluorouracil—were the most active established agents against breast malignancy. Over the years, both these men had used them with considerable success. "I do see some real positives. She tolerates this combination extremely well, there've been almost no side effects to speak of."

"Christ, Stillman, the tumor's growing right through the stuff! If I didn't know better, I'd think the chemo was actually feeding the malignancy!"

Stillman nodded. "And how aware are they of her progress at the White House?"

"They're not idiots, Marty. You don't think much of Burke, neither do I, but he is an M.D. He can read X rays."

The latest X rays were what had them both so concerned. Not only was the tumor in her lung growing, it now appeared as a nodular density.

"Well, then, he also shouldn't expect magic," countered Stillman, with quiet vehemence.

"Ah, but that's the thing of it—they do. They're looking for you to treat her with a goddamn magic wand." Markell rose to his feet. "It's time to try and give it to them. I want to go experimental. Let's talk about the results of your protocol."

Caught short, Stillman took a moment to collect himself. "Well," he said, smiling, "I haven't killed anybody."

He was gratified to see Markell smile back. "That's not exactly the kind of endorsement I had in mind."

"Maybe not. But in experimental breast treatments around here lately, that makes it unique."

"I agree, you were on target about that." Markell shook his head. "That's all our friends at the White House would have needed right now, a public stink about some kid doctor at the ACF hyping his results."

"On breast cancer."

"Where's Logan going, anyway?"

"I have no idea. One of them's still around, though—Reston, the one who came clean. He's got promise, why not give him a break?"

Markell looked at him with sudden impatience; who the hell did Stillman think he was kidding with this show of ersatz magnanimity? "We've already had this conversation, Greg. What I want to hear about now is dyronium nitrate. Tell me about your results."

"Look, I believe in this drug. Let's begin with that."

"Why? On the basis of what data?"

"We don't have all our data in yet. But we've already had some encouraging responses. No appreciable tumor shrinkage, but seventeen of the thirty-eight women on the protocol have shown considerable periods of stabilization."

"How considerable?"

"In several cases, we're at six months and counting."

Markell sat back down behind his desk. Briefly, he seemed to focus on an abstract painting at the far end of his large office. "I know you want to be a hero on this one, Greg," he said, "I know that you want to make her well."

"Isn't that what *they* want?"

He nodded. "But I think it's time to think about cutting losses. Let's put her on this stuff of yours. Maybe she won't get better—but your job right now is to see to it she doesn't get worse."

T hree days after he arrived, a Monday morning, Logan closed the door of the small den and settled onto the faded green love-seat that had been there as long as he could remember. On a small table beside him sat the same black rotary phone. Glancing down at the yellow legal pad in his lap, he picked up the receiver.

His plan was simple enough. There were twenty-seven comprehensive cancer centers in the United States; each so designated by the ACF for its record in basic research and the range of clinical trials and community programs it sponsored. Before this week was over, he intended to hit every one of them.

As an intellectual proposition, Logan knew not to be overly optimistic; if nothing else, the experience he'd just lived through had taught him how quickly a seeming sure thing can blow up in one's face. Still, he couldn't help himself. He'd been around, he knew his relative worth in the biomedical community. Hadn't he, a mere year and a half before, been among the prize recruits in the nation? And—never mind the recent unpleasantness—it was reasonable to assume that his time at the ACF could only have increased his market value.

His first call, to the Washington Memorial Cancer Center in St. Louis, quickly confirmed that feeling. Here, as at a dozen other institutions around the country, Logan enjoyed the advantage of already knowing a higher-up—in this case a crackerjack oncologist named Bradley Merritt, formerly associated with Claremont Hospital.

Since he ran into one of those automated phone systems that refused to deal with his rotary phone, it took Logan several minutes to reach his office. But when he did, Merritt had his secretary put through the call immediately.

"Dan Logan," he said, with a heartiness Logan had never before associated with him, "what a terrific surprise!"

"Well, Brad, just thought I'd say hello," he tried to respond in kind.

"Believe it or not, I was talking about you just the other day—about how many of the best and the brightest seem to come out of that place." He laughed. "I probably should've appreciated it more at the time."

There was more small talk about Claremont and assorted souls they'd both known there, before Merritt flipped the subject to today. "I assume you're not calling just to reminisce."

Logan chuckled. "No—much as I enjoy it. Frankly, I want to find out how things are over there. The sorts of research you're involved in, the quality of the work environment."

"You're asking if there are any openings?"

"I always like to keep my ears open. And my options."

"What about the ACF? You've got to have—what?—another year or so on that contract." There was no trace of suspicion in this. In fact, Logan had the impression he was trying to restrain his enthusiasm.

"Oh, we don't exactly see eye to eye on some things. They know I'm looking around." A variation on what he'd decided would be his standard explanation.

"When could you come aboard?"

"Uh, I don't know." Caught by surprise, Logan paused a moment. "Probably pretty soon. But, I should tell you, this is the first call I've made. I'm going to want to see what else is out there."

"You're not going to do better than here. A top-notch facility, quality people. . . . The governing philosophy is to go after the best—then give them the lab space, and the freedom, to pursue their passions."

Logan couldn't believe it: the guy was *desperate* for him. What Merritt couldn't know was how appealing it sounded. Logan ached for a lab where he could pursue independent research—and one line of inquiry in particular. "Sounds good," he acknowledged blandly.

"Look, Dan, do me a favor. Don't call anyone else today. Let me speak to the director here and see what kind of package we can put together. Will you do that for me?"

"I guess so." Logan chuckled. "Only, what am I supposed to do now with the rest of the day?"

"Thanks, Dan, really. Just sit tight. I'll get back to you."

The call came that evening, shortly after dinner. Logan took it in the same room. As soon as he heard Merritt's voice, stripped of all animation, he knew something had gone terribly wrong.

"Uh, listen, Dan," he began, "I've spoken to our top guys."

"Yeah . . . ?"

"It seems we're in a holding pattern right now. No new hires at all."

"Oh. I see."

"Look, I'm terribly sorry. I hope I didn't lead you on."

"Not at all." No need to prolong this; it was agony for both of them.

"Good. Look, I'm sure you'll land something terrific."

"Oh, yeah."

But the knot in Logan's stomach meant he already suspected otherwise. On some level, this is what he'd been fearing—that, somehow, he'd been tainted.

Over the next two days, he called every one of the remaining eleven institutions in which he knew a senior staffer on a first-name basis. At most, he had no trouble accepting what he heard: sorry, money was tight, they just weren't hiring. But at no fewer than four, ranging from Scripps-Morgan in southern California to Boston's Revere Hospital, the St. Louis experience was repeated with only minor variation; strong initial enthusiasm unaccountably dissipating within twenty-four hours.

But, then, he knew what was happening—it was just a matter of facing it. At every one of those institutions, someone had checked in with the ACF.

"Look, Nick, just tell me what's going on?" Logan finally erupted when his last in-house source called with the bad news. "Who got to you guys?"

"That has nothing to do with it," came the mealy-mouthed reply. "You know how these things are, decisions that seem made get unmade."

Anyway, what was the point? Logan already knew the answer.

There was only one office at the ACF to which such calls would have been directed: that of Raymond Larsen.

By Thursday morning, as he set about cold-calling the second group of institutions on his list—those in which he would be known, if at all, only by reputation—Logan had reached a decision. At least in this initial approach, he would make no mention of his association with the ACF, acknowledging it only if the matter was raised on the other end. True enough, this could cause logistical problems. How to account for the previous eighteen months? How, indeed, to present himself as sufficiently credentialed as a cancer researcher to make a case for himself as a potential employee? Still, given the apparent alternatives—certain rejection versus at least the slim possibility of moving to the next step—the choice seemed obvious.

Then, again, by the end of that morning, he was convinced the point was moot. The five calls he made to assorted department of oncology heads and cancer center directors, or, more precisely, to their secretaries and assistants, produced not even a flicker of interest. More than that, in a couple of instances, judging from the knowing tone on the other end, he had the impression that his call had been *expected*.

Could it be that Larsen was actually seeking out potential employees and blacklisting him? Why? Could those bastards really be so vindictive they'd want to *bury* him?

Or—this was equally a possibility—maybe he just starting to lose it. Making these calls *was* hard, a violent assault on his already battered ego; seeing himself as victim was, in its way, safer. It was certainly easier. Sometimes now he found himself overcome by a wave of hopelessness so intense that for minutes at a time he couldn't bring himself to move, let alone pick up the phone. *What miserably wrong turn had his life taken that had him sitting here day after day, staring at those damn pine-paneled walls and the pictures his father had stuck up of dogs playing cards, getting crapped on by people who didn't know the first thing about him?*

Thursday afternoon, at one of these low ebbs, he even came close to calling Dr. Sidney Karpe, the eminent private practitioner who'd so assiduously wooed him before he'd decided to go to the ACF. But, no—what was he thinking? Karpe had been furious at the time; he'd *relish* the opportunity to get even, and then spend the next six months dining on the story of the little bastard who'd tried to come crawling back after he couldn't cut it at the ACF.

Instead, he picked up the phone and dialed 011 39 6—the country and city codes for Italy and Rome—followed by the six digits Sabrina had scribbled down in his address book. Instituto Regina Elena.

It took several minutes for the receptionist to track her down. As he waited, Logan could hear the sounds of a busy hospital, at once familiar and exotic: footfalls on a hard corridor, the chime of nearby elevators arriving and departing, a "Dottore Ferlito" being paged over the PA system; occasionally, young women—nurses?—exchanging scraps of conversation, the language so melodic, it might have been poetry. Logan tried to imagine the scene, but with little success. All he could summon up were the grim Italian hospitals in vintage movies, where all the nurses were nuns in white habits.

"Logan, it is you!"

"Who else?" He'd thought about this moment for days; now that it was here, he was determined not to show her the depth of his distress. "I've been missing you, Sabrina. A lot."

"I also, dear one." She laughed, a marvelous sound. "You see, it is so easy for me to say from far away."

"You sound great. You doing okay?"

"Yes, I think so."

The distance made it somewhat awkward, but less so than he'd feared.

"So I guess it's been an adjustment."

"Not so much. We have electricity here also, Logan, even some of the modern drugs."

"I meant in a positive way—that it's not the ACF."

"No. Thank goodness." She paused and her voice fell. "I must tell you something, Logan. Larsen, he called the *direttore* of this hospital, saying bad things about me. Untrue things."

He was less caught by surprise than he pretended. "That son of a bitch! How'd he respond?"

"*She*. Her name is Antonella Torrucci. She told him to go screw his own face, she doesn't want to hear this. She knows me for years, far better than him."

He laughed, imagining Larsen's reaction at the receiving end.

"That's great! One small victory for humankind!" Then, despite himself, "I envy you."

There was a brief awkward silence. "And you, Logan? What's happening?"

"I'm still looking. I'm working on it."

"You are okay?"

"Of course."

But he suspected she'd already guessed that he wasn't, and it left him with an empty, helpless feeling. There was another pause.

"Listen, Logan, I must go. I am on duty."

"I'll call you soon. As soon as I know something."

"Ciaò, my love." He heard a kissing sound. *"Ti amo."*

A moment later Logan was staring down at his yellow pad. There remained seven institutions on the list. But by now, he wasn't even sure it was worth the trouble trying them.

John Reston was frustrated. He hadn't expected it to be like this. Hadn't he done his penance, offered up mea culpas till they were coming out of his ears? Yet still they didn't trust him. What did he have to do to put the past behind him, bring them Logan's head on a fucking platter with an apple in its mouth? Others at his level, a lot less sharp than he, were right at the center of the work on Stillman's protocol, a sure road to glory. And here was he, still in Kratsas's lab, still doing shit work.

So when he got the call to report to Stillman's office, he made it over in less than five minutes.

"Close the door," said Stillman, "take a seat."

Reston perched on the edge of it. "I was hoping you'd call. I was going to come over and see you."

"Good, I like that attitude. Because I've got important plans for you."

"Thank God, I'm going stir crazy down there." Reston smiled. He was about to hear about Stillman's wonder drug. At long last, he was being ushered into the charmed circle.

Stillman hesitated, seeming to study his face. "Tell me about Compound J."

"Compound J?" Reston was more than just baffled, he was mortified. Wouldn't they ever let him forget Compound J?

"And the other one. What'd you call it, Compound J-lite?"

"I guess you could say it was sort of like being on the *Titanic*—with someone else at the helm."

"You participated in the research, didn't you?"

"It was Logan's baby. Always."

Stillman leaned forward. "But Dr. Logan's gone, isn't he? And so is Dr. Como. You're here."

Reston sat there blankly. For the life of him, he couldn't figure what the senior man was getting at. "The whole thing was a disaster," he said. "All I want to do now is forget about it."

"I'm interested in your honest feeling about these compounds. As one who was personally involved."

"I think they stink. I think they're killers."

"No, Doctor," he said, with sudden impatience, "no one else is here, I want you to level with me. What are their strengths and liabilities? Why was the decision made to go back to the lab in the first place? What structural problems were identified with the molecule?"

Reston hesitated and Stillman moved quickly to reassure him. "I promise you, should we resume research on these compounds, you shall continue to play a prominent role. You can take that as a personal guarantee."

It took a moment to penetrate. "You're thinking of doing more work on Compound J? *Why?*"

"I'm not dogmatic, I'm a scientist. The drug did show some activity."

Reston laughed uneasily. "Too goddamn much activity."

"Yes, of course." From the top drawer of his desk he removed a sketch. Reston recognized it as the chemical structure for Compound J. "Clearly, in your conversations, you discussed ways of mitigating the toxicity problem. I'd like to know what they were."

"But aren't you focused on your own protocol?"

In the split second it took Stillman to answer—"I can do both"— Reston began to suspect the truth. *This fucker's own drug doesn't work!*

But simultaneously, Stillman was reaching a disturbing conclusion of his own. "Tell me, Doctor, do you even know the chemical structure of Compound J-lite?"

There was an undercurrent of menace to the question, and Reston caught it. But there was no way he could bluff this one. "I lived and breathed Compound J for almost a year," he said, falling back on bravado instead. "Short of Logan, I know more about the stuff than anyone."

"Uh-huh."

"The work in the lab isn't exactly my strong suit, but I took notes."

Stillman didn't believe him, not for a second. Fleetingly, he wondered just how much this guy might shoot off his mouth. "Good, I'll want to see those."

"I think I still have them around somewhere. I dumped a lot of the protocol stuff."

"Sure, bad memories and all." Stillman smiled congenially. "As I say, so far it's only a vague possibility. But if we do pursue this, you'll be key."

"Good." The meeting was clearly over, and Reston rose to his feet. "Till then, maybe you can find me something else worth doing around here."

"Absolutely, I'll see to it." Stillman nodded. "In the meantime, of course, we never had this conversation."

Throughout the latter half of his stay, Logan's father had been uncharacteristically restrained. After the call from St. Louis, the one which had left his son so crestfallen, he'd not asked even once about the progress of the search.

"So . . . ?" he finally put it to Logan on Saturday morning, as they drove down Webster Avenue, the town's main street, in his six-year-old Chevy.

Here it comes, thought Logan. "So *what?*"

They were en route to the library, one of his father's weekly routines. A voracious but indiscriminate reader, he'd haul home ten or twelve volumes per trip, everything from Herodotus to Jackie Collins.

"So what the hell are your plans? Or do you plan to make a career of feeling sorry for yourself?"

Teeth gritted, Logan said nothing. He just stared out the window at the passing storefronts, so much shabbier than he remembered them. *No question, this guy'd give Seth Shein a run for his money any day.*

"Dad, when are you going to lay off? Why don't you just let people live their own lives?"

"Don't be a fool. You sound like your sister."

"I'm going back to New York, all right? I'm probably going to take a job that I'm incredibly overqualified for!"

He'd reached the decision just the evening before, and called Ruben Perez to make sure the spot was still open. The pay was minimal, just $34,000 per year, but working was better than not working.

"And whose fault is that supposed to be?" asked his father.

He sighed wearily. "No one's, Dad, no one's fault. I guess I'll be leaving in a couple of days."

"You know, I'll never forget that nickel cadmium storage battery you rigged up for the science fair. Useless, but very interesting. It showed a lot of promise."

"Right. Thanks."

Over the years, his father had brought up the storage battery regularly, as if all of Logan's subsequent accomplishments paled by comparison. Invention had been the older man's own early passion, as well as his most enduring source of disappointment. Forty years before, while in the Navy, he'd concocted an industrial-strength cleaning fluid—but failed to have it properly patented. A few years later, it was in general use in factories and shipyards, and someone else was cashing in.

"I'll bet you think I did a lot of things wrong, don't you?" he asked suddenly.

Logan looked at him, staring straight ahead at the road. *Him? Everything.* "Look, there's no sense in getting into any of that. I'm sure you did the best you could."

"Damn right I did!" He pressed slightly on the accelerator. "Sure, I know I might've done more with myself. You don't think it bugs me?"

Logan turned back to him in surprise. Never before had he heard such an admission from his father.

"I look at this business of you and the ACF," he continued, "and it just tees me off. They're trying to do the same thing to you they did to me."

"Thanks, Dad."

"I just think it's awful. The world is full of miserable bastards who think they can get away with anything."

"You're right." Logan nodded, feeling better than he had in weeks. "That's it exactly."

"Well . . . you just keep doing your work, that's what counts."

Logan nodded. "I know."

"That's the best way to fight 'em. It's what I should've done." His father fell silent for a few seconds. "And how about staying in a little better touch? Your mother misses you."

D an Logan was relieved to find that his prospective new boss was more than just a money-grubbing cynic. Alex Severson had abso-lute faith in his idea: what he took to be a novel method of targeting HIV-infected cells while bypassing healthy ones. Having patented it, the young biochemist had devoted the past year and a half to raising money for his own start-up biotech company, HIV-EX.

The problem—and Logan saw this almost as quickly—was that the guy was a far better promoter than he was a scientist. Like so many others behind small biotech companies, Severson was trying to stuff something down Nature's throat—in this case, the notion that a drug delivery system might be made to seek and destroy selected cells while leaving others untouched. Appealing as such an idea might be in theory, plausible as it was to hopeful and unsophisticated investors, Logan knew that in practice it was close to an impossibility. Already in his brief career, he'd seen countless similar ideas bite the dust.

Which made for an awkward situation. Given his reservations about Severson's project, Logan just wasn't sure he could bring to the job the commitment the other had every right to expect. Nor, frankly, was he crazy about the idea of being subordinate to someone of such obviously limited gifts.

On the other hand, Severson seemed desperate to have him; so much so, the young entrepreneur was ready to augment the modest salary with stock in his company—plus, far more significant in Logan's view, unlimited use of the lab during off hours.

"I understand you're a creative guy," assured Severson. "That's why I want you."

"I'll tell you the truth," Logan told him, struggling with it even as they talked, "I'm very tempted. I'm just really not sure there's enough work here for the two of us." He glanced around the converted loft space that was HIV-EX world headquarters, trying to conceal his distress; the equipment, what little there was, looked to be reconditioned surplus. "Wouldn't there be a lot of replication of effort?"

"None at all," Severson dismissed this. "You'll be my director of basic research, I defer to your greater skills in the lab."

"And you?"

"I'm president and CEO, I don't even *want* to hang around this place. My job is to get out there and round up money."

"How much have you raised so far?"

Severson gave him two thumbs up. "Nine hundred forty thousand and counting. I'm finding I'm pretty good at it."

Logan could see that. He was increasingly aware that in what is known as the real world the distinction between reality and wishful thinking can be remarkably tenuous. As a salesman Severson didn't just spin a good story—more vitally, he believed it himself.

Logan figured, in fact, that it was this very capacity for self-delusion that now had Severson regarding him as a prestige hire.

"Look," he was saying now, moving into hard-sell mode, "I know how this place must look to a guy like you. We don't throw money at equipment, we don't buy three of something if one will do. But lean and mean has its advantages, starting with the fact that you'll pretty much be your own boss. Could you ever say that at the ACF?" He smiled, and Logan wondered if he might know something of his recent past after all. But, no—if that were the case, he wouldn't be here. "The fact is, I'm one helluva great guy to work for. You do the work and I'm happy, period, end of story. Ask Perez."

No question, the pitch had its points—not the least of which was the chance to work closely with his old friend. Since Ruben, the company's only other on-site employee, was a sort of all-purpose assistant in the lab, the two of them would be together almost constantly.

As soon as they were alone, Logan threw an arm over his friend's shoulder. "So that's the big bonus of being here, your company?"

"Eight hours a day, every day." Perez laughed. "Just remember, I got seniority. If it's a conflict between the Mets and the Yankees on the radio, we go with the Yanks."

"Fine," said Logan. "If you're gonna play hardball"—he paused to give his friend a chance to grimace—"I'm gonna make *you* listen to classical music."

Perez smirked. "And I thought things around here couldn't get any worse."

Logan's gaze took in his surroundings, fixing on the phony wood paneling, buckling in the middle, that lined an entire wall. "They can't."

"You're right, this is the Bowery of biomedical research. But, you know what? No one gives you any shit here either. Personally, I'll take it over Claremont Hospital any day."

"The Bowery, nice. As in: nowhere lower to sink."

"I wouldn't say that," said Perez, faintly impatient. "Working the hospital on Riker's Island might be lower. Look, it's a job, not a career." And a job, moreover, that Perez had put himself out to secure for him.

Logan nodded. "I know you're right. I've just gotta keep thinking that."

Sabrina had to make the trip, if only to satisfy her intense curiosity. True enough, she had nothing more than an address: Philusstrasse 29. A call to the local directory had failed to locate even a telephone number. More ominously, her own letters to Herr Kistner had gone unanswered.

Still, she couldn't let it rest there, not knowing for sure. The first Friday in December, not due back at the hospital till Sunday, she headed out to the airport and bought a ticket for Cologne.

When she arrived in early afternoon, she was surprised to find the temperature a good twenty degrees cooler than that in Rome.

"Bringen Sie mich bitte zum Kölner Dom," she instructed the cabbie. *Take me to the cathedral, please.*

As they entered the city proper, brilliantly decked out for Christmas, there the historic building suddenly loomed, majestic, in the midst of square miles of postwar construction.

"Wie ist es passiert? Wie hat er ürberlebt?" How did it happen? How did it survive?

He shrugged. "I am too young, I wasn't here. But they say the English pilots were under orders not to hit the cathedral. They say that after a while people knew to run there whenever there was an air raid. Are you going to go inside?"

"I don't have time just now. Please, if you could just circle around it so I can have a look."

When he stopped at a light at the edge of the crowded square, she handed him a slip of paper with the address. "Is this very far?"

"*Nein, Fräulein.* Just a little bit over in that direction."

It turned out to be a brick building of four stories. She half believed the name wouldn't be there, but there it was, the first of eight listed on the directory: R. Kistner. He was on the ground floor.

She pushed the buzzer. Though she could hear it ring in an apartment just off the lobby on the other side of the glass front door, there was no response. She rang again. Nothing.

Dispirited, she stood there a long moment. What now? Perhaps she should find a hotel room and come back later. Or leave a note.

She wandered outside into the cold, and was hit with another blast of frigid air. On a bench across the street huddled several figures. Shivering, she hurried toward them.

"*Entschuldigen Sie, bitte,*" she said to the one closest at hand, an elderly woman. *Excuse me.*

The woman did not move.

"I am trying to find someone. Perhaps you can help."

She gazed up at her with watery eyes. "You are not from around here."

"No." She hesitated. "His name is Rudolf Kistner. He lives in that building."

The woman looked at her companions. "No. I do not know."

"Perhaps"—Sabrina turned hopefully to the others, a man and a woman, equally bundled up—"one of you might know."

Neither even looked in her direction.

"We do not know," said the woman.

"Thank you." Sabrina started moving off. "I will leave him a note."

Having composed it and wedged it into Kistner's mailbox, she again left the building. She was searching the street for a cab when she became aware of the old man from the bench coming toward her. Though he used a cane, he moved remarkably well. Stepping aside, she watched him enter the lobby; then, though aware of her eyes upon him, proceed to the mailbox and begin reading her note.

"Herr Kistner?" she said, pushing through the front door.

He looked at her a moment; then back down at the note.

"I can *tell* you who I am. I am from the American Cancer Foundation!"

Slowly he unwrapped his muff. The face that emerged was ancient, a thousand furrows beneath a shock of snow-white hair. If she'd had to guess, she'd have put his age at past ninety.

"In America?"

She nodded. "I have written you letters. I've been working on the study you inquired about. With Dr. Logan? Why didn't you speak to me out there?"

He ignored this. "And you are who? His assistant?"

Sabrina was wise enough not to take offense; it was likely that in his entire career in the lab, the old man before her had never worked with a woman as an equal.

"Actually, his associate."

"I am very old. I do not enjoy visitors."

"In your letters, you inquired about our progress. Since I happened to be in Cologne, I thought I might be able to tell you."

Unused to telling lies, Sabrina found that even this modest one came with great difficulty. But she'd come too far to risk being turned away now.

His damp, pale blue eyes opened a bit wider. "I will make an exception."

Wordlessly, he led her through the lobby and into the living room of his tidy apartment. She was reminded of her grandmother's place in Livorno; the same heavy turn-of-the-century furniture and odd assortment of Oriental rugs on the floor, the same musty odor and shelves heavy with leather-bound books.

"Forgive me," he said, turning almost courtly. "The housekeeper comes only once a week. May I get you some tea?"

"No, thank you."

He took a seat in a stiff-backed chair. She noticed on the table before him an electronic chess board. He was midway through a game.

"Do you play?" he asked.

"Just a little."

"Care to make a move?" He turned the game toward her.

Flushing slightly, she studied the board; she wasn't ready for such a test. "Pawn to King-six."

He smiled—she'd passed. *"Gut, sehr gut."* He looked up at her. "Now, please, tell me about your protocol. Your Dr. Logan did not give many details."

"We have had," she replied, choosing her words carefully, "very encouraging results. The drug is active, of this there is no doubt."

He leaned forward, as alert as any rabid fan at a sporting event. "Yes, I see."

"Unfortunately, toxicity remains a problem."

"Of course. As always. Can you give me the details? How many women have you had on this test?"

So she began at the beginning, in broad strokes recounting the entire history of the Compound J protocol, leaving out only the final, humbling chapters. The impression with which she deliberately left him was that the experiment was ongoing—and that both she and Logan were still running it.

"This brings me to something I wish to ask you," she said. "It is about Mikio Nakano, the Japanese chemist. In the letters you wrote of him with great admiration."

She thought she saw him start. "Yes? Perhaps I did."

"Can you tell me what happened to him? And to his work?"

He shook his head. *"Nein, nein.* I do not know. After he left our laboratory, I did not see him."

She gazed at him curiously. "But," she said, feeling in her pocket for the Xerox copy of the letter, "you wrote something to Dr. Logan. You wrote"—she studied the page—" 'I know he did not stop working on this problem.' " She looked up. "Is this not so, Herr Kistner?"

Again, he shook his head. "It was very long ago, I am sorry."

"But how did you know?" she pressed. "Were there rumors of such a thing? Did you perhaps hear about it somewhere?"

"No, I did not hear. I am old." Grasping the arms of his chair, he slowly lifted himself to his feet. "Sometimes I write things, even I do not know why."

Sabrina understood she was being dismissed. "I'm sorry to keep asking you this, Herr Kistner, but it is important. You have no idea what became of this man Nakano?"

"No, I am very sorry, miss." Taking up his cane, he started leading the way toward the door.

As they walked, Sabrina withdrew a business card. "Please," she said, handing it to him, "just one favor. If you do recall anything else, you will let me know?"

He held the card close to his face and squinted; then turned to her in surprise. "The Instituto Regina Elena in Rome?"

She nodded. "Our study had problems. You see, I am no longer welcome at the ACF. Neither is Dr. Logan."

Logan's spirits picked up somewhat once they got started. Obliged to spend at least a couple of hours each day in the P-3 facility, strictly isolated from the rest of the lab because it housed live HIV, he had to go about his work with the utmost precision and vigilance; any slip was potentially disastrous. It was not for nothing that, by statute, no sharp objects were permitted in this area, nor could any equipment be removed from it without exhaustive cleaning. Depression was an indulgence he could simply not afford.

Still, demanding as it was, the work would never be challenging. In other labs around the country, the P-3 facilities were thought of as the place to be, epicenters of cutting-edge AIDS research. At HIV-EX, what passed for pioneering work—Severson's own—had already been completed. The tasks that fell to Dan Logan were less those of a talented biochemist than a competent technician. In essence, his function was simply to prepare solutions of Severson's material and various anti-HIV drugs; then monitor their progress against a mix of normal cells and live HIV to establish whether HIV-EX technology was an advance over existing delivery systems. He was under no illusion that he would find significant data to support the thesis.

It was only after normal working hours that he was able to spread his creative wings. For at last, he was free to get back to work on Compound J.

Yet the primitive conditions held him back. Before, everywhere he'd worked, lab animals had been available virtually for the asking, with tumors preinduced by support staff. Here, animals had to be ordered from a breeding lab in Massachusetts, untreated. Because they had to be paid for out of pocket, Logan decided on immunosuppressed rats, which at fifteen bucks per (ninety dollars, plus shipping for a minimum order of six), were roughly one third the cost of rabbits. The human tumor cell line necessary to induce cancer had to be obtained through a suburban Washington outfit called the American Tissue Type Collection.

"Christ," exclaimed Logan, filling out the order form, "from the sound of it, you'd think they sold ladies' dainty underthings. I won't even know how to grow the tumors in the damn rats when everything gets here. I've never done that kind of shit work."

"I have," said Perez dryly.

"Well, there you are," said Logan, trying to make the best of it, "you've got to help me out."

From the outset, Perez had resisted the notion that he serve as Logan's assistant. Although he was untutored in high-level chemistry, he was blessed with considerable common sense, so he quickly grasped the obvious: Even if, theoretically, such a miracle drug could be concocted, the chances that it could happen here, in this miserable excuse for a lab, with him, Perez, as the entire support staff, were close to nonexistent.

"The truth is," he challenged, "you don't even know what you're looking for, do you? It's totally hit and miss."

"No, the basic structure for the compound is there."

"There are how many changes you could make in that molecule, ten thousand? A hundred thousand? Even under the best of circumstances, in the best of labs, that could take years. You're talking needles and haystacks. Hell, hayfields."

"Except we've got a head start—Compound J-lite."

"Dan, that's a death drug. It rots livers!"

"I'm not convinced of that." He paused meaningfully. "Atlas was in with those animals, Ruben, I'd bet my life on it."

"So what if he was? You're saying he murdered your bunnies? That's what you think?"

Absolutely, FUCKING right! Bet the farm on it, buddy! "Well," he said, a stab at moderation, "it's what I hope to find out."

This is why Perez had begun to fear for his friend's equilibrium.

Hadn't Compound J inflicted enough damage already? The guy's career was a shambles, his personal life all but nonexistent. Logan was self-destructive, anyone could see it. What better proof could there be than his lunatic insistence on pursuing this thing?

"Look, Dan, why don't you drop it," he asked, "at least for now? Just lay low for a while, relax, do your work."

"I can't, Ruben. You know why."

"Right, yeah. Because the stuff works."

"Yes, because it *works*! It's active, we proved that." He looked at Perez beseechingly. "C'mon, Ruben, I need you, I can't do this alone."

Perez didn't want to be unkind—he just wanted to force upon the guy some semblance of reality. If Logan was determined to play Don Quixote, he wasn't simply going to slide into the role of Sancho Panza.

"Look," said Logan, "I know what you're saying. Really. Don't you think I know where I stand?"

"I don't. Tell me."

Logan exhaled deeply. He thought about this all the time—sadly, bitterly—but he'd never once said it aloud. "I have no standing in the scientific community. *None*. Even if we make progress with the drug, right now I'm not even in a position to get it tested. It's possible I never will be." He looked levelly at his friend. "You know how that bastard Shein always refers to the ACF?"

"How?"

"As the big leagues. Which leaves me, I guess, playing on a sandlot somewhere—washed up by thirty. Satisfied?"

"No," said Perez softly, his heart going out to his friend, "I'm not satisfied. I feel bad for you, man."

"Good." He managed a smile. "I'm not proud, I'll take the sympathy vote. Think of it as therapy for me, Ruben. Creative play. It'll keep me off the streets."

He never formally agreed. But when the rats arrived a few days later, in cardboard boxes with vents and screens, it was Perez who immediately took charge. "What the hell's wrong with you, they can't live in these. Go out to a pet shop and get me some decent cages."

Logan grinned. "Will do."

"And some Purina Rat Chow."

Logan paused. *"Rat Chow?"*

"It costs a little more, but it's worth it." He hoisted a rat from its box; hairless and immunosuppressed, it was even less appealing-looking than its sewer-dwelling cousins. "These bastards are condemned, think of it as a couple of weeks' worth of last meals."

The breast-tumor cell line came the next day, packed in dry ice, and went immediately into a culture flask. A week later, Logan harvested the cells, mixed them in a saline solution, then watched his friend shoot half a milliliter into a tail vein of each of the six rats.

Within a week, the first tumors were visible; small bumps on the skin surface. Within five days, these would blossom into rock-solid protuberances the color of Bazooka bubble gum.

"Bastard," observed Perez, sarcastically, studying the doomed animals, "you'll do anything for science, won't you?"

"The question is how many times I'm going to have to prove it." Logan clapped his friend on the back. "C'mon, let's us mix up a new batch of Compound J-lite."

The procedure was identical to the one Logan had followed earlier —only this time, without the time pressure, they proceeded at a somewhat more leisurely pace.

They spread it out over five days, remaining in the lab every night that week till ten-thirty or eleven; sometimes, after breaking for dinner, returning for two or three hours more. Soon, despite himself, Perez began to find himself engaged by the process. What for Logan was routine, became for Perez a crash course in advanced biological chemistry.

Then, again, he came to it with the one trait that can never be taught: an ability to focus on the right questions.

"What was it about Mrs. Kober?" he asked the last night as they waited for the newly formulated compound to cool down. "Why did she live and none of the others? Why'd the stuff work on her in the first place?"

Logan had been wondering the same thing for nearly five months now. "I don't know. I've gone over and over the charts. I've even kept in touch with her to make sure she's *still* okay." He shrugged. "Not even an earache."

"It has to be something, right? These things don't happen for no reason at all."

"No. Only, sometimes the reason's so complicated we pretend they do. Those are the ones we write off as 'idiosyncratic.' "

"Not me. Not you either."

He laughed. "You sound like Sabrina. Again."

"Ah, the highest of all compliments."

"You think I talk about her too much?" Logan looked concerned. "Do I make an idiot of myself?"

"Nah." He waved it away. "I'm glad you think I come close to filling her shoes." He shot his friend a smile. "At least in the lab."

"Yeah? You don't know what we've *done* in the lab." He paused. "Anyway, I hope you don't get attached to animals like she does." He indicated the rat cages in the corner. "Almost time to start dosing our friends."

They hadn't made love now in nearly three months. She didn't feel like it—and, obviously, under the circumstances, John didn't press. "Hey," she said, laying her book on the bedside table and taking his hand, "it's a *much* better excuse than claiming to have a little headache, isn't it?"

"You never claimed that," he replied, smiling, once again grateful it hadn't touched her sense of humor.

"See, I should have. Then you wouldn't be asking me so many questions now."

"Does it hurt a lot?" he asked softly.

"There you go again."

He stroked her face. "Tell me how it feels."

This stiff-upper-lip stuff was starting to wear her down. "I guess it feels just about the way I look."

That needed no elaboration. Although her fears about losing her hair had passed—the two cycles of standard chemo had left it only slightly thinner—she'd never imagined anyone could appear so perpetually fatigued. No matter how much sleep she got, it was never enough to dispel the rings beneath her eyes; they'd become as much a part of her revised face as her nose and lips. Nor, it seemed, was sunlight able anymore to lend her pale, tired features so much as a suggestion of their former color.

"So it doesn't hurt so much now? There's no actual pain?"

"Only when I look in the mirror." She reached to him and took his hand. "Oh, John . . . I try so hard not to complain. Please let me know if I ever start reminding you of Camille."

He smiled. "I don't think there's much chance of that."

"But you know what? Lots of times I want to complain, I *feel* melodramatic." She paused and made the face she always did when annoyed with herself; only, now it seemed less amused than anguished. "See, listen to me now! Oh, God, let's talk about something else."

But, of course, more and more these days, attempts at normal conversation—even when the subject at hand was some fascinating detail of his day—tended to lead back to the same place. A story about the latest secret dispatch from the Middle East peace negotiations would end up being about the alleged medicinal properties of hummus; an anecdote about a recalcitrant congressional leader turned into one about a relative of the legislator who'd been treated at the ACF.

Still, she had no need for concern on this score: the crisis had the opposite of a chilling effect on their bond. Though, even with his wife, John had never been particularly comfortable with emotional exchange, generally giving no more of himself than a situation demanded, now, suddenly, he found himself making excuses to linger at her side; more in the present than perhaps he'd ever been.

"You want me to turn out the light?" he asked. "Probably you should get some sleep."

"Yes, please."

He reached over and flicked off the bedside lamp.

"John?" she said tentatively.

"What, my love?"

"You don't have to spend the night in here."

"I know that." He paused. "Are you worried about the calls waking you up?"

He'd never liked to defer; he had a standing order that he was to be awakened with any news deemed by aides to be even marginally important.

"No." She laughed softly. "I just wanted to make sure you really wanted to. You know how I hate pity."

"Don't worry, you don't inspire it."

"I worry about embarrassing you. I worry about letting you down."

He rolled over on his side to face her. "Please, Elizabeth, I'm the one who should be embarrassed, putting you through all this pretense. I hate it. Sometimes I just want to say 'Screw it!' "

"No. I'm managing all right. Just keep me away from long flights of stairs. I'm running out of excuses for why I get winded."

"You mean more to me than anything, you know that."

She laughed, but the laugh quickly turned into a cough. "No, I don't! And in the position you're in, I *shouldn't*!"

He kissed her lightly on the cheek and took her in his arms. "You can't help yourself, can you?—always with a wiseass remark."

"Not wiseass, true. I don't try to fool myself, John, and I don't resent you for it."

"What is it, anyway, about the stairs? What does your doctor say?"

"Stillman?" He couldn't see her face, but the distaste was clear in the way she spoke the name. "Something about the tumor preventing fluid from draining from the lungs, so it fills up the air sacs. Actually, it's pretty interesting, if it were happening to someone else. I wish I didn't have to always drag things like that out of him."

"Elizabeth, he's the absolute best. Everyone says so."

"Maybe."

"No maybe about it. He is the number-one specialist at the leading cancer institute in the world."

"Okay. But it's been an education—and not just about air sacs in the lungs."

"Meaning?"

"When it comes right down to it, they have no idea how to beat something like this. It's just trial and error. That's the big secret they keep from the rest of us."

They lay in silence for a long while, just holding hands. Suddenly he was aware that she was crying.

"Elizabeth?"

"Never mind. It's just me being stupid again."

He took her in his arms again, her face damp against his. "You're thinking about the children?"

She nodded. "It's so trite. I so much want to be there when they get married. I want to see my grandchildren." Burying her face against his shoulder, she began to sob in earnest.

"Shhhh," he comforted, stroking her hair. "It's going to be all right."

They both knew it was a lie, of course. But this time, safe in his arms, terrified, she let it pass.

Perez arrived at the lab before Logan, so it was he who discovered the mess: cabinets ransacked, drawers overturned, broken glass from smashed beakers and test tubes everywhere.

As soon as Logan entered ten minutes later, he went ashen. "Oh, Jesus!"

"Yeah, I know." Perez surveyed the wreckage. "Don't worry, they didn't touch the HIV. They missed the P-3 facility entirely."

"What about the rats?"

"No problem. Better than ever."

In fact, already, three days after their first daily dose, the animals were showing marked improvement. The tumors had begun to soften and shrink. Just like the first time.

Logan hurried back to the storeroom to see for himself. It was true, the animals were thriving, the cages appeared not to have been touched.

Returning to the lab, he sat down heavily in a chair. "I can't believe this. I fucking can't believe it!"

Perez, sweeping up, paused to face him. "Hey, it was junkies, man. It happens—especially in a neighborhood like this."

"I know." He knew he had to play this cool; already Perez regarded him as a raving paranoid.

"It's the world, no way to stop it. We even had a couple of break-ins like this up in Claremont, with all our security." He resumed sweeping. "All this stuff can be replaced. Just be grateful there wasn't any real damage."

Logan couldn't help himself. "We'll see."

"What the hell's that supposed to mean?" But, of course, Perez already knew. "Aw, shit, man, drop it, will you? It was *junkies*."

"Why isn't anything missing?"

"We were lucky."

"Junkies wouldn't take *anything*?"

"I'm not even gonna have this conversation with you, Logan. There's something sick about it—you turn even good news bad."

"You're probably right," Logan allowed. "I hope so."

"You're a paranoid!"

"We'll see."

"You know why I was most afraid of this?" demanded Perez, three mornings later, holding one of the six dead rats in his hands.

Logan stared at it. "Because I'd say I was right."

"Because you'd take this single fucking piece of data—dead rats—and fucking misinterpret it! There ain't no sabotage, Logan. Face it, the drug killed the animals, just like it did before. It doesn't work!"

"Then why's Stillman so interested in it? Why was he willing to forgive everything if we'd work on it for him?"

"Oh, man, can't you see what a stretch that is? He's a cancer researcher, he's gonna be interested in any active drug."

"Why've they tried to destroy me?"

"Don't exaggerate, Dan. They don't like you—it's a different thing. In their position you'd probably do the same to them."

"That's a lie!"

Perez laid the dead rat aside. "This is pointless. You gonna want to waste more money autopsying these guys?"

He shook his head.

"Logan, ask yourself: What would they even gain by doing something like that? You've told me yourself how rare it is that a drug active in lab animals works in human beings."

"I want to run the experiment again," Logan suddenly decided.

Perez threw up his hands. "Oh, shit."

"We've still got some of the compound left, I'll order more rats today."

"Forget it. I want no part of any of this."

"Please, Ruben, I need you. We can't keep them here—and I don't think my place is much safer."

"In my apartment? Logan, I'm trying to get my social life going again."

"*Please*, Ruben, for me. I'm *begging* you."

It was no exaggeration. "You're way over the top, man. You're just *gone*."

But already Perez was thinking about where to stick the cages to hold down the smell.

The letter arrived ten weeks after Sabrina's return from Cologne. Even if the envelope hadn't borne a characteristically austere German stamp—a grim latter-day statesman, as opposed to the birds, flowers, or Roman pottery that graced Italian mail—she'd have recognized the handwriting; slightly shaky yet still evocative of turn-of-the-century elegance.

Rudolf Kistner!

She closed her office door before sitting down to read it.

> My dear Doctor Como:
> Greetings and best wishes. Before all else, I must offer appreciation for your kindnesses on your recent visit. Thank you so much for the many details of your protocol with Dr. Logan.
> I sincerely hope you did not find me rude. I do not receive many visitors. Perhaps I am out of practice. Since your visit I have thought much about the question you ask me. Even now, I do not know if I can give the answers you seek. It is so long ago—a different age, a different way of thinking. I hope you can understand this.
> Herr Doktor Nakano was a very great chemist. The work he did was important work. But it is my duty to tell you he was not treated as he should have been in this country, and this is the shame of all of Germany.
> Was Herr Nakano my friend? I have thought much on this question also these last days. Surely, at the time I did not regard him as such. He was a master chemist, I only a young admirer—one of many who worked at the Christian Thomas Company. Not one time did I ever visit his home. Nor did I even learn until after he was made to leave Christian Thomas that Frau Nakano was of the Jewish faith. This was in 1936. After this I did not see him again.
> You must understand that I did not support the views of the National Socialists. Few in our laboratory did. We held Professor Nakano in only the highest esteem and his personal affairs

were not our affair. Some even continued to correspond with him after he left for Frankfurt. It is in this way that I learned of his continued work on the compound.

Personally, I was not one who wrote to him. This is why I was so surprised to receive from him a letter in November of 1938. I still have this letter, at the time he was living at Bornheimerstrasse 138. It was quite short, only that he wished for help in leaving Germany. I do not know why he chose me. Perhaps he wrote many similar letters to many people. Perhaps he recalled I had a friend at the Swedish legation.

Of course, I could do nothing. You must understand that at the time it was not possible. My own late wife said she believed this was the great sadness of my life. I think not. Yet it is true that even now it troubles me. For Professor Nakano's work was truly of the highest order.

This is why I now write you, as earlier I wrote Dr. Logan. Perhaps it is not too late to see his work recognized at last.

Though it was not yet 5:00 A.M. New York time, Sabrina picked up the phone and dialed Logan's number.

"Sabrina?" he managed, struggling from a deep sleep. "Is something wrong?"

"Logan, you must hear this."

She read him the letter and waited for a reply.

Still groggy, he hesitated. "He didn't say anything about the research."

"You do not think this is important?" she asked.

"I don't know. What do you think?"

"I think I should go to Frankfurt today. This afternoon."

Catching a three-forty flight out of Rome's Leonardo da Vinci Airport, she landed at the Frankfurt International Airport almost precisely two hours later. By six-thirty she was standing before the building occupied, sixty years before, by Mikio Nakano.

Like the surrounding neighborhood, the three-story, granite-fronted house had seen far better days; the heavy iron knocker on the front door and brass handrail leading up the front steps bespoke classic nineteenth-century burgher taste, but now the building had a decided shabbiness around the edges. Several large windows had been cracked and inexpertly repaired, the patch of garden was overgrown, even the knocker and rail needed a coat of paint.

The street itself, quiet and narrow, featured perhaps a dozen such houses, most now occupied by more than one family. The street was so little traveled that Sabrina's taxi, pulling before the house, had interrupted a raucous game of soccer.

Briefly, Sabrina turned from the house to watch the game. A dozen or so children were involved, German and Turk, boys and, she was pleased to note, spiritedly defending one of the goals, a girl.

Smiling, she turned back to the house, walked up the steps, and rang the bell. A middle-aged woman with bright yellow dyed hair answered it.

"*Ja, bitte?*"

"I was wondering, please, do you know where I might find the owner of this house?"

For a moment it seemed the woman was confused: what could this strange, elegant foreigner be doing at her door? "*Der Eigentümer?*" she replied finally. *The owner?*

Sabrina smiled, to establish she was not bringing trouble. "I had an old friend who lived here many years ago. I am trying to discover what's become of him."

The woman stared at her a moment more. Then, calling over her shoulder, "*Mutter, komm bitte.*" She turned away and repeated the word more loudly. "Mother!"

"*Ja.*"

"There is someone to see you."

A moment later an elderly woman, frail but with an exceptionally kind face, came shuffling into view. She was wearing a tattered bathrobe, and Sabrina was embarrassed to have imposed on her.

Slowly, she explained again why she was here.

"But *I* am the owner," came the old woman's reply. "Tell me what it is you want."

Sabrina suppressed her excitement. "This person lived here quite a long time ago."

"Yes?"

"Before the war."

She shook her head. "*Nein, nein.* I have been the owner only three years, you see. Since my dear husband died."

"Ah, I see. I'm sorry. Could you tell me, please, how long did your husband—"

"Only since 1969. He bought it as an investment." She smiled. "Not the best investment, but I manage."

Sabrina realized this was hopeless. "And you do not know from whom he bought it?"

She waved her hands. "A man, Herr Klaus. He also is gone, many years."

"Well, thank you so much for your time."

She nodded. *"Die Krieg ist seit langer Zeit vorbei."* The war is a long time past. "We do not think of those days much anymore."

Well, thought Sabrina, back on the sidewalk, what now? She had not expected anything to fall in her lap, of course. Yet, somehow, she'd let herself imagine that once she was here, a direction of inquiry would magically reveal itself.

She watched the soccer game a few minutes longer before, out of the corner of her eye, she saw approaching an elderly woman pushing a stroller.

"Excuse me, madam."

Again she saw how Germans of a certain age are reflexively on guard around strangers. The woman slowed down slightly but made no reply.

"Perhaps you can help me," said Sabrina, falling into step beside her. "I am inquiring after a Japanese man who once lived here." She indicated the building. "In this house."

"Nein, auf keinen Fall," came the emphatic reply as she picked up her pace.

Still, lacking any alternative, this now became Sabrina's modus operandi. She began randomly approaching passersby on the street, anyone who looked to be over sixty-five, repeating the question.

Given Sabrina's temperament, this was nothing less than an ordeal; a matter of forcing herself, *daring herself,* to follow through. But she began finding it a bit easier when she assumed a more general line of inquiry, pretending to be a graduate student researching the recent history of the city. She heard about chronic shortages during the war; about children and grandchildren raised in these houses; and, several times, about how the influx of Turkish guest workers had made things worse than ever before. "Look around you," one woman put it to her with sharp annoyance, indicating with her hand. It was now close to 8:00 P.M., and in the gathering darkness, Sabrina could no longer pick out the detail on the houses. "Once, everything here was respectable. But these people, they have no respect for property—and we are the ones who must pay."

"Surely there have always been foreigners here, even before," observed Sabrina.

The woman shook her head. *"Nein, nur Deutsche."* Only Germans.

"I have been told there was a Japanese, a famous scientist, who lived on this very street."

She cast Sabrina a look, at once surprised and disapproving. "I do not know." She began moving off. "One should know not to listen to rumors."

"Entschuldigung." Pardon me.

Sabrina wheeled around. There stood the girl from the soccer game, her pretty face framed by a tangle of dirty blond hair.

"You wish to know about this district? The people who have lived here?"

"Yes. This is of great interest to me."

"Come, my grandfather will tell you. He has lived here many years, all his life in the same house."

Sabrina nodded. "Where is he?"

"Not far." She extended a small hand. "My name is Agneta."

She shook it. *"Ich heisse Sabrina."*

Wordlessly, the child led her around a corner and down several residential streets, before emerging onto a more widely traveled thoroughfare. Here were a number of modest commercial establishments. All but one were closed for the day: a small shop, its interior shielded from view by strings of beads covering the windows. It was only when they entered that Sabrina saw it was a Middle Eastern–style coffeehouse, patronized by men of the local immigrant community.

Peering through the acrid smoke, she picked up only one clearly recognizable German in the place—the individual toward whose corner table Agneta was leading her.

He stood to greet the child, his surprisingly youthful countenance erupting in a grin. "Come to visit your old grandpapa or just after another pastry?"

His companion at the table, a middle-aged Turk, smiled broadly, showing several gold teeth.

"Grandpapa, this is Sabrina. She has questions about the neighborhood."

"Well, then"—he gestured expansively with a workingman's hands—"sit down. You have come to the right person."

"Thank you," she said, taking a seat.

"And where are you from?" he asked, picking up the accent.

"Italy. I am Italian."

"Ah, a very nice place, very warm people." He indicated the small cup of thick black brew on the table before him. "Please, you must have some Turkish coffee. For me, it is an addiction."

He ordered the coffee and sweet pastry for his granddaughter. "Now, what is it you wish to know? I am seventy-one years old, before that you must find it in a book."

He was so willing, Sabrina impulsively decided to abandon her ruse. "I am told that many years ago, before the war, a Japanese man lived on your street. A scientist."

Instantly, the old man's face softened. "Ah, yes. The professor. It is so long since I have thought of him."

"Professor Nakano."

"Yes, that is it. Such a nice man. I was only a boy, of course. He lived with the family of his wife, Jewish people. He also had a laboratory there, in the basement. Everyone knew of him."

Sabrina gave a convincing impression of complete calm. "So I have heard. That is what I am trying to find out, what happened to him, to his work."

"Ah, I see." He fell silent and took a sip from his cup. "You know, of course, those were bad times, very difficult."

"Yes, I understand."

"We, the children of this neighborhood, we liked the professor very much. He used to give us hard candy." He glanced at his granddaughter. "You must understand, there were not many National Socialists in this district. My own parents, your great-grandparents, were Social Democrats."

"Did they know anything of the professor's work?" asked Sabrina.

"Only that it was very important, very impressive."

"I understand that in 1938 he was trying to leave."

He nodded slowly. "Yes, of course, they all were. You have heard of *Kristallnacht*? When the Nazi gangs came after the Jews? It was then they destroyed his laboratory. Everyone heard of it, even the children, it was very sad to us after all his hard work. This is when he sent away his things."

"Pardon?" Involuntarily, Sabrina leaned slightly forward. "What things?"

"Not only him, many Jews in the quarter. After *Kristallnacht*, they began sending their valuables, what was left, out of the country. I know about this because my older brother, he helped carry some of their trunks to the shipping office." He turned again to the girl, adding with pride, "Your great-uncle Helmut, who died in the war. The professor's trunk was one of the first, the very next day. I recall it very well, my brother said he was in a frenzy. Normally he was such a calm fellow."

"It went to the shipping office?"

He nodded. "Beside the old City Hall. Poor souls, they could not get out themselves, but they saved what they could."

"Surely, they would have records there, then."

He smiled indulgently. "*Nein.* The center city was completely destroyed."

"Do you know if Professor Nakano got out?"

"Of course not." He paused. "You must remember, his family was Jewish. He was not the sort of fellow who would leave them behind."

The coffee was making Sabrina's head spin—or was it what she was hearing?

"Soon afterward," he continued, "many of the Jews in the quarter were taken away. And the professor with them. It was said they were sent to Dachau."

Though none of this was surprising, Sabrina was unprepared for the force with which it registered. She knew almost nothing about Mikio Nakano, had never so much as seen a picture of him. Yet over the past year, working on the compound, she'd begun to feel an intimate kinship with him. Later that evening, thinking about the thugs destroying his lab, imagining it, she would not even try to hold back the tears.

"The professor's trunk was sent to America," the old man added now, trying to be helpful.

"You are certain of this?"

He nodded. "He had, I believe, a brother-in-law. Many of these people had family there who had gotten out earlier."

She hesitated, almost afraid to ask the obvious question. "Do you happen to recall the family name of the professor's wife?"

"I am thinking about that as we are talking. It was so long ago and I was so young. But, yes. I believe it was . . . Falzheim. You know, like the town near Stuttgart?"

"**F**alzheim," mused Logan. "Can you believe it, she got the name from a former neighbor, someone who actually *remembered* Nakano?" Ruben Perez didn't even pretend to be impressed. "So you have the name of his in-laws—maybe. So what?"

"It's a start," shot back Logan. "A *good* start. The guy'd been working on this process for twenty years! Supposedly he made real headway."

"Right. And he wrote it all down and it's just waiting somewhere for you to find it." He walked across the room and picked up the local telephone book. "Manhattan. Isn't this where most of the German-Jewish refugees back then settled?"

Annoyed, Logan took it from him and flipped to the appropriate page; not at all to his surprise, there was no such name. "I didn't say it was going to be that easy."

Perez laughed. "Too bad. Next you could've found the cure for AIDS. That's probably about to float up in a bottle at Jones Beach."

The hardest part was that, for once, his friend's skepticism only reflected his own. Logan knew how farfetched this possibility was. On the other hand, he also knew—far better than Perez ever could—how extraordinarily difficult this compound was to decipher. At the very least, this was a lead worth pursuing.

"But who knows," said Logan, snapping the phone book shut, "you could be right in principle. It seems to be a pretty distinctive name."

He started for the door.

"Where you going?

"Forty-second Street, the main library there."

"What for?"

"You ought to get out more, Ruben. They've got phone books from all over the place there. Could be it'll turn up in Detroit or Miami."

Now it was Perez's turn to flash annoyance. "C'mon, man, I was just pullin' your chain. You gotta stop it with this shit, we got work to do."

"What are you gonna do, report me? I'll be back in a few hours."

That estimate proved way off. Though there were perhaps seventy directories at the Central Research Library, from large and medium-sized cities throughout America, it took no more than fifteen seconds to locate on each the page where the name Falzheim might have been—but wasn't. Even including the round trip by subway, he was back at the office in an hour and a half.

"Ah, shit," he said, marching through the door, "facing you is gonna be even worse than coming up empty. So let's have the wisecracks now and get it over with."

But to his surprise, Perez just turned from the bench where he was working and nodded soberly toward the far end of the room.

Logan was stunned. There, atop a stool, sat Allen Atlas.

"Hello, Dan," said Atlas. He indicated the woeful surroundings. "Nice place."

"What do you want?"

"Nothing much. Just to talk."

"Sorry," he said coldly, "I've got work to do."

"I appreciate that. Actually, that's what I want to talk to you about —work."

Though the guy fairly oozed sincerity, Logan couldn't help but feel he was being mocked. "I've got nothing to talk to you about, *nothing*. Let's not try to pretend that what's happened didn't happen."

Atlas nodded toward Perez. "Maybe we could have this conversation someplace else?"

"Don't worry, he already knows all about you."

"Just ten minutes, that's all it'll take. I promise, you won't be sorry."

To himself at least, Logan didn't deny he was intrigued. What was the son of a bitch after? He glanced at his watch. "Ten minutes."

* * *

"All right," Logan said, as they entered the bar two doors down from HIV-EX, "you're down to six."

Atlas smiled. "You should've warned me you've got the slowest elevator in New York."

"Your problem." They sat down in an empty booth. "Now, what do you want?"

"Wait a sec, will you. Won't you at least let me order us something to drink?"

He returned a minute later with two beers and placed one on the table before Logan. "Drink up, it's on the ACF."

"No, thanks."

"C'mon, Logan, this is no easier for me than it is for you. Let's just make nice for a few minutes and see what we can do for one another."

"Screw you, Atlas. I didn't come looking for you." Logan took a quick swig of beer and glanced at his watch. "Two minutes."

Atlas held up both hands, a gesture of surrender. "You're right, you didn't." He paused. "I'm just trying to say that there've been some real second thoughts at the ACF about what happened to you guys. Dr. Stillman, for one, recognizes it could've been handled a lot better."

Logan leaned forward, his eyes narrow. "Which part are you talking about, Allen? How they fucked us at the hearing, or how they fucked me when I went looking for another job?"

"That's your imagination, Logan, we had nothing to do with that."

"Sorry. Time's up."

"Wait!" Atlas grabbed his arm. "Look, Stillman's ready to bury the hatchet. You want a better job, the ACF can help you out."

"Why, Atlas? All of a sudden they're growing consciences down there instead of tumors?"

"We're doing what we've always done, trying to cure cancer. Dr. Stillman wants you to know he's had a chance to go over your data a lot more carefully. He thinks your Compound J has some promise. He'd like to talk it over with you."

"Tell me something I don't know, Atlas. Tell him I'm always more touched when he asks personally." He shook his arm free. "And tell him I'm happy where I am."

"What the fuck is wrong with you?" snapped Atlas, all pretense of cordiality gone. "You're gonna lose any talent you've got in a dump like that! And any shot at a reputation."

Logan stood up and came close to saying it: *Hey, asshole, don't worry about my talent. It's YOU trying to rip ME off.* But instead he just walked out the door.

Atlas hurried after him outside. "Hey, Logan!"

Logan wheeled to face him. "That's final, Atlas. No negotiation." This was starting to give him the kind of pleasure he thought he'd never again experience in science. "But do tell him how much I love being kissed up to."

"I will." Disconcertingly, he was smiling again. "Just one more thing—I'm real sorry about your friend Reston?"

"What about him?"

"Didn't you hear?" He paused meaningfully. "They found his body in his office the other day. Barbiturates. Apparently he got tired of living."

Logan just watched as Atlas turned and walked off in the other direction.

Amy answered the phone on the first ring. As soon as he heard her voice —flat, detatched—he realized she was in bad shape.

"Amy? It's Dan Logan."

"Hi. How are you?"

"I'm okay. How are *you?*" He paused. "I heard about what happened."

"I'm doing okay, better. It's been almost a week. I'm going back to work tomorrow."

"I'm so, so sorry. You know, even after everything that happened he was still—"

"Yeah, I know."

"—my friend. I don't think it was ever personal."

"Well, thanks," she said. "Look, Dan, it was nice of you to call."

Logan was caught short. He didn't want to get off, not yet. There were too many questions demanding answers. Desperately, he plunged ahead, seeking the vital young woman he knew. "Allen Atlas told me."

"Atlas?"

"He was in New York today, on business. I could hardly believe it.

It just seems so completely out of character. Do you have any explanation for it? Did he leave a note?"

"Please, Dan, I don't want to talk about it."

"I don't mean to get so personal, but it's important."

"Really, I just don't."

"Why not?"

"Good-bye, Dan. Thank you for calling."

Hanging up the phone, Logan turned to Perez, sweeping up the far corner of the lab. "She wouldn't tell me a thing."

"It's not easy being the girlfriend. She probably feels guilty about not picking up the signals."

"You think so?"

"I've seen it lots of times. It's sad, 'cause it's not really their fault."

Logan thought it over a moment. "This isn't one of those cases. Something's off." He paused. "She doesn't think he killed himself."

Perez stopped his sweeping. "What are you telling me? Did she say that?"

"No. But I know her. I also knew him." He stopped. "There's also the way Atlas told me about it."

"The *way* he told you about it?"

"Almost like, I don't know . . . a threat."

"Oh, come *on*, your damn imagination's working overtime again. Just stop it, man, you're really starting to worry me big time."

This gave Logan pause. Perez's judgment was rock solid. "You think so?"

"Look, the guy did himself in. Period. You know better than anyone how that place crushes people. That other one, the one you found . . ."

"Barbara Lukas?"

"Was that a fake too? What do they do down there, murder people for being pains-in-the-ass?"

Logan smiled. "I'm going home. This is one time you might actually be right."

"I'll take that as a compliment," he said, shrugging it away. "C'mon, you've had a rough day, I'll buy you dinner."

"Another time. What I need now's some peace and quiet." He laughed. "Or maybe you think that's just my imagination too?"

* * *

But twenty minutes later, when he arrived at his studio apartment, kidding around was the farthest thing from his mind. Heading home, he'd been seized by so powerful a sense of anxiety that, once inside, he ran to the medicine cabinet for a mild sedative. He was perspiring heavily. He took his pulse: 120. What was going on here? Distractedly, aware he was hungry, he opened a can of baked beans. He was just slitting open a package of hot dogs when he was hit with a sharp pain in the right lower quadrant.

Within a minute the shooting pains were coming regularly, every fifteen or twenty seconds, powerful enough to make him double over in pain. He staggered to the next room and collapsed on the bed.

Now there came a terrific pounding in his head, so intense, it all but crowded out thought. Yet he was so weak he could scarcely even move. Struggling to maintain control, seeking clarity, he managed to bring his hands to his temple and squeeze.

Could this be a flu? But, no, it had just come on too fast, and the symptoms were incongruent.

Appendicitis? Invariably that starts in the midepigastrium, not working its way down to the right lower quadrant for a good twenty-four hours. And this wasn't tenderness—it was pain.

Food poisoning? What had he eaten today? His mind raced. For breakfast, only a bowl of Rice Krispies and orange juice. For lunch—what?—some chicken noodle soup, a bagel with jelly, tea. He'd just taken the sedative—could that have something to do with it?

Wait a second . . . the beer with Atlas!

The panic suddenly welling up within was even greater than the pain. Could that have set off the anxiety? Was it possible the further reaction was then triggered by the sedative? Or was that just mad speculation? His head swam, he felt himself losing consciousness. He had to get to a hospital, had to get this shit out of his system! Pushing down on the bed with all his strength, he raised himself to his hands and knees.

But it was too much. He actually saw the blackness coming and felt it begin to wash over him.

* * *

When he awoke, the room was still dark. The clock on the bedside table read 3:23 A.M. He was, he realized with a start, still fully dressed, down to his shoes. Tentatively, he lifted an arm, then his head; then he sat up.

Slowly, he got off the bed and started toward the kitchen. But before he'd taken five steps, the terror hit with tidal force. So physically traumatic an experience *always* leaves after effects—at the very least, wooziness and disorientation. But now there was nothing. Except for slight hunger pangs, he felt absolutely wonderful; better, in fact, than he'd felt in months. Like a finely conditioned athlete on a natural high.

This was as frightening as anything yet. He'd always taken his body for granted, but even it seemed beyond his control.

The thought, once it presented itself, was impossible to shake: Atlas!—and he'd meant it only as a warning.

The early hour wasn't the only reason he didn't tell Perez what he was going to do. Acutely aware his friend regarded him as delusional on the subject of the ACF, Logan preferred to not even imagine how he'd react to a snap predawn decision to take off for Washington, D.C.

Picking up his car at the lot on Eleventh Avenue where he had long-term parking, Logan headed into the Lincoln Tunnel just as dawn was breaking. Doing seventy-five most of the way, stopping just once for gas, he made it to downtown Washington in less than four and a half hours, pulling up before the FCC Building on M Street just after ten.

Too late. The sidewalks, which only moments before had been alive with government functionaries hurrying to work in the boxy, nondescript office buildings lining the broad avenue, now were nearly empty.

Logan wheeled around a corner and headed right, toward Pennsylvania Avenue and his alternative destination: the National Archives.

What he needed was a volume called *The Martin Allen Directory of European SS Arrivals, 1890–1940, Port of New York*. He'd learned the day before, ironically enough in the New York Public Library, that it was available only here.

"Are you looking for a particular voyage?" asked the officious young man who handed it to him.

"Actually, I'm looking for a specific name. I don't know the date they sailed, or even the exact year."

The young man gave a tight smile. "I hope you have a lot of time."

Since the book provided just a record of departures and arrivals—

the individual passenger lists being available only on microfilm—Logan was reduced to playing probabilities. In all likelihood, German-Jewish refugees exiting Germany would have left via Hamburg, the country's principal port. It was also probable—assuming the cause of their departure was the rise of Nazism—that they'd have left between January 1933, when Hitler was named German chancellor, and late 1938. And though there were several companies that had worked the route between northern Germany and New York, Logan decided to concentrate on by far the most prominent: the Hamburg-Amerika line.

Still, throughout almost the entire period, Hamburg-Amerika had three ships running out of Hamburg simultaneously—the *Potsdam*, the *Bremen*, and the *Lübeck*, each making approximately fifteen round trips annually. The sheer volume was staggering. Worse, when he requested the first microfilm reel bearing passenger rosters, he discovered that the lists, numbering as many as fifteen hundred names apiece, were handwritten—and not in alphabetical order.

It was the very definition of tedium, reading down those long columns of names, hour after hour; individuals and family groupings by the thousands, the *tens* of thousands, all but indistinguishable from one another. He'd chosen to work ship by ship, starting with the *Bremen*. More than once, aware that his attention had wavered—that his eye had seen but his brain not registered—Logan had to go back to the top of a list and begin again. He could not take the chance that he'd missed the single name he was after.

Falzheim.

Working through the morning, he did not find it. The closest approximation, which he dutifully jotted down, was *Pfaltzstein, Ernst.*

By midafternoon, having moved on to the *Potsdam*, he was up to August 1934, when he made note of a second name that seemed close. *Forcheim, Leopold;* immediately followed by *Forcheim, Hilda* and *Forcheim, Greta.* A whole little Forcheim clan, he realized, and pressed on.

An hour later, dizzy with fatigue, he took a break and dialed the lab.

"You're in Washington?" exclaimed Perez. "What the hell for?"

"Look, just do me a favor. Do you have that phone book handy?"

"Oh, Christ, man. You went down there for *that?*"

"I just want to try a couple of names on you. You got a Pfaltzstein? With a *P?*"

"What?"

He spelled it.

Logan heard the pages rustling. "No way. You know something, I oughta have you locked up."

"How about Forcheim? With an *F.*"

He sighed. "Hey, yeah—I got one."

"Where?"

"Up in my neighborhood, Washington Heights. 802 W. 190th St."

Logan wrote it down. "Good. Thanks."

"You gonna keep looking?"

"I think so. I'll give you a call when I get home."

But it was already past four o'clock. In less than half an hour, Logan headed from the building and hailed a cab. He couldn't chance missing her again.

He had the driver let him off at the Foggy Bottom Metro station on Twenty-third Street and moved around a nearby corner. The spot allowed him an unimpeded view of pedestrians approaching the station from the direction of Amy's building on M.

He waited about ten minutes, and there she suddenly was; moving briskly but, as he had hoped, alone. He began walking slowly toward her.

"Amy?" he said, feigning delight at a chance encounter.

Startled, she reflexively smiled. "Hi." Then, she recognized him; and to his surprise, the smile turned genuine. "I had a feeling you were coming."

Taking his elbow, she led him briskly back around the corner.

"Where are we going?"

"I'm trying to figure out where we can talk."

"I got the idea you didn't want to."

"You caught me at a bad time—at home." She glanced over her shoulder.

"What, you think you're being followed?"

"I don't know. Probably we should just keep walking." She laughed uneasily. "You can tell I'm not very good at this."

"Amy, what happened to John?"

She said nothing, merely increased her pace, making a left onto L, then another onto Twenty-second; then turning quickly to look behind her again. "What'd Atlas say to you?"

"That they found him in his office. That he'd done it with pills."

"That's what they told me too."

"You don't believe it?"

"I guess I do." She looked deeply pained. "Dan, you knew John, did he ever seem the suicidal type to you?"

"No. That's what struck me." Hell, he'd rarely known anyone so astonishingly unburdened by self-doubt or moral unease—even when he should have been.

"I don't know, I don't know what to believe." She said nothing for half a block. "They were after him for information. About Compound J. They were pushing him really hard."

Logan's blood went cold. "Stillman?"

She nodded. "They wanted to know how the stuff worked, things he just couldn't tell them. Because—let's face it—he hadn't been that involved."

"Right." Logan could almost see it: the cocky, insecure Reston—that *jerk*—eager to give them what they wanted, desperate to play the big man, but powerless to do so. He tried to make the question sound innocuous. "Why did they want to know?"

She shrugged. "But obviously, they thought more of Compound J than they pretended. And you know John, that's how he got back at them."

"What do you mean?"

"He challenged them about it, *taunted* them." She smiled mirthlessly. "At least that's what he told me. He might have been exaggerating."

Having walked five blocks, turning corners apparently at random, they suddenly found themselves on busy Connecticut Avenue.

Now that she'd let it all out, Amy was visibly more relaxed. Even her apprehension about being trailed seemed gone. She indicated a nearby bar-restaurant. "I think I need a drink."

But the conversation had had the opposite effect on Logan. Though years of medical training had taught him to maintain a calm front, his mouth was dry and he felt weightless on his feet. "Not me, I'll take a rain check."

She started to turn away. "Don't be too hard on him, Dan. He was a bastard, but he never hurt anyone intentionally."

What the hell did *that* mean? "See you, Amy. Watch yourself."

"Funny, I was going to say the same thing to you."

As soon as she'd disappeared into the bar, he jerked around, scanning the busy street. Nothing—but how would he know otherwise?

It was early evening now. This was a hip area, lots of nice shops and good restaurants. Couples fresh from work were everywhere; the men with loosened ties, many of the women having exchanged their work shoes for comfortable running shoes. Without thinking about it, he darted into a bookstore.

At least he'd be safe here. But abruptly he thought of Georgi Markov, the Bulgarian dissident murdered by the KGB in London. He'd read a good deal on the case: how they'd stuck him at a bus stop with the point of an umbrella, using a plant lectin called ricin, almost undetectable by traditional forensic techniques. What, he wondered, had they used on Reston?

What had Atlas fed *him*?

It could have been anything. Toxins distilled from near-extinct Amazonian plants, retrieved by botanists contracted by the ACF to scavenge for new anticancer drugs. Materials so rare and poisonous that millionths of a microgram could kill, and yet leave no apparent trace. He knew full well higher-ups at the ACF had readier access to such compounds than any intelligence branch of any government on earth.

Logan walked quickly from the shop. His car was still in the underground garage by the National Archives. When the cabbie dropped him at the entrance, he ran to it without looking back.

Seated behind the wheel, he tried to collect himself. This was crazy, he wasn't doing himself any good.

Maybe it was simply his state of mind, but suddenly he knew what he had to do.

It took him no more than twenty minutes to reach Seth Shein's home in Arlington. Pulling up before the large Tudor, he saw Shein's red

Range Rover at the head of the driveway. The car, seemingly so out of character, was a source of immense pride to the senior man.

Heading up the walk, Logan knew he still wasn't thinking clearly. What did he expect to come of this? An honest explanation? Reassurance of some kind?

He was still considering when Alice Shein opened the door. He saw her shocked dismay. "Seth," she shouted. "Seth, come here!"

"What the hell is it?" Logan heard him shout back. "I'm busy."

A moment later he appeared at the door in baggy trousers and a work shirt, hammer in hand. Seeing Logan, he recoiled—but recovered immediately. "Logan, you look like shit."

Just for an instant, the younger man was overwhelmed by doubt. "I need to know what's going on," he said, fighting for control.

"With you?" Shein replied. "Not much, from the looks of it." He looked his visitor over contemptuously. "Don't think I'm gonna ask you in. No one invited you here."

Defiantly, Logan elbowed past him into the house, then wheeled on him. "What happened to Reston?"

"You're trespassing, Logan," Shein said mildly. "And you still look like shit."

"What happened to Reston? What'd they give to him?"

"Reston finally figured out what a nothing he was and did something about it. End of story." He snorted. "We're all better off without him, including him."

"Why're they killing my lab animals?"

"*Killing your lab animals?*" Shein laughed out loud. "You got it wrong, Logan—*you* killed those animals. What the hell's happening to your mind, you're embarrassing yourself!"

Logan's response was spontaneous, almost primal. "You motherfucker!" he shouted. "You say you're interested in helping people! You don't give a fuck about anyone but yourself!"

"So what? Look at you—obviously, you don't even give a fuck about that."

The sight of Shein standing there with that smug smile was too much; abruptly, Logan snapped. Knocking the hammer from his hand, he slammed Shein against the open front door. "You bastard," said Logan, breathing hard. "You wreck people's lives and don't give it a second thought!"

Pinned tight against the door, Shein was still smiling. "Untrue. I only wreck 'em if it's the most attractive alternative." He looked into his eyes. "What are you gonna do, Logan, beat me up? That's your whole problem, you're outta control. You're worse than just a loser, you're a crybaby."

Logan's fingers dug into Shein's arms as he tightened his grip. Shein winced—but his voice didn't waver. "Accept it, Logan, you just weren't good enough."

"You fucker. You know damn well that Compound J works!"

"My God," taunted Shein, "I never thought my judgment could be so off—you're pathetic."

"Why else are you still interested? Why else was Stillman after Reston about it?"

"You're outta your head, Logan, you're a fuckin' maniac."

Logan shook him violently. "Tell me, goddamn you!"

"Let go of me," he shouted.

Logan did so.

"Good," said Shein, rubbing his upper arm. "Now get the hell outta here and crawl back in your hole. I got a kitchen cabinet to fix."

"I'm not going anywhere until you tell me the truth!"

"Alice," he suddenly called out.

Looking up, Logan saw Mrs. Shein standing at the top of the staircase, terrified.

"Call the cops," instructed Shein. "No, make it the federal marshals . . . tell 'em we got a psycho here threatening a guy with security clearance."

Quickly, Alice darted into another room.

"I swear," said Logan softly, "you're not going to get away with this."

"Of course I will. Some of us are just winners."

Suddenly, Logan lashed out with his fist, hitting him square in the face. Shein crumpled to the floor, a thin stream of blood trickling from his nose.

"Nice," said Shein, wiping his nose deliberately with his sleeve, "a sucker punch. You're as honest in a fight as you are in the lab." He called again to his wife. "Tell 'em to hurry. Also that he's driving a beat-up white Ford—a real piece of crap."

Turning, totally spent, Logan walked quickly out the door.

Shein remained on the floor, watching Logan drive off.

But now, staggering to his feet, he headed for his office. *Did he have the home number of the ACF pharmacist in his address book?*

Yes, there it was! Seizing the phone, Shein punched it in.

Someone was following him—he was sure of it! For nearly fifty miles, from the start of the New Jersey Turnpike leaving Delaware to beyond Trenton, the headlights remained constantly at the same distance behind him; switching lanes as he did, seeming to mirror his every change of speed.

Pulling off at a rest stop, he did not leave the car—just sat and waited, staring into his rearview mirror, the exit ramp in full view behind him. Nothing—just a steady flow of cars driving up to the pumps and then off into the night. After ten minutes, he eased back onto the turnpike.

He snapped on the radio. Listening—even to a late-night talk-radio crazy going on about the JFK assassination—steadied his nerves. It at least provided the illusion he wasn't entirely alone.

Then, suddenly, just outside of New Brunswick, it was back. Or—he couldn't be sure—maybe this was a different car. This one stayed with him for ten minutes, fifteen. But when he slowed down to take the first available exit—8—it zoomed right past him, a boxy Volvo wagon. A family car.

Had his eyes been playing tricks on him? Or—worse—was it his mind?

It occurred to him, an oddly comforting thought, that he'd had only four or five hours' sleep over the past two days; his perceptions might be off simply as a physiological result. Thinking about it, he was hit by a wave of exhaustion.

Briefly, he considered spending the rest of the night at a motel. But, no, he was no more than an hour and a half from the city. And—if they were out there—why make it easier on them?

He traveled the rest of the way in the right-hand lane, at a steady fifty-five. Dropping off the car at the lot, he caught a cab and made it home by 1:30 A.M.

The flashing red light at his bedside indicated he had only one message. He was not surprised it was from Perez.

"Hey, Logan, what are you doing to me, man? Lemme hear from you as soon as you get back. *Immediately!* I don't care how late!"

Kicking off his shoes, Logan collapsed on the bed. *What time is it in Italy?* he wondered. But before he'd even done the math, he was asleep.

At that moment, Seth Shein was wide awake, his every sense on full alert. His eye moved from one to another of the four files open before him on his desk at the ACF, each distinctly labeled in black marker: RHOME, KOBER, WILLIAMS, DIETZ.

Again, he picked up the Dietz autopsy report, almost identical to those of Williams and Rhome: "Fulminent hepatic necrosis . . . pleural effusion . . . question of pericardial tamponade." Each of these women had gone from apparent good health to total physiological decompensation and death in a matter of a few hours; their livers shut down, their lungs no longer performing, their hearts weakened beyond hope.

But what about Kober? She'd had the same initial positive reaction to the drug as the others. Why in her case had there been no comparable devastation afterward?

He chuckled to himself. In a way, it was too bad she *hadn't* died— that way he'd have an autopsy report on *her* for comparative purposes.

Already, he'd carefully examined all the women's treatment schedules. They'd been close to identical. Kober had not missed any treatments, as one line of inquiry had led him to speculate; nor had her dosage ever been even marginally reduced. Like the others, she'd received her full complement of Compound J—two grams' worth, every other week for over four months.

Idly, he flipped through the Kober file; then, for the third time, pulled out her CAT scan.

He held the film over his head so it was illuminated by the overhead light. There were eight pictures, each representing a slice of the patient's body at a different level. The liver, homogeneous, took up almost one entire picture; in the next, he once again noted the upper pole of the left kidney, the kidney hilum, the indentation in it where the blood vessels enter and exit. Then . . . wait a minute, what was this? Where was the upper pole of the *right* kidney?

Quickly, he turned to the notes on her initial examination. Here was confirmation: this woman has only one kidney!

Shein laid the file aside and leaned back in his chair. On the face of it, this made no sense at all. In fact, it was *backward*. Like many drugs, Compound J was eliminated via the kidneys. Lacking a kidney, she'd have had *more* drug in her body than the others, not less. Given the drug's established toxicity, she should've gotten sick and died sooner!

He cupped his hands behind his head and closed his eyes. This was always the part where it got to be *fun*.

He didn't quite have it yet, but it was coming.

Logan awoke with a jolt, the telephone jangling in his ear. The room was still semi-dark. He fumbled for the receiver.

"Christ, Ruben, gimme a break. What time is it?"

But on the other end there was only silence.

"Ruben?"

He heard the click as someone hung up.

Instantly, the drowsiness was gone. He dialed Perez's number—and woke him.

"Dan?" he asked, his voice heavy with sleep. "You just got back?"

"Late last night."

"Why the hell you calling me now?"

"Ruben, listen to me. Something's going on." Suddenly, he thought better of it: what if his phone was tapped? "Wait, just stay there."

"Where am I going?" asked Perez wearily.

Logan slammed down the phone and, wild-eyed, throwing some clothes into an overnight bag, dashed out the door.

"Ruben?" he said, ten minutes later, into the receiver of a pay phone.

"Logan, you're totally fuckin' up my life."

"Stay there. I'm coming over!"

He caught the uptown A train at Canal Street and, sitting among the earliest of the morning commuters, hid behind an open *New York Times*. At this hour, the trip took less than half an hour. It was not yet seven when he pressed the buzzer in Perez's building—and woke him again.

"Look, Ruben, I'm sorry," he said, facing him across his tiny living room. "I know this is tough on you."

In the far corner, the rats scurried in their cages; the tumors, induced a week earlier, were visible even from where Logan sat. In a few days, they'd begin dosing them with the drug.

Perez, in a bathrobe, leaned forward in his chair and rubbed his eyes with both hands. "What is it now?"

Briefly, in broad strokes, Logan told him about his experiences in Washington.

His friend took it in soberly, aware of the sharp decline of Logan's emotional state in just two days.

"Listen, Dan," he said softly when he was through, "I just want you to think about what you're saying to me. Really *think* about it." He paused, groping for the right words. "Look, I hear you. I know what the girlfriend told you must've been pretty scary. But think about where she's coming from, all right? The guy she loved just killed himself."

Logan shook his head emphatically. "No. It isn't that. You don't know these people, Ruben."

"It's the fuckin' ACF, Dan! They don't DO this kind of thing." He threw out his arms imploringly. "Don't you know what you did, man, you decked Seth Shein!"

"He's part of it. He's as bad as any of them."

Perez sighed. This guy needed help, and he was no shrink. "Look," he said, rising to his feet, "I gotta get ready for work. You do too."

"I don't think so, Ruben. Not today."

"Jesus, Logan, you need this job! Even Severson can run outta patience."

"I know." But Logan remained where he was. "Would you mind if I stayed here? Just for a few days?"

Perez disappeared into the bedroom and returned with a key. He tossed it to Logan. "Your funeral. What're you gonna do for clothes?"

Logan nodded at the overnight bag. "But I was kind of rushed. I only brought a couple of things."

"Man, don't you got any other friends?" He shook his head wearily. "Gimme the key to your place, I'll pick up some stuff for you after work."

* * *

Perez had been gone a half hour before Logan focused on it. Rummaging in his jacket pocket, he was unable to find the crumpled scrap of paper on which he'd written the day before. But there it was in the phone book: Forcheim G. 802 W. 190th St. Not many blocks away.

Logan showered and pulled on the clothes he'd brought in his overnight bag—jeans and a short-sleeved shirt. They would have to do.

He decided to walk, down Broadway and up a long, curving hill. The building was perhaps twelve stories high, opposite an old age home. The names on the panel in the entryway reflected the changing face of the neighborhood, a near equal mix of German-Jewish and Hispanic, with a couple of Russian names as well.

Forcheim. Apt. 3C. He pushed the buzzer and waited.

"Yes?"

"Ms. Forcheim?"

"Yes?"

What now? "My name is Dr. Daniel Logan. I know this might sound strange, but I'm looking for—"

"Pardon?"

Feeling incredibly foolish, he began shouting. "I'm trying to find out about a man named Nakano—"

He heard the slight click that signaled she'd snapped off the intercom. "Shit," he muttered, and pressed the buzzer again. No response. He pressed again. And again.

A resident of the building, seeing him standing there, muttering to himself, inserted her key and hurried quickly through the plate glass door, taking care he wasn't able to follow.

"*Damn* it," he said, aloud, and was about to turn away, when through the glass he saw the elevator door in the lobby open.

Coming toward him was a woman—probably in her mid-sixties, wearing a baggy housedress, but possessing one of the most beautiful faces he'd ever seen: jet-black hair, lustrous skin, dark eyes slightly crescent shaped. As she got closer, he saw the eyes were astonishingly bright.

He knew it even before she opened the door. "He was my father."

Twenty minutes later, he sat on her faded couch, a cup of tea on the low table before him, as she wound up her story. It seems she was less than a

year old when she came to America with her aunt and uncle, her
mother's younger brother. The plan was that eventually her own parents
would join them. "But my mother's parents, my grandparents, were too
old to leave, they didn't want to. Someone had to stay with them, and I
suppose everyone thought because my father was not Jewish . . ."

"It would be safe."

"I don't think anyone had any idea then how bad it would get."
Momentarily, she looked as if she might cry. "I was lucky, actually. I had
my aunt and uncle. They adopted me. I was never alone. My aunt just
died last year. I took care of her."

Logan glanced about the room, busy with colorful fabrics, plants,
framed photos. His gaze fixed on the small portrait in a wrought iron
frame on the window ledge beside him. It showed a youngish Oriental
man wearing black-rimmed glasses and a serious expression. "This is
him?"

"Yes." She smiled. "But I have others where he doesn't look so
stern—one where he's playing with me. When it became clear they
weren't getting out, they sent us an album."

"He was a very gifted man," said Logan, trying to nudge the subject
in another direction, "a very great scientist."

"Would you like to see it?"

"Of course."

"I keep it right here." She reached into a shelf beside her and
withdrew an album with a faded fabric cover. "This is how they used to
make them then, to last."

Opening it, Logan was instantly transported to another time, the
Frankfurt of pre-Hitler Germany. That vanished world was the backdrop
of many of the black-and-white pictures, carefully mounted and labeled
in an elegant hand; elegant little shops and well-tended parks and peace-
ful streets. But, above all, he picked up a sense of the young family in the
foreground. Mikio Nakano, usually in a business suit, but occasionally
showing a mischievous or even a silly side; the woman before him, as a
chubby infant; her darkly pretty young mother.

"What was your mother's name?" asked Logan.

"Emma. Isn't she pretty?" It was apparent this was important to her
even now.

"Very."

"She was a piano teacher, did you know that? That's how they met. With all his work, he decided to take up the piano." She laughed. "I have all the details. My mother also sent over her diary. Would you like to see it?"

"I would." For, in fact, the particulars of this family's life were starting to engage him.

"Actually, it's four volumes. She wrote down everything."

She went to a closet across the room and carried them over. For the next quarter hour, as she hung over his shoulder, commenting, he perused the pages of flowing script.

"It's remarkable," he said finally, gently closing the book, "what a treasure." He paused. "I was wondering, by any chance did your father also keep a diary?"

"My father?" She shook her head. "Not really, I don't think he had the time."

"I mean about his work."

"Ohh." She thought a moment. "Actually, yes, I think there is something, a journal of some sort. . . ."

Getting up, she went to a closet across the room and began rummaging about. "Most of it I can't make heads or tails of, of course. All those numbers and letters." She stood on tiptoes and gingerly pulled down a box from the crowded top shelf. "I think it's in here. Yes, here it is."

In her hands she held a black-and-white marble composition book, similar to those Logan himself had used in school. "I hope you'll excuse the disorder. But I usually find what I'm looking for."

She handed it to him. Casually, as if simply perusing another interesting artifact, he opened it. What he saw on the first page sent a shiver down his spine. A rendering of the precise compound with which Logan had been working.

"I hope it's helpful," she was saying.

He flipped to the next page and then on to the one after that; then, more rapidly, scanned perhaps ten more. What he was seeing was a series of brief entries, three or four to the page. Occasionally an entry was accompanied by a sketch of a chemical model, annotated and dated. The story being told here was riveting—that of the evolution of a brilliant scientist's thinking as he struggled, over the course of more than two decades, with a problem of almost unimaginable complexity.

Excitedly, apprehensively, Logan skipped to the back of the notebook. The final dozen pages were blank. But on the one that preceded them, there it was: the fully realized compound!

Logan quickly deciphered the German words above it. *"Es funktioniert!"* It works! It was dated 26/10/38. Two weeks before *Kristallnacht.*

"Would you mind if I borrow this?" asked Logan, trying to maintain a veneer of calm.

She looked suddenly concerned. "It's very important to me."

"I understand. Of course." *How to put this?* "I just think you should know your father did some remarkable work here."

"Really?" She lit up. "That's wonderful to hear."

"Only for a day or two, I just want to make a copy of it." He began fumbling in his jacket for his wallet. "I'll leave you my driver's licence, my credit cards . . ."

With a sudden laugh, she relented. "Never mind, of course you can. I never imagined anyone would ever be interested."

S omeone else might have dreaded this confrontation. Seth Shein relished it. In his long tenure at the ACF, never before had he had such an opportunity, and there'd surely never be one like it again.

He had to make the most of it—even if that meant winging it.

"Say, Stillman," he said, strolling into his rival's office unannounced, "haven't seen much of you lately."

Gregory Sillman looked up from the paper he'd been working on, his lip instantly curling in a sneer. "Who the hell let you in here?"

"Just wonderin' what you been up to." He noticed Stillman had slipped his forearm over the page before him. "Colleague to colleague."

"Get the hell out of here!" Stillman snapped the button on his intercom. "Martha!" There was no response. "Martha, goddamn it!"

"I think she might be downstairs in the cafeteria," offered Shein, innocently. "I think that's where I just saw her." He took a seat. "So . . . you wanna tell me what you been workin' on?"

Stillman rose to his feet. "I'm in no mood for your idiocy, Shein." He started moving toward him. "Now get out!"

"Maybe that's the wrong question. What I mean to ask is—who've you been treating with Compound J?"

He stopped in his tracks, less angry now than seemingly bewildered. "What?"

"Simple question. I looked at the records down in the pharmacy. It seems you've checked out fifteen grams of the stuff. Who for?"

"For research purposes, of course," he said. But, knowing who he was dealing with, he wasn't able to manage complete conviction. "I've never denied Compound J seems to have some activity."

Shein snorted. "Don't insult my intelligence," he said, his voice taking on a dangerous edge. "You can do anything else—all right?—but don't insult my intelligence. We're talkin' fifteen fuckin' grams! How many mice you planning to dose, a hundred thousand?"

"Shein, that's the most irresponsible kind of speculation!"

Shein hesitated a long moment, appearing to consider this. "You know what Logan thinks?" he picked up, his tone almost conspiratorial. "He thinks you murdered his lab animals. He thinks you were so desperate to discredit his research, you poisoned his fuckin' lab animals! So that you could take over."

"You're throwing Logan at me? A guy who faked his data? He's got his head up his ass."

Shein nodded decisively. "You're right, I agree with you—Compound J-lite is incredibly toxic stuff. No way you killed those lab animals." He smiled; it was impossible to tell he was operating on pure intuition. "Just the women."

"What? What the fuck are you—"

"Simple enough with these new poisons, Greg. Was it chrisanthe-toxin—*that* destroys the liver. All you'd have to do is get a thousanth of a microgram into the IV line. Or, better yet, into the chocolates the Italian babe was always slipping her patients."

Stillman came back with a brittle laugh. "Compound J killed those women, Shein. It's an established fact."

"No, Greg, Compound J doesn't have that kind of toxicity. You know that. Why else would you take the chance of feeding it to someone else?"

The other man hesitated, his face suddenly drained of color.

Jackpot!

"I'm not even going to dignify that with a response," said Stillman finally.

"Greg, you already have." Shein smiled confidentially. "She must be pretty big stuff for you to go to so much trouble. I figure none of the conventional stuff worked, right? So what were you gonna use—*your* stuff, that'd had zero responses? Compound J may be hit and miss, it's had some problems, but at least it's active."

"Where do you come up with this crap?"

"Take a look at Kober's file, Greg. The woman only has one kidney . . .

"What the hell do I care?"

"It means she had more Compound J in her system, not less. The stuff didn't kill her—it probably saved her. It helped her fight off the toxin."

"You're psychotic, Shein, you're delusional! Do you *know* what you're suggesting?"

"Well, Greg, I know this: We got three dead ladies and Compound J didn't kill 'em. Just as a matter of professional interest—did you use the same toxin on Reston? The fucker was quite a loose cannon, wasn't he?"

"Jesus H. Christ!" Throwing up his hands, Stillman returned to his desk chair and sat down heavily.

Shein had never imagined there'd come a time when he'd see his rival so helpless, so utterly vulnerable—and he moved in for the kill. "It's okay if you don't wanna tell me. He's only been buried—what?—a week. No problem exhuming the body and running a few tests."

"Shein, look, we've had plenty of problems, you and I. But what are you trying to do to me here? We're both in the same business, we're both out to cure cancer."

"I assume you're just talking theoretically here, right?"

"What are you trying to do, wreck the ACF? I'm not saying there's a word of truth to this—there's not. But I promise you, if you pursue it, that's what you're going to do. You're going to fuck up everything we've worked for. And, let me tell you, it couldn't come at a worse time."

Shein leaned forward. "Oh, yeah? Why's that?"

Stillman closed his eyes and breathed in deeply.

"C'mon, Greg," he urged gently, almost seductively, "out with it. You know I'm gonna get it anyhow."

Stillman stared at him miserably. Then he picked up the file on his desk and handed it over.

Logan had been poring over the notebook in Perez's living room for over four hours, but he was still as light-headed with excitement as at the start. Though he'd never been especially religious, he now could say he understood the definition of a spiritual experience. For what he held in his hands was close to holy—the life work of a scientist as remarkable as any he'd ever studied in the classic texts. Work of potentially incalculable benefit to humankind.

The telephone rang, startling him.

"Logan? I hope you're not chewing up the carpets."

"Ruben, where are you?"

"At your place. How much stuff you want me to bring over?"

Nothing could've been of less importance to him. "I don't know, at least a few days' worth."

"Great," said his friend, wearily.

"Oh—could you also bring my German-English dictionary? It's on the shelf next to the couch." Logan had been having trouble deciphering some of Nakano's more complicated notes.

"What for?"

"Please, I'll tell you when you get here."

"I see it. It looks like a *heavy* mother! Logan, I have a lot of junk to carry already."

"Take a cab, I'll pay for it. Please, just hurry."

Logan turned back to the notebook. It was nothing short of remarkable in its detail, a complete record of the development of the compound from theory to realization. He could see how Nakano had built on small successes as he went; yet, too, how reluctant he'd been to discard certain key ideas that seemed virtual truisms and how slow to embrace others that appeared, at first blush, extraordinarily unlikely.

Logan understood. Nakano had also been convinced at first the toxicity was linked to the length of the polymer's bridge—in fact, had persisted in that belief for a dozen frustrating years. It was only his belated discovery that the problem lay elsewhere—in the unlikeliest of places—that enabled him to press forward; and even then, ten more years were required to reach completion.

Logan studied the final series of drawings with particular care. All that had been required was a slight repositioning of the sulfonate groups, on the head and tail modules of Compound J. The compound Nakano discovered was, in fact, an isomer of Compound J: it had exactly the same number of atoms in its chemical composition, but its parts were arranged slightly differently.

It was as if the molecule were a deck of cards in which, for a particular trick to work, the cards had to be in a precise order. Logan himself had had several cards out of sequence. He might have gone on working for a hundred years—a thousand!—and never gotten it right.

He heard the click of a key in the door and looked up.

"Well," announced Perez, a shopping bag in each hand and the dictionary under his arm, "just call me the Bag Man of Washington Heights."

"Ruben, c'mere. I have to show you something."

"Will you let me close the door, for Chrissakes?"

He had just done so and was heading toward the couch when there came the sound of heavy footfalls in the hallway outside, immediately followed by a violent pounding on the door.

"What the fuck?" exclaimed Perez, quickly moving for the baseball bat he kept in the corner.

In a panic, Logan slammed shut the notebook and slipped it beneath a cushion of the couch.

Abruptly, the door crashed open, kicked in by one of the four burly men who came rushing in. Three of them had guns drawn.

"Which one of you is Logan?"

"Who the hell are you?" demanded Perez.

"Keep your mouth shut!"

Logan noticed the head man had a small photograph in his hand. It was identical to the one on his ID card at the ACF. Instantly, he knew: these guys were ACF security.

"I am," he accepted the inevitable. "I'm Dan Logan."

"Who's he?"

"He's my friend, he didn't do anything."

"He goes too," came the command.

"What about these?" One of the men indicated the rats.

The leader didn't hesitate. "Take 'em."

Both men were jostled out of the apartment and down the stairs, where two cars waited, engines running.

"My fault, man," called Perez, before he was pushed into one car. "I was a fuckin' idiot!"

Logan couldn't manage a reply before he disappeared into the second—a Volvo. *No way,* he reflected miserably, *ALL mine.*

He was placed on the back floor, invisible to passersby. "My friend didn't do anything," he repeated. "He doesn't know about any of this."

But he had no doubt that if they were ready to eliminate him to steal Compound J, Perez, caught in the crossfire, didn't have a chance.

"Don't worry about it," said the guy in charge.

"How'd you find me?" Though, in fact, he was just trying to reassure himself these people were human enough to make conversation.

"No talking, Doctor. Those are our orders."

Anyway, the answer seemed clear. Having staked out his place, he figured, they'd followed Perez uptown.

For the next thirty-five or forty minutes they drove in silence, across—he surmised, looking up from his position on the floor—the George Washington Bridge—and on into New Jersey. When they came to a halt and he was helped from the car, he was surprised to find they were at the edge of the tarmac in what appeared to be a rural airport. But now he found himself hustled aboard a plane on the adjacent runway, a Learjet. A few moments later they were airborne.

Again, he was kept from the window, an exercise that struck him as completely pointless.

"I know where we're going," he said quietly.

Neither of the men flanking him replied.

"At least give me the satisfaction of knowing I'm right."

Nothing.

"Screw you!" he said, summoning up his final reserve of defiance. "Screw you all!"

They came down at a similar airfield—Virginia, he guessed, by the look of the terrain—and he was made to lie down in the back of another car, a Buick sedan.

"Hope you're not too uncomfortable," said the head man, the first time he'd spoken since New York.

But by now, in his despair, Logan took this as nothing more than an effort by the guy to absolve his conscience. He'd all but accepted the inevitable. "Look, asshole, where I'm going, I'm not worried about a little discomfort."

For another half hour there was silence—until someone tapped him on the shoulder. "Okay, you can sit up now."

With difficulty, he struggled in the cramped space to his knees, then two pairs of hands helped lift him to the backseat.

"Why," he said, shaking them off, "you want me to see the place where—"

He stopped in midsentence, jaw literally going slack. What loomed before him was so staggering, for a moment he was actually unable to process it. They'd just driven through a gate and were heading up a drive toward the imposing structure.

"Is that the . . ."

"Yessir, of course. The White House."

They halted at the East entrance and Logan was helped from the car.

"Again, I'm very sorry for the inconvenience, sir," said the senior man. "There was concern you might try to evade us, and our job was to bring you here as quickly as possible. I hope you understand."

He got back in the car and it drove off. Instantly, another man was at Logan's side. "Right this way, please, Doctor."

He escorted him into the building, around a corner, and then up a narrow staircase.

"Excuse me," said Logan, "but isn't this where—"

He nodded. "The private quarters, yessir. Please follow me."

He led the way down a long corridor, knocking at a door close to the end.

"Come in," called the familiar voice.

His escort opened the door and stepped aside to let Logan pass. There, in what appeared to be a sort of sitting room, waited Kenneth Markell, Raymond Larsen, and Seth Shein!

By now Logan was almost beyond surprise. He just stared at them.

"Dr. Logan," nodded Markell in greeting, as if the meeting of this group, in this place, were the most natural thing in the world.

Suddenly conscious he was still dressed in his T-shirt and jeans, Logan folded his arms before him. "What am I doing here?"

"We've got a situation," said Markell.

Logan turned to Shein. "Why am I here?"

"Hey," replied Shein, with what he'd once have taken as an ingratiating smile, "don't ask me, I only work here."

"A *situation*," repeated Markell. "And it occurred to us that you might help." He paused. "Mrs. Rivers has a chemotherapy-refractory cancer. I'm afraid it's bad."

The First Lady? Logan's mind raced. It made perfect sense, of *course* —yet somehow he was again caught short. He'd always liked Elizabeth Rivers, he'd voted for her husband. What Markell was telling him was that she was doomed; they'd tried all the chemo they could and nothing had worked. "I'm sorry."

"The upshot is that she's willing to try any alternative therapy we deem appropriate. The President concurs in that view. The situation is quite desperate."

"We understand," added Shein, "that you've continued to work on Compound J."

He looked from one to the other. "How do you know that?"

"As I expect you know, Doctor, it's our business to keep tabs on such things," replied Markell. "Part of our responsibility."

The break-in—it wasn't only Stillman! These sons of bitches! These monsters! Yet instead of anger, what he felt bubbling up within was something like pure joy. "Yes, of course, I'd almost forgotten how things work at the ACF."

Logan waited for a reaction to this provocation, then gave a small smile when none came. It was true: THEY needed HIM. HE was in control here, HE had the power. "Where's my friend? They took my friend also."

"He's fine. There are security implications to this, of course; we didn't want the police or the press involved. We had to be certain he was aware of that."

Logan nodded. "Shouldn't there be someone else here?"

"Who would that be?" asked Markell, all innocence.

"Dr. Stillman. Or did he object to my being called in?"

Markell looked at Shein, who seemed pleased to field the question. "Dr. Stillman is leaving the ACF for greener pastures. He has accepted an offer to be the director of the Southwest Regional Cancer Center in Phoenix. That far away enough for you, Logan?"

"Dr. Stillman was the original doctor on this case," added Markell quickly. "Unfortunately, he did not agree with the course we wished to pursue. But we remain on excellent terms. I expect no negative fallout for the Foundation."

Throughout it all, Larsen, having taken a seat in the corner, looked as if he wanted nothing so much as to disappear into thin air. Now, Logan confidently turned his way. "How about you, Dr. Larsen? Do you agree with this course of action?"

Larsen cast a worried glance toward Markell. "Actually, I'm new to the case myself. But, yes, it strikes me as fully appropriate."

"It does? You're saying you've changed your mind about this compound? And me? You're offering me an apology?"

Larsen shifted miserably in his chair. "I am interested in what is best for the American Cancer Foundation," he replied stiffly. "That is my policy. As always."

"Ah, but that isn't what I'm asking. Don't you remember, we have a history together, you and me."

"Doctor," cut in Markell, "is this absolutely necessary? There are times to put aside personal feelings in the interest of the general good."

"Hey, c'mon," spoke up Shein, throwing an arm around the younger man's shoulder, "Logan's got a point and we know it. You"—he pointed a finger at Larsen—"treated him like shit. If he wants to see you grovel a little, I, for one, can't blame him." He smiled amiably at his colleagues. "Why don't you let me have a few minutes alone with Dr. Logan?"

Markell nodded. "Absolutely."

Shein steered Logan toward the adjacent bathroom and closed the door behind them.

"Great." He laughed, jerking a thumb toward the room they'd just left. "I enjoyed that as much as you did." He rubbed his jaw. "And a lot more than the last time we got together."

"How'd all this happen?" asked Logan coolly.

Shein shrugged. "Hey, didn't I tell you I'm your guy? And now here we are, back in the saddle again—the Lone Ranger and Tonto." He dropped his voice even lower. "You know the best part? It's a no-lose proposition. If she responds, we get the credit. If she dies, Stillman, out there where the buffalo roam, takes the blame. I mean, you should see her in there, so weak she can hardly move. The fucker wasted five months on totally useless treatment!"

"Markell's willing to back that?"

"What choice does he have? You got a desperate man in there."

Logan smiled. "Sounds good. Let's go back and talk turkey."

"Well?" asked Markell when they emerged.

"You're right. Obviously, we have to do everything we can." Logan paused thoughtfully, then looked directly at Shein. "I'm going to want to head up my own team, of course."

Shein blanched. For the first time in Logan's experience, he appeared wholly at a loss for words.

"I understand," agreed Markell.

"I'll pick my own people—starting with Dr. Como and Ruben Perez."

"Of course. Whoever you feel you need."

"What about the FDA? We're going to be working with an untested compound."

Markell waved this away. "That can be handled. Just tell me how much of the stuff you need fabricated, we've got guys who can get it to you tomorrow."

"Good." Logan looked from Markell, to Larsen, to Shein. "Thank you, gentlemen. Now, where do I get some fresh clothes? I'd like to see my patient."

O n an evening almost precisely ten months later, Logan felt a tap on his shoulder.

"Mrs. Rivers," he said, surprised.

"I believe you promised me a dance, Doctor."

"It must've been one of those lies doctors tell to buck up patients." He grinned sheepishly, aware of the dozens of pairs of eyes on them. "I don't want to embarrass you in front of all these people."

"That's the same thing he always says to me," noted Sabrina, "and nobody looks at us. This is a guy who just does not know how to have fun."

"Well, I don't embarrass easily. C'mon, here comes a slow song. Don't worry, I'll lead."

She took his hand and led him toward the crowded dance floor, other revelers clearing a path as they went.

"You *should* dance with her," she teased, "she's the best-looking woman here."

"So . . ." he changed the subject, gazing around the vast hotel ballroom, "how long do you have to stay at each party?"

She laughed. "Who knows, I just do what I'm told. Believe me, *seven* inaugural balls wasn't my idea."

"Anyway," he offered, "I guess congratulations are in order."

"Thank you—but doesn't that go both ways? It looks to me like you guys are quite a success story yourselves."

He smiled. "Right." The reference was to his recent appointment as Director of Basic Research at New York's prestigious Roosevelt Cancer

Research Institute—with Sabrina named Director of Clinical Trials. "They're keeping us pretty busy."

"I just hope you'll be available, if needed."

"Of course."

Logan was relieved to hear her say it. She looked stupendous and—in this he took even greater pride—her CAT scans had been clean for over five months. But he knew as well as anyone that with this disease, it is tempting fate to think in terms of definitive cures: for some time to come, she would have to be closely monitored.

"Word is you plan to put the drug into a major clinical trial."

"Yes, there's still a lot about this compound we need to know. I'd like to get a couple of hundred patients signed on to move things along."

"Have you put in for the patent?"

He grinned. "How close are you to the IRS?"

"Don't worry, I can be trusted."

"Anyway, three quarters of the profits are going to Nakano's daughter. Believe me, money was never the point."

Elizabeth Rivers looked at him closely and nodded. "I know that."

"I don't know how to have fun?" demanded Logan, opening the hotel room door. *"Me?* You got me confused with someone else, lady."

Sabrina laughed. "All right, I admit, this kind of fun you know."

He gazed at her with a mix of tenderness and lust. She was wearing a black Versace gown, as drop-dead sexy as it was elegant. "C'mere."

"Just wait a second, please. I need to take off these fancy jewels, no? They are rented."

He removed his tuxedo jacket and shoes and collapsed onto the oversized bed. Idly, he picked up the remote and switched it on. "Almost ready? You're driving me crazy here."

"You are already crazy, Logan. This is one of the things I love about you." She took off her second earring and carefully laid it on the bureau. "There. Ready." She moved to the bed and fell into his arms.

They were so lost in a passionate kiss, the words in the background didn't even register.

"Authoritative sources at the renowned American Cancer Foundation announced today . . ."